GOLLA

Also by Naomi Jacob in Futura

THE FOUNDER OF THE HOUSE
'THAT WILD LIE...'
YOUNG EMMANUEL
FOUR GENERATIONS
PRIVATE GOLLANTZ
GOLLANTZ, LONDON, PARIS, MILAN

NAOMI JACOB

Gollantz & Partners

THE GOLLANTZ SAGA 7

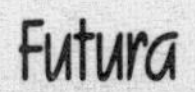

A Futura Book

First published in 1958
New hardback edition published in Great Britain in 1985
by Judy Piatkus (Publishers) Limited

This edition published in 1986
by Futura Publications, a Division of
Macdonald & Co (Publishers) Ltd
London & Sydney

ISBN 0 7088 2694 6

Printed and bound in Great Britain by
Collins, Glasgow

Futura Publications
A Division of
Macdonald & Co (Publishers) Ltd
Maxwell House
74 Worship Street
London EC2A 2EN

A BPCC plc Company

To
EVELYN
(Mrs. Eustace Benn)
in affection and admiration
Mickle

1

Emmanuel leaned back in his chair and sighed, a sigh of contentment. On his desk—that desk which had once belonged to Disraeli—lay the marked catalogues of the Cathcart sales, one which would take place in London, the other at the family place in Hertfordshire. Emmanuel had expected that the family would have to sell their wonderful old pictures, their china, silver and books. The old earl had died only six years ago, his son who inherited had lived only eighteen months, and the estate could not stand the drain of two lots of death duty.

Hard luck just the same! He hated to think of these collections of lovely things being broken up and dispersed. Well, he would buy some of the pictures, and possibly some of the more exquisite pieces of furniture in London ; Simeon could go down to Selton and bid for silver, any rare books—though they hung fire in these days—china and the like.

Simeon was distinctly sound. His father remembered the day he had told him that he wished to come into the firm, and that he had bought Chaffers book on silver marks! Since then the boy had studied, and gathered knowledge at every opportunity. Emmanuel doubted if even old Arbuthnot could question any decision of Simeon's.

How old was he now? Emmanuel Gollantz had never found it easy to remember dates except when it came to dealing with pictures. What a long time ago it seemed since he stood in his flat in Milan and imagined that a cat had got into Juliet's bedroom ; how angry he had felt that apparently neither the doctor nor the nurse had the sense to turn it out. The thin cry proved to be Simeon announcing his entrance to a world which he apparently disliked.

What a queer life his had been, Emmanuel reflected. First his

—virtual—banishment from England, when he had accepted it to save his mother distress because he adored her and Bernstein had said that she must be spared all worry. He remembered his first little shop in Milan, when he had engaged Guido Moroni as his assistant; Guido who was now his partner, who ran the gallery in Milan so admirably; Guido who used to clean his nails with an old dagger, who was inclined to breathe garlic over you, and who now was one of the most fastidious men imaginable.

Juliet had come there, looking for old wallpapers for her villa at Como. His 'Lovely Juliet' who had captured his heart, who would always remain in her special niche in his memory, aloof and apart. He had begged her to marry him, and she had refused. Not because—he knew that now—she had not loved him, but because she was the wife of Vernon Seyre who refused to divorce her, and had been the mistress of the dead Leon Hast. So she had turned Emmanuel away and he had gone back to England.

His face was grave as his thoughts were reflected in his expression. How terribly unhappy he had been; then he had married Viva Heriot. Viva was, and always would be, wonderful. They had been very happy, at first, until he immersed himself too much in his work—because the thought of Juliet Forbes came so often to his mind, because he grew apprehensive, and found that only by working until he was tired to death could he close his eyes without seeing Juliet's lovely face.

Then she had come to England, and he had heard her sing, he had met her again, and knew that nothing had changed. Viva had been wonderful about it, and Emmanuel went back to Milan. It was there that Viva had come to see him, and told him that she wanted him to let her divorce him—she wanted to marry 'Toby' Tatten.

Emmanuel liked Tatten; admittedly he was—to put it mildly—limited in his outlook, in his interests, but he was a good fellow and he and Viva married and were very happy. Seyre had divorced Juliet, and married someone else, an American, Emmanuel thought.

He and Juliet were married by the British Consul in Milan. A year was granted to them—Emmanuel's 'perfect year'. He had never known that such happiness was possible. Simeon was born, Juliet recovered, went to Paris to sing and returned with a cold. She had said. 'Paris is never lucky for me. I always catch cold there. This is nothing, in two days I shall be well.'

In four days she was dead, and Emmanuel's life, that perfect life which he had loved, was over. How kind people had been, trying to help him, and to lift him out of the ghastly depression which overwhelmed him.

As his mind wandered back, his handsome face lost its look of contentment. That particular wound had gone too deep; all through his life, however well the scar might seem to have healed, memories stabbed it into life again. He clenched his hands—those fine hands with their sensitive fingers, with the ring which old Emmanuel had from his father in Vienna, which he in his turn had given to his son Max, and Max had handed on to his elder son, Emmanuel.

Emmanuel looked suddenly a little older, his hair seemed to have become more silvered at the temples, his mouth—that well-cut, but rather full mouth which was part of the legacy from his Jewish ancestors—drooped at the corners.

His grandfather, old Emmanuel, who had become a figure which was almost legendary, had once said to him, 'Ve are Jews, my dear poy. Very vell, I don't believe t'at you or your brudder hev effer been to *shule* in your lives, but you remain Jews. T'isn't *shule* makes Jews, it is blood.

'Remember Jews are sed people, melancholy people. One moment t'ay laugh, the next a leetle cloud comes over the sun, and they—sigh, and allow depression to take possession of t'em. It is part of t'eir 'eritage. Part of t'eir history, t'eir memories are too long, too vivid.

'English people—and 'ow much I like t'em—seeng "Look, if you please for the silver lining!" Jews look, but t'ey don't find it! Ah, vell, my dear poy, we must accept eet. Maybe it is why we Jews sometimes turn to material t'ings. Maybe put too much trust in—vell, in chust—*t'ings*. T'ings ve can handle, t'ings ve can place upon a value, no? Beauty—ah, ve are ver' sensitive to t'at. No metter if it is pictures, furniture, or even'—his grandson remembered how he had smiled—'loffley vimmen. Not in bed vays, in cheneral decent Jews don't like—vat do you call t'em? —harlots. I am a ver' old man, I hev loffed my life, but neffer hev I found it possible to pay money for one, two, three—even more—hours of vot is called—loff!

'Oh, I hev seen beautiful vimmen, hev admired t'em, yes, hev even had the chance to go and climb into their beds—for a price.' He shuddered. 'The price was alvays too high! "T'ank you," I hev said, "and now—good night." My poy, I hev neffer liked to use the toot'brush of some odder person!'

The sudden ache had subsided, and he forced his memory to move forward. He had married Viva—for the second time—after a decent interval when 'Toby' Tatten had been killed in a riding accident. It had been a wonderful success. He had loved her dearly, he admired her, found her stimulating, she was a wonderful companion, and interested in his affairs without ever attempting to direct him. No, Viva was a splendid and wonderful woman, a great companion to any man, and he was profoundly grateful.

They had gone to live at Ordingly, the big house which old Emmanuel had bought outside London. Angela—his beloved mother—had lived there with them. She and Viva were very close, and when Angela was taken ill, Viva had been marvellous to her.

Emmanuel's face clouded again. He remembered so well when his mother first became ill, Meyer Bernstein, who had been their doctor—although he was now a famous physician he was still willing to drive out to Ordingly to attend any of the Gollantz for whatever ailment—had seen her, and afterwards talked to Emmanuel.

'What illness?—No illness to which I can put a name,' he said. 'She is *tired*, yes, and I think lonely without your father, the good Max. She has no pain, she has no suffering—and shall have none, I promise.'

'But my mother is not old,' Emmanuel protested.

Bernstein smiled. 'Old, what is old? Angela is seventy-t'ree. Women live to be a hundred, and get a kind telegram from the Queen, congratulating them. Perhaps some of them have lived like cows, calmly, eating and sleeping. Angela has *lived*. She has crowded so much into each year, she has suffered, she has carried the burdens of other people, old Emmanuel, then Max, later your dear Juliet—ah, she suffered over that, I can tell you! Your—*accident*, and Julian going to America.'

Emmanuel said, 'She adored Julian!'

'When you adore someone, make an idol of them and then find their clay feet—that hurts badly, Emmanuel. Poor old Bill Masters—who had been in love with her for years and years—she misses him. No, the life of Angela has not been an easy one. If she is tired, then, my dear boy, let her rest.'

Angela had been content to lie in her big bed, with the wide window which looked over the big trees of Ordingly, which she loved and which Max had loved also, and just allow life to slip away.

'I'm not ill,' she had told Viva, 'I'm tired. I want to rest—sometimes I think that it is the longest rest possible that I am waiting for. I don't really mind a great deal—I don't mind at all. You'll take care of my dear Emmanuel, Julian is a rich man in these days, and Bill is content with his work and his wife—oh, dear! Viva, I do find her so dull! No, my small flock are quite safe. I've known such splendid people—it's nice to lie here and watch the pageant pass—some of them such swaggering people like Leon Hast—how I disliked him—some of them magnificent, like my dear old Emmanuel, some straight and upright like Max, some kind and rather heavy in hand like Bill Masters—so many of them. There, I shall go to sleep and see my pageant go past. Good night, Viva.'

She slept and never woke, and to Emmanuel it was like the end of the world. He had always known that his brother Julian was her favourite son, that was why he had shielded Julian so often, taken the blame for things which he had not done—simply to preserve Angela's illusions about Julian.

He remembered how for the third time he had seen a long procession of cars move slowly away from the big porch at Ordingly. The day had been beautiful, the kind of day which used to make Angela say 'It's good to be alive!'

So many of his father's relatives had come. They had all liked Angela, many of them had loved her. They had flown from Austria, from Germany—older and thinner, and perhaps less prosperous than he remembered them, bearing marks of suffering on their faces. Louis Lara and his wife, the almost fabulous Olympia, had come from Paris; Paoli Mancini with his magnificent wife, Iva Alfano, and little Guido Moroni from Milano; little Gilbert—who had been Juliet's accompanist, white haired, and stooping—so many people who had held their places in Angela's life. Her own families—from the shires—Drews, Wilmots and the rest.

At the last moment a young man had arrived. Tall, slim, the replica of his father years ago—Julian's son, Max, who had flown from America. His manners were good, and the boyish charm which Emmanuel remembered from an earlier visit had developed into an urbane self-assurance. But Emmanuel's old memories of all that he had suffered at Julian's hands were so strong that he found it difficult to accept the young man without some feeling of repugnance.

He explained that his father would have come with him, but he was suffering from one of his periodic attacks of acute pain from his back. Emmanuel reflected that Julian had always suffered from 'one of his periodic attacks' when he was faced with doing something which he disliked. He also remembered his brother's terrible fear of death, which almost amounted to an obsession. His face looked grim, his mouth set, as he said, 'I think that we ought to be moving,' and offered his arm to Viva.

That night he felt that Ordingly was empty—felt for the first time the complete realization that Angela had gone, and remembered the line 'My house is left unto me desolate'.

Viva had been very gentle, almost unexpectedly gentle, and understanding. He had tried to tell her how grateful he was to her, she had listened, a little tender smile on her lips, her eyes very kind as she watched him.

'My dear, I can do so little,' she said.

'You do so much, Viva. I am so gr-rateful. I feel that I've been ver-ry ill, and sick people are tedious, no matter how much you love them.'

'You have been ill,' she agreed, 'you've been a sick man. Now, you will begin to get better, stronger. That doesn't mean that you forget; it means that you've adjusted yourself to things. Emmanuel, how much longer is Max going to stay here? He's been here for over a month.'

He looked at her sharply. 'You don't like him?'

'I didn't say so. He's a modern product, I suppose. Everything moves round Max Gollantz. He's sufficiently attractive, but he's another Julian. Damned selfish, damned self-centred. He tells me that his father and grandfather—how well I remember old

Van der Hoyt!—write telling him to look around, to get ideas. "We're always going for new ideas at Van der Hoyt, Inc.," he said. I can't say that I've seen him doing much looking around since he came here.'

She had gone on to say that she needed a holiday, that Emmanuel needed one, that they'd shut up Ordingly. 'Keep on the servants, of course—let them take their holidays in rotation. I can arrange that with Mrs. Cowley. If Max wants to stay in England, let him take a small flat—in London.'

He had agreed, for he had found Max Gollantz's presence something of a trial although he was a nice enough lad. His manners were good enough and he didn't give much trouble, but it was obvious that he and Simeon disliked each other, and Bill—easy-going Bill—didn't care for him.

Bill said, 'Oh, damn it, didn't we have sufficient to go through with his pernicious father, without having this replica foisted on us!'

Yet there was nothing definitely wrong with Max; Emmanuel mentally exhorted himself to be unprejudiced and fair. It was just that he brought back Julian too vividly. After all, you couldn't blame the fellow for that!

He and Viva had gone for their holiday. They had gone back to Lake Garda where they had spent their second honeymoon, and had stayed at the same hotel. He remembered how two little dogs had come and 'made compliments' to him; now there was only one, and she walked more slowly, and seemed to sleep a good deal. The peace of the lake, with the mountains in the distance, the soft air, all conspired to soothe him, and refresh him. Guido came over to see him and declared that when he retired—'the which I shall never do!'—he would build himself a villa on the shores of the lake, and 'like Catullus inscribe poetry of the most melancholy and of great beauty'.

As they drove home, Viva said: 'My Emmanuel, you're better; much as I admire your interesting pallor, I am attracted by the faint tan which you have acquired. I shall get you some when we get to London, it's made up by all the best chemists acting on the statement that "handsome men are slightly bronzed".'

Max had transferred himself to a small and expensive flat in King Street, St. James's. Emmanuel flung himself into his work, feeling that once again he was charged with energy. Simeon said, 'I say, you do look well!' Hannah Rosenfeldt nodded and beamed, 'So! Again we have that man we know, eh? You will face work—and there is much—with a good, courageous heart, no?'

It was soon after their return that Viva told him she wanted to 'have a small string of horses'.

'If you had said pearls,' Emmanuel smiled, 'I should have understood.'

'I should never ask for a *small* string of pearls. Anyway, I have enough to supply half the oysters in Scott's. No, I've not got enough to do. Mrs. Cowley is wonderful, everything runs like clockwork, the servants seem very contented. What with a new cinema in the village, and the bus service running as it does, and your bit of brilliance in getting that extra car to take them in relays to town, their lives are one long round of gaiety and fun. And why the devil shouldn't they be! I'm all for it.'

Carteret had talked to her; he didn't advise a big string, he would find her a first-rate lot to make a good start, and keep an eye on them whenever she needed advice. There were plenty of loose boxes at Ordingly; Emmanuel rode very seldom, and even with Viva's two horses there was still ample room. They would be no expense to anyone but herself, 'and soon they'll begin to make money for me! Do you mind, Emmanuel?'

Of course he didn't mind, in fact he had begun to take a great interest in the beautiful creatures. He chose her racing colours, pale grey with yellow hoops. When she had her first win, at a small race-meeting at Tollermere, he was as proud as if she had won the classic races—all of them in the same year.

'Their names are a little str-range, don't you think? R-roaring Gal—and she is so pr-retty too. I have a gr-reat affection for little Miss R-roaring Gal.'

Viva nodded. 'She's a useful little thing, but it's Hereward who is going to do really big things. Just watch him! As 'Buster' Carteret says, we shall all be putting our shirts on Hereward.'

Hereward was a fine gelding, even Emmanuel could see that; more, he was good tempered, friendly, and appeared to have no objectionable traits.

There Emmanuel sat, in his austere but splendid office; admittedly it was restrained splendour; it was always kept scrupulously tidy, perhaps most things in it were just a little, as Simeon said, 'over life size', but to Emmanuel that fact gave them an additional air of solidity.

'After all,' he had told Simeon, 'we Gollantzes, the firm, are a little more than life size! How many people have we in the workshops? Forty, eh? And the upholstery? Twenty-four, eh! Repairing, painting, and a dozen other things as well. Three men scour-ring all over the world for treasures, and it all began with your great-gr-randfather opening show-r-rooms in Campden Hill.'

Simeon smiled at him across the big desk, 'I don't think that either old Emmanuel or Grandfather Max will be able to find much fault with us.'

'I should never wish that either of them should, in any way, Simeon. I am very pr-roud of our business—it is unique.'

The telephone buzzed and Simeon said, 'I'll take it, Father.' He listened, then said, 'Very well, I'll come at once.' He turned back to his father. 'Someone to see me—what a bore, just as I fancied you and I could get down to talk about the sale at Selton.'

Emmanuel watched him go, moving easily, closing the heavy door without either effort or clumsiness. No one would suspect that the boy had lost one foot in that air-raid. Simeon had always kept himself physically fit, he had never put on weight—Bill Gollantz was the only one of the family who had done that, and Bill didn't care—never had cared—for strenuous exercise of any kind. Simeon rode, played golf, went swimming, and even went dancing with his wife. Emmanuel smiled with satisfaction. He'd have hated to have had a fat, overweight son.

The inter-house telephone buzzed, Simeon's voice said—keyed in its slightly official tone which he used in business interviews: 'Sir, would you see the gentleman I have here with me? Yes, I know' as his father expostulated that he saw no one without an appointment—'but it—well, it's important. Thank you, at once then.'

A moment later he heard Simeon's knock and his son entered, followed by a young man of about his own age, possibly a little older. He was tall, well built but slim—as slim as Simeon himself—with hair that had a tendency to curl, which Emmanuel noticed was rigorously repressed. His features were well cut, and his eyes very clear and intelligent. His clothes were sufficiently well cut, but it was a provincial cut.

He waved the young man to a chair, and said, 'Now, what can we do for you, Mr.——?'

Simeon leaned over the desk and handed his father a card. Emmanuel raised his eyeglass and examined it.

'Charles Emmanuel Gollantz, 28 Milson Street, Dullton.'

He laid down the card. 'What a strange coincidence—your name I mean. I imagined that I was the only Emmanuel Gollantz.'

The young man answered, and his voice, while not exactly dialect, held the inflexions of the North Country.

'It's my name too, sir, it's the name—at least Gollantz is—that I was born with. I can prove it, sir ; I've got all the proofs with me—my own birth certificate, my mother's marriage lines, all in order.'

'But—' for a moment Emmanuel was shaken out of his usual composure—'but tell me your father's name, please.'

'Julian Edward Gollantz, sir.'

Simeon watched his father's face. It was expressionless. Perhaps the lips were set a little more firmly than usual, but there was no other sign of emotion. When he spoke his voice was steady, not over-loud and expressing no surprise whatever. Simeon thought how much he admired Emmanuel.

He repeated, 'Ah—Julian Edward Gollantz. Yes, I see. Simeon, I am sure that you have work which is pr-ressing. Don't let us detain you.' Then he smiled, and the other young Gollantz thought what a kindly smile it was, and wished, suddenly, that he had a father to smile at him in that way. Not that Mum wasn't wonderful, and still attractive, but she had remarried and although her husband—who was a master-plumber—had met with considerable success and had been able to leave her in comfortable circumstances young Gollantz had always resented him. Not that he hadn't been kind ; but he never felt that Thomas Watson really believed that Julian Gollantz had married his mother in accordance with the prescribed legal methods. He had never dared to say so to Mum, for she had a fiery temper, and would have gone off the deep-end properly, but he had always felt that—somewhere—a doubt existed in Watson's not particularly active brain.

'Your name is Gollantz,' she had said to her son, 'and it's a fine family, and rolling in money. Not that I want you to get any of it. I believe in men making their own road in the world. I've never been in touch with them, never pressed any claims, but I've always kept all the proofs, and when the time comes—we'll use them. When the time comes, then you shall have them and take them to London. Your father's brother is a Bart. Your grandfather, Max, he was a Bart, too. Your grandmother—I saw her once and bonny she was—died six months ago. No, when the time comes you shall go and make yourself known to your family.'

He had been quite content, he had his own ideas about what he wanted to do, and he had been apprenticed to Digby Ferrers, the auctioneer and valuer, a man who was highly regarded in Dullton. He had worked hard, and Ferrers had praised him for his industry and application, but when he thought of selling—possibly for the rest of his life—solid second-hand furniture, ugly tables of the Victorian era, 'what-nots' and hideous bedsteads, his heart sank a little.

He was under thirty now, his apprenticeship was served, and he was even permitted to mount the rostrum and wield the auctioneer's hammer. Some of it was amusing enough; people said that he had 'a way with him', but he was tired of ugly furniture, horrible lithographs—usually sold in lots of five or six in tarnished gilt frames—jugs, basins and 'accessories', as he always added hastily; but the old fashioned chamber-pots always got a laugh. He longed to be selling Chippendale, Hepplewhite, and Sheraton. When he announced, 'A very useful lot of china-dishes, plates, cups and saucers—what offers?' he thought of the great sale-rooms in London where two small china figures would be shown, 'a most valuable and interesting pair. Shepherd and shepherdess, Chelsea, of the best period. Both bearing the gold anchor mark. Both completely undamaged in any way. This is an occasion, these figures are unique, and—' with a small discreet laugh—'I have been selling china for many years now, but "unique" is a word I use very, very seldom. Now, shall we say—to make a start—a hundred guineas?'

So as his discontent grew, he told Mum, and confessed he

wanted to go to London, and see if Emmanuel Gollantz could not find a position for him where he might study what he called 'real furniture' and 'real china'.

She listened, gravely and attentively. 'Aye, lad, I think that the time has come. Get yourself fitted out nicely—don't pull a poor mouth before these grand folks. Hold your head up, and remember you're as good as what they are. I'll get all the papers ready for you.'

Now, he sat in this wonderful room, while behind a marvellous desk Emmanuel Gollantz faced him. Charles had never come in contact with such a man, had never seen such composure, never understood before the full meaning of the word 'noncommittal'. Here was a man who didn't give himself away; he had given no sign as to what effect Charles's announcement might have made upon him. He was calm, restrained and yet perfectly courteous. His face was impassive, but, when you met his eyes, there was kindness in their depths.

Now he said: 'Naturally, you will realize that this is a—shall we say?—ver-ry astonishing statement. It will be necessary in common fairness for me to investigate it thoroughly. Not,' hastily, 'that I doubt its ver-racity, but one must not take such things on tr-rust even if you regard the person who advances these claims as completely tr-rustworthy.'

Charles said, 'That's all right, sir. I'll leave you all the papers, but—I haven't made any claims, neither shall I!'

The well-marked eyebrows lifted a fraction, 'No?'

'Certainly not. Mum and I have sufficient to live on, but I've got a favour to ask—I'll go into that later, if I may, sir. It's nothing to do with money, I promise you that.'

Emmanuel's smile broke out. 'From what I have heard, I think that this favour, if it is within my power, will most certainly be gr-ranted. Now will you come here tomorrow to meet my brother, William, who is a solicitor? Shall we say at twelve o'clock? If you will go along to my son's office, you can discuss with him where you can stay. Until tomorrow then.'

He did not offer to shake hands, as Charles rather expected him to do, for everyone in Dullton shook hands on the slightest provocation, but his smile was very warm and friendly.

Charles said, 'Would you care for me to leave the papers with you, sir?'

Emmanuel shook his head. 'That's kind of you, but I think not. You shall entrust them to my brother, William, tomorrow officially. Again—good-bye.'

The door had scarcely closed behind him when the telephone buzzed.

'Miss Rosenfeldt is here, Sir Emmanuel. Can you see her?'

'Certainly, and send in tea, please.'

Hannah Rosenfeldt entered a moment later. She was immense, her face was that of a very obvious Jewess, her eyes full of intelligence. Her hands were small and beautiful, her figure non-existent. Emmanuel had known her all his life. She had been secretary to his grandfather and his father ; now, when she was over sixty, she still came down to the *salon*—the galleries—four times a week. She went round all the show rooms, her keen eyes taking in everything, the slightest hint of tarnish on silver, a trace of dust on a plate, lack of polish on one of the exquisite pieces of furniture, and Hannah Rosenfeldt saw it—and dealt with the person responsible.

Reuben Davis, who had the firm's affairs and accounts at his finger-tips, never hesitated to turn to her for advice, even though there were times when she could be almost harshly critical. Everyone feared her, and everyone liked and trusted her.

For years she had lived with Emmanuel and Simeon in Heber Square ; then when Simeon married, she had taken a tiny house in Chelsea, had installed a perfect pianoforte, a radio, and a most expensive long-playing gramophone, for music was—after the Gollantz family—her passion. She dressed expensively but with little attention to prevailing fashions ; she preferred rich, stiff silks, and fine velvets, and rarely wore anything except dark colours.

Emmanuel came forward to meet her and taking her hand he led her to a chair. 'Tea will be here in a moment. How pleasant to see you, Hannah. Last time you were in the galler-ries you didn't honour me.'

'I hed no time, it was necessary for me to explain, in detail, what is meant by—clean silver. Emagine it, a George the Third tea-pot, with still plate powder clinging to the hendle! Tea-pots are the devil! If they are of china, then there is probably dirt gathered round the place where the handle joins the tea-pot ; if it is cups—again where the handle joins the cup! T'ese people—

ganefs who take the salaries of Prime Ministers, and do twice as much harm! I lose patience with the vorld! Now, tell me, how are t'ings with you?'

Tea was brought and the tray was placed on a small table beside Miss Rosenfeldt, who immediately inspected the handles of the cups, and nodded a grudging approval. The door closed, and she said, 'How are you? And Vifa?'

'Both well,' Emmanuel assured her, 'but today, Hannah, I have had a visit from someone who—I honestly believe—is a member of the family. A son of my br-rother Julian.'

'Ugh! That one! Already you have one son of his making himself a play-boy in London. Where does this other one come from, tell me?'

Carefully, dispassionately, Emmanuel told her the story. She listened, then said, 'In all probability a bastard, eh?'

'I don't think so. He had his mother's marriage lines, his own birth certificate. His mother was a chorus girl in a Manchester pantomime. She met Julian—I suppose—when he was going so much to that place where he stood for Parliament. It's not far from Manchester. He is coming here in the morning to meet Bill and myself.'

He sipped his tea with appreciation. 'I liked him. He must be a few years older than Simeon. His clothes were—terr-rible, and his tie beyond belief, but he was well set-up, decent manners, and assured me that he was not here to "make claims".'

'What then is he here for, tell me?' she asked.

'Apparently to establish the fact that he is a Gollantz and that we r-recognize him as such.'

'And if he is one of you, Max Gollantz is a bastard, and Julian is not legally married to the Van der Hoyt woman, so?' She sighed gustily. 'I emagined that we were finished with Julian, but no, he pursues you, always there is something new to cause worry and disturbance. Trouble—always at the back is this Julian; unhappiness, always Julian has caused it, has engineered it. Care must be exercised, Emmanuel, great care. And Max Gollantz, what does he do with himself all day? Spend money, no?'

'A good deal, I imagine. He takes Viva out dancing; she enjoys that, he dances beautifully, she says. But what he actually *does*, I have no idea. He told me that he was looking for ideas for Van der Hoyt, Inc. I have not heard what he has found.'

Hannah drank the last drops of her tea, and set down her cup.

'He will find nothing good, this one. Through him you will find nothing but trouble. Watch carefully, Emmanuel. I once said how like old Emmanuel you were—but that you lacked the *hard core* which he had. Cultivate that hard core, you'll need it. There I must go, I have friends coming in this evening to play Schubert and Mozart. I listen and all everyday things seem to dissolve into thin air; only melodies—such melodies—remain. Good-bye and *mazeltov*.'

He went back to his chair, telephoned on his private line to his brother Bill, and told him very briefly about the visit from Charles Gollantz.

Bill puffed and blew a little, for he was growing very stout, taking after the Jaffes, on his father's side of the family. 'At twelve, eh? Lunch with me afterwards, will you? Good.'

'Will you handle it alone or with Charles Wilmot?'

'Charles? Oh, he's away in some place in Italy, Abano, taking mud baths for his rheumatism. I'll tackle it. Good-bye.'

2

Emmanuel walked over to Simeon's office, where his son was alone, working at some figures. He looked up as his father entered, and smiled.

'The young man has gone?' Emmanuel asked.

'Yes, a few minutes ago. Father, I *like* him. There's something straight about him. Admittedly his accent is—well, it's a bit strange, and his tie is a disaster. I've told him where to go and get another before he meets Uncle Bill in the morning. He took it awfully well and said, "It would be nice if you could put me wise to a few things. I would like"—and he gave a kind of gulp—"to go to a really tip-top tailor while I'm in Town." D'you think that it would be all right if I took him along to Camforth's?'

Emmanuel said, rather drily, 'If he can afford Camforth's, why not?'

'I thought of asking him to stay with Daphne and me, Dad.'

'No, no! I hope that you didn't, Simeon. Once this affair is settled, then if you wish to that is your business, but until then —it is wiser not to.'

'He had an address, some small hotel in Kensington. His mother gave him the name, he said.'

Emmanuel rose. 'I'm going. It's been a long day, and I want to think things over. It is all going to be ver-ry difficult. Give my love to Daphne.'

As he drove home, he watched Edgware Road slip past; he liked Edgware Road, liked its bustle and air of vulgarity; he liked Maida Vale too, though he regretted the demolition of some of the handsome old houses he had known. Kilburn always seemed too crowded, and he was relieved when he began to get into roads which had fields on either side, where houses might be springing up very fast but where there were still trees, and an occasional old house. Then the last stretch before he reached Ordingly; he slowed down a little for this was his favourite stretch of road. How many times had he driven slowly along here, and tried to work out his daily problems? Some of them had been trivial, things which, when he had viewed them calmly, had no real importance. Others required more thought and deep consideration. Worries concerning Angela, his father, the necessity of solving the problem of his brother Julian and himself living under the same roof at Ordingly, his father's belief—which had never been completely shaken—that he was hard and unforgiving towards his brother. That faint distrust regarding Juliet; his father had liked her and admired her as an artist, but he had deplored that his eldest son should have married a woman—however beautiful, however talented—who had been the mistress of Leon Hast. All those things he had worried over when he was driving along that last stretch of road which led to Ordingly.

Now there was this new puzzle to be solved, the question of Charles Emmanuel Gollantz. If they accepted him, if his proofs and claims were valid, what would be the position? Was Julian to be denounced as a bigamist? For that matter his first wife had married again, someone called Thomas Watson. Had she, too, committed bigamy? There was something distinctly likeable about the young man, despite his queer accent and his deplorable clothes. There had been considerable dignity in his tone when he reminded Emmanuel that he was making no 'claims'. Old Emmanuel and Max Gollantz would have approved of that!

Well, it was all beyond him. Nothing to be done except wait and see how Bill would deal with this problem in the morning. There was something very reassuring about Bill, he was solid—both physically and morally. He was astute, and he was—at the same time—essentially kind.

Emmanuel drove faster, conscious that he was tired and longing to get home and talk to Viva. He knew that though Bill and Simeon both liked and admired Viva, whom they regarded as being a little hard, hard like a well-cut diamond or a highly polished piece of steel. Emmanuel had learnt that her hardness was one of the most superficial things about her. Fundamentally her heart was very warm and—at times—very soft.

He turned the car into the drive, and through to the big yard where the garages were, as well as the loose boxes. The yard always gave Emmanuel a little thrill of pleasure ; the paving stones were kept so meticulously clean, and if anyone were sufficiently careless or unfortunate as to leave traces of oil from a car, Andy Miller regarded it as an offence which should be punished by law.

Miller was a small, wizened-looking man, with a face wrinkled like an old apple. His legs were slightly bandy, and his eyes like gimlets. His knowledge of horses was profound, his affection and admiration for them unlimited. 'Buster' Carteret had sent him to Viva and he had taken to her at once.

Viva had offered him a small cottage situated in the park, he had shaken his head, and looked slightly disgusted.

'Bean't there no loft as could be furnished. I like ter sleep wi' me 'osses, not miles away.'

'And Tom and Fred, you don't want them to sleep in one of the lofts?'

'It's a matter o' less importance nor nowt *wheer* they sleep, so's they're 'ere when I want 'em i' t' marnin'.'

Now Andy watched Emmanuel drive in very neatly, and stood waiting for him as he left the garage.

'Good day, Andy,' Emmanuel said.

'An' t' same to you, sir. I'll say one thing abart you, if it's t' last words I speak—I've known a few gents i' my time, an' very few can get a biggish car, like wot yours is, inter a garridge as neat as what you do.'

Emmanuel smiled. 'Thank you, Andy. I appreciate that very much.'

'Think on,' Andy continued, 'I don't say the same about all as comes 'ere. Young Simeon's kereful, 'er ladyship—well, she's what I call a very stylish driver—takes risks but,' impressively, 'they come off. Yon nevvy o' yourn, Max—'oly terror. Bang, whizz, crash, bump! That's 'im. I shouted at 'im last time 'e was 'ere, "Mind my ruddy paint, can't you?" 'E gave me a dirty luke! Told me 'e wanted 'is car cleanin'. Garrod was out wi' you, 'er ladyship was out wi' young 'Arris. "Let Tom or Fred do it," 'e sed, "they've nothing to do." I tole 'im proper—Tom an' Fred would only 'ave nothink to do when Andy Miller 'ad drawn 'is last breath and gone to 'is Maker. I tell you straight, sir, I'll not 'ave 'im 'anging abart round *my* 'osses. Said as 'e'd like a canter on 'Ereward!' Andy drew a deep breath at the very thought of the audacious proposal.

'What did you say?' Emmanuel asked.

'I said,' his voice was impressive, 'I said as I ondly 'oped as 'is 'ead never ached while he was given permission to ride 'Ereward, by me—*or* 'er ladyship. That's what I told 'im.'

'Very trying,' Emmanuel agreed. 'Well, Andy, her ladyship's lucky to have you to look after the horses. Good-bye, Andy.'

'Goo'-bye, sir.'

Emmanuel walked out of the big yard, and went towards the house. Ordingly was a handsome building, without holding any particular architectural features. Good, flat-fronted late Georgian, with a rather fine and dignified porch added some years after the actual house was built. He mounted the wide steps which led to the terrace. He had always liked the wide terrace, with its stone balustrade, decorated at intervals with huge stone vases which were always filled wih growing flowers.

Anderson, the gardener, said, 'One thing he's fussy about—them vawses. "Keep 'em filled," them's his orders. Likes to see something bright.'

Reaching the top of the steps, Emmanuel liked to linger for a moment, and turn back to look over the land which was his, the land which his father had loved, which old Emmanuel had bought for a home for his family and his descendants. He loved the wide spreading trees, the smooth lawns, the glimpse of the old red-brick walls—now weathered to a colour which was almost a soft rose—of the kitchen gardens. In the distance a silver ribbon showed where the river flowed; that river where he had fished, and boated and punted when he was younger.

A good place, a safe place, he reflected, a place where a man could sink his roots deep, where he could feel that he was home. He had been offered huge sums to induce him to sell some of the land, and he had refused them all. He didn't want additional money, he wanted to keep Ordingly.

He had been fortunate both in his business and in his speculations; even though he felt the burden of taxation weigh heavily, he could shoulder it. Simeon had his mother's money, it had been left to Emmanuel who had refused to touch a penny of it. Simeon was a rich young man, for Juliet had made a great deal of money, and in addition Leon Hast—people said that he had been a millionaire—had left her his entire fortune.

Viva was well endowed, and when her mother, Lady Heriot, Aunt Beatrice—once Miss Beatrice Grantley of the old 'Gaiety' —died she would have more. Not that he didn't want Aunt Beatrice to live for years; she was one of the few people who really amused him with her Edwardian slang and phrases.

Hawkins must have seen his figure through the glass door, for Emmanuel heard it open, and heard, too, the scrabble of feet. He looked down, and smiled. There were three small dogs circling round him, Viva's two Pekes—Ping and Pong—and his own Pug, Smog. All three black faces were alight with realized expectancy; they had waited for him, and their hopes were realized.

He asked them questions concerning their day's doings—had they been good, had they eaten their dinners, how many wild boars had they killed in the park? They listened, their heads on one side, their wide mouths stretching from ear to ear.

He stooped and stroked them in rotation, then said, 'Now, let's go in.' They rushed in before him and flung themselves down on the big rug in the hall as if exhausted by their efforts.

Emmanuel said to Hawkins, 'No manners, have they? They might at least let me come in first, don't you think?'

Hawkins replied that he had always heard that Pekes were haughty, and that he supposed that Pugs had much the same temperament. He added that her ladyship was in her bedroom.

He walked up the wide staircase with its low steps, and along the corridor to Viva's room. He knocked, his face already softening, his mouth almost breaking into a smile. He heard her voice, very clear, bidding him to come in.

She had been too wise to even hint that she might have liked Angela's room, that had been left without any change whatever. Her own satisfied her very well, with its wide windows commanding a splendid view. When Emmanuel entered Viva was sitting at her dressing-table; the light caught her hair and showed it very golden. He bent down and kissed her cheek, lightly, and then kissed her again on her bare shoulder.

'Hello, my pet. You're late, aren't you?'

'Your loquacious Miller kept me chatting, and then I had a word with the dogs. I think you're lucky having Miller.'

'So do I! Would you like some tea?'

'I had a cup with Hannah Rosenfeldt. I might not say no—at least not very emphatically—to a whisky-and-soda. Shall I ring? You're dressing early, aren't you?'

'Max telephoned. He wants to take me to a dance—he called it a ball—an immense affair in aid of some stupendous charity. You don't mind, do you?'

Emmanuel, his face grave, said, 'Darling, of course I don't mind, but this is the second time this week you've been out dancing with him. Just be a little careful, won't you? I don't want to have him—losing his heart, always supposing that he has one.'

Viva laughed, 'Idiot!' Then to Hawkins who had entered with a tray, 'Put it there on that table.' She turned back to Emmanuel, 'He's a child. Do try to remember that I'm well over forty!'

'My eyes, and they are remarkably good, tell me that obviously that is the perfect age! I don't want you to be—bothered, that's all.'

She took the cocktail which Emmanuel handed to her, and her eyes met his, smiling. 'Come with me, then,' she said. 'Give me your protection!'

'I can't, I've too much to do. Anyway, I haven't a ticket.'

'Oh, this work! My hated rival! I'll guarantee to get a ticket—they're always glad to sell an extra one. Can't you come?'

He shook his head. 'I'd love to, but I've a heavy day tomorrow and a whole lot of stuff to go through——' He leaned down and kissed her. 'The old stor-ry, "I could not love thee dear so much——" '

Viva shrugged her shoulders. 'My dear, it's not like you to be so lacking in originality. You'll assure me next that you have been faithful to me, "in your fashion", which means that Gollantz business must come first.'

But her lips smiled and her eyes were very tender. She had realized long ago that he allowed nothing to come between him and the work which he had in hand. Years ago she had resented it—she had tried to make him jealous, had actually quarrelled about his devotion to his work ; now she had grown wiser and more tolerant. Possibly she loved and understood him better.

When Emmanuel had bathed and changed he joined Viva in the drawing-room, to find young Max with her. His smooth elegance always irritated Emmanuel a little ; true, the fellow wore his clothes well, was always immaculate, but there was a sort of self-satisfaction which seemed to emanate from him.

Viva said, 'Max has brought his car, so he can drive me up to Town.'

'I'd rather you took Garrod,' Emmanuel said. 'He's done nothing today, I drove myself. If Max drives back with you he can collect his car.'

Max looked suddenly sulky. 'I'd rather drive up in my car.'

'Then do,' Emmanuel replied with great suavity, 'and Viva can drive in ours.'

'Seems terribly elaborate, taking two cars and a driver.'

'Possibly—we're rather elaborate people.'

He watched his nephew, letting his mind rush forward to what might transpire tomorrow when Bill examined the proofs which Charles had brought with him. If they were watertight it would shatter this young man's small world, damage his self-esteem badly, except that, like his father, he was probably endowed with the ability to rise above such things, or at least to turn them to his own advantage, as Julian had done with everything which had seemed to be a disaster. He remembered how Julian had once boasted that he was only 'baffled to fight better'. He remembered, too, how Bill had raised his eyebrows and said, 'Did you say—fight better?'

During dinner Viva felt that there was a strained atmosphere, Emmanuel was studiously polite to his nephew, but he invariably seemed to ask questions which produced unsatisfactory replies.

She said, 'You're looking tired, Max.'

He nodded. 'I believe that I am. I've got a new flivver—new car.'

'Always exhausting having to choose a new car,' Emmanuel said casually.

'Well, your British cars are so good, seems like you can't go wrong, and yet you've got to be selective.'

'Quite. And you have—selected . . . ?'

'I've got a Bentley.'

Again Emmanuel nodded. 'A very pleasant little car.'

He sipped his wine, then added, 'I should like one myself, but they're too expensive for me. Worth it, I'm sure, but——' he shrugged his shoulders.

'Yours is a—what is it?'

'His is a slightly middle-aged Sunbeam, mine's a Sunbeam-Talbot,' Viva said.

Emmanuel smiled across the table at her. 'As a race-horse owner, my wife must have a good car, to inspire public confidence. And have you found any brilliant ideas to take back to America?'

'I'm on the track of several things.'

'Splendid! You must tell me about some of them—one day.'

The atmosphere was growing more and more frigid, Viva felt, and the air seemed to be filled with antagonism. This smooth-haired fellow with his immaculate clothes and handsome face was obviously on the defensive.

'Oh, for God's sake,' she thought, 'don't let's have another family feud. Max is a play-boy, and there is nothing Emmanuel hates so much. I doubt if he's done a stroke of actual work since he came to England.' She said, 'Let's have coffee in the drawing-room,' and rose abruptly.

Max held the door open for her. Like most American young men he had excellent manners. He thought, 'Gosh, she's lovely. May not be all that young, but she's got style, finish. Damn that pretentious prig for making her take his ancient Sunbeam and a chauffeur! I don't wonder that my father loathes him—under all that smooth manner he's as hard as nails.'

They drank their coffee, which Emmanuel made himself. Max, watching, stigmatized it as 'another affectation'. Made in some Italian machine. It was admirable coffee, but Max thought, 'Beastly foreign contraption! He learnt that when he was living with that singing tart of his in Milan—which he always calls—Milano. What a darned shame that Simeon will get this place and the title. I'll swear that if he was born in wedlock it was by the skin of his teeth. My father's told me as much. I'd have been the third baronet—or the fourth if my father inherited first. Damn' shame.'

Hawkins entered. 'The car is there, m'lady.'

'Tell him to wait five minutes,' Viva said. 'Emmanuel, give me a liqueur—yes, brandy, and another cup of your coffee. No one,' she said to Max, 'makes coffee as Emmanuel does.'

Emmanuel, handing her the little glass, gave his small ceremonious bow. 'If it pleases you, then my life has not been wasted—thank you.'

It was Emmanuel who brought her cape and put it round her, saying, 'Have a wonderful time—and don't be too late.' Then leaning forward a little he said very softly, 'You look wonderful tonight—as always.'

He ran down the steps to see that the big fur rug was tucked round her. She protested that it was not cold, but he insisted. Max watched how deftly his hands moved; he never seemed to fumble, every movement was swift and exact. Then with a 'Good night, Max' and a 'Have a good time, darling', he shut the door, calling, 'All right. Garrod, off you go.'

Emmanuel went back to his study, and sat down at his desk. He opened his brief-case, and laid the papers which it contained before him. He tried to immerse himself in his work, conscious that he was tired and that he felt lonely. He had hoped for a long evening during which he might have discussed with Viva what he was already calling in his own mind 'The case of the new claimant'. Viva might not be intellectual, but she had a keen and sharp intelligence, inherited, Emmanuel suspected, from her mother, the one-time Gaiety girl, and most certainly not from her father who had been one of the most stupid men imaginable, and during his later years, a complete drunkard into the bargain.

He wished that he didn't dislike Max so much. It was stupid to dislike the fellow; he was the result of his upbringing, of the spoilt way in which he had been brought up, with too much money, and his good looks hailed as atoning for everything. Vaguely he wondered what Angela would have made of him.

Would she have given him the unstinted love which she had always given to Julian, or with her added years might she have realized that he was an idler, and something of a 'four flusher'?

All speculation, all profitless. Emmanuel turned back to his work and concentrated almost fiercely on it.

He finished his checking of costs, his assessments of values, his final instructions for Simeon about the lots for which he wished him to bid at the coming big sale. So absorbed was he that he did not hear Hawkins bring in the tray for drinks, nor see him set it down on the small table beside the big chair at the fireside. Hawkins must have lit the fire, for it was burning brightly, the fir-cones spluttering a little, giving out blue flames as they were consumed. Emmanuel looked at the clock on his desk; the time was nearly two o'clock. He stretched his hands high above his head and yawned, then rose and walked to the big chair by the fire.

He would wait for Viva; she might not be too tired for a talk, and it would make him feel happier if she knew about the interview which was to take place next—no, *this* morning.

He poured out a drink, threw two small logs on the fire, then lit a cigarette and lay back suddenly relaxed and pleasantly tired. Then rising, he switched off all the lights except the one on the table by his side, picked up a new book and began to flick over the pages. He did not realize that his eyelids were very heavy, that they slowly closed, or that his hand allowed the new book to lie neglected on his knees as he slipped into sleep.

Viva had come in very quietly; the time was nearly three. She stood looking down at Emmanuel, and felt a wave of tenderness sweep over her. He looked older than his years, his temples were silvered, and there were slight hollows under his eyes. His beautiful hands, those hands which he inherited from the first Emmanuel, lay limply on his knees.

She remembered, as she watched him, how at one time she had been desperately in love with him; then they had realized that they were totally unsuited to each other. She had asked for a divorce and he had given it to her. She remarried, dear little 'Toby' Tatten. Then after his death she had married Emmanuel again. Her love was no longer the furious, over-heated love of youth; it was temperate, but, she felt, almost limitless in its depth. He meant everything to her, and her one regret—which she had never voiced to him—was that it was unlikely and improbable that she could ever give him a child.

'I don't know,' she mused as she watched his tired, sleeping face, 'why I can't be like Sarah, Abraham's wife, who had a son at some extraordinary age! It seems unfair that those ancient people should have been given chances which we don't get—oh, damn!'

Emmanuel stirred, shook his head as if to dispel sleep, and opened his eyes. 'Hello, darling—you're back. How nice! I believe that I went to sleep.'

'Asleep! I heard your snores at the end of the drive. No, sweet, you looked all in. I wish that I hadn't wakened you. One drink each and then bedtime. I hate those great unwieldy dances. Oh it was sufficiently well done, I'll admit. Too well done for my escort. I left him at his flat, and thought that I'd send Harris over with his car in the morning.'

Emmanuel handed her a whisky-and-soda, frowning. 'You mean that he had too much to drink? The damned young cad, I think a few well-chosen words are due to Mr. Max Gollantz.'

'No, don't say anything. I'd perhaps been rather harsh, and he was sulking. I imagine that he isn't used to being checked for anything. He more or less betook himself to the buffet and emerged very much the worse for wear. Oh, I was all right. I met plenty of people I knew; your ancient wife isn't quite relegated to the ranks of chaperons—though no one indulges in them in these days, it seems—or dowagers. In fact the popular taste seems to be for the woman who is—past her first youth. I wish you could have seen Lady Fexton—you know, Millicent Fexton, she must be sixty-five if she's a day—prancing about with men young enough to be her grandsons. You're looking terribly serious, Emmanuel—nothing wrong?'

'I'm annoyed at Max's behaviour, and I've got something of a pill waiting for me in the morning. I'll tell you, as br-riefly as possible.'

He told her of the visit which Charles Emmanuel Gollantz had paid him, of his mother and her second marriage. Viva whistled.

'Looks to me as if both Julian and this lad's mother have

wandered into ranks of bigamists. It will be something of a headache for Bill to sort that out. Julian's got away with everything short of murder—and that only by the Grace of God who gave you such a thick skull, my pet—and it's time that he had to face some of the music. He's slid out of everything most conveniently—for himself—until now.'

Emmanuel frowned. 'I somehow can't feel like that,' he said slowly. 'No one dislikes my brother more than I do, but this is going to affect other people as well—his wife, his son, old Van der Hoyt—I don't suppose that it will affect this other chap's mother—there'll be extenuating circumstances and lapse of time, but it's going to hit young Max pretty hard.'

Viva finished her drink and handed Emmanuel the empty glass. 'Queer fish you are! I don't believe that you've got a bit of malice in you, or real resentment.'

'What good would it do me to harbour either malice or resentment? I don't like my brother, never r-really have done, but to find a certain satisfaction in this unfortunate business changes nothing, wipes out nothing; it only means that I consume a certain amount of nervous energy in indulging in a r-rather poor kind of satisfaction.'

'Yet as Jews, don't you believe in "an eye for an eye"?' she asked.

'Darling, our Jewish blood has been considerably watered down, hasn't it? Then if Julian did put out my eye metaphorically speaking, it won't give me my eye back to put out one of his, will it? There, it's too late—or too early to have discussions; Bill will look at me in the morning and wonder what on earth I was doing to get sunken eyed.'

'I believe that Bill and his wife have dinner, play a game of bezique, drink hot lemon and congratulate themselves on being tucked up in bed by half past ten every night of their lives,' Viva said. 'There, good night, darling, and if I'm still asleep when you leave, don't let them wake me. Elderly women must have their rest! Bless you, I love you very much.'

Emmanuel undressed slowly, he drew back the curtains and looked out on the wide lawn and the great trees beyond. He loved the peace of it, the silence of the night which still remained a friendly silence. To ears attuned to the country—and Ordingly was still 'country'—there were always small noises, little rustlings, a stir in the long grass, even the dim shape of some little animal scuttering across the lawn. Now he saw one of Andy Miller's much loved stable cats majestically stalk over the short turf, stepping daintily as if it disliked the dampness of the dew on its paws. Emmanuel sighed contentedly. He always felt better for these nightly doses of silence, for that was how he thought of them. They seemed to iron out the creases left in his mind by the worries of the day.

He walked to his dressing-table, opened one of the small drawers, and took out a small, black bound book. It was a Bible which had been given to him when he was in the Army. He was not, and never had been a religious man in the conventional sense of the word, but he had read the New Testament with grave and sincere attention.

There had been a time when he remembered that he had come very near to hating his brother Julian with an emotion which was both intense and vindictive. He had lain in bed, when he was recovering from the attack which Julian had made on him at the Galleries, and found himself actually planning how he might have his revenge on his brother.

Then when he began to be able to totter about his room, he had found the shabby little Bible, its covers rubbed through being carried in his haversack with the rest of his collection of small personal effects. He remembered many passages which he had read and admired. He sat down and turned the pages idly, allowing his eyes to rest on a verse here and there. The language pleased him, the beauty of it soothed him, and during the days which followed he found himself turning again and again to the little Book.

He read again the reply to the question as to how often it was incumbent to forgive your brother, the reference to 'an eye for an eye,' and the qualification, 'But I say unto you——' He had refrained from taking any actual revenge on Julian because of his mother, his beloved Angela. He had once said to Bill that he liked giving presents, and this was a 'present which I feel I have given Angela'.

Bill grumbled, 'Yes, but she doesn't know about it, so she doesn't know that she's had a present, old boy.'

Emmanuel had found the injunction, 'First be reconciled to your brother, then offer thy gift.'

He smiled now, when he remembered how that sentence had made him feel slightly deflated, how he had realized that he had almost begun to think himself something of a fine and unselfish fellow on account of what he had done.

As boys they had all been brought up in the Church of England. Angela had insisted and as Max—their father—was, except in the matter of giving generously to the Jewish charities, the most *link* of Jews, he had agreed. Anyway, Emmanuel remembered Max would have done practically anything to please Angela. Emmanuel had been confirmed, and still remembered—with the same acute embarrassment which he had felt at the time—the 'Talks' which the Head had given to such boys as were being prepared for confirmation.

He recalled those early evenings in the Head's library, all of them sitting in a big semi-circle, 'Like Christy minstrels before a show,' as Faversham had said. Not that any of them had made fun of the instruction which was given to them; they listened attentively, even respectfully; they rarely discussed what had been said afterwards. There was a great deal of talk about cleanliness, the Head was strong on it 'Physical cleanliness which naturally we all practise, mental cleanliness—which many of us *don't* practise, and spiritual cleanliness. A clean body and a clean mind.' There had really been very little about actual religion. The Sacraments were a prop and stay. 'It is difficult,' the Head said, 'to take the Sacrament if you've behaved in a way of which you *know* God would disapprove.'

'*The* Sacrament?' said young Fitzmaurice, who was a Catholic, and was driven to the Catholic church in the nearest town with Flower and MacMurdoch every Sunday in a cab specially hired for the purpose, 'what d'you mean?'

Gibbons said, 'Well, there are two—Baptism and the Holy Communion.'

Fitzmaurice grinned. 'You're let off lightly! There are *seven*! What do you say to that?'

Gibbons retorted. 'That you make a kind of habit of them!' and everyone had laughed.

Confirmation had made very little impression on Emmanuel Gollantz; he had gone to Communion every month while he was at school. When he left he had practically forgotten all about it. Now, this shabby little Book had come to mean something to him. He had not the least intention of renouncing his Faith, for even though he supposed that he was a Christian, a member of the Church of England, he always thought of himself as a Jew.

Emmanuel was intelligent; more, he was grateful for benefits received, and through this Jesus of Nazareth he knew that he had found solutions to many of his problems. How did he regard this Jesus? As he closed the Book and got into bed, he lay with his eyes closed, trying to come to some conclusion.

'The greatest Psychiatrist there had ever been,' he thought. 'Someone who understood what men *might* be but who made allowances for what they are.'

He closed his eyes, for they were heavy with sleep. His last thought was, 'I don't want to worship Him. But I do want to understand Him, to know Him and to profit by His wisdom. I can't actually love Julian, but I can teach myself not to be vindictive, not to find satisfaction by humiliating him. Not only because I could ever feel full of brotherly love towards him, but because—well, what is over is over; no one can take my past happiness from me, or the happiness which I enjoy with Viva. To be consumed with hate—which at one time I always was—is to limit myself, my appreciation of the good things and the happiness which have come my way.

'I can't devote time and energy to hating Julian, that would prevent my enjoyment of listening to the trees whispering, of seeing a big cat walk daintily over damp grass, the faint sound of that energetic little river as it comes pouring over the—oh, artificial—waterfall.

'I should be so busy concentrating on my hymn of hate, that I should rob myself of so many pleasures. No—it's all a tedious muddle, but with Bill's help we'll straighten it out—with as little hurt to everyone as possible.' He yawned. 'I believe that fellow Charles will feel almost as I do. . . .'

So he drifted into sleep, was called the next morning, and because he had trained himself to be satisfied with very few hours' sleep, he woke refreshed and renewed.

Lady Gollantz, her maid told him, was still asleep, and he left a message that he would telephone during the morning.

He walked down to the waiting car, erect and unruffled. Hawkins, watching him, said to Viva's maid who was standing near him, 'That's a proper gentleman, that is. Never knew his grandfather, but I knew Sir Max, and he was just the same as our gentleman. Chips off the old block, and a damned good block, if you ask me.'

Hortense, whose real name was Ellen, said, 'Yet they're Jews, aren't they? Supposed to be mean as sin.'

Hawkins eyed her coldly. 'Only by ignorant and provincial people.'

3

Emmanuel walked down to the waiting car. Viva had been right, it did look a little elderly, although it was kept in perfect condition and was obviously, as he told himself, 'a tried and trusted servant'.

He nodded to his chauffeur. 'You drive,' he said, 'I'll sit at the back, I've got some thinking to do.'

The man had been with him for many years, a fresh-faced fellow who was devoted to his master. He said, 'Beats me, Sir Emmanuel, how your brains stand up to all the thinking you give them to do. I told Miller the other day, I said, "Mine would have given way under the strain", and so they would.'

Emmanuel's eyes twinkled. 'What did Miller say?'

Garrod grinned. 'Said that they wouldn't have, because I'd got none to put a strain on! He's what you might call caustic, is Miller, sir.'

'He's a rattling good fellow. I'd trust Miller anywhere.'

Emmanuel leaned back in the corner of the car, and allowed himself to relax. In spite of his short night, he felt refreshed and revitalized. Today was going to be difficult but he felt instinctively that things were going to work out smoothly. He had liked Charles Emmanuel Gollantz; he might speak with a decided accent, he might refer to his mother as 'Mum', his clothes were distinctly unfortunate and his tie terrible, but he had a queer dignity, and Emmanuel sighed with relief, and thought again, 'It's going to be all right.'

He let his thoughts wander, and allowed himself one of his rare mental luxuries—that of thinking how fortunate he was; in spite of all the 'slings and arrows' he was fortunate. He had suffered the agonies of bereavement, but now the wound only ached intermittently. Viva was the most perfect companion, she was charming to look at, and she had for him—he knew—an affection which was deep and sincere.

His work—he smiled as he remembered how much he loved and enjoyed his work, and how much he would have disliked to have adopted any other profession. Beautiful things—he let the words trickle slowly through his consciousness, they meant so much to him. Jewels he knew little of, in fact he had no great love for them. He admired the deep red heart of a ruby, the cold perfection of a fine diamond, the clear green of a flawless emerald, the restrained loveliness of a sapphire which only showed its depth and colour under chosen circumstances. Opals he detested, found them slightly meretricious; pearls were his favourite jewels, there was a soft radiance about them which satisfied him almost completely. But he had never taken much interest in jewels. He loved old silver, smooth and shining gently; he loved old pewter too. There was something charmingly mellow in old pewter, though the designs were invariably simple and showed no great workmanship. Silver was different—there you might find exquisite workmanship, beauty which passed, at first sight, almost unnoticed. Gold—he shrugged his shoulders—except in a few rare specimens, small boxes, set with stones, the early musical boxes which gave out charming tinkling tunes of melodies which had grown a little faded like very old brocade, an occasional vase or cup—gold seemed to be hard, and a trifle ostentatious. As for gold dinner services—pah! he preferred a good Crown Derby or Royal Worcester any day!

His real loves were pictures and furniture. There he felt happy; more, he knew that he was an expert. But although he might be able to assess the value of a lovely painting with complete correctness, that never detracted from the joy which he felt when he stood before one of those masterpieces which he had seen so often, and of which he never tired. Colour fascinated and held him, the blue of Breughel and Boucher, the old gold and rich damask hues of Paolo Veronese, the quieter tones of the Dutch masters, Vermeer of Delft—how he loved 'The Courtesan'!—the great sweeps of Raphael's lines, so bold, so generous, the limitless sadness of El Greco, the deep profound greens of Giorgione. He drew a deep breath; he was driving to London but his spirit was wandering round half the galleries of the world. He remembered how what were then called 'the French modernists' had burst upon him. Manet, Monet, Sisley, Renoir—oh, those paintings of his of the life of the cafés in Paris, those adorable ladies of the *demi-monde*! Seurat, with his 'atmospheric' paintings; Monticelli, who they said painted with a spoon! He remembered his early adventures among pictures, the time when he had come to old Emmanuel so proudly, bringing what he fimly believed was a genuine Bellini! He remembered how, when he was in Italy, he had fallen completely in love with two Madonnas of Moretto's. They didn't look in the least like Madonnas, they were splendid, autocratic creatures—no, one was Saint Margaret! How lovely they were. Then he had begun to understand wood, and now that was his chief—or almost his chief—interest. Fine, well-seasoned wood, solid age-old oak, mahogany—there was something reassuring about mahogany—the delicacy of walnut, rosewood, elm and the rest. Always excepting ebony, which he disliked and found unsympathetic. Beautiful forms executed in wood—the great names of the grand old designers, the grace of Empire before it became debased and over decorated. Ah, there was almost unlimited satisfaction in wood.

His lips curved into a smile. Furniture and pictures, a man might have less satisfactory interests. They had driven through Knightsbridge, and there was 'Number One London' on his left, and before him Piccadilly. Bond Street, the finest street in the world, even though they were doing their best to spoil it, to rob it of its character. The car slowed down and stopped. Garrod opened the door. Emmanuel ran his eyes over the exterior of the Gollantz Galleries. He always derived a sense of pleasurable satisfaction from the sight of the beautifully arranged windows.

He nodded his thanks to Garrod, then produced a very crisp note, and handed it to him. 'Go to Moyses Stevens and order some flowers to be sent to Lady Heriot. Something striking, with a good scent if possible—I know her tastes. I'll telephone to Lady Gollantz and ask her to be so kind as to call for me here.' He laughed. 'The rest of the day's your own.'

'Thank you, sir. Then I'll go straight back to Ordingly. Very good.'

He walked into the building, remembering how his brother

Julian had always referred to it as 'the shop'; Firby, the commissionaire, touched his hat and gave Emmanuel a 'good morning'. Emmanuel went to his office, and hanging up his hat and coat in the little room which his grandfather had insisted on building—'Neffer vill ellow my office to look like the vay a cloak-r-room does!' he had said—he came back to his desk and telephoned for Simeon.

Simeon came in. He looked well, his face glowed with health, his eyes were dancing with excitement.

'I was so glad to know that you were here, Father. I wanted to see you very much. I've some terrific news for you! Terrific!'

'Then why not sit down and impart it to me?'

'I'm almost too excited to sit still. Father, Daphne told me this morning that she is certain that she's going to have—yes—a baby! She wanted to be quite sure, and now she is, and—well, it's rather wonderful, isn't it?'

Emmanuel, more moved than he cared to show, stretched out his hand.

Simeon took it in his. Emmanuel said, 'It is wonderful. I offer you my sincere congr-ratulations. Please give my pr-rofound love to Daphne. I don't know that I r-really care for having—gr-randparenthood thr-rust upon me, I don't feel like a gr-randfather——' His smile faded, and when he spoke again his voice was very gentle. 'It is str-range to imagine your beloved mother as a gr-randmother! Take every care of Daphne, Simeon.'

'Be certain of that, Father. If it's a boy—as we hope—we would of course like to call him Emmanuel—with your permission.'

His father gave him one of his queer, very courteous bows. 'I give my full permission, and I am flattered. Thank you both. I think that, early as it is, this is an occasion which demands a bottle of wine, no? Bill will be here pr-resently, to discuss this unfortunate affair of young Charles Gollantz. Tell Miss Hawkins to send along a bottle of our good friend The Widow, '89. Go and see to it yourself, please, Simeon, Miss Hawkins is admirable but inclined to over-chill. Four—for Hannah must join us, of course—no, five, if young Gollantz arr-rives it will please him to be asked to join us. Thank you, Simeon. Oh, and Simeon'—as his son had his hand on the door handle—'the finest glasses, for this is an occasion.'

He telephoned to his secretary. 'The letters—does there seem anything of gr-reat importance? No? Then let them wait. Is Miss Rosenfeldt in this mor-rning? Then, if you please ask her to join me here. Thank you.'

Lilian Morrison sighed a trifle sentimentally as she hung up the receiver.

'Oh, I do hope it's nothing to worry him! What a pet he is —always so polite—always "if you please" and "thank you". Oh, dear!'

Hannah Rosenfeldt arrived at the door of Emmanuel's office at the same moment as Bill Gollantz. Together they entered, and Emmanuel thought that their size made even his large office seem cramped and full to overflowing.

Emmanuel greeted them. 'I am so glad that you have come,' he said. 'You both understand the firm, and should know of any changes which may take place in the near future.'

Hannah said, 'Changes, please? What changes do you propose?'

'To install an additional member in the firm,' Emmanuel said calmly.

Bill said, 'You're crazy! Are you short of money, want fresh capital?'

'As far as I know this proposed member will not have a penny!'

Hannah said, 'Possibly great experience, no?'

'None at all, I believe.'

It was at that moment that the door opened to admit Charles Emmanuel Gollantz. He stood for a moment uncertain; he thought that he had intruded, burst in upon a private gathering. There stood Emmanuel Gollantz, tall, smiling, holding a glass in his upraised hand. Charles thought, 'By Gum, how handsome he is! God must have broken the mould when they made him!' There was Simeon, smiling that lovely warm, friendly smile of his—which, had Charles known, he inherited from his mother. An enormously stout woman, obviously a Jewess, with a keen, intelligent face, and a very large—not to say fat—man, leaning back on his chair.

Emmanuel caught sight of him. 'Ah! Come in. Just in time. Simeon, another glass. We are drinking the health of a new member of the family! Please, join us.'

Hannah Rosenfeldt drank and said, '*Mazeltov!*'

Charles sipped his champagne and muttered, 'The best of luck.'

The fat man said, 'The two mean the same thing,' and drained his glass.

There was a brief silence, and Emmanuel said, reverting to his rather grave manner, 'I have just r-received the news that I am to be—a gr-randfather.'

Charles looked at Simeon. 'Congratulations, I'm sure.'

The fat man set down his glass. 'While I appreciate the sentimental value of this gathering, might I remind you all that I am here on business? In other words—Simeon, clear the decks!'

'Right, Uncle Bill.' Neatly and carefully he collected glasses, and set them on the salver. The stout woman rose, and she and Simeon walked towards the door. She turned back and spoke to Emmanuel.

'I want you to see a Chippendale bureau. They want us to buy it.'

'Who?' Emmanuel's voice had changed, it was crisp, incisive.

'Manfred's.'

'We're not buying. How much of it is Chippendale?'

'None of it! Very well.'

The door closed, and Bill Gollantz heaved a sigh of relief.

'These social occasions! Now, let's get down to brass tacks.'

He drew his chair up to the table, and became suddenly, the astute man of law. Even, Charles thought, his face changed a little, became less heavy and fleshy, his expression keen and alive.

'Now, these papers,' he said. 'I've looked through them. They appear to be in order.'

Charles replied, 'I have every reason to believe that they are, sir.'

'Quite, but I must—you appreciate that—verify them.' He rustled through the papers with his thick but sensitive fingers. 'Your birth certificate, the marriage lines, even your mother's birth certificate. Very good. I shall send someone to verify them all.' He smiled and his heavy face looked kind and friendly. 'No offence, but these things are necessary. I should have the report tomorrow. Now!' his voice was very clear, 'what do you intend to do—should these papers prove to be authentic?'

Charles glanced at Emmanuel, sitting with his finger-tips pressed together, calm and impassive. He turned back to the lawyer.

'Well, sir, nothing very much. I want to be able to call myself Gollantz. I'm known as Charles Hughes, at the moment. That was my mother's name before she married. But I *am* a Gollantz, and I don't like folks speculating as to whether I'm a bastard or not. I'd not make any scandal, I'd do it by deed-poll. I could call myself Watson—that was my step-father's name—but somehow I don't want to. Then there's a favour I should wish to ask Sir Emmanuel. That's all.'

'You're not asking for money?'

'No, sir. I've made my own way so far, and my mother has more than a sufficiency. I can manage very well.'

Bill puffed heavily, 'Quite. Commendable. Very. Now, I am prepared to admit that—provided these documents are satisfactory—my brother committed bigamy, which would render his son illegitimate. But,' he held up an admonishing finger, 'he could also aver that your mother did the same in marrying Mr.—er—Watson.'

'After a long period of years and silence, she married Watson, yes. But she was assured that the long passage of years might be taken as proof of Julian Gollantz's demise.'

Bill wagged his head. 'Always a snag about those wretched suppositions! What steps did she take to trace him? Did she advertise? Did she do a hundred other things to make certain?'

Charles said, 'I doubt it, sir. Frankly, she was glad to be rid of him.'

For the first time during the interview, Emmanuel threw back his head and laughed. 'How often have we all felt exactly the same!' he said.

Bill shot a glance at him. 'That's an improper remark to make.'

'But a tr-rue one. Come now, Bill, admit it.'

'As Bill Gollantz—possibly; as your legal adviser—certainly not.'

Emmanuel said, 'I'm lunching with you at the Savoy, remember.' He added, 'I've told them to telephone to ask Viva to join us.'

As Bill heaved himself to his feet Emmanuel thought, 'He's getting exactly like Simeon Jaffe!'

'Delightful. I adore Viva, she brings a little sparkle into the Gollantz family. We're a dull lot. She acts like a cork swizzed round in a glass of champagne when it's lost its sparkle. I'll be there. Good-bye, young man, and I am convinced—off the record—that it's going to be all right.'

Charles said, 'Thank you, sir.'

Bill stared at him, his eyes narrowed. 'I must say that I shall be happy when it's all cleared up and you can say Uncle Bill—or just plain Bill.'

'Again, thank you, sir.'

He lumbered out, and Emmanuel said, 'Sit down, I want to talk to you. D'you r-realize that you're prepared to do a—pr-retty big thing?'

Charles shook his head. 'Not as I see it. I don't want to spoil another fellow's chances. I've not been brought up in—well, a public school atmosphere, and I don't know a lot about social things. I've never known my father, but from what my mu—mother has told me, he seems to be an out-and-out cad. I've never seen him, I never want to see him. I want to make my own way—and I believe that I can. I want to ask you, sir, to use your influence to get me apprenticed—or whatever is the right term—to a firm of really tip-top auctioneers. Not specialists like Christie's, but a good firm where I can learn the—well, the higher branches of the business.'

Emmanuel nodded, slowly, frowning a little. This was so unlike Julian!

'And that is all—literally all—that you want?'

'That's so.'

'It means study, examinations, possibly—and I advise this—voice production. It's pr-retty hard work to stand on a rostrum hour after hour and keep your voice clear unless you've had it trained.' He smiled suddenly. 'I believe in you, I'm behind you. I can arrange to place you with a firm. I'm willing to be r-responsible for your fees while you're training. Bill—my brother—is a lawyer, he's got to be cautious, but I believe that he feels as I do.

'Now if ever-rything works out r-right, I propose that you should be the grandson of my father's brother, Algernon. Your father—Frank Gollantz—died in the First World War. He had changed his name, but we can pr-rove that you have a r-right to claim Algernon as your grandfather. How's that?'

'All right by me, sir.'

'Algernon was, I believe, a r-rather unpleasant fellow.'

Charles smiled. 'I doubt if that description wouldn't fit my father.'

Emmanuel nodded. 'It would. Now, you'll have to live in Town.'

The young man said eagerly, 'My mother'—he got it right that time—'will sell the house in Dullton, we'll get a flat in London. Not terribly large, but—well, nice. She's ready to come once this is settled, and she would like to be known as Mrs. Gollantz, sir.'

'That's my brother Bill's side.' He hesitated. 'If it's all satisfactory, I should esteem it a favour if you'd allow me to gr-rant you an allowance. Nothing pr-rincely, but just to ease the wheels I mean.'

The door opened suddenly and a woman entered. Charles Gollantz thought that he had never seen anyone who was so attractive. Tall, fair, with very large, bright eyes, dressed in a way which he could only describe as 'smashing'.

Emmanuel leapt to his feet, and went to her, saying, 'Viva, this is a wonderful surprise!'

She said, 'You're lunching with Bill, I'm invited. It's ten minutes to one—and who is this, please?'

Emmanuel bent and kissed her cheek. 'This is your—kinsman, Charles Gollantz.'

Charles bowed, and Viva stretched out her hand saying, 'I'm delighted.'

Charles took her hand and longed to raise it to his lips as he had seen heroes in musical comedy do when they met someone whose beauty or attraction left words inadequate. Instead he said, 'It's a great pleasure.'

'Are you joining us for luncheon?' she asked.

Emmanuel answered for him, 'No. You see, Viva, Bill is—what they call—acting for me. He is there to attempt to prove the claims which this young man makes false. Therefore, it would be unwise for us to be seen all lunching together.'

Viva made a gesture of impatience. 'What ghastly rubbish!

Still, there it is and I suppose the young man must be sent off to have luncheon—in solitude—at Lyons or some place of that kind.'

'Simeon has asked me to have lunch——'

'Luncheon,' she interrupted him. 'Our beloved old Emmanuel always said that lunch was something which you ate out of a paper packet. Where are you having luncheon with Simeon? He's nice, isn't he? Emmanuel, go and get your hat and coat.'

Charles stood watching her, fascinated. Not very young, in fact you could call her on the verge of middle age, but—he sought for a phrase—groomed to a hair! That was it. Her clothes, her hair, her skin—she used make-up that was obvious, but it was used with skill and discretion. Her clothes, quiet and unostentatious, appeared to him to be all that clothes ought to be.

She met his eyes and smiled. 'Now after this luncheon with Emmanuel and Bill, I shall be cast out to either go home, or go to a matinée. Why not call for me at the Savoy—you know where it is, don't you?'

Charles nodded. 'Yes, I know that much about London, though not much more.'

'Say at half past two then. By that time the brothers Gollantz will both be champing at the bit, longing to get back to their own business. I'll have my car, and I'll show you something of London.'

'I say, that is kind' He hesitated, then made a little gesture which indicated his clothes. 'But—shall I do?'

'Do?' Viva laughed, 'do—what, do—whom? You mean your clothes! My good boy, wait until you've seen some of the men who walk into the Savoy! It's a very nice suit. Your tailor's been a little generous over the neck, but that's something Simeon's tailor can put right.'

'He took me to his tailor yesterday, I've ordered——' At that moment Emmanuel came out from the little cloak-room, smiling, and rubbing his hands which still looked cold from recent washing.

'We shall have to turn on the heating,' he said, 'it gets chilly. Oh, how I hate cold water! Now, are you r-ready, darling?'

'Am I ready!' she turned, appealing to Charles. 'I've been

waiting for hours. I have an appointment at half past two. I'll drive you to the Savoy in my car.'

'Where are you going at half past two?'

'Charles is calling for me. I'm showing him something of London. Good-bye, Charles—for the moment.'

Emmanuel said, 'I'll see you tomorrow. I'm convinced that the report fr-rom Bill's sleuths will be all r-right. I am seeing Mastock of Kennerley and Mastock this afternoon—the big autioneers. See you here about eleven. Yes, go and find Simeon.'

As they drove to the Savoy, Emmanuel asked, 'What do you think of him?'

'He's what Julian might have been like if he'd been a decent fellow. I liked him at once. What's he going to do—if his claims are sound?'

'That's what I like so much about the chap,' Emmanuel said, 'he doesn't want anything. He doesn't want to inform Julian; I proposed, that being the case, we'd better say that he was the grandson of Algernon, who was my dear father's elder brother.'

'One of the family bad hats, eh? And money?'

'Says he wants to earn it for himself. He's saved apparently, and his mother—an ex-chorus girl—is comfortably off. All he wants is to get into a first-class firm of auctioneers, and to go to Simeon's tailor.'

'Modest enough in all conscience. Well, we delivered Master Max's car. He was not visible—still asleep I imagine. The sooner that little tick goes back to his fond papa, and, no doubt, his equally fond mama, the better. Damn that taxi! In fact damn everything on the road except me! There you are, precious, I've got you here all in one piece.'

Emmanuel smiled. 'Most creditable!'

Viva's own chauffeur was waiting, and she gave her orders crisply and exactly. 'Take her to some parking-place, have your luncheon, and be back here at half past two. Then you can go off, I'll drive myself.'

'Very good, m'lady.'

'Have a decent luncheon, remember.'

'Yes, m'lady.'

As they walked to the American Bar, Emmanuel slipped his hand through her arm. 'Angel,' he said, 'don't turn this young man's head, will you?' She turned to him, smiling. 'Who—my driver? Good heavens!'

'You know very well I wasn't r-referring to him. No, to this young Charles. He's probably never met anyone like you in his life——'

She laughed, 'Have you?'

'I'll answer that question some other time. But you are a—well—a turner of heads to these young men. That's what's happened to the wretched Max, unpleasant fellow though he is.'

'Now,' she challenged, 'say—"Remember I warned you".'

'I've no intention of saying anything of the kind. Be nice, friendly to him, but don't let him get his head filled with r-romantic ideas.'

'Darling, be yourself, and consider my age!'

'Be yourself and remember that age for you is something which does not exist. There's Bill!'

Viva asked as they sipped their cocktails, 'What do you think of the new arrival, Bill?'

'What matters is what I think of his claims, and I'm bound to admit they seem sound to me. I've people now on their way to various places to verify them. I think—privately—that the papers—certificates, and so forth—are watertight. Can't quite understand the fellow making no demands, that puzzles me a bit, I admit. Not like a son of Julian's to be so self-abnegating.'

Viva said, 'He has a mother as well as a blackguardly father, Bill. She was—like my own mother—a chorus girl, and when they're good, well, they are pretty damn' good. I like this lad, I'm certain that he's straight.'

Over luncheon Bill asked about the horses, and Viva was enthusiastic. Old 'Buster' Carteret had done her a wonderful turn when he sent her Andy Miller.

'We've entered Hereward for the Calmering Cup.'

Bill whistled softly. 'That's asking something big, isn't it? He was first at Melford, but that's a potty kind of meeting; he was unplaced at Redcar, and third at some other small meeting.'

Viva nodded. 'Knowledgeable fellow you are! I knew he wouldn't do anything at Redcar, so did Miller. The going was heavy, and he doesn't like it. Given good dry weather, and he'll show them his heels in the Calmering.'

Bill grunted, 'Hope you're right. And the others——?'

'White Knight—he's a good, unspectacular beast. He'll never set the Thames on fire, but he'll—well, more than earn his keep in smaller races. Roaring Gal—she's a real roaring gal too—has the heart of a lion.'

Emmanuel said, 'I've heard that lions aren't really very brave, Viva.'

'Then of whatever animal has a great heart. Next season, she's really going places. "Buster" Carteret wants me to see a mare next week, he can't praise her sufficiently. Says she has the best turn of speed he's seen in years. But Hereward is the boy I'm pinning my hopes on at the moment.'

They found Charles waiting in the entrance hall. Simeon had given him a wonderful luncheon, all the things he liked best—roast beef, and Yorkshire pudding, which was not quite as they made it in the north, but very good, and apple pie and Stilton cheese.

Emmanuel said gravely, 'Now could it possibly have been Simpson's, I wonder?'

Bill added, 'Or the Cock in Fleet Street?'

Charles said, 'I think the name was Simpson's. Anyway it was jolly good.'

Viva cried, 'Take no notice, Charles. That's the Gollantz idea of being funny. Of course it was Simpson's. If I hadn't been here they'd have gone on for hours, naming every possible and impossible place in Town.'

'Can you call for me, about half past five?' Emmanuel asked.

'Not only I can—but I will,' she returned. 'There, good-bye my precious. Good-bye, Bill—your Edith ought to make you take more exercise.'

'Haven't time, Viva, too busy winning the daily crust.'

As she settled herself at the wheel, she said, 'They're two of the nicest men who ever happened. Emmanuel's almost too good to be true, and yet you realize that his goodness is true, every bit of it. The horror, my dear Charles, is your father, who is, without exception, the most poisonous thing in creation.'

'I haven't the least intention of claiming him as my father,' Charles said. 'Mr. Gollantz will have to brief me in detail as to whom I am supposed to be. I don't know much about it—someone called Algernon was—or is—going to be adopted as it were as my grandfather, I believe.'

Viva turned neatly into the Aldwych. 'That's going to be all right,' she assured him. 'Bill will give you some immense document to study which will cover every eventuality. Now, you know this part of course. That theatre on the corner is where my mother used to appear—as Miss Beatrice Grantley. I believe my grandfather was a greengrocer in the New Cut. She'll tell you all about it when you meet. She'll adore to meet your mother—you must get her to come and stay with us once this silly argument—which isn't an argument at all—is settled. Come and see my horses.'

His face glowed. 'Horses—I love 'em. I've always thought that one day I'd buy a horse. Do everything for it myself y'know, grooming, feeding, everything. Tell me about yours, please.'

She had turned again, and was making her way skilfully through the crowded street. 'There's Ludgate Hill, and Saint Paul's——'

'I recognized them.'

'Now we'll go on—east of Aldgate Pump. Watch the names over the shops. The English ones begin to change to Jewish, Polish and so forth. There's the Pump—now we're in the East End. We'll drive down as far as China Town and then you shall take me to tea——'

'In China Town?'

'No, I don't think so. One day we might come and sample some Chinese food, go to the Prospect of Whitby and make general sightseers of ourselves. You and Simeon and his wife and me—Emmanuel would hate it. He's all on the side of comfort, not to say over-civilized luxury.'

Charles was watching the strange names on the shop fronts curiously.

'There seem to be more foreigners than English here,' he said.

Viva laughed. 'Don't forget that you're partly a foreigner yourself. This Gollantz family—they are like the scattered tribes of Israel. Paris, Italy, Vienna, Holland—Heaven only knows where else. You only see the Foreign Contingent—that's what Emmanuel's darling mother used to call them—gathered together for family festivals—weddings, funerals and the like. At intervals Emmanuel tells me that he must go to Budapest for a couple of days—taking a top hat with him, because the cousin of his great-uncle—he has never seen the great-uncle or his cousin—has died and he must be present at the funeral. They've a great sense of family.'

'Somehow,' Charles said, 'here—it's Whitechapel isn't it?—everything seems more colourful. The people can't all be foreigners, but they seem to have imbibed the vitality of the foreigners. Even the men selling fruit appear to me to put extra energy into what they're doing. Is it down here that there's a street called Petticoat Lane? I've heard of that.'

'They call it Middlesex Street in these days—for some reason best known to the L.C.C. We'll go there some Sunday morning, and buy smoked salmon—I think you get the best in London in Petticoat Lane. Here you are, Commercial Road, and this is where China Town begins. There's the Asiatic Seamen's Home—funny how those Lascars always trail along in single file. Now we'll turn back to the West End, and have some tea at Gunter's before I go to pick up my hard-working—and adorable—husband.'

Charles, as he helped her out of the car, said, 'I've read about Gunter's—in books. It's where rich people take their children to have special ices, isn't it?'

'It wasn't here then—I remember it in Berkeley Square, and my mother knew it when it was in Oxford Street. I come here because I can generally find a place to park. Come in, and you shall have your ice if you feel that it would be a suitable experience! No? Then we'll fly to tea and cakes. There, now begin to tell me all about Lancashire, and your work and ambitions—I warn you, I have an insatiable curiosity.'

4

Bill said, 'I'm perfectly satisfied. You've a right to use the name—Gollantz. I've got a full briefing for you, so that if people ask questions—which they've no damn' right to do—you can answer them. I advise you to study it carefully, and then have it put in your bank for safety. Ah, here's Emmanuel. Well, old boy, it's all settled—everything has been audited and found correct.'

Emmanuel held out his hand to Charles. 'Delighted, Charles. Thank you, Bill. Well, young fellow, I've an invitation asking you to come out to Ordingly for the week-end. If you'd write to your mother, you might enclose Viva's letter, she didn't know the address, neither did I. We'd like your mother to come down with you. Think she will?'

'I imagine she'll be delighted, sir.'

Emmanuel went to his big chair, and turned to his brother.

'Just one thing, Bill. I feel very deeply that we ought to—well, make some financial attempts at squaring this account with Charles. Only I wish that precious brother of ours could be made to take a share—the lion's share—in it.'

'Did you ever know the time when Julian didn't get off scot-free?'

Charles made a movement, and laid his hand on the desk. His face was scarlet, his eyes looked suddenly very hard and intensely blue.

'It's very kind of you—both of you,' he said, 'but as I told you the first time we met, I don't want anything, neither does my mother. You've both done quite enough, more than enough. I'm grateful and more than grateful—you've been generosity itself—but I didn't come here after money. I came here to—to establish myself. So, with all respect, I'd rather you didn't mention this matter again.'

Emmanuel nodded. 'I admire your spirit. I can tell you that I've seen George Mastock, and he would like you to call on him at five. On this I insist—I pay your articles. It will mean hard work, but they're the best firm I know. Now, go and improve your knowledge of London.'

He smiled, that smile which lit up his rather grave face, and gave Charles the assurance of his friendship.

His colour had died down, he no longer stood tense, he was able to return Emmanuel's smile.

Bill heaved himself out of his chair 'This is the first time that the family have got something for nothing!'

'Nothing, sir!' Charles exclaimed. 'I don't call it nothing.'

'Well, for virtually nothing. We've a new member of the family who won't let us down.'

He nodded his 'good-bye' and lumbered out.

Emmanuel said, 'My dear brother—and he's one of the best chaps imaginable—is exactly like a great uncle, Simeon Jaffe. He left me his Milan galleries. We must send you there, as part of your education. Also it is part of that same education to meet my partner—Guido Moroni. There, off you go. See Mastock at five, and the best of luck.'

Charles rushed back to his hotel, wrote to his mother, and wondered if his dinner-jacket was all right for the week-end. His shirts were creditable, he always went to Manchester for them—Ohm and Webster—an odd name, but their shirts were beyond reproach.

He bought two new black ties—thankful that he had learnt to tie a bow properly—and lunched at a restaurant which looked inexpensive, and proved to be nothing of the kind. True the food was admirable, but the amount of the bill staggered him. As he was drinking his coffee, he saw Simeon, lunching with a stout man who was obviously on the point of leaving. Simeon saw him and waved. Presently he came over, his face wreathed in smiles.

'I've heard from my father that everything is absolutely all right. Believe me, he's as pleased as I am. I've been lunching with the dreary old egoist Marcus Harrison. Now I've promised to have coffee with young Max'—he dropped his voice a little—'to whom you have behaved so generously. Can he join us? You ought to meet him, he'll be at Ordingly next week-end, and you and I might clear the decks, eh?'

Charles said, 'Oh—just one thing. Those tails I'm having made, they won't be ready. Can I pass in a dinner-jacket?'

'Can you pass? My father will probably wear a plum-coloured velvet smoking-jacket. It's not a full-dress do—it's really because my great-aunt Beatrice is longing to meet your mother. Ah, there's Max!'

A young man, a very handsome young man, came towards them ; Simeon caught his breath for a second—this young man and Charles might have been twins. The same slim figures and the same very bright blue eyes.

He came across the restaurant slowly, stopping to speak with various people, all of whom seemed delighted to see him.

Charles thought, 'So this is my brother! I wish that I could come into a restaurant as he does—so easily, with such self-confidence. I wish I could wear clothes as he does! He's had everything since he was born.' Then, with a sense of revulsion at his drift towards self-pity, he added mentally, 'So have I: the grandest mother in the world, who gave me everything, who worked and slaved in third-rate theatres when she grew too old to get work in the first-class ones. What's the matter with me? I'm glad to be who I am, I'd hate to be—my brother!'

Max joined them and said, in a voice with a marked American accent, 'Hello, how are you? Yes, thanks, coffee and a brandy. Introduce me, please.'

Simeon said, 'This is a cousin—Charles Gollantz. Charles—this is Max Gollantz, another cousin.'

Max stared and said, 'How d'you do?'

Charles replied, 'Very well, thank you. How are you?'

Then blushed to his eyebrows because he had once been told that the proper reply to 'How do you do?' was—'How do you do?' He saw Max's eyebrows go up a little.

'I never knew there were any more cousins,' Max said. 'I thought you and I were the whole shoot.'

Simeon shook his head. 'No, old Emmanuel had a son—Algernon. His son was Frank——'

'Yes, killed in the First World War.'

'Exactly. Well, he left a son—— he broke off. 'I say this is very boring for you, Charles. Sorry.'

Max said, 'He married Lady Stansfield, didn't he?'

'She wasn't Lady Stansfield then, she married Stansfield after Frank was killed.'

Max was frowning, he seemed to be trying to remember something, and was annoyed that—whatever it was—it eluded him. Suddenly he snapped his fingers. 'I've got it, wasn't she killed in a motor crash with,' his eyes narrowed a little, 'a fellow called—damn it! Ah, I've remembered, Hast, a Jewish antique dealer?'

Charles scented that something lay beneath all this, and envied Simeon his calm and aplomb. Simeon sipped his coffee and then nodded gently.

'Only partially correct. Hast was probably one of the greatest art experts in the world.'

Max lit a cigarette with great care; for some reason Charles held his breath. He felt that he was waiting for a storm to break in a great clap of thunder.

'But,' and Max turned to Charles, 'you're not the son of Leon Hast? This is all most confusing.' His voice was very smooth, and his American accent more pronounced than usual when he smiled and said, 'I just don't get it—then who was your father?'

It was Simeon who broke in. 'His father was the grandson of old Emmanuel, his grandfather was Algernon—for whom the family has no great regard. Now can we let the matter drop? I'm growing desperately bored with all this family-tree business.'

To Charles it seemed like a snake striking, when Max asked, 'Did you ever know Hast, Simeon?'

'No—I wasn't born when he died.' The voice was still under complete control.

'Of course, I forgot, you're not Viva's son!'

'My mother was Juliet Forbes, the singer. She died when I was a year old.'

Charles leaned forward and spoke eagerly. 'She must have been wonderful. I have some records of hers at home. Some of them are in Italian, but there are the songs of Purcell which my mother loves. She takes as much care of those records as she would of jewels. There is such a——'

He felt Max's eyes, looking coldly at him, and realized that he had been talking very fast. 'They really are quite wonderful,' he ended a trifle lamely.

Simeon said, 'I must be getting back. Would you care,' he turned to Charles, a new quality of warmth in his voice, 'to come with me and see some prints we've just had submitted to us? I don't know much about them, but my father thinks highly of them.'

As they walked out of the restaurant, Charles gave a sigh of relief. At one juncture he had felt that the storm was practically unavoidable, but it seemed to have cleared and the atmosphere was calmer.

Max laughed suddenly. 'I remember my father used to say—"must get back to the shop".' He turned to Charles. 'For a time he was in charge of the silver there.'

Again Charles felt that sense of chill, as Simeon said, 'I know that he did, I always felt that it was a singularly witty remark. My father, for some reason, disliked it. Coming our way, Max—towards the shop?'

'No, I've business in the City, Cheerie-bye.'

As they walked slowly up Arlington Street and waited to cross Piccadilly, Simeon said, 'One day someone will land their fist in that young man's face, and the person at the other end will be me. I'm looking forward to the week-end to see how Aunt Beatrice deals with him. Write to your mother immediately, won't you? Do you think she'll come?'

'She'll be over the moon. And if I might just tell her—well, who your mother was—she'd be so thrilled. She's like a girl over the people she loves and admires.' Impulsively, he added, 'I do want you all to like her.'

Later, after he had seen the famous prints, he listened to Emmanuel talking about them, his big magnifying-glass in hand, and marvelled at the knowledge which this man possessed, how easily he marshalled his facts, and when he left the Galleries he wondered if he could ever hope to gain such knowledge or to have the ability to present his information to a listening public. It was not only that Emmanuel spoke with assurance, but he was able to present his facts lightly, even amusingly.

When Simeon had asked him why they were so often asked to buy prints which had the mounts cut, Emmanuel leaned back in his big chair and said, 'Because British legislation has never yet made that a major crime. One day, they will realize—those law-makers—that these criminals are destroying one of the nation's assets, and a suitable punishment will be allocated to that particular and very horrid violation.' Then, his fine fingers lightly pressed together, he had told them a story of an old lady who had come to him with four very fine Bartolozzi prints. They were beautifully framed in oval frames, with the mounts completely cut away.

Charles said, 'Did you buy them, sir?'

Emmanuel nodded. 'Indeed I did. You may not believe it, but even antique dealers have hearts. She'd believed in them for years, and I couldn't disillusion her. I paid—well, the price they would have commanded had they been uncut, I sold them for —I think—a pound for the four. She was a charming old lady, her name was Miranda Belairs. I remember that I asked her to take tea with me, and that she felt that I was—what do you say in these days?—a big bad wolf. But how charming Mir-randa Belairs! She was entrancing!

'Ah, Charles, even in Bond Str-reet, we have our moments of romance.'

Simeon eyed him narrowly. 'Papa, how much of that story is true?'

Completely unmoved, his father answered, 'Pr-ractically all of it.'

Now Charles walked away from the dignified Galleries towards his rooms in King Street ; there he sat down to write to his mother. He sent on the invitation to Ordingly for the coming week-end, and begged that she would send or bring his dress shirts and extra silk socks. She must telegraph the time of her arrival and he would meet her.

They were very close, this mother and son, her flamboyance might be obvious but there was a warmth and kindliness about her which he loved.

She had known when to keep her own counsel, she had held her head—and a very handsome head it was—high, she had worked and accepted the fact that she must be content with engagements at second-class theatres because she was growing too old and too stout for the first-class pantomimes.

Sitting there, in his comfortable sitting-room, he lapsed into the dialect of his own county: 'Naay, Ah've never lacked owt, never!'

She had married Thomas Watson, and been a splendid wife to him. Charles had found him a kindly, insignificant little man, who was filled with admiration for his wife. Their home had been comfortable, for she boasted, 'When it was necessary I could kick as high as anyone—aye, as high as Lottie Collins herself! But when it comes to cooking—my cakes are as light as the feet of any Tiller Girl who ever crossed the stage.' Now, through this strange twist of fate's wheel, she was to come to Ordingly, to meet Lady Heriot.

Still half musing, he finished his letter, and in his neat, methodical fashion, stamped it and carried it out to lay it on the table on the landing where Vickers would collect it and post it in time for the country post.

Then he walked back and sat down in the big, ugly, comfortable chair by the side of a bright coal fire. Simeon had found him these rooms, and Charles gained whole-hearted enjoyment from them. True, they were completely unimaginative, even ugly, but they were well kept, and both Vickers and his wife treated him admirably.

He had never met such a couple before and they interested him profoundly. Vickers would appear sometimes in a linen jacket of blue with a narrow white stripe, at others even assuming a green baize apron, when he invariably explained, 'At the moment, sir, I am cleaning my silver.' Later he was immaculate in a short black jacket with striped trousers, and a very correct black tie.

He had been, so he told Charles, butler to Lord Crawshay, and later, 'when financial matters grew restricted as they have done to all—or practically all—the real gentry, I was butler valet to the Honourable Lionel Browne—with an "e" of course. Later my wife—who although always head-housemaid, had what the French call a "flair" for cooking—decided to retire. Very far-sighted lady, my wife. She said, "Really comfortable rooms for gentlemen, and we'll see that they are gentlemen!"

'Her aunt, a certain Mrs. Baker, died and left her a houseful of furniture. She had a very select boarding-house in Hove.

We were fortunate. The Hon. Lionel interested himself, and his uncle, the Duke of Hansfield, is one of the ground landlords, and—well, we've been here for nearly fifteen years. I'm afraid that I've run on somewhat, as the saying goes; I offer my apologies, sir. It is difficult to resist a sympathetic listener.'

Charles liked them both. He liked the regularity, the knowledge that his morning cup of tea was placed on his bedside table exactly as the clocks were striking eight. He had gone to the bathroom one morning to find the water less hot than he liked. Quite cheerfully he had said to Vickers, 'The water's a bit on the chilly side this morning, eh?'

Vickers had eyed him reprovingly. 'Might I suggest, sir, that you are ten minutes earlier than usual? Mr. Fane has only this moment vacated the bathroom. The water requires a certain time to attain the desired temperature, if you will forgive me for saying so.'

After that Charles had watched his clock carefully, and never impinged on the time allowed for the ablutions of the Hon. Clarence Fane.

Now, conscious that the warmth of the fire was exceedingly pleasant, and that he was thankful that he was in his own warm room and not tramping about in the cold and slightly foggy streets, Charles leaned back. He reviewed the past month, and wondered if any fellow ever had such surprising luck. He had always realized that his claim to be Charles Emmanuel Gollantz was just and completely well founded, but he had felt slightly apprehensive as to how the Gollantz family might receive him—an unknown claimant to their name.

Not that he had 'claimed' anything—on that both he and 'Mum' had been determined from the beginning. Recognition, for her sake and his, was what he was determined upon. There might have been a certain suspicion, doubt, coldness—instead he had found them all ready to be friendly and more than friendly.

Simeon, whom he had met first, had been interested and completely charming; later, when he was taken to meet the head of the house, the great Sir Emmanuel Gollantz, Baronet, he decided that never had any man impressed him as he did.

Charles had admired him whole-heartedly and completely from the moment he saw him. There had been a kind of cool friendliness, even a hint of caution in his manner. While he never implied a doubt, yet he hinted that everything must be sifted and examined. Never for one moment had he made Charles feel that he was regarded as an impostor, and when he had stated that he was making no 'claims' he fancied that he saw a glint of approval in Emmanuel's eyes.

He felt that from that moment the man accepted him ; it was as if he had registered, 'That gains my approval—that is the Gollantz touch.'

Emmanuel had insisted upon paying his fees to the finest and most exclusive firm of auctioneers in London, and when Charles had tried to thank him, had dismissed the whole thing with a slight wave of his hand. Then Lady Gollantz had appeared on the scene, and when he thought of her Charles knew that his heart beat rather faster. He had never met such a woman ; she seemed to him to be the epitome of all a woman should be. She was lovely, she was gay, she was friendly. Now she had invited him to come to Ordingly for the week-end, and to bring his mother with him. He had known many girls, for he was a friendly fellow and popular.

There was a phrase—usual in the north—that two young people who were obviously attracted to each other were 'going together'. Nothing was implied which was in the least derogatory to either of them. It simply meant that they were—for the time being—chosen companions. Sometimes the association ended in a marriage, but if it faded out no one was held blameworthy.

He had 'gone together' with Phoebe Morrison. She was a dear little girl, a typist at Baum and Terrys, and, as they said, 'well thought of'. Pretty, intelligent to a certain extent, Charles had enjoyed going with her for long—rather dreary—walks on Saturdays or Sundays. He had taken her to the local theatre once a week—seats in the 'dress circle'. He had taken tickets for the more select of the subscription dances, sending a taxi for her and ordering one to take her home.

And then, for the remainder of the week, he had to all intents and purposes, forgotten her. He had never attempted to make love to her. When they met and parted he had kissed her affectionately but with restraint. Vaguely—very vaguely—he had thought of marriage, of a nice, well-furnished home—but since he came to London, the idea had faded into the dim distance.

There was an innate decency about Charles Gollantz, and he could see with admirable clarity into the future.

He said to himself, as he sat there, staring into the bright fire, 'I've not time to think of anyone else--and I know that there is no future in it for me. I don't even dream of one. She's devoted to the Head of the House—and he is to her. She's just come into my life, she's filled my mind completely—whether I shall ever be able to gct everything clear again, I don't know.

'I have an allegiance to him'—he always thought of Emmanuel as 'him'—'and I'd never make a false step. There's no earthly reason why she should consider me in any way except as a rather extraneous member of the family. It's only that she's driven the thought of any other woman completely out of my mind, my heart, my consciousness.'

He sat staring into the bright heart of the fire, his mind a blank. He was still fairly young, and life at the moment was proving a slight puzzle to him. He had plenty of grit, determination; he was sufficiently intelligent to understand that the Gollantzes, however kindly and friendly they were, must realize that there were gaps in his education, in his social senses, which came to them perfectly naturally. They had always lived in fine, dignified houses, surrounded by beautiful things; they had moved in an atmosphere which—in spite of its business aspects—held a certain ease.

Charles had always known considerable physical comfort; when his mother married Thomas Watson, their home had been solidly well furnished and there had been no scarcity of money, but the whole family had been satisfied with a life practically devoid of any elegance.

Now; although his rooms were heavily furnished with Victorian furniture, they contained a certain dignity which had been missing in his home at Dullton. Charles had visited as many of the 'stately homes of England' as possible; he had paid his half-crown on days when those houses were opcned to the public, and had gazed with awe and amazement at the lovely old furniture, the china, pictures, and wondered—though vaguely at first—what it must be like to live in beautiful surroundings. He had known that his imagination was fired, he longed to understand exquisite furniture, to appreciate china and pictures. That was why, in spite of the fact that Ferrers had been satisfied—and more than satisfied—with him, he had always wanted to get out of the rut of small provincial town sale rooms.

Mum, bless her, had encouraged him. When he had talked to her of his ambitions, she had nodded gravely, and had said later, 'It's not to be wondered at, luv. It's in your blood to love these things.' Then, when he began to ask questions, she had told him the whole story, had shown him her 'marriage lines' —'for I never was a bad girl in my life, ducks'—and had encouraged him to go to London to see Emmanuel Gollantz.

And now, Charles leaned back in his chair, and stretched his arms, now he was invited to Ordingly, and so was Mum—but he must remember not to call her 'Mum'. He would not only see a beautiful house, but he would be staying there as a guest, not just visiting for an hour on payment of half a crown.

Viva Gollantz, that lovely woman who occupied his mind, would be there, and he'd show that detestable young man, Max Gollantz, that he could behave decently, and hide his feelings, and be merely an attentive, and appreciative guest.

As he thought of Max Gollantz, Charles's pleasant face—so like Max's but lacking in some small quality which made Max a very handsome fellow and Charles merely a good-looking one —hardened. How he disliked him! When they had met Charles had realized that Max regarded him as somehow inferior to himself. There had been a kind of vague sneer in all that he said, and at their first meeting it had only been through Simeon's tact and discretion that a scene had been avoided.

Charles was not easily roused, but the veiled insolence of Max Gollantz had touched him to the raw, and he would have given a good deal to have driven his fist into the handsome, arrogant face. It had been Simeon's quiet, firm voice which had killed the impulse before it was born.

'I must be on my guard,' he thought. 'He hasn't played his last card. I believe he thinks there is something fishy in the family's acceptance of me. I won't spoil it! He'll go back to America, and let him take his doubts and suspicions with him. I can take his insinuations; I don't care a damn for his doubts and to keep my temper—and if necessary I can refer him to that mountain of a man, William Gollantz—is the least that I can do to show my devotion to the Head of the House.'

The week-end came, he met his mother at the great, gloomy, echoing station, and thought how charming she looked. She might be—indeed was—stout, but her clothes were well cut and restrained. He heard her pleasant warm Lancashire voice with a little thrill of love and even emotion.

'Now, luv,' she said, 'this is grand, isn't it? To think of us going to stay at that grand house! I've seen pictures of it in some of the really swanky papers. When do we go, luv?'

'I'll drive you down tomorrow, Mum dear. Tonight I've booked a room for you at the Savoy. I'll come along and we'll dine early, and then I've got seats for a musical. You'll like that?'

She squeezed his arm affectionately. 'I'd like most anything if I was with you, bless you. But, Charlie, the Savoy!'

He laughed. 'I suggested to Simeon that I'd get you a room at—well, I suggested a couple of hotels. He said, "I say, Charles—not for your mother!" Then he telephoned to the Savoy!'

In the taxi she said, a trifle anxiously, 'Are they dreadfully swanky?'

'Not a little bit, I promise. It's just that—well, they've always been used to certain things and I suppose they can't imagine anything else. But they're not a bit swanky. Not a bit like—for instance—the Harbingers at Dullton Towers.'

'Pooh! Them!' she retorted, 'jumped up nothings!'

'I think,' he said slowly, 'that Emmanuel Gollantz is the grandest man I've ever met. Handsome, so quiet, and yet as he talks to you, you can *feel* his uprightness and integrity. When he smiles, it seems as if all the warmth imaginable shines in his eyes. His son is grand too—he lost a foot in the war, but you'd scarcely notice it, and he never grouses about it. There's another brother—that is Sir Emmanuel's brother—William. He's a lawyer. Immense, like an elephant, but you realize that there's all the astuteness in the world in his character. Lady Gollantz—she's the daughter of your old friend——'

'Well, Charlie, not all that much of a friend. She was really something—I was just chorus. But she was always kind and nice was Beatrice Grantley, and lovely to look at. Her daughter sent me such a kind note inviting me for this week-end—that's the one you sent on to me.'

He nodded. 'Mum, darling, they're all nice, barring——' He hesitated, and she said, 'Aye, go on, lad. Tell me.'

'Barring young Max Gollantz. The son of Julian who lives in America. He loathes me, and I can't honestly say that much love is lost on either side.'

Mrs. Watson uttered a sound which might be described as a 'snort'.

'He'd need give himself airs, that one!'

'He will probably be at Ordingly this week-end, so we shall have to be civil to him, darling.'

'I hope I know how to behave myself, Charlie, when I'm a guest in someone else's house,' she said with dignity. 'Have no fears for me.'

Rose Watson enjoyed her evening; she had all a North-countrywoman's appreciation of good food, she enjoyed light and bright music, and when Charles said, 'Would you care to dance, Mum dear?' she beamed with pleasure. He was surprised how smoothly and easily she moved, for she was a fairly heavy woman. Her movements were completely graceful and she was as light as a feather.

'Lovely dancer you are, darling,' he said.

She chuckled. 'Not forgotten my old training, ducky. Still imagine that Mrs. John Tiller is standing in the wings, ready to make that penetrating hissing noise through her teeth if any girl wasn't doing her best. I can hear her now—"S-s't!"'

When he left her, she kissed him and said, 'Thanks for a lovely time, Charlie. If you're short of cash, I can let you have some. No? Then I'll be ready at lunch-time. Lunching in Town, are we? Right. Pick me up here when you're ready. I want to send a note to Mrs. Hilton, and another to that stuck-up Miss Mayhew, just to show them where I'm staying. There, good night, luv, and God bless.'

Saturday was bright and sunny, and Charles knew that his spirits were rising with every mile of the road which led to Ordingly. He drove well, and his small Austin behaved perfectly.

His mother said, 'I like this car—I suppose they all drive very posh cars, eh?'

'Lady Gollantz has a smart car, I forget what it is, Max has a brand new Bentley, and Sir Emmanuel has a rather large, rather antique Daimler—yes, I'm sure it's a Daimler. Now, look, when we pass this curve in the road, you'll catch sight of Ordingly in the trees on the right—Simeon told me. Look! There it is! Georgian. Old Emmanuel bought it, and Max and his wife lived there for the rest of their lives.' He was growing excited and rather nervous, and she heard both the excitement and the nervousness in his voice. 'Lady Gollantz has a small string of horses—you like horses, don't you?'

She laughed. 'I don't know much about them, luv, except the kind you have in panto. I mind in panto at Rochdale once, the Fairy was in love with the hind legs of the horse—two brothers played the horse, Len and Wilf Something-or-other. We were always falling over the Fairy and the Hind Legs in dark corners of the stage—we could have killed them!'

Charles turned the car neatly through the lodge gates, and drove slowly up the drive.

Rose breathed, 'Eh, it's a lovely house!'

Charles thought, conscious of a thrill of pride, 'It's the family home, and I'm accepted as one of the family. I'd not change places with the greatest duke in the land.'

5

He was surprised. and faintly ashamed of being so, at the ease with which his mother accepted her new surroundings. The rather old butler was suave and respectful. Did Mrs. Watson wish to go to her room? Mrs. Watson did. A maid appeared and escorted her, a young man in restrained livery carried her bags.

Viva Gollantz always boasted that she had no difficulty in finding and keeping good servants. Her mother—Lady Heriot—said the same.

The butler turned to Charles. 'Lady Gollantz will be here in a moment, sir. If you care to go to your room, I will have your bag sent up.'

The impression that Charles had of the house was that the colours everywhere were subdued without being dull or dingy. There seemed to him a predominance of pale grey, pale yellow. Light wood devoid of high French polish, and a sense of space.

His room was not particularly large, but the window looked out on to the park lands, and as his ancestor—old Emmanuel Gollantz—had done, he looked out at the splendid trees, and saw the silver ribbon of a stream making its way through the green of the more distant fields. Nearer, the gardens still held the last of the autumn flowers. There were bright bushes which could withstand the cold, and the wide terrace showed tiny lines of herbs growing between the old flagstones. He drew a deep breath, and sighed, 'It's beautiful—beautiful.'

He washed away the dust of his drive, smoothed his hair, and then heard a gong—faint and melodious. He knew that his mother would prefer to 'make her entrance' alone, and so walked slowly down the wide staircase to the hall, admiring its black and white marble paving, its fine old chests, and those rugs which were shabby with much use, but still retained their glowing colours.

Viva was standing before the huge log fire, and Charles thought that the leaping flames of the burning wood caught her bright hair and burnished it. She turned as he came down the stairs, calling in her particularly clear voice, 'Ah, Charles, welcome to Ordingly. Come and meet my mother—who has only honoured us this week-end because she wants to meet *your* mother again.'

Charles saw a large, handsome woman, magnificently—if a little ostentatiously—dressed, who held out a hand literally weighed down with splendid rings.

She said, 'This is nice—how are ye? Charles, is it? I shall call you Charlie. No one except me ever calls Emmanuel "Manny". I do, and I always shall.'

Viva said, 'I hate it, Mama. It sounds like a Whitechapel tailor!'

'He likes it, and I like it, so'—she laughed—'what's the odds so long as we're happy. Have you brought Rose Hallet with you, Charlie?'

'I think she's coming down the stairs now, Lady Heriot.'

Lady Heriot rose, and waved her ringed hand to Charles's mother who was coming down the wide staircase.

'Hello, Rose,' she called, 'overture and beginners, please. You'll miss your entrance, Miss Hallet, and that means a fine, y'know.'

He saw his mother's face break into a smile as she reached the hall and said, 'Miss Grantley, please—it's not your cue. Lady Gollantz, I'm so delighted to be here. It was very kind of you to ask me. Charles'—(her son thought, 'Isn't she clever! Charles—not Charlie!')—'says that you have all been so kind to him, and I'm grateful.'

'We have done nothing, Mrs. Watson. Now please go and talk to my mother, who is only here because she wants to meet you again. Tea?'

'Please.' She sat down on the big sofa beside Lady Heriot.

'No tea for me, Viv—I'll have a whisky-and-soda. Tea—well, it doesn't suit me. Now, Rose, give me all the news. I'm buried in what calls itself society, and I get bored to death. Oh, who do you think I met a few days ago in Fortnum's?—you'd never guess—dear Claire Romaine! Looking grand, dear, and as amusing as ever. We've seen some changes, Rose ducky, haven't we? The good old days—them was the days!'

'I always say so, but Beatrice, I was never in your street, y'know. You were the—well, the tops. It's nice of you to remember me.'

Lady Heriot threw back her head and shouted with laughter. 'Don't come that stuff, Rose. "As friends we met, as friends we part, as friends we meet again!"'

Viva smiled at Charles. 'They seem to get on quite well, eh?'

'I think my mother gets on with everyone, Lady Gollantz.'

'And you?'

'I hope—as we say in the north—in the main.'

She smiled back at him, then turned suddenly, and he saw that Emmanuel had entered the hall through a door which must have led to another part of the house. Charles, watching Viva Gollantz, thought that he had never seen a woman's face show so much love; not that she widened her smile, but there was an air of tranquil content, as if with his coming Emmanuel had brought a sense of completeness.

He came over and leaned forward to kiss her lightly on the cheek, then with a 'Hello, Charles, nice to see you', he moved on to greet Lady Heriot and Mrs. Watson.

The former screamed, 'Manny, your hands are frozen! What have you been doing?'

'Washing them in cold water,' he told her, 'because my wife is a firm believer in rigid economy and won't allow all the radiators to be turned on.'

Viva said, 'The man's an infernal liar! It's because he's so parsimonious and only buys the cheapest and worst coal.'

Rose Watson laughed. 'In these days,' she said, 'none of it's cheap, and the best is just the same as the worst.'

'Thank you, ma'am,' Emmanuel said. 'Charles, please note that your mother is on my side. It's freezing hard tonight, by the way.'

'Ice?' Viva exclaimed. 'When will the lake hold?'

'When will the possible ice on the lake hold—that's what you mean, isn't it? Not yet—so if the frost continues all night, don't try to persuade Charles to take you sliding! You hear that, Charles? I forbid it.'

This was the first time Charles had seen Emmanuel wearing country clothes, and he thought how much better he looked in them than any other man he had seen. His suit seemed to have reached exactly the right age—it was neither too new nor too shabby. His brown shoes were the colour of ripe horse chestnuts, and there was a touch of colour in his usually pale cheeks.

'Have you all had tea? Is it cold, Viva, or still fit to drink?'

'It's still hot, Manny,' Lady Heriot assured him. 'Rose had a second cup. Viva was too busy chattering to Charlie.'

Emmanuel poured out a cup and sipped it with grave attention. 'It's what I call warm and wet, Aunt Beatrice, and that's about all that can be said for it.'

Viva said, in that lazy voice which Charles found so attractive, 'Order some fresh tea.'

Emmanuel raised his eyebrows in mock horror. 'And possibly jeopardize my chance of buying better coal! Perish the thought!'

She said fondly, 'You poor mutt!'

Emmanuel asked where Simeon was, and Viva told him that he had telephoned that his wife was not feeling very well; if she felt better later he would come.

'These young husbands are all the same!' Lady Heriot announced. 'When their wives are going to have a baby it's the first baby ever born, she is the most vulnerable person, and every slight pain or ache is looked upon as a major catastrophe.' She gave an exaggerated sigh. 'My husband never suffered in that way, he paid more attention to his brood mares!'

Viva said, 'Mama! that may be true, knowing my respected father I am inclined to agree with you, but don't let's advertise it. Anyway, Max is coming.'

'Max Gollantz?' Rose asked.

Emmanuel said, 'The same. He will arrive in his new Bentley, wearing a Savile Row suit of clothes, and—by Gemini, that must be him,' as the bell rang through the big hall. The butler entered, and Emmanuel said, 'Hawkins, if that's Mr. Gollantz bring him here, and then take away this clutter of tea and bring us something to drink before we go up to change.'

Charles was conscious of an alteration in the friendly atmosphere; it seemed as though a chill wind had swept through the hall. Emmanuel stood more erect, that Lady Heriot looked slightly truculent—he wondered what Viva had told her, his mother twisted her handkerchief in her fingers—and Max entered.

'I say, sorry if I'm late. Viva, how are you? Ages since I saw you. Uncle Emmanuel—it's nice to be here.'

Lady Heriot said, 'So you're Max Gollantz. My name is Heriot.'

Max bowed—beautifully—'I am delighted——'

'And this lady is my very old friend, Mrs. Watson. The mother of our Charlie, there. You're like your father.'

'So I have been told.'

'Not so good looking—you're like Charlie too. How is your father?' She shot out her remarks like a machine-gun. 'I've not seen him for years.'

'He was very well when I left New York.'

Hawkins had come in with the subdued young footman. They had removed the tea-tray, and substituted a trolley which, it seemed to Charles, held bottles of all kinds and descriptions.

Lady Heriot nodded to Emmanuel. 'Whisky-and-soda for me, Manny. What about you, Rose? Pink gin? That's a frightful tipple, old girl.' Then turning back to Max, 'Doing well—I mean your father?'

'He is in partnership with my grandfather—Van der Hoyt Inc.'

She said irritably, 'What in Heaven's name is "Inc."?'

'Incorporated, Lady Heriot.'

'And what are you doing, gallivanting about London?'

'Making various purchases—new productions—which Van der Hoyt's can use.'

'Grand—you look a bit of a knut, I'll say that.'

He looked puzzled. 'A nut?'

She turned to Rose Watson, and grinned. 'These young things—in our day we knew what a knut was—we spelt it with a "k" didn't we, Rose? Poor Basil Hallam! Remember "Bric-a-Brac"?'

Max turned away and went over to Viva, who had listened with a certain amusement. She nodded, saying, 'Help yourself. My mother is something of an *enfant terrible*, but she has a heart of gold. I adore her.'

Charles, who had moved away, watched Max; his eyes devoured Viva, and Charles felt a sudden rush of fury. Lady Heriot and his mother were neither of them unused to male admiration, and here was this fellow making it plain to everyone that he was crazy about Viva.

'I'll lay any money,' he thought, 'that both Mum and Lady Heriot notice it! *And* comment on it. Still, I'd give something for his ease and certainty.'

He was thankful when Emmanuel returned, and laid his hand on Charles's shoulder saying, 'Just a quick one and then the first gong will be making the night hideous.' Lowering his voice he added, 'If this frost holds, don't let Viva persuade you to take her on the lake—there are springs there, and it takes a good deal of frost to make it really safe.'

'I promise, sir.'

That night when they went upstairs, Rose said to her son, 'Come and let's have a last little bedtime chat, Charlie.'

An electric fire was burning, and when Rose had taken off her dress and put on a dressing-gown mother and son sat on either side of the fire, both content and happy in each other's company.

Rose said, 'We might have a last little night-cap, Charlie, eh? They think of everything here, there is whisky and soda on the little table. Well, that was a grand evening, I enjoyed every minute of it. Lady's Heriot's just as big a card as she always was, full of life! Her daughter's a lovely looking woman, isn't she? Funny to think that she and that nice Sir Emmanuel were married, divorced and then remarried. Devoted seemingly. I'll tell you something else: that Max, who, I might tell you, I didn't properly take to, can't keep his eyes off her. Fairly eating her with them, he was. Rude I call it.'

'So you didn't "take to" the Magnificent Max?' Charles spoke idly, feeling relaxed and pleasantly tired; he had enjoyed his evening, and after catching Viva Gollantz's expression when her husband came in, he had—as he told himself—'taken himself in hand'. There must be no more of this schoolboyish romantic idiocy. He could and would always admire her, and be grateful to her for the way she had accepted him and his mother, but sentimental yearnings—'Silly idiot I might have made of myself, and infuriated the Head of the House!'—must be firmly suppressed.

Rose sipped her whisky-and-soda reflectively. 'No, I can't say I cared a lot for him. I suppose actually he's your half-brother?'

Charles nodded. 'I believe so. Only I stipulated that I didn't wish him to know.'

'You were right too. I know Julian, he's a vindictive beast, and you never know where he won't try to rake up bother. He'd try to prove that my marriage to Mr. Watson wasn't legal, that I ought to have taken greater pains to discover if he was still alive. No, let well alone, lad. There, you're dropping with sleep. Away to your bed. Good night.'

People straggled down to breakfast, helped themselves to food which was kept hot on the side table, read Sunday newspapers, or merely sat staring out of the long windows as Charles did, feeling his love for Ordingly growing minute by minute. Then his eyes wandered to the portrait which was hung over the huge fireplace. An old man, handsome, dignified, dressed in a style which was old fashioned but still full of elegance. His chin was stretched a little over the white strip of collar and the high satin stock, with its black pearl pin. His beautiful hands were clasped on the head of a malacca cane with a large carved ivory knob. The face, Charles felt, was at once kindly and critical. He could not imagine old Emmanuel Gollantz having tolerated, at any time, what was mean, base or unworthy. There was arrogance in the fine high-bridged nose ; the heavy-lidded eyes were still—even in old age—keen and bright, the chin jutted a little, the lips were rather full and yet sensitive. Charles, examing the picture, gave a little sigh of satisfaction.

A voice said, 'You're looking at Sargent's portrait of my grandfather. I never thought him a great artist—Sargent—he never *drew* properly. But his trick of catching the personality of his sitter was quite wonderful, and he applied his paint well. Yes, in spite of everything, I like the portrait. Remember,' Emmanuel was helping himself to eggs and bacon as he spoke, 'that if it were offered to me in a sale room, I might—if I happened to be in a good temper—give thirty guineas for it—not more.'

He came to the table and sat down. Charles watched him, admiration in his eyes.

He said, 'He must have been a great man, sir.'

'He was indeed. His understanding was tremendous, his kindness was inexhaustible. He was gener-rous, but never ostentatious in his gener-rosity. If you have finished your br-reakfast, pray light a cigarette. Turn a little in your chair, for on this other wall are the por-rtraits of my father and mother. De Laszlo painted her—charming isn't it, though slightly too photographic, I admit. My father was painted by Lavery—good, solid work, without any gr-reat imagination. That would have pleased my father. In fact it *did* please him. He was a "solid" man. In his way he was as notable a character as my gr-randfather.' He paused, and laughed softly. 'These people—for my mother was an angel—take some living up to, Charles.'

Charles met his eyes, and said, 'I'll do my best, sir.'

Emmanuel answered, 'Thank you, I know that. Just give me another cup of coffee, will you? Now, I shall join you in a cigar-rette. The first one is the perfect one of the day.'

'I was sitting here—before I began to stare at your grandfather's portrait, thinking that Ordingly is as nearly perfect as anything I have ever seen,' Charles told him.

Emmanuel leaned back in his chair, and smiled. 'Yes, I'm fond of it, and so is my wife. My gr-randfather bought it, and my father and mother lived here for most of their married life—and died here. There have been dark moments here, but' —he shrugged his shoulders—'we have survived them. Would you care to come with me and see some of the pieces I have collected? My wife collects horses—and does it very cleverly; I collect such pieces of furniture with which I fall in love, oh, desper-rately in love, and cannot bear to see them go where they won't have a r-really good home.'

He rose and walked out, Charles following him, Emmanuel led him to various rooms, talking of chairs, tables and cabinets as if he really loved them. Once or twice he said, 'R-run your fingers lightly over that wood—car-ress it.' Or opening a cabinet, and taking out some little figure, 'Just hold that. Capo di Monte. What a lovely patina. Here, a little piece of "bisque" —so often they were finished with a base which had a high polish.' He talked easily, and Charles felt that he was being instructed by a master.

When finally they reached Emmanuel's library, and sat there in the splendid carved Chippendale chairs, he said, 'That was wonderful. Thank you, sir.' Charles sighed. 'I wonder if I shall ever be able to possess half your knowledge?'

'That depends so much on how great is your desire to learn.'

'And appreciate, surely?'

'Undoubtedly. I have heard my grandfather say that when he was in r-real doubt concerning some piece of china or furniture, he had tr-rained himself to shut his eyes and, as he said, "Allow his fingers to see".' The clock on the wide mantelpiece chimed and Emmanuel started. 'Twelve o'clock alr-ready. How bored you must have been, with my talking all the time! Come and have a glass of sherry before my wife descends on us, and takes us off to see her horses.'

They had been, as Lady Heriot told them, 'Beaten to it!' She held out her glass to Emmanuel saying, 'Thanks, Manny, fill it up will you? Then I suppose we're off to see Viva's gee-gees, eh?'

'And it is becoming more and more of a favour for Miller to let me take visitors to see them,' Viva said. 'I've never known a man so watchful. Carrots—their Sunday treat, scrubbed in the kitchen here—aren't good enough, he scrubs them himself in the saddle-room. I believe that he weighs every one of them to make sure none of the horses is getting one calorie—or whatever it is they do get in carrots—too many.'

Her mother said, 'Let's get cracking. Charlie, will your mother want a coat? She says "No", but I think she'd be better well rugged up.'

Rose protested, said that she was 'tough', and after some small discussion they went out to the stables. The day was bright and there was some pale sunshine. Charles, walking beside his mother, knew that his eyes were taking in everything. Max was walking with Viva, and she turned and called over her shoulder, 'The frost is still holding, we'll have those skates on yet, Charles!'

'You won't!' Emmanuel retorted, 'I have an ally in Charles.'

They came to the big courtyard, it was the first time Charles had ever visited such stables and loose boxes. The old paved yard looked as if it were washed with meticulous care—as indeed it was—every morning. The whole place smelt of cleanliness, and the little man wearing perfectly cut riding breeches and a tweed coat looked as clean and neat as the place which was his special domain.

''Mornin', ma'am,' to Viva; a broad smile to Lady Heriot and 'Very nice ter see you 'ere again, m'lady.' He eyed Max a trifle coldly, and his voice, though respectful, had lost its warmth as he greeted him.

Emmanuel said, 'Rose, may I introduce my wife's trainer, Andy Miller? This is my nephew, Charles Gollantz.'

Miller gave his stiff ceremonious bow to Rose, and muttered, ''Appy an' honoured, Ah'm sure. How d' do, sir. Now shall we, as Jorrocks says, "cut the cackle an' cum to the 'osses"?'

Charles was entranced. He followed Miller into the saddle-room, where Fred and Tom, both bearing waistcoats with long black sleeves, were polishing bits, or cleaning saddles.

Charles thought, 'It's Sunday morning, this is an act Miller's put on. Knowing there were visitors he was certain that they'd be brought here, and he wants to do credit to his owner. I like him, he's going to do everything to make a good show. He's from the north, Yorkshire, I fancy.'

Lady Heriot was saying to his mother, 'Andy Miller—I've known him since Hyde Park was in a flower-pot. Straight as a die! Viva's damned lucky to have got him—thanks to "Buster" Carteret.'

'An' this 'ere is my store an' my kitching. I like to see my 'osses food pervided, as you might say, under my eyes. In this game, you 'ave ter regard everyone as a possible enemy! Except your owner, and your stable-boys.'

Emmanuel said, 'Does that include me, Miller?'

'I 'ave to admit that it does, sir—more or less. Now, comin' ter the loose boxes, the first 'oss is our old pal, White Knight. That's a 'oss with a 'eart of gold, like wot a lion is. 'E's not fast, but he's faithful. 'E'd run till he dropped, if you treat 'im right. Yes, ma'am, I've a few carrots ready for you to feed to 'em.'

Emmanuel took one of the small, pink carrots, and offered it to the horse, who took it gently, and crunched it with appreciation.

'We've entered him—with Hereward—for the Calmering. Hereward is always happier when White Knight is with him.'

Lady Heriot asked, 'Got a chance, Miller, this Hereward of yours?'

'We think, m'lady, that 'e 'as a very fine chance.'

She laughed. 'The stable putting their money on him, eh?'

'I'm risking a quid each way, m'lady—and I don't like taking risks!'

'A cert?'

'Nothink's a cert, m'lady, till the 'oss is past the post. Now, 'ere's Snow Prince—nice 'oss, but 'e's lazy.' He turned to Viva. 'We'll never do much with 'im—he's a Selling Plater, ma'am. Now, this 'un Great 'eart he's more of the character of White Knight—willing, an' he has a pretty turn of speed. Little light, m'lady, as no doubt you've observed, but pervided the goin' isn't too heavy, he'll go places will this 'un. Good shoulders, plenty of staying-power, an' 'is hoofs are good and 'is hocks is good. That's right, ma'am, give 'em the carrots, it's their Sunday mornin' treat.'

Rose asked, 'Do you always have straw plaited along the edge of the boxes?'

'Allus, in a stable wheer Ah'm in charge, ma'am. Now, this is Roarin' Gal—'ooever called 'er that, didn't know 'er, for she's as gentle as a lamb. She did very well for us at Ripon, and quite well at Stockton. Not racing 'er this spring, she's in foal to Cay Drake—Sir Archibald Culner's—a grand 'oss, and Roarin' Gal will do 'im and uz credit.'

He paused until Viva had given the mare her carrot, then with the air of a conjurer presenting his finest and most admired trick, he said, 'An' 'ere, m'lady, we 'ave Hereward.' He turned to Emmanuel, saying, 'And there, sir, you 'ave a fine 'oss. A 'oss of quality. Puts me in mind of a coloured print I 'ave, of Ellington out of Flying Dutchman, wot won the Derby many years ago. Same nice small 'ead, lots of power, a good do-er.'

'What's his record, Miller?' Lady Heriot asked. 'Good?'

'First, unplaced and third, m'lady—which was just what we wanted. He'll show his form in the Calmering, or I'm no judge! Give 'im a little carrot, m'lady, then you can say that you once fed carrot to a future Derby winner—as that's what I figure 'im to be.'

'Don't overtrain him, Miller,' Beatrice Heriot said. 'I've known a lot of horses ruined by over-anxiety.'

'Not uz, m'lady. Takin' it nice and easy. Reg'lar, of course. The owner 'as booked Freddie Calft to ride 'im. Little Tom Willis, 'im as you saw in the saddle-room, will ride White Knight.'

Speaking for almost the first time, Max said, 'I once ventured to say that I should like a canter on him. I was treated as if I'd insulted a member of the Royal Family!'

With considerable dignity Miller answered him, 'Sir, 'ad I not understood that your knowledge of 'orseflesh was what you might call in the elementary stage, I'd 'ave said a good bit more.'

In a voice which was filled with ill-suppressed fury, Max retorted, 'Say, I like that! I've ridden all my life. I'm considered a pretty good horseman.'

'Did you once ride Simeon's Crusader—and let him down?' Emmanuel asked, his tone dangerously pleasant.

'That was years ago! How did you know?'

'I fancy that Miss Rosenfeldt found you and Simeon having something of an argument about it. As you say, it is some years ago—probably you have improved since then. Yes, he's a fine chap, this Hereward. I don't often go to race-meetings, but I shall go to Calmering, and—what's the expression?—put my shirt on him.'

'You can, Sir Emmanuel. You'll get enough back to buy yourself a dozen shirts, or my name isn't Andy Miller.'

Viva and Emmanuel remained for a few moments talking to the little North-country trainer as the others walked away. Max slouched along, his hands in his pockets, while Lady Heriot chattered incessantly of fillies, geldings, sires and dams, weights and jockeys—half of which was Greek to Charles and, he believed, to his mother. He felt completely content; except for Max the visit to Ordingly had been a joy. He told himself that he loved Viva Gollantz, that he would always love her, but that he had got his feelings for her into focus. In fact, he could almost smile at himself for having even momentarily indulged in hopes for the future—a future which should hold Viva and himself. What incredible stupidity, what damned insolence! Viva herself had answered him, when he had watched her face as she saw Emmanuel enter the hall. More plainly than words could have done she had told him—told everyone who was capable of reading the meaning of her expression, and were not too stupid, too filled with self-esteem to be unable to read what her face depicted so plainly.

Charles was leaving just before dinner. Rose was nervous of his driving back to London in the dark, and although he protested that after all in late November it was dark by tea-time, she still looked worried. So he had given her his promise, saying, 'All right, Mum dear, I'll even give up the chance of a good dinner to satisfy you!'

'That's my kind lad. I'm a silly old fool, but when I get these fancies into my head—well, they stick! I'm driving up in the morning or just after lunch on Monday with Lady Heriot. She's asked me to stay with her a couple of days before I go back home. My word, Charlie, your old mum's seeing life, isn't she? Staying here, and then going to stop with Beatrice Grantley. I'll make them open their eyes when I get back, mark my words.'

'Who is looking after Thomas?' Charles asked.

She returned indignantly, 'Now, lad, you can't imagine me not having arranged everything for Thomas? Mrs. Smithers, who does for me, is sleeping in while I'm away. She loves Thomas as if he was her own child—why, come to that a lot better'n some folk love their children. Nay, no call to fash yourself over Thomas!'

Charles laughed, 'Now that my mind is set at rest, you can go off gallivanting a little longer. Have you let Mrs. Smithers know you won't be back for a few days?'

'I sent a telegram. I asked Viva where the post office was—thinking that even on Sundays it might be open for an hour or two. She said—in that "grand" way—"Just write it out, Rose, and we'll telephone it through to London—it saves time." Mind it's not being swanky, it's just, I suppose, that they've always been used to having things done the road they want them.'

'The privileged classes as the Socialists would say,' Charles said.

Rose bristled slightly. 'Well, they've a right to a few privileges. Look at the taxes they pay, look what they hand out in charity—aye, and do it willingly—look at the people they employ, and pay well for their work. If you ask me, Charlie, England will be a lot worse off in many ways without these same privileged classes. I can't see any of them thinking that some woman who has worked for them honestly and faithfully can live on an Old Age Pension without a bit of extra help!'

'I thought that you didn't like these jumped-up people!'

'No more I do! But I like folks with roots, who are proud—aye, proud—to fulfil their obligations. Well, it's been a lovely experience. And we're asked for Christmas—how'd you like that, Charlie luv?'

'Splendidly. I believe they make great things of Christmas. Rather strange when you remember that Emmanuel is really at least half a Jew.'

'Plenty of Jews are a lot better Christians nor some as call themselves Christian. The proof of a man's real religion is the road he lives his life—remember that, my lad. Come to that you've got a strain of Jew in you yourself, think on.'

He put his arm round her plump shoulders and kissed her. 'Believe me, I'm glad of it, darling.'

6

Charles was ready to leave. He carried his bag down to the hall, where Hawkins was bringing in the trolley laden with various drinks. The butler looked at him slightly reprovingly.

'No call for you to carry your bag, sir, Frank could have done that.' Then less severely, 'If I might say so, I trust that we shall have the pleasure of seeing you and Mrs. Watson here again.'

'Christmas,' Charles said, smiling. 'Tell me, where is everyone?'

'I believe, sir, that Lady Heriot and Mrs. Watson are still in their rooms,' Hawkins replied with the admirable if slightly overdone caution of a well-trained butler. 'Sir Emmanuel is attending to correspondence in the library, and Lady Gollantz went through into the conservatory some moments ago.'

Charles walked through the big drawing-room and into the warm, humid air of the conservatory. It was a long, rather narrow place, where the moist heat seemed to enhance the scent of the flowers. Charles disliked the heaviness, it seemed to envelop him in a thick, heavily scented blanket.

Where he stood, the conservatory was in darkness, but at the farther end there was one electric light burning, and in the radius of light cast by it, two people were standing—Viva and Max. For a few seconds Charles hesitated, then Viva's voice, as always very clear, could be heard.

'Max, I will not have this! I will not be followed and pestered. I will not be stared at as if I were some exhibit in a show! It's becoming intolerable.'

Max murmured something which Charles did not catch, and Viva continued, 'No, of course not—how can you expect me to love someone who is young enough to be my son, apart from the fact that I have——'

Very carefully Charles found an empty flower-pot, which he dropped with a great clatter, saying firmly and loudly, 'Oh, damn!' He called, 'Is that you, Viva, because I shall have to get away. Hawkins has the drinks ready in the hall.'

He fancied that he saw Max turn away and leave the conservatory by another door. Viva called, 'Coming now! Did I hear you trying to break up the happy home?' She came towards him.

'Sorry, I knocked over a flower-pot in the dark.'

She met his eyes very steadily. 'That was very clever of you—and then you announced your presence by one of the most heart-felt "Damns" I have ever heard. Well, come along and let me give you a stirrup cup.'

By the time they reached the hall, the rest of the party were there, Max looking completely unperturbed as he stood sipping a cocktail.

Lady Heriot shook Charles's hand warmly. 'Nice to have met you,' she said. 'Leave wine alone, it's too expensive; fast women and slow horses have played the devil with too many young men—you don't sing?'

He grinned. 'Not a note——'

'Ah, then song offers no inducements. Come and have a bite with your mother and me tomorrow about eight—or no, make it seven and we can go on to a show. I'll fix it. I'll be seein' you, as the girl said—no, all right, Viva, I won't tell him that one.'

His mother kissed him, whispering, 'Drive carefully, won't you, Charlie. Until tomorrow, eh?'

Max, busy lighting a cigarette with extreme care, nodded, and mumbled that they would be 'running across' each other no doubt in the near future. Viva and Emmanuel went with him to the big door, where they stood watching him, her arm through Emmanuel's, both smiling. She called, 'At Christmas—we'll have that skating then!'

Emmanuel said, 'Charles, remember that you're on my side!'

He drove back to London carefully, for the roads were not too good, and in some places there was ice, and he hated driving on ice. It had been a wonderful two days. Not only had he loved the easy dignity of it all, but he felt that he had been allowed to be officially 'one of the family'. His admiration for Emmanuel had increased, his love for Viva had been transmuted from something which might have become furtive and altogether objectionable into a real affection and admiration. He admitted that these feelings might also contain a certain amount of romance—Viva was still a beautiful woman, she had charm and vivacity, and a kindness and warmth of heart which were unmistakable.

He did not regret his entrance into the long conservatory. It had not been premeditated, and he therefore had not the slightest reason to be ashamed. He had heard what he had heard because he had been momentarily at a loss to know what course he should pursue. He had heard Viva's clear voice raised in protest, and had realized that Max—as he himself had been —was in love with her. He had thrown down an empty flowerpot, and seen Max—almost like a shadow—glide away through the other door. But he had gone—that was the main thing!

And now? Max no doubt realized that he must have heard something. How much or how little would remain a matter of conjecture, but of one thing Charles was certain: Max—from now on—would hate him, and what was far, far more important, would undoubtedly nurse a grievance against Viva, because she had repulsed him.

He had sensed that in Max there was a vindictive quality which was completely absent in Emmanuel, or for that matter in any of the Gollantz except—and this was speculation—his own father, Julian. He recalled yesterday's visit to the stables, when Miller had voiced his perfectly civil rebuke, and Emmanuel's little recollection of some fight between Max and Simeon. He remembered how Max had slouched off, his hands deep in his great-coat pockets, speaking to no one, merely walking alone nursing his grievance against Miller, Emmanuel and probably against Simeon as well.

Charles imagined that Max had been spoilt and over-indulged all his life. Money had never mattered very much, and he had been allowed to savour everything which—for the moment—interested him. Expensive cars, changed each year for others even more expensive; clothes from the most exclusive tailors, holidays when one luxurious house was changed for another;

lovely women, no matter what their age, flattered and pleased at attentions paid to them by the grandson of the millionaire Van der Hoyt.

'All the same,' Charles thought, 'I may understand why he is as he is, but I've made an enemy of him. He hates my being accepted at Ordingly, he is jealous that Viva is friendly to me, and that Emmanuel interests himself in my welfare. All right, Max, as we say in the north, I'm not so green as I'm cabbage looking. I'll look after myself, and happen a few more people as well if you try any funny business. Don't tread on my toes, and I won't tread on yours. . . . Hello, Baker Street. The little bus has done well.'

He dined the following night with Lady Heriot and his mother, and after hurrying through an excellent dinner went on to one of the most successful musicals in Town.

Beatrice Heriot disliked it. She whispered to Rose Watson, 'Can you imagine Gertie Miller, or Ella Terriss or Evie Greene giving us this rubbish?'

'It would have sounded very different.'

'It wouldn't have "sounded at all"—they'd not have sung it!' During the interval she insisted on a visit to the bar, where the manager came to her, smiling. 'Lady Heriot, this is a pleasure. . . .'

'For you or for me?' she demanded.

'I trust for both of us.'

She tilted her chin. 'Say you're not sure, my friend.' She introduced him to Rose Watson, saying, 'Ask her what she thinks.'

Rose said, 'Well, it's not quite my style of musical comedy. . . .'

'But,' he protested, 'this is not a musical comedy, this is a —musical. One of the greatest successes London has ever seen.'

Lady Heriot took her whisky-and-soda from Charles, nodded her thanks, then said, 'Well—a rose by any other name could still smell nasty.'

'Her Majesty has been to see it, and Princess Margaret has been twice.'

Rose sighed. 'They're both young—they never heard José Collins or Lily Elsie.'

'Or Marie Tempest, or Winifred Hare, or a dozen more,'

Beatrice added. 'Now, have a drink before the bell goes. Yes, it's all right, my friend and I are both "pros" and we can ask a man to have a drink with us. Charlie dear, see to it, will you? Well, old boy, glad your theatre's full, even if I don't like the show. Write me down as a "has been".'

She was so full of actual kindness that no one ever disliked her for her outspokenness, and now she beamed on them all, as she said, 'Down the hatch,' adding, 'Jolly good luck to your show, old boy. I'll send the younger generation to see it. There's the bell—goo' night, old boy, the best of luck.'

Later, when they sat in her drawing-room, furnished with satin-covered chairs so heavily 'buttoned' that they seemed to defy comfort and yet, strangely enough were extremely comfortable, Charles listened to their conversation, feeling that the pages of musical-comedy history were being turned for him. He heard names that were only vaguely familiar, those of Mary Stuart, or Nell Gwyn. Yet it held him entranced, and when Lady Heriot went to the wildly over-decorated grand piano, sat down and sang—and her voice was still tuneful and her enunciation perfect—'She was the Miller's Daughter' and 'Under the Deodar', he was charmed.

'Melodies,' she said, 'that's what we can't get now. Very few men that I know can write 'em. That darling Ivor Novello now, he's had melody in his blood. Listen to this——'

He went back to his rooms, his head ringing with the music that he had heard.

Rose returned to Dullton—so called not because the inhabitants regarded it as 'dull' but because a small, rather insignificant river named Dull flowed through it. Charles became immersed in his work; he was packing his brain full of knowledge, not only of pictures, furniture and china, but with the more technical points of auctioneering. Night after night he sat with his books round him, trying to amass and store away all the things which would fit him for the life he had chosen.

There were times when Viva's golden head came between him and the pages of the book he was studying, times when he felt that he could still hear her voice, see the quick turn of her head, or the smooth movement of her body as she moved to pour out tea or hand someone a big silver box filled with cigarettes. It didn't hurt, he knew that his infatuation for her had been fundamentally unworthy, and he reminded himself of 'the desire of the moth for the star', of his admiration for Emmanuel, and went back to his books contented.

On Saturdays, when he was free from his duties at the offices of Kennerley and Mastock, he walked about London. He grew to know which street markets were worth visiting and which were a mere waste of time. He was gathering, slowly and without great expense, a little collection of china and one or two pieces of old silver.

In Middlesex Street—once the famous Petticoat Lane—he had found a small plaque in an oval frame. The poor thing had been damaged, but there was still colour and glimpses of fine patina. It was a portrait of a man, in admiral's uniform, in profile. Charles examined it, and decided that it was Admiral Blake.

'Who is this?' he asked the stall-holder.

The little man answered, 'Thet? Why—Nelson!'

'Nelson?'

'Thet's why 'e's 'ad it done side fice, ter 'ide 'is blind eye. Blimey, Guv'nor, we all like ter 'ide our de-fects, don't we?'

Farringdon Market, over there at Shepherd's Bush, in the streets leading off Edgware Road—in all these he had found small pieces, possibly of no great value but capable of giving him great pleasure. To bring them home, wash them with the greatest care, and place them in his room gave Charles untold delight. It seemed to him that they took on a new lustre, a fresh beauty because they knew that they had been bought by someone who admired, loved and appreciated them.

One Saturday, when Christmas was only three weeks away, he wandered to Clerkenwell. He passed many rather shabby little shops, and at last found one which, though very dirty, displayed in its window a set of ivory chessmen. Charles stopped, peered through the dirty glass, and decided that they were good —if the whole set were there.

Emmanuel played chess, and Charles could see, in imagination, his fine fingers hovering above these carved pieces as he decided upon his next move. He walked into the shop. A small, scruffy man was behind the littered counter. He was busily employed in cleaning his nails with a tram ticket.

He looked up, 'Yus? Want anyfink?'

'I should like to see those chessmen in the window, if I may.'

'Seems you've see n'em already. Orlrite, I'll git 'em.' He shuffled to the window, and brought back the pieces. 'Perfec',' he said, as he spilt them on to the counter in a way which made Charles almost grit his teeth in horror. 'Antiques, them is. Gen-u-ine. Prob-'ly over a 'undered years old. Take a luke at this 'un,' he handed Charles a magnificent castle, '*you* never saw a set like this i' yore life.'

'Is there a board?' Charles interrupted.

'A board! Gor' luv uz, mister, buy one o' them in Woolworths! It's the pieces as matter. An' perfect, not one missing. Play chess?' Charles had never played chess in his life, but he said bravely, 'I've been playing chess for years. Do you?'

'Me! 'Corse I do—ask anyone in Clerkenwell what Joseph 'Indes knows abart chess. Know the answer? I'll tell yer. It 'ul be, "'Im, knows bloody everythink!" That's me—Joseph 'Indes.'

'And the price, Mr. Hindes?'

The little man screwed up his eyes. 'You a dealer?'

'No, merely a chess player. If I had time and you had a board we might have had a game, eh?'

'I'd 'a beat you, mister. Nah, the price. Well, say fifteen, eh?' Charles looked at the pieces. They were beautiful, the carving was fine and exquisite. 'Fifteen—just set them out, will you, let's make sure they're all there.'

With certain, if dirty fingers, the little man set the pieces out, naming them as he did so. 'Theer you are, mister—all "Sir Garnet", not one missin'. Fifteen pahnds.'

Charles replied, 'Ten—on the nail.'

'Blimey, it's bloody robbery—ten! Makes me larf. Say—twelve.'

Charles, his eyes on the beautiful things, his mind thinking how carefully and tenderly he would clean them, how tomorrow—no, it was Sunday—on Monday, he would have the finest board imaginable made for them, nodded. 'Right, make it twelve.'

'Done, an' it's a proper Christmas present as I'm makin' you, did you but know it.' He began to wrap the pieces in some dirty newspaper, but Charles repressed his longing to cry, 'Let me do it'.

Hindes, obviously pleased with his work, said, 'Theer—travel safe ter Timbuktu like the road I've wrapped 'em. Nothink like newspaper—an' the older the better.' He counted the notes which Charles gave him and said, with a sudden change of manner, 'Don't want a receipt, do yer?'

'No, don't bother. That's all right.' He thought, 'I bet any money these were never come by honestly. What do I care? I believe he'll like them.'

'Mind if I have a look round?' he asked. 'Might not be anything, but I love—poking about.'

'Go on, mister, 'ave yer luke rhand. Nothink much, but there's some pickshures over there—'ad 'em for years. I don't bother wi' pickshures meself. Over in that Johnnie 'Orner—tike yer time.'

Hindes was right. The shelves, all deplorably dusty, held nothing in the least attractive. There were a few tattered books, mostly of the mildly pornographic type, some cracked tea-cups without saucers.

He came to some canvases stacked in 'the Johnnie 'Orner' and began to turn them over. They were filthy and Charles was conscious that his hands were rapidly becoming so. He glanced at the dreadful paintings of improbable flowers in hideous vases, the head of a girl so badly painted that she looked as if she were suffering from acute toothache, a landscape with mountains in the distance covered with what might have been mist or snow, with a few cows scattered about the foreground for good measure.

Hindes looked up from his paper. 'I tole yer theer was nothink much. I've a pickshure 'enging in my sitting-room as *is* a pickshure. Two ladies standing on the edge of a marble swimming-pool. It's by a' artist called Taddermer. It's suthink, but I'd not sell it, not for a 'undered pahnds.'

Charles murmured, 'Ah—fine artist,' and pulled out a small painting and peered at it. The painting, like the others, was almost obscured by dirt, and he could well believe Hindes when he said they had been there for years, but through the filth he could see dim figures—skating. As he carried the canvas over to the window, Hindes glanced up and tendered advice.

'Bit mucky, eh? Spit on it. Finest thing ter clean 'em—spit.'

Charles thought, 'It would take a hell of a lot of it to clean this one!' However, he carefully spat on his handkerchief and rubbed the canvas gently. Yes—a winter scene, skating figures, a house—he could make out this much in the corner which he had cleaned. Once cleaned properly, well framed, this might be the very present for Viva for Christmas. It probably had little or no value, but at all events it would amuse her.

'How much?' he asked Hindes.

'Thet? Ten bob, mister.'

'I'll take it. Got a piece of newspaper so that I can wrap it up?'

'Mite 'ave. I'll luke. Yes, 'ere you are.' He handed Charles a paper which was almost as dirty as the picture itself. 'Tike it 'ome, an' you can read the piper whil yer 'ave yer tea, eh?'

Charles paid, and with the chessmen in an untidy parcel, tied with a piece of string which was almost like a ship's cable for size, he bade Hindes 'Good afternoon' and walked out.

Hindes called, 'Come again, anytime. Mite 'ave suthink—never know. S'long.'

He stood for a moment on the pavement outside the shop, glad to breathe the fresh air again, for the shop had been unbearably stuffy and fusty. There were few people about, and he glanced round wondering if he was likely to pick up a taxi. Turning to the left, he saw a figure emerge from a shop which looked more prosperous than the others in that rather mean street. Instinctively—though for the life of him he could not have said why—Charles drew back into the shelter of Hindes's shop door.

The figure, tall, elegantly dressed, moving with a certainty and decision which Charles realized he had envied more than once, crossed the road. His half-brother—Max Gollantz! What in heaven's name was he doing in an obscure chemist's shop in Clerkenwell? As the figure disappeared, Charles thought, 'He knows his way, there's no hanging about to wait for a taxi, he knows where he can find one. This isn't the first time he's been here.'

He walked forward, encumbered as he was with his parcels, and very conscious of his dirty hands, towards the chemist's shop. It was small, but looked clean and well kept. Charles entered, and found behind the counter a smallish man, with a high forehead and spectacles with very thick lenses.

'Vot can I do for you, saire?' the man asked.

'A tube of toothpaste, please. No, I don't mind what kind.' as the man hesitated, 'some reasonably good make.'

The man nodded. 'Eet is not goot to use any kind of toothpaste. Much better is—powder. But to take anysing—thet shows a lack of r-real interest in the tee't.' He wrapped up the tube which he had selected, and handed it to Charles.

Charles said, 'That gentleman who left your shop a few minutes ago, was it Mr. Brownleigh? I only caught a glimpse of him, but I fancied that it was Mr. Brownleigh.'

The man shook his head. 'Br-rownleigh? No, or maybe it vas. I don't know the gentleman's name. I never see him before. He vantet to buy'—there was a faint pause, and Charles thought, 'You old liar!'—'to buy carr-roway seeds to put in cakes. I don't have them. I send him to anudder shop. I am kemist.'

'Quite, my mistake no doubt.' He paid for his tube of toothpaste and walked away, his mind filled with speculations. He remembered that Max had said he was collecting various 'toilet accessories' which might sell in the United States; was this where he had found them? Possibly the foreign chemist did some laboratory work as a kind of side-line. Still, it was strange that Max should come all the way to Clerkenwell to find a suitable chemist.

Then a crawling taxi came past and Charles hailed it and with his precious parcels drove back to his rooms.

He stopped once on the way to buy at an oil shop a small, very fine soft sponge and a cake of soap.

Vickers eyed his clumsily packed parcels with slight disfavour.

Charles said, 'I've been routing about in a junk shop, Vickers. My hands are filthy and I'm dying for tea—and are there any muffins or crumpets?'

Vickers unbent a little. 'I have no doubt, sir, that Mrs. Vickers can oblige. Shall I take the parcels?'

Charles laughed. 'And get as dirty as I am? No! I'll go and wash and afterwards, perhaps, you'll give me your opinion of my purchases and your advice on how to get rid of some of the dirt on them.'

'I shall be delighted, sir, to put whatever small knowledge I have at your service.'

'Splendid! Then bring in the muffins or crumpets. I'm nearly starving.'

He sat by the fire, eating hot muffins with the appetite of a schoolboy. He had propped the picture up in a chair and his eyes kept wandering towards it. It was difficult to see it quite clearly through the layers of dirt, but he could see the skating figures, and his thoughts went back to Viva. Perhaps, in spite of his determination to drive away all romantic emotions regarding her, there was still something rather tender and even sentimental about his feeling for her. Possibly it was not altogether unpleasant to indulge in a retrospective regret—thoughts of 'what might have been' and other ideas which beset young men without a great deal of worldly experience. Had he been a reader of poetry, he would no doubt have found many quotations to suit his mood. His thoughts, however, did not affect his appetite.

Vickers came to take away his tea-tray, and Charles showed him the ivory chessmen. Vickers, setting down the tray, gave them his whole attention.

'If I may express an opinion, sir, these are very fine. Beautiful work and as far as the eye of a person who is in no way an expert may be relied on, in perfect condition. Mrs. Vickers will be only too delighted to wash them for you, using a soft brush—camel hair—to get into the corners. No trouble at all, I assure you. As it happens all our gentlemen are dining out this evening—I don't know about you, sir?—and she will have, as you might say, almost unlimited time at her disposal.'

Charles said, 'I'm dining out, Vickers. I'd be grateful.'

'Pray don't mention it, sir. Mrs. Vickers is as fond of beautiful things as I am. We have an ivory model of the Taj Mahal, which her aunt left her. Kept under a glass case, she'd not part with it for all the tea in China, as the saying goes. Now sir, we'll see about this painting of yours, with your permission.'

He carried away the tea-things and the chessmen, and returned later with several old newspapers, a white table-cover, various soft clean dusters, a basin and a can of hot water.

After advising Charles to remove his jacket and pull up his cuffs, he issued his advice and instructions.

'The sponge, sir, squeezed practically dry. Now rub it on the soap. Now apply it very gently to the picture itself. That's the way! Again and again, the dirt won't come off at once—it's taken years to put it there, and it takes a long time to remove it—particularly London dirt.'

Charles worked slowly and carefully. A skating scene, with beautifully painted figures, full of life, gradually emerged. Some trees, almost bare of any leaves, an old house—or inn—and the whole bathed in a lovely clear, cold light—the light of a winter's day.

Charles looked at it and sighed with satistaction. Vickers handed him a dry, soft cloth. 'I should remove any moisture, sir.'

Charles said, 'It's a beautiful picture, don't you think?'

'If I might express an opinion, it is the Dutch School, and it reminds me forcibly of a painting one of my former employers had, by a Dutchmen called Breughel. A very well-known painter.' He allowed himself to smile, saying, 'What a find, sir, if you've found a Breughel! They're worth a mint of money. I assure you that is correct.'

'Anyway, it's a charming picture,' Charles said, 'and thank you for your help and co-operation.'

Vickers was already clearing away the water and cloths. 'It's a pleasure, sir, to have been present with you when you went on this voyage of discovery. And now, if you are dining out, sir, might I suggest that it is time for you to think about dressing?'

He was meeting Simeon in the American Bar at the Savoy. Charles was a few minutes late, and Simeon came towards him, his face shining with pleasure.

'Such a surprise! Who do you think are here—two of my oldest and dearest friends. How I wish that Daphne could have joined us, but she is shy of going out much at this time.'

'And the friends?' Charles asked.

'Louis Lara and his marvellous wife who was—years ago—one of the most famous dancers in the world—Olympia!'

As they drank their cocktails, Simeon told him about the Laras, how, many years ago, when Emmanuel first started his little shop in Milan—'before the arrival of Simeon Jaffe from Vienna'—Louis Lara, also a dealer in antiques and now a world-wide authority on pictures, had worked with him.

'Louis, my father, and dear Guido Moroni were tremendous friends, a friendship which has grown with the years. Now Louis is my father's partner in the Paris Galleries, and Guido manages the Galleries in Milano. During the German occupation in Paris, Olympia and Iva Alfano—another friend of whom I shall tell you one day—did wonderful work in the underground movement. They insist that we dine with them—they will meet us here. Ah, here they are! How happy this makes me!'

He was talking excitedly, and Charles felt that there was something still left of his early upbringing in Italy, or perhaps it was the warmth of his strain of Jewish blood. He went to meet Louis Lara and his immensely stout but still beautiful wife, the famous Olympia.

Lara was tall and very slim, so unbelievably elegant that his clothes seemed to have been moulded on to his body. His soft shirt was pleated in tiny tucks, his handkerchief was of crêpe de chine with a narrow black border, and his black tie was bordered with white. He was handsome, smooth, with kindly yet astute eyes. His face, while not 'marred by race', obviously betrayed the fact that his Jewish blood predominated.

His wife, still lovely, displayed a neck and shoulders which Charles felt were quite perfect. Her dress was magnificent, her jewels—though restrained—were quite incredible.

Simeon introduced Charles and Olympia gave him her hand and a brilliant smile. Lara said, 'Thees ess a most surprising pleasure. To know of another Gollantz in this terrible world is to feel that—without a doubt—the world is a better place in vhich to live.'

Their dinner was a vivacious affair. Olympia emerged from her somewhat statuesque aloofness and calm, her husband chattered of his work, of Paris, and was amusing. They were both delighted at the prospect of Simeon becoming a father, Madame Lara even removing—very carefully—a tear from the corner of each of her magnificent eyes so that they should not fall and damage her elaborate and carefully applied make-up.

They asked Charles what he was doing, and when he told

them, Laura cried, 'Alvays thees businesses draw us—furniture, china, pictures, are in our blood.'

'I bought a picture today,' Charles told him, and described the dirty little shop in Clerkenwell. 'I carried it to my rooms, and with the help of the ex-butler who runs the house I cleaned it.'

Louis Lara almost shot out of his chair. 'With what did you do this cleaning, please?' When Charles told him, he gave an immense sigh of relief. 'Now tell me, is it good? Of what is the subject?'

He listened intently, nodding his head from time to time, asking pertinent questions, some of which were so technical that Charles had to admit that he did not know the answer.

Simeon said, 'Could it be a Breughel, Louis?'

'I think not. But listen, tomorrow we drive to Ordingly, for luncheon with the beloved Emmanuel and his wife. May I call at your rooms and see this picture, in the morning—shall we say at eleven? Receive me, if you vish, in your pyjamas, and I shall leave my wife in the car to wait for me. I am filled with excitement. Mind, I may be wrong, it may prove to be only one of these abominable copies! We shall see—we shall 'ope.'

Simeon said, 'And the ivory chessmen?'

Lara shrugged his elegant shoulders. 'Not of particular interest to me—though I shall be happy to see them. Now, you shall see my wife and I dance togesser. 'Ow sad that dear Carr-oll Gibbons is not wiz us any longer. Such a nice man—such a clever artist. Olympia, may I have this great pleasure?

7

Charles woke conscious of a feeling of expectancy and excitement. As he emerged from the mists of very sound and youthful sleep he remembered. His picture—his present for Viva for Christmas—Louis Lara's promise to come that morning on his way to Ordingly to give his opinion of the painting. He sprang out of bed, bathed, shaved and dressed very quickly. At breakfast he told Vickers of the impending visit. Vickers was suitably if restrainedly impressed.

'Might I suggest, sir, that Mrs. Vickers prepares some of her black coffee, and that we offer a nice liqueur brandy? Her coffee is admirable and I happen to know that the French regard drinking coffee—if one may say so—as a rite.'

Back in the kitchen, he told his wife, 'He's fussing about like the vicar's wife at the annual sale of work. Gone out to buy some flowers! That's because Madame Lara might possibly accompany her husband. Remember Olympia, Phoebe? Famous dancer, and if all one heard was true, no better'n she should have been. However, seems that she's settled down.'

Charles found his flowers, and brought them home in triumph. Mum always said that he could arrange flowers beautifully, and he put his whole heart into making these look their very best.

Eleven o'clock came, and at half past eleven Louis and his wife arrived. Vickers announced them as he might have announced guests at a Lord Mayor's reception.

'Monsieur and Madame Louis Lara, sir.'

She was swathed in magnificent furs, Louis wore a splendid coat with a fur lining and huge astrakhan collar. As Charles escorted her to the most comfortable arm-chair, she beamed at him, and then said pensively, 'W'at a 'ideous room! 'Ow can you leeve 'ere, tell me?'

Charles said, 'It's ugly I know, but it's comfortable, and they look after me very well.'

Vickers entered, and bowing offered her coffee.

'Bleck coffee! 'Oo makes this, pleaze?' she demanded.

'My wife, madame, and it is generally highly esteemed.'

'Louis, w'at is t'is—esteemed?'

'Held to be very excellent, darling. As I am sure that it ees.'

She sipped it, a trifle noisily. 'Eet is as bleck coffee should be, 'ot as 'ell, strrong as love, bleck as night. Yes, and a small *fine* also. *Merci!*'

Louis, his eyes wandering round the room, saw the chessmen. He darted towards them.

'They are nice, Charles, ver' nice. Not for me. Might be for Emmanuel.'

'As a matter of fact I bought them for his Christmas present.'

'Ah! So a leetle secret, no? I must not mention them to 'eem, eh?'

'Please—no, sir.'

'And now—the painting! I am all excitement! Is this a present for Christmas also for some person?'

'For Lady Gollantz, and also a secret.'

Louis made a gesture as if he turned a large key in his chest. 'It will be re-regarded so! Now, my impatience grows.'

Charles brought out the picture, and set it on a chair, while Louis produced a small magnifying-glass from his waistcoat pocket, and taking off his heavy coat, leaned forward to examine it. He peered, he took out a fine linen handkerchief and wiped his forehead very delicately. He nodded, then said, 'Your cleaning 'as not harmed 'eem at all! 'E will be bettaire when 'e is cleaned by a professional, but 'eet is not bad, no. My compliments.'

His wife almost screamed, 'Louis—cretin—tell Charlee if it is any good. To hell with the cleaning! It is a ver' schairming painting, 'ooever made it.'

Louis said, 'Simeon wondered eef it could be a Breughel. No, eet is not by either of the Breughels. Eet is by a pupil of Pieter—the elder Breughel. His name—' his words came very slowly as if he weighed every one, 'his name,' he repeated, 'was Hendrik Avercamp. He lived from 1586 until—' he snapped his fingers—'an—I recall now—1634. Now, are you proud of yourself, Chairlee?'

'You mean that it is valuable?'

'I will buy it at this very minute eef you wish to sell.'

Olympia said, 'What prrice you'll giff 'eem, my old Jew?'

Louis smiled at her fondly. 'I don't know if 'e wants to sell.'

Charles said, 'No, really I don't. I bought it for a present. I paid ten shillings for it, and it's going to be properly cleaned and framed and—it's going to *be* a present.'

''E is a gallant young man!' Olympia asserted. 'Giff me again coffee. Chairlie, are you in loff with 'er?'

Charles knew that his face flamed suddenly and felt furious with himself. Louis Lara shook his head at his wife in mild reproof. 'Olympia, you embarrass the poor fellow! T'ese are questions one does not ask.'

She shrugged her shoulders. 'In England my 'usband always bekoms more Engleesh gentleman every day. Only in Paris is 'e human once again. I ask w'at questions I wish.'

Recovering his equanimity Charles said, 'And why not? No, I'm not in love with her, but I happen to know that she loves skating, so I bought this picture for her.'

'She is charming, this Viva Gollantz,' Olympia said, 'but not so charming that she vill offer us t'anks, Louis, if we are late for luncheon. Kom! *Au revoir*, Chairlee. When you kom to Paris you must stay at our *appartement*. I shall give you coffee as good as you 'ave given us.'

As they drove away Louis called, 'I shall keep your secret, but show the picture to Emmanuel.'

On Monday morning he telephoned to the office and asked if he might have an hour's grace as he had to see Sir Emmanuel on business. Permission given, he set off for the Bond Street Galleries, the painting under his arm. He went to Simeon's office, and asked if he thought Emmanuel would see him.

Simeon glanced at his watch. 'When that shows ten o'clock, my father will arrive.' He grinned. 'Never a moment before or a moment after. Of course he'll see you. Sit down and have a cigarette.'

Simeon was right. A commissionaire opened the office door,

saying, 'Sir Emmanuel has arrived, Mr. Simeon.' Simeon nodded, then took out his watch and held it out for Charles's inspection. 'What did I tell you? Ten, exactly.'

He went to his father's room and returned to tell Charles that Emmanuel was waiting for him. The sight of his fine, mobile face, his whole air of being fastidious in everything, always gave Charles a feeling of pleasure.

'Good morning, Charles. Simeon tells me that you have a picture which you want to show me. What is it?' His eyes twinkled. 'Not a Bellini, no? No, that was a little joke of my grandfather's. I once imagined that I had found a Bellini, and he went to gr-reat pains to instruct me that it was nothing of the kind. Now, show me your find. Louis—I'm so glad that you met him—is one of my best fr-riends. They left for Paris this morning. Now!'

Charles set up the picture. Emmanuel leaned back in his chair, his fingers-tips laid together, his face impassive. Once or twice he nodded, then rose and taking out his glass—which Charles imagined was as much a part of him as his clothes—he walked towards the painting.

Suddenly he swung round. 'Who cleaned this?'

'I did, sir.'

'Ah, of course it must go to our own man, Clapham. Did Louis express any opinion as to the artist?'

'He mentioned someone called Avercamp.'

'Undoubtedly he was right—regarding pictures he invariably is—and very pleasant, too. Now, Charles, I propose to have it cleaned and properly framed, and then—I'll offer you twelve hundred—guineas of course—for it. Also, you can take it to anyone else to get a valuation if you wish. How's that?'

Charles flushed, and wished fervently that he could rid himself of the detestable habit. Emmanuel continued, 'I should suggest some small recognition to the man who sold it—nothing excessive, he doesn't deserve it, to have kept that beautiful thing in filth and dirt for years. Criminal!'

'If you saw the shop, sir, you'd not blame him. It's just a lot of junk! But I don't want to sell it. I bought it for a present.'

'But you can't afford to give presents worth over a thousand pounds! Present indeed! Some girl—who won't appreciate it, and would much rather have a dinner-dance at the Savoy. Charles—have sense.'

'Sir, it cost me ten shillings, and I wanted it *then* for a present, and I still want it for that, and that only. It's for Lady Gollantz, because she likes skating. Only don't tell her—it's a surprise for Christmas.'

Emmanuel returned to his chair, he sat down, saying, 'Well, I *am* damned. It's a most generous thing to do—I warn you that Viva won't r-really appreciate it, she doesn't understand pictures, but she'll like it, and,' he smiled, 'I shall be happy to think that it hangs in my house. Thank you, Charles. Now, Simeon, send it to Clapham, and tell him to clean it—sorr-ry Charles, from my point of view it is still lamentably dirty. So leave it here, will you, and when next you see it—well you'll realize what a tr-reasure you have found. I shall attend to the framing myself. There, you must get back to work and so must I. A cup of Hannah's excellent coffee first? Yes?' He telephoned from his desk. 'Is Miss Rosenfeldt there? Ah, Hannah, can we have three cups of your wonderful coffee? Or make it four if you want to see something very delightful.'

He sat there, leaning back, smiling at them both impartially. He asked after Simeon's wife in a way which was neither mechanical nor sentimental, he talked to Charles about his work, giving him advice about new text-books which he regarded as sound.

Emmanuel's talk was always at its best when he sat at his desk, in the room which held so many memories for him. It seemed to Charles that his fine face softened, that his lips were more ready to smile. As he spoke of Charles's forthcoming visit it was obvious that he looked forward to the Christmas festivities with a pleasure which held something completely youthful.

Simeon asked, 'Is Max coming?'

'Max, as befits the grandson of a millionaire—or he may be a multi-millionaire for all I know, is disporting himself on the Riviera, from there he goes to Switzerland for Winter Sports. He plans to be back for the start of flat r-racing. When does it start, Simeon?'

'March twenty-fifth, I believe; the Calmering is run on the twenty-seventh, I remember that!'

'Naturally, that's when Hereward makes his formal debut. I'd give anything—yes, anything—to have him win, it means so much to Viva.'

Simeon said, 'Of course she's flying high, Papa.'

Emmanuel smiled. 'Nothing but the best for Viva—look who she chose for her husband—*twice*! Ah, Hannah, thank you, now look at this!'

The elderly Jewish woman, almost as cumbersome in her movements as Bill Gollantz, walked over and stared at the picture.

Emmanuel said, 'Well?'

'It's very dirty!'

Reprovingly, he said, 'Hannah, Hannah, can't you see under the dirt?'

She nodded. 'Only just! Flemish—Dutch—Breughel influence—about 1650? Umph. You got something very good there, Emmanuel.' She screwed up her eyes, still peering at the picture. 'It's coming! Avercamp, no?'

'That's what years of training under three generations of Gollantz does!' Emmanuel cried in triumph. 'The woman's a marvel. Yes, you've said it. Now, your coffee.'

She sat down, and sighed, laying her plump hands on her wide-spread knees. 'Now, tell me the story—I have no doubts that there is one.'

With mock reticence Emmanuel shook his head. 'There is—but it is not mine to tell. The owner won't sell. I offered to buy.'

'Raise your offer—they'll all sell if you offer enough, you know that as well as I do already.'

'I'm afraid he won't, I know my man. He only wanted an opinion.'

She shrugged her massive shoulders. 'Then charge him for that. You don't run the Galleries as a philanthropic affair, no? These people—they'll bring you coloured magazine reproductions for a valuation next!'

Emmanuel sipped his coffee, his eyes dancing with amusement. 'Your coffee, Hannah, like yourself, impr-roves with the years! You come to Ordingly for Christmas, Hannah?'

'I hope that I shall be forgiven for celebrating a Christian festival—me, a—moderately—good Jewess. Yes, I shall be there

—I've not missed for more years than I care to count.'

'And now—my work is waiting, and yours too—one little bit of news: our dear Guido Moroni will be over for Christmas! I am sure that he will br-ring with him the largest "Motta" he can find and'—he shuddered—'I have never liked them, not even soaked in white wine.' He turned to Charles, 'How would you like to go to Milano after Christmas, spend a few weeks there, and,' he laughed, 'find me an old master—only don't pay more than two hundred lire for it?'

'Would my firm let me go, sir?' Charles could scarcely hide the eagerness in his voice.

'Oh, I think so,' Emmanuel said easily. 'I'll arrange it. Don't worry. Now—work, my dears.'

Charles never forgot that first Christmas at Ordingly. He drove there with his mother, who was in a state of wild expectancy. The day was fine and there were even shafts of rather wan sunlight filtering through the bare branches of the trees. Rose chattered gaily, her North-country vowels falling pleasantly, and bringing a sense of warmth to his ears.

'It's going to be a proper party, Charlie,' she assured him. 'I had a letter from Beatrice Heriot, telling me all about it. This great friend of Sir Emmanuel's is coming over—Signor Moroni. They seem to think the whole world of him. It's almost like going—well, home for Christmas. The folks in Dulltor are properly jealous. Why, I even had one of their reporters from the *Gazette* to ask how I was spending Christmas! I just said, all grand, "With Sir Emmanuel and Lady Gollantz, Lady Heriot—and others," and left it at that. I've got two new dresses, Charlie. Went into Manchester to Kendal Milnes—oh, they were helpful. I hope you'll like them.'

'I'd like sackcloth if you were dressed in it, Mum,' he said, and meant it.

When they arrived at Ordingly, even Hawkins seemed to have unbent a little for Christmas. The rather acrid smell of evergreens met them as they entered the hall; there were swags of holly stretched across the ceiling, a scent which gradually, as the heat from the big logs burning in the open hearth, increased as the hours passed.

Lady Heriot screamed, 'Hello Rose, hello Charlie! Happy Christmas!'

Viva came forward, bringing with her two men who were strangers to Charles. One was small, elegant in the manner of Louis Lara, with thick dark hair heavily streaked with grey; the other a little, rather shrunken man with white hair and eyes which peered at you from behind strong glasses. His voice was very gentle, and the touch of his hand friendly.

They were Guido Moroni and someone called Gilbert—Charles never heard him called anything except 'Gilly' and always forgot to ask what his name actually was afterwards. Then he was introduced to 'Buster' Carteret, another old friend welcomed for the festivities.

Viva said, 'Tonight is *our* night, so it's glad rags, Charles. Tomorrow it's the dance in the billiards room for the servants—it's their night—so you can be ready to dance with Hortense, and you—Rose—with Frank, who I assure you in a dinner-jacket is a most personable young man. Bill is coming, and when he "takes the floor" with Mrs. Plumley—that's the cook, I tremble to think what is going to happen. If we were wise we should all fly to the old air-raid shelter, for the house might easily tumble about our ears. Yes, Simeon and Daphne are coming, though she won't dance of course.'

There was a general and genuine feeling of good fellowship everywhere. Servants smiled at their employers, and the employers smiled back. There was a sense of relaxed discipline everywhere. Emmanuel moved among them dispensing drinks, looking as if he had thrown off years.

He said to Charles, 'I am glad to tell you that the ice is definitely holding, so tomorrow—unless we have a sudden thaw—which the glass seems to think is unlikely—you can go skating with my wife, and I shall not have to watch you in the role—which no doubt you would fill admirably—of gallant rescuer.'

Young Simeon, standing near, whispered to Charles, 'He always talks like that when he's being amusing. It's an old trick of his, he used to do it to amuse me when I was a kid—using long words and rather stilted phrases.'

Charles, following Emmanuel with his eyes said, 'Oh, he's grand!'

'I must warn you, it means church in the morning—that's

an old custom which my grandmother started. The whole lot of us troop there, then of course we go to see the horses—that's another custom, maintained even when there were only two or three of them. "The stables after church"—it's part of English country life. After that luncheon, and when that is over if you can face skating with Viva I'll take my hat off to you!'

Charles said, 'Consider it off already!'

Dinner was magnificent; the great Christmas tree in the hall, shone and glittered. Rose Watson exclaimed, 'Oh, how luvely!' and Viva with a wave of her hand indicated Hawkins. 'His doing!' she said.

He replied, 'Thank you, m'lady, I'm sure.'

Charles stood back to watch them all. He knew his pulses beat more quickly when he remembered that these were 'his family' and that they had accepted him as part of them. 'The clan'—possibly not all of them united by blood ties, but most certainly by affection.

Little Moroni, darting about, beaming on everything, paying excessive compliments in rather distorted English to the women; Bill Gollantz moving about ponderously and yet with a certain lightness so often to be found in excessively stout people; his wife, Edith, attractive, but—Charles felt—not quite 'fitting in'. She was, Charles felt, seeking for a word, just a little prim, yet she appeared to be devoted to her immense husband and he to her. Simeon was hovering round his attractive wife, Daphne, anxious and yet proud.

Gilly, another onlooker, was watching Simeon, his mouth very tender. 'Ah, how like Juliet he is! He has her tenderness, her ability to radiate love.' The little white-haired man's smile faded, and he took off his thick glasses and wiped them on a large white handkerchief.

His eyes went to Emmanuel, and his thoughts filled with happiness, though they still held something of regret.

'My dear young man—not so young any longer, but still the same admirable young man. Happy with your charming Viva, I know that, and so you ought to be, but how often do your thoughts fly back to those days when we—you and Juliet and I—were together. Your life ended when she died, but, thank God, you have made a new one—a happy one—though it will never efface the joy, the grief, the intoxication, and the misery of that other life with "Lovely Juliet".'

His love for Emmanuel was great. After Juliet died it was Gilly who had come to his flat, and greatly daring, had opened her piano and begun to play some of the music she had loved best. He remembered how Emmanuel had come in and stood transfixed, his face livid with fury. 'No one must play here, Gilly!' he had said, his voice cold as ice.

Gilly remembered how he had summoned all his courage, and had continued to play; how Emmanuel had sunk into a chair, his head in his hands; the music had continued, and when Gilly stopped he saw that Emmanuel's pale face was blotted with tears. Gilly had walked over to where he sat, and said, 'My dear young man, we must never forget her—she is someone to be remembered always.'

Then there were those three women, Lady Heriot, someone called Mrs. Watson, and Hannah Rosenfeldt. He knew Viva's mother had been a Gaiety girl, and he suspected Mrs. Watson had come from the theatre. Both were resplendent, both were talking vivaciously. Emmanuel obviously liked them, for as he passed he bent and said something to them in a low voice which caused Lady Heriot to exclaim, 'Manny, you're awful—isn't he, Rose—awful!' The third woman, Hannah Rosenfeldt, he knew as the Jewess who had stood so staunchly by Emmanuel when he had faced desperate troubles, when he had taken the blame for his brother Julian's faults on to his own shoulders because he had been warned that his mother—Max Gollantz's wife—must never be worried or subjected to any shock. Yes, Hannah Rosenfeldt had been a fine and wonderful friend.

And this new young man standing near him, watching everyone, with a faint smile of quiet enjoyment on his face. That face was vaguely familiar.

'Charles Gollantz,' Viva had said, and Gilly frowned, trying to remember to which branch of the family he could belong. Vaguely he was like Julian—whom Gilly had always loathed—but there was a kindliness in this man's face which was quite foreign to Julian's. He must ask Emmanuel when the opportunity arose.

Emmanuel, moving among his guests, wearing the clothes

which he liked best, a high beautifully folded white stock, a rather elaborate waistcoat, and knee breeches, with silk stockings ending in shoes with small silver buckles, felt a great warmth in his heart.

Viva was looking magnificent, her dress became her, and she laughed and smiled easily. He thought how deeply and sincerely he loved her. He knew that he wasn't 'easy'; he allowed himself to become too absorbed in his work—that, among other reasons, was what had split their first marriage. Now, both grown older, they were better able to make adjustments. Viva liked to dance, she loved rushing about, excitement was life to her. That was why the idea of racing had made such an appeal to her. He went his own, rather dull way, working hard, and when he and Viva were together one was interested in the news which the other had to give. Not merely politely interested, but definitely and completely interested.

He remembered their second honeymoon, when they had stayed at the Bella Riva at Fasano on Lake Garda. Viva had gone to her room, and he had wandered into the beautiful garden. He had met two small dogs, who were kind and friendly. He went back to Viva and told her that they had spoken to him.

'What did they say?' she asked.

He shook his head. 'They spoke Italian.'

'Then translate for me.'

'They asked, "How are you Emmanuel, please", and I replied, "I am that rarest of things—a completely happy man". They ran away laughing.'

And he had been right, he was completely happy; there had been sadness, as when Max died, when his beloved mother died, but those other memories which used at one time to torture him—memories of Juliet—had become transmuted into something beautiful and tender, warm and kind.

Now this new young man, not quite as good looking as his father, had come on the scene, and Emmanuel had tried and tested him. He had not yet failed. He might not be so spectacular as Max, but he was infinitely better stuff. He thought, 'And when I lay down my arms, he and my dear Simeon will keep the tradition going. They will stand as Old Emmanuel, as my father—and, please God, as I have tried to—for integrity and decency. Yes, dear little dogs at the Bella Riva, I can still tell you that I am a happy man.'

Hannah Rosenfeldt, sitting comfortably in a huge chair, because in these days her legs were not adapted to standing too long, watched the gathering with benevolent eyes.

They followed Emmanuel, moving around to see that his guests were properly supplied. His two little dogs followed close on his heels, they too had eyes only for him. When he stopped they stopped, gazing up at him with melting, adoring eyes. She sighed. There had been in the past so much storm and stress, and now it seemed that the House of Gollantz had reached 'the haven where they would be'. There was only one fly in the ointment—this Max Gollantz. 'Like his father,' she mused, 'he is a viper. That he is a bastard means nothing to me. This man Charles will make his way without leaning on the House. The other—I watch, and I wait. Pah, I am an old fat Yiddish woman! What is there left for me to do? My work, except for my visits to the Galleries, is over. Yet, I stay, for one day again it may be that these dear, strange people—Christians, but still good Jews in that they hold to all that is best in our Faith—will need me.'

Hawkins entered and in the festive spirit, announced, 'M'lords, ladies and gentlemen, dinner is served!'

Viva called, 'Hawkins, where's the Lord—who is he?'

The meal was hilarious. Emmanuel rose and after the turtle soup, which he himself did not touch, took the carving knife and fork and went through the motions of carving the huge turkey. He turned to Charles and smiled. 'I can't carve—never could—so they do it in the kitchen and put it together so as not to allow me to disgrace myself. Look, it falls apart!'

Later the lights were put out, and only the flickering candles on the table left, when Hawkins brought in a Christmas pudding which was surrounded in the blue flames of brandy.

Lady Heriot cried, 'And mince pies, Viva. Every one you eat before New Year means a happy month. For luck——'

Hawkins said, 'They are here, m'lady. Might I suggest that the pudding is also lucky? Be careful, m'lady, there are various tokens inside.'

Viva, a glass of champagne in her hand, stood up. 'Everyone—here's to Hereward and the flat racing.'

Emmanuel called, 'Hawkins, you and Frank must drink that toast, two more glasses! Now—Hereward!'

The stout Carteret echoed, 'Hereward. One of the finest I've ever seen.'

They trooped back into the hall, and Emmanuel began fussing round the Christmas tree.

Moroni said to Charles, 'Here are evidences that the Master is in his elements, yes?'

'He seems to enjoy it all,' Charles agreed.

'I shall confide something to you,' Moroni went on. 'To have him in full enjoyments, it is necessary for him to be making himself servants for others. This is his nature.'

Emmanuel began to take the presents from the tree and pass them to Simeon to distribute. The hall was filled with murmurs of satisfaction or little shrieks of delight, and Viva unwrapped the picture, Moroni could only restrain himself with difficulty.

'Please to show me! *Dio mio*—who found this and how! Emmanuel, tell me, who cleaned this work, it is done with admirableness, and the frame, this is an old frame, not one of modern commerce, yes?'

'Clapham cleaned it, and between us we found the frame: it's contemporary—or practically. You like Charles's present, Viva?'

'It's beautiful, and as a reward, Charles shall take me skating tomorrow! Charles, I am delighted! One day—tomorrow perhaps—you must tell me how you found it. We must stop Emmanuel, or he will deliver a short but pithy lecture on the painter—frankly I don't care a damn who painted it, I only know that it is beautiful and I shall treasure it all my life.'

The tree was stripped of all but its glittering Christmas toys, and when Hawkins arrived with Frank carrying a great silver tureen filled with steaming punch, and proceeded to serve everyone, Emmanuel ordered the tree to be taken out ready for the Ball on Christmas Night.

Rose sipped it with appreciation. 'Champion,' she told Charles. 'Only one thing needed—frumenty, served like we do in the North.'

'Creed wheat, luv.'

'Boiled wheat!'

Rose Watson laughed. 'Nay, there's a difference between creeing and boiling, luv. We serve it with neat whisky in little tiny glasses. Plenty only take one helping of the frumenty, but most of them come back again for another tot of whisky.'

Hawkins came to Viva. 'The choir are in the servants' hall, m'lady.'

'Bring them up, Hawkins. Now, Mama, get your handkerchief ready. Mama always sheds a few tears over the carols.'

'And is not ashamed of doing it, either!'

The choir trooped in, arranging themselves in a semicircle, while the schoolmaster who was also the organist, shook hands with Viva, Emmanuel and Simeon.

Gilbert asked him, 'Are you conducting? Would you care for me to play the accompaniments?'

For a moment the organist looked hesitant, then his face cleared. 'Why, it's Mr. Gilbert. That's most kind, and a great honour I should add. Now all of you, remember you've got a great pianist playing for you. Thank you, Mr. Gilbert—"Holy Night". Just give them a chord if you will.'

Charles never forgot that first Christmas Eve at Ordingly, the voices rising and falling, the listeners intent and many of them more than a little moved by the beautiful old words and music. Lady Heriot and his mother were openly wiping their eyes, and from time to time 'Buster' Carteret brushed his eyes with the back of his immense hand. When Gilly crashed out the magnificent opening chords of 'Come all ye faithful' Charles heard Guido Moroni draw a long gasping breath, and heard him murmur what sounded like a very short prayer. Again the voices rose in the most splendid of all hymns, and even above the boys' and men's voices could be heard Guido's strong true tenor. As a voice it was no better than a dozen you might hear in the streets of Milano any day, as errand boys sang as they went about their work, but it held the quality which Italian voices seem to draw from the sunshine and the good red wine.

'*Adeste fideles,*

'*Laeti triumphantes;*

'*Venite, venite* in Bethlehem.'

'Buster' Carteret murmured, 'That was—well—just something!' Gilbert rejoining them, asked, 'Was that my old-young friend Guido singing so beautifully for us?' Turning to Emmanuel he praised the singing of the choir and the organist for the training he had given them. Then he turned back to the piano, seated himself, and called, 'Now Guido, you will sing "Candele" for us, and you musicians can sing the second verse in English. Now, Guido!'

'Sì, maestro.'

Gilbert played the air, and Bill Gollantz said, 'Damn it, "Auld Lang Syne"! Never knew any other country sang that!'

His wife said rather primly, 'You live and learn, Bill.'

Charles felt that she disapproved a little of the whole thing—and felt that they were all over-sentimental and emotional. Guido was singing again. Although his thick hair was streaked with white, he looked very young, and there was an almost childish innocence in his expression. The choir hurriedly masticated large slices of Christmas cake or mince pie and were ready to join in the second verse. At the line 'Here's a hand my trusty friend,' Charles saw Emmanuel take Hannah Rosenfeldt's hand in his, and saw him lean down and kiss her. The sight, the little incident over so quickly and so unselfconscious, moved him deeply.

Guido ended on a high, admittedly rather forced falsetto note, and Gilbert turned and made a grimace at him.

'God gave you a voice, Guido, He never gave you that horrid note!'

'I am sorry, Maestro. *Mea culpa, mea maxima culpa!*'

The boys and men filed out, each shaking hands with Emmanuel who pressed coin of the realm into their palms. The organist asked, as Charles felt certain that he asked every year, 'Shall we have the pleasure of seeing you and your guests at Church tomorrow?'

'Indeed you will—have your choir not already admonished us to "Come to Bethlehem"?'

The great evening was over, and people began to drift away to their rooms. Emmanuel's two little dogs sighed with relief; they hated parties and thought them unnecessary. It was strange to Charles to see Emmanuel and Guido both kiss Simeon on both cheeks as they wished him good night and a Happy Christmas.

Viva said, 'Charles, give me a last drink. Mama—you'll have one?'

'Rath-*er*! I'm too old for all this emotion—these people like Gilly, and Guido, yes—and all the Gollantz family, thrive on it! Thanks, Charlie.'

At last, Emmanuel and Viva climbed the stairs, the little dogs close on their heels. Hawkins came in for the last time to methodically turn out the lights, then he too left, and the big hall was empty.

8

As they walked across the park to the little Norman Church, Viva said to Charles, 'Funny crowd when you come to think of it. There's Guido—staunch Roman Catholic, and I've an idea that Gilly is too—Bill and Emmanuel Gollantz are Jews—though I doubt if they've ever been in a synagogue in their lives; Hannah Rosenfeldt is orthodox—to a point—you'll see she'll stand all through the service until the sermon. Me—heaven only knows what I am, I only know that I'm better for marrying Emmanuel. But what a mixed bag! What are you and Rose?'

'I suppose I'm C. of E., but I've always felt that my mother leaned towards the non-conformists. Do you think it matters?'

She frowned. 'I'm hanged if I know, Charles. To some people it does matter tremendously. I read the other day that Jenny Lind—and she was a strictly good woman if you like—said that it was really difficult for her to speak to anyone she knew was a Catholic. That's completely outside my comprehension. I suspect that Bill Gollantz's wife doesn't care for this mixed bag! Oh, she's nice enough, but I never feel—though it's a word I hate—"cosy" with her.'

They were nearing the porch of the church, and she called, 'Bill, Emmanuel, remember to take your hats off!'

Bill grinned at her. 'Remember that you've got no real part in the service—you should be up in a gallery somewhere.'

Her mother answered, 'Some of the best in the audience sit in the gallery, Bill, just remember that.'

Charles heard the whispers of the congregation as they walked to the big Gollantz pew, saw that Emmanuel turned as he passed and gave a smiling salutation to one and another. They filed in, some of them overflowed into the second pew, and Charles heard the sound of voices in the vestry. The murmur of a short prayer, then united voices responding with a long drawn out, 'A—men.' Then the procession of choir boys and men choristers, the curate, and the handsome, portly vicar.

Guido whispered, 'I find the Protestant missal so complex. Kindly help.'

Charles found his place for him, and handed him the big prayer book, smiling a little. 'I expect we should think the same of yours.'

Guido murmured, 'I am filled with gratitude—many thanks.'

Once more Guido's strong, untrained voice rang out in the noble Latin of the great Christmas hymn. Simeon wondered if the organist had given instructions to the choir, that if Guido began to sing they should lower their voices, for while he sang, utterly oblivious of his listening audience, they sang very softly and with great sweetness.

Gilly, sitting in the big pew, turned and whispered, 'No falsetto!'

The rest of the congregation had listened entranced, not only the strength of his voice, but the fact that he had sung in Latin had impressed them. They whispered, 'One of Sir Emmanuel's Italian friends!' or 'Eh, that weer a grand voice, that weer.'

As they came out of church people were waiting in little groups. Charles watched, his heart glowing with pride. ''Appy Christmas, sir'; 'M'lady, a lovely Christmas tew yew.' Others, of possibly higher social standing, but with hearts as warm, came to shake hands with Emmanuel and his wife. Simeon thought, 'I suppose all this kind of thing would be regarded as subservience by a Socialistic state. They'd be wrong. It's not only that they want to pay respect to my father and his wife—it's to give themselves the pleasure of doing it. They're his friends, Viva is a friend, and they want to wish them well.' He watched Emmanuel's pleasant smile, listened to Viva's clear voice, asking questions, offering congratulations, demanding to know if this and that sick person was receiving everything necessary. There was no hint of patronage, it was a meeting of friends; there was the impulse to be helpful, the anxiety to do all that was possible for one's friends.

Charles said, 'Wonderful to watch, eh?'

Simeon nodded. 'I think so, and all this friendship isn't

bought—it's earned! Makes you feel rather proud.'

Someone touched Simeon's arm, it was little Andy Miller.

'Mr. Simeon, 'appy Christmas. Eh, that foreign gentleman sang a treat. Minded me of once when Ah was in Rome. I'd taken over a couple of 'osses for Prince Doria. I went to Saint Peter's—it was Christmas Day o' course—an' 'eard them sing that hymn. It tuke me right back, Mr. Simeon.'

Simeon said, 'You'll meet Signor Moroni, he'll be around at the stables before luncheon.'

'Ah'll be prhard. But Ah wanted ter ax you about this ball ter night. Las' year Ah weer i' bed wi' 'flu, but Ah'm all right this year. Now Ah've gotten a dinner jacket, will that be all right? Ah've had it for over twenty year, but Ah don't want ter cut a poor figure before everyone.'

Simeon smiled at the anxious rather wizened face which stared up at him.

'Absolutely all right. We should all be wearing them, but my father is afraid of Hawkin's critical eye, and my mother is nervous of Mrs. Cowley. So we shall all turn out in tails—because we're rather cowardly.'

Miller nodded, 'Ah understand. Well, so long as Ah don't have ter dance wi' Mrs. Plumley, that's all Sir Garnet. They're waiting for you, Mr. Simeon.'

When they visited the stables, Miller graciously allowed them to offer very small, beautifully scrubbed carrots to the horses, and he was duly presented to all the guests, offering his hand to 'Buster' Carteret saying, 'Nice ter see you, Major. How d'yer feel about our 'osses? Nice little bunch, eh, sir?'

'Damn nice little string. I've a promising filly I want Lady Gollantz to have a look at—I believe she'll do things and go places.'

'An' Hereward, sir, 'ow d'you find him?'

Carteret nodded. 'I'm not worried about him. He's all right.'

'Proper light of 'er ladyship's eyes that one!'

'Mistaire Miller,' Moroni said, 'all my life I hev been nairvois of ze 'orse. But not your horses. They are clearly—to me—angels and dreams of beauty.'

'Like wot your singing was, sir, in church this morning,' Andy told him. 'Proper luvely—tuke me right back ter Roma one Christmas Day. Swear ter you sir, Ah 'ad tears in my eyes listening ter you. Ah offer 'eartfelt thanks.'

'I am eshamed that I had so poor a voice to offer, Mistaire Miller. Maybe you'll be at the ball tonight. Then—when I can tear you away from the lovely ladies 'oo will wish to dance wiz you, we shall talk about the music—Bellini, Puccini, the great Verdi—yes? Now *arrivederci.*'

He moved away and Miller whispered hoarsely to Charles, 'Proper gent, that. Only bother I've never 'eard of those pals of 'is. Suppose 'e thinks Ah know them, Mr. Charles?'

Luncheon over, Emmanuel retired to talk business with Guido, Gilly disappeared, Bill Gollantz and his wife with 'Buster' Carteret disappeared also into the drawing-room, while Simeon went to Daphne to assure himself that she actually rested.

Viva said, 'Sluggards, aren't they? Come and skate, Charles.'

The grass crackled crisply as they walked over it to the little lake. The air was cold but beautifully clear, and Viva was in the highest spirits. A young man whom she called Watkins, who, it transpired later, was an under-gardener, put on their skates.

She said, 'Nice of you to turn up, Watkins, on Christmas Day.'

'Nay, m'lady, it's a bit of a relief. To my mind Christmas Day is a dowleyish kinder day. You eat over much at dinner, and if you don't get out you sit and watch TV. and as like as not go to sleep.'

He fastened on their skates, and stood watching them as they slid off on the smooth, newly brushed ice. He admired Viva, and in a short astrakhan jacket and cap to match, she looked particularly attractive. All the servants liked her ; her standards of efficiency were high ; but she was always ready to praise when work was done well.

Watkins, watching her now, mused, 'If there was more like her, always ready with a "Please" and a "Thank you", folks 'ud be able ter get servants—aye, and keep 'em.'

The cold air had whipped colour into Viva's cheeks ; she looked almost startlingly attractive, and quite young. Charles guessed that she was well over forty, but she certainly did not look it.

She said, 'You skate well, don't you?'

'I love it. Most winters I've gone off to the lakes—when there's been a hard frost, and sometimes I've skated on one of the little tarns most of the day—all alone, trying to really make a decent skater of myself. I'd love to go in for winter sports too.'

'We'll go next year,' she cried delightedly. 'We'll make Emmanuel come too, root him out of his old Galleries. Please heaven by that time the odious Max will have gone home to his precious father—who is even more odious.' She stopped short. 'Sorry, Charles—I didn't mean to be offensive.'

'I don't mind. I've never seen the man, and I never wish too, either.'

She said, 'Can you waltz?'

'Not awfully well, but I'll try.'

The attempt was better than he had dared to expect. As they moved smoothly and easily, Viva smiled at him, her glowing face not far from his own.

'Heavenly,' she said. 'There! We'll try again later. Do you like Max?'

'Candidly, no, and Max doesn't like me. I fancy he's not quite satisfied that I'm not an impostor, not really a Gollantz.'

'Max will never like anyone,' Viva assured him. 'He's like his father in that—and in other things as well. Do you know that Julian once tried to kill Emmanuel?' Charles gave an exclamation of horror. 'Yes, it's quite true. If you look closely at Emmanuel's forehead, you can just see the end of a scar—his hair hides the rest. It's a long story, you must get Simeon to tell you one day—or Bill if you can get him to talk. He was trying to double-cross Emmanuel—he was in the Galleries at the time buying silver. Emmanuel managed to smooth over two little games of Julian's, who was using false silver marks and wasn't quite clever enough. Finally Emmanuel—who might forgive most things, but not anything crooked which touched his beloved Galleries—began to draw the net pretty tight for his beastly brother. There was a row one night, very late. Julian used to go to the Galleries at night, using the little steel door. It's never used now. Emmanuel caught Julian, who banged him on the head with an old silver tankard. Simeon and Bill found him lying in a pool of blood. Julian—because of Angela, his mother, who had a weak heart—was hustled out of England, and Emmanuel lay for weeks, here at Ordingly, literally hovering between life and death.

'Julian has never come to England since, and if he did he'd never come to Ordingly—except over my dead body! Let's waltz again, Charles. It's a horrid story and forgive me for having inflicted it on you. That's right—now you've got it—splendid!'

Their eyes met, and Viva said, 'You've gone quite white, Charles. You're fond of Emmanuel, aren't you?' Charles nodded. 'He likes you—he has plans for you. These Jews are great schemers, remember that! No, I loathe Max. Emmanuel doesn't like him much—but he's more tolerant than I am. Bill dislikes him, and little Andy Miller hates the sight of him. Max is sore with me. You must have guessed why when you came into the conservatory that evening—you did, didn't you?'

'Well—yes, I suppose I did—that was why I knocked over the flower-pot.'

She laughed. 'I thought so. Imagine it—compare Max and Emmanuel! Is it likely that I—over forty—*well* over forty—would look at him!' She broke off. 'There's a seat over there. Just wave to Watkins to come and take our skates off—this elderly woman is growing tired.'

'Elderly woman!' Charles laughed. 'It's all right if I give him something?'

'He'll be delighted.' Watkins came up at the double, and helped her to the seat. 'It's been lovely, Watkins. I hope that we've not kept you too long.'

'Pleasure, m'lady. If the frost holds—an' it looks like it will—will you be skating tomorrow? If so I'll get the ice brushed ready for you.'

She turned to Charles. 'Shall we? You don't have to be back in Town until Tuesday, do you? Yes, we'll skate tomorrow if the frost holds.'

'Very good, m'lady. Thank you, sir—very kind of you.'

They walked back over the frosty grass. Charles wondered if he should tell her of seeing Max in Clerkenwell, then decided against it. He had, after all, a perfect right to go where he pleased and it was his own business. There remained, at the back of his mind, a queer distrust of Max Gollantz—something about him which Rose Watson would have said 'wasn't jannock'. As they drew nearer to the big dignified house, Viva said, 'I don't know why, you can put it down to my being really a very silly woman—which without doubt I am—but that wretched Max makes me nervous. He's like his father, they're both vindictive. That type of Jew doesn't make friends except for material gain. The other type—old Emmanuel, Max—Emmanuel's father—Emmanuel himself, Simeon and I think you, Charles—though all the Jewish blood in the later generations has become pretty diluted—make friends who love them, friends they value.

'Max hates me, because I wouldn't tolerate his—pawing, whenever we were alone, because—to put it quite frankly—when he suggested that I might have a definite affair with him, I smacked his face. It may be true that "hell hath no fury like a woman scorned" but it's just as true of a man. He hates you because he can't understand "where you come in" and he's afraid you may get something—money, position, anything—that he wants. His feeling for you is jealousy.

'He hates Emmanuel because he is always rather coldly polite. He hates Andy Miller because he wouldn't hear of allowing him to ride Hereward. So he goes about nursing all these little hates until they grow into a huge grievance.' She laid her hand on Charles's arm. 'Don't allow him to pick a quarrel with you. That's what he'd like to do. Ah, we're home. Thanks for a lovely afternoon. Go on and call the dogs out. Emmanuel will have been immersed with Guido and they must have a little run.' Charles ran up the steps, and although the dogs seemed to think that it was totally unnecessary to leave the big wood fire, they followed him, and when they saw Viva, they indulged in a wild and almost hysterical greeting.

The afternoon was rapidly changing into early dusk. Over the park Charles could see wisps of mist gathering in the bare branches of the trees. He stood on the terrace, his blood still tingling pleasantly after the exercise he had taken, and watched Viva racing with the little dogs. At intervals, for the sheer joy of living, one of them would roll over in the frost-covered grass, then leap to its feet and race madly after its mistress. She turned back and came towards him.

'Lovely. What a glorious afternoon! Now, let's have tea—

never mind if the others are still asleep, we'll have it, and send in some to my hard-working husband and his nice little Italian. I adore Guido, he was best man at our second wedding.' She flung her coat, hat and gloves on to the big settle, and told Charles to ring.

When Hawkins came, he noticed her bright colour, and smiled. 'Have you enjoyed your skating expedition, m'lady? If I may say so you look as if you had. Tea, m'lady? Mrs. Plumley thought that crumpets might be acceptable.'

Viva beamed at him, 'Crumpets! Mrs. Plumley knows that I adore them. Thank her, Hawkins. Yes, here for me and Mr. Charles, and send in some tea to Sir Emmanuel in the library. The rest of them can have it when they wake up. I suspect they're all still asleep.'

So Charles and Viva Gollantz sat there with the great wood fire flaming and crackling, while the little dogs waited expectantly for the biscuit which was their daily ration at tea-time.

Viva ate crumpets with unconcealed enjoyment. 'Bad for my figure, but when you get to my age you don't really care a great deal. Yes, another please. Tell me about Dullton, about your home, anything, but talk to me.'

He began to tell of the town where he had lived, of his occasional visits to Manchester to hear a concert or to see a play which attracted him. When he spoke of artists he admired, Viva thought that his voice sounded almost boyish; he was wildly enthusiastic, and she realized that whatever self-consciousness he had, it disappeared when he spoke of either music or the theatre.

'John Barbirolli—there's a conductor for you! And more, look what he's done to raise the standard of orchestral playing! I haven't heard them all—the ones who are famous internationally, but surely he is the finest in Europe. He isn't completely English, is he? I have records of Toscanini. I'd like you to hear them—I've a good gramophone. They are something—well, out of this world. How I should have loved to have seen him conduct.' He sighed. 'It's too late to hope for that now.

'I'm greedy, you see. I want to hear the best things. I want to hear opera in Milan at the Scala, in Rome, to hear the finest singers—I suppose you've heard them all?'

She nodded, making a small grimace. 'Charles, at the risk of making you completely disillusioned about me, I'm not really terribly musical. Grand Opera is incomprehensible to me—wasn't it King Edward the Seventh who said that if he ever had to sit through a second Grand Opera he'd abdicate? Well, I understand exactly how he felt. I like to listen to Gilly playing the piano, I don't say that I understand it but it is charming and soothing; but to hear and watch some heavy-weight Teuton soprano bawling her head off when she ought to be at Tring on a diet of orange juice getting her weight down, revolts me.'

'It's a strange medium really,' Charles admitted, 'acting and singing. Someone once told me that in Wagner's operas they actually change the scenery to the conductor's beat.'

Viva held out her hand. 'Pass me that cigarette-box. Oh, Wagner, I only once heard an opera of his, and I loathed it. A fat Venus behaving as badly as she dared with some awful youngish man, and a lot of attendant sprites. Then a concert somewhere or other, when the young man behaved very rudely and interrupted everyone else who tried to sing, and then a lot of dreary monks walking about on a mountain singing the same song again and again. Oh, it was terrible. I think in the end most of them died, and not before time!'

Charles heard voices. 'I think the sleepers have awakened,' he said.

'Ring for more tea for them, will you? Hello, sluggards all—sleeping beauties or what will you, rested after your non-existent labours?'

Gilly, coming down the wide stairs, said, 'You wrong me at least, Viva. I have been writing Christmas letters, taking advantage of your beautiful note-paper. It increases my prestige to have my friends know that I am staying at Ordingly, that the railway station is Ordingly, the post office the same and the telephone number Ordingly twelve.'

Charles dressed early and wandered along to his mother's room to talk to her. She beamed at him, her comely face shining with affection.

'This is nice, Charlie. It's a lovely party, everyone's as nice as they can be, but I never seem to get you alone. Now, luv, what 'ud you say if I sold up at Dullton and came to London and we took a nice—not over big—flat? Lukes to me as if you'll be in London a lot, and—well, I must say I like the life, the bustle, plenty of theatres, and the latest films. I should get a good bit for the house—it's freehold, and they're hard to come by. I believe that old Lizzie 'ud come with me. She's not so young but she's got plenty of go in her yet, and she thinks a lot of both of us. What do you think, Charlie luv?'

He smiled back at her anxious face. 'Mum, I think it's a wonderful idea, but you mustn't just "put on an act". You must really want to come, and feel that you'd be happy. I must be assured of that.'

She sent him back his smile, a smile of such warmth and affection that it made his eyes sting suddenly. 'Charlie luv, I'd be with you—that's enough said, eh?'

There was a knock on the door, and Viva's maid, Hortense, entered. 'M'Lady send me to 'ook you up, madame. Vat pleze veel you vear?'

'D'you know, Hortense, I think the mauve——' Rose said. 'Charlie, turn your back while I get hooked up. Pretty colour isn't it?'

He nodded. 'Yes, mauve is pretty, but I like you in something more definite. Still, I'm sure you'll look wonderful. There, Hortense, get on with the good work.'

A minute later Hortense cried, 'Mistaire Charles, all is accomplished. And now, a 'appy thought.' She handed a cellophane box to Rose, saying, 'Wiz the res'peks of Mrs. Cowley and Mr. 'Awkins, madame. A stray for you to wear at the ball.'

Charles said, 'Charming, but it's "spray" not "stray"!'

'Oh, *la la,*' she replied, 'vot is chust a vord—nossing!'

Rose looked at the spray of orchids, holding them against her dress. 'When I was young we always wore them pinned upside-down—the flowers hanging; how do they wear them now, I wonder. It's so long since anyone sent me flowers.'

Hortense said, 'Permit—I shall make. So and so! Pairfect!'

Then, 'Eef there is nossing other madame requires, I fly.'

Rose said, 'That's right—you fly, and thank you very much. The flowers look beautiful that way.'

When the door had closed she came to Charles and laid her hand on his shoulder. 'Look, Charlie boy, things are going to change for you, my luv. You're going to have great chances, don't grow away from your mum, will you? I mean, all these years we've been so close, and although I'd never want to stand in your light, I couldn't bear to feel that you were—well, growing away from me.'

'How could I, Mum dear, you're everything to me. Never, never be in the least bit afraid of anything like that. If I get chances, I hope that I shall have the wit and brains to take them, but they won't make the slightest difference to us. You silly, silly woman—how could you even imagine it?'

'It's all this—grand living, Charlie.'

'Rubbish, darling. Why you yourself take to it like a duck to water.'

'So do you, and it has been known that ducks swim away, luv.'

He laughed. 'Not this one, it happens to know where it is well off!'

'And if you married someone grand, posh, Charlie?'

'I'd say, "This is my best wedding present to you, my mother!"'

She kissed his cheek, 'Eh, you talk luvely sometimes, Charlie. Now, that nice Sir Emmanuel has been talking to me—fancy came to ask me—nice thought, eh?—if I minded you going to Milan and staying with that dear little Italian gentleman, Mr. Moroni. To live in his flat, where Sir Emmanuel lived at one time—and a sad time it was for him in many ways, poor fellow, though he seems happy enough now—and go about with him, visit this Gallery they have there, go to places round about and, he said, "study, study, study, Mrs. Watson."

'He said, "I've talked to George Mastock—an old friend of mine—and it is all arranged for Charles to go for a couple of months." Said it in that grand, easy fashion like these people do—it's not swank, it's not conceit, it's just that they're—*sure*. Oh, he talked a lot more—very interested in you, luv—but the rest he'll tell you himself.'

Charles said, 'It's exciting—good of you not to mind, dear. Only I want to be back by March the twenty-seventh. I want to see Hereward win!'

'Got much on him, Charlie?'

He grinned. 'Well—more than I can afford to lose. But that Major Carteret and Miller seem to think he's a cert. Oh, don't think that I'm going to turn into a gambler, darling, it's just that—it's his first big race and—we want to stand solid behind Viva.'

'I'm not afraid, you've gotten a good headpiece, luv. Now, I heard the gong and we'd better go down. Sure you like my dress?'

'I like your dress, your flowers, your hair—everything about you!'

Emmanuel looked tired, he had talked business all the afternoon with Guido, but he was in high spirits. He teased Hawkins, 'No flowers for the men, eh? Why not some buttonholes for us, Hawkins? I'm hurt.'

'Sir Emmanuel, with all due respect I have never felt that the wearing of buttonholes by gentlemen in full evening dress was—if I may say so—quite *de rigeur*. The true elegance of the costume, sir, lies in its complete simplicity and even severity. Thank you, sir.'

Beatrice Heriot said, 'And, by Jove, he's right. I've seen men with things like cauliflowers in their claw-hammer coats and I always said to myself—"no class" or "pansy boys". Not that I'm any class myself, but I've learnt to know what's what and who's who. Yes, thanks Guido, I'll have another whisky-and-soda.'

The dinner was simple, for Viva knew that all the servants were what her mother called 'prinking'. Frank served the coffee, and they sat drinking it in the big hall, until Hawkins came to announce that everything was ready for the ball 'to commence'.

'Buster' Carteret said, 'B'gosh, he's immaculate! Did you notice his coat? It's far better than mine! Gad, he's a wonder is old Hawkins.'

The huge billiards room was filled with people, chattering excitedly. Viva, Rose and Lady Heriot had put on their finest gowns, but when Mrs. Cowley, the housekeeper, came forward to greet them, nothing could have exceeded her dignity or the beauty of her very stiff, rich claret coloured silk dress.

Viva thanked her and Hawkins for their flowers, and Mrs. Cowley murmured, 'A little trifle of appreciation, m'lady.'

Emmanuel said, 'The band ready? Then—the grand march.' He explained to Guido, 'We always have this first, then the dancing follows, it gives us all an opportunity to show off our paces! I take Mrs. Cowley, Viva goes with Hawkins, Bill—take Mrs. Plumley, Guido—Mademoiselle Hortense. The rest of you go and find your partners, but Rose—I'd like you to take Andy Miller. There—are we ready——?' He called to the band leader, 'Now a nice, fairly dignified march. Thank you.'

Andy Miller, wearing a suit which was palpably years old, and of a slightly antique cut, said to Rose Watson, 'From t'north, aren't you, ma'am?'

'And proud of it!' she returned. 'Same as you, eh?'

'Me—— Rochdale, same as Gracie Fields. That *is* something to be proud of, ma'am. Just take a luke at them, ma'am, as they walk round. Luke at 'er ladyship—laughing and chatting wi' Hawkins, watch Sir Emmanuel—speaking to Mrs. Cowley like as if she was a duchess. Mr. Charles—we all like Mr. Charles—making Annie—she's the second 'ousemaid—laff. Madam, that's class, that's what comes from being bred in a good stable. Blood, ma'am, blood, and being in the stud buke. Even Mr. Bill—he oughter get some of that weight off of 'im—but he's got dignity. 'Is wife's walking with Frank, the footman.'

Rose looked at the tall young man, pacing so correctly at the side of Mrs. Bill Gollantz, and thought how personable he looked, and what a pleasant way he had of listening attentively whenever his partner spoke. 'Queer,' she mused, 'the way things happen. It's just chance or fate or whatever you call it, that my Charlie isn't a footman, and that nice-looking Frank isn't belonging to some fine family like what this one is.'

Then the actual dancing began. Hawkins and Mrs. Cowley had stipulated that there should be some 'old-fashioned waltzes' as being more fitting to their age and dignity.

One of the gardeners had suggested that 'Rock an' roll' might be a nice change. Mrs. Cowley had hissed through her teeth, Mrs. Plumley breathed deeply, and Hawkins spoke, with dignity, his manner pontifical. 'I can excuse that suggestion, Harris, as I don't think you've been with us very long, have you? Otherwise you would know that nothing of that kind is permitted here. This is not some shilling hop at the local dance hall, this is a party when *we* have the honour of sharing the festivities with Sir Emmanuel and her ladyship. Am I expressing your feelings correctly Mrs. Cowley—Mrs. Plumley?'

The vast Mrs. Plumley breathed, 'Let me catch anyone rocking and rolling, I'll rock and roll them to some tune!'

Simeon, even with his artificial foot, could dance a little, but he soon tired, and once his duty dances were over, he contented himself with leaning against the bar watching. Next year there'd be a new Gollantz; he grinned happily at the thought. This year Charles had been added to the family, next year—he hoped Daphne's child would be a boy—another Emmanuel. A tall young man standing near him was drinking a glass of lemonade. Simeon fancied that his face was familiar, but couldn't quite place him.

He said, 'Good dance, eh?'

The young man set down his glass and replied, 'Topping.'

'You staying in the house or just come for the dance?'

The other stared for a second, then said, 'I live here, sir. I'm Frank, the footman.'

For a moment Simeon felt embarrassed, then he said, 'Then let me tell you, Frank, that's a damned nice dinner-jacket of yours.'

'Thank you, Mr. Simeon. I'm a great believer in good clothes. When I saw Mr. Miller—although mind, we all like and respect him—his clothes gave me quite a shock. They did indeed.'

'He's getting a new rig-out when Hereward wins the Calmering!'

'You think Hereward's a cert, sir?'

'I don't know a great deal about it, but Miller, and Calft—who is going to ride him and came last week to have a look at him with Major Carteret, they all seem pretty certain.'

'So are Fred and Tom—Tom's going to ride White Knight. We're all having something on Hereward.' He finished his drink, and with an 'Excuse me, sir, my partner is waiting for me,' walked off.

Emmanuel came up and joined his son. 'Not dancing, Simeon?'

'I've done my duty, Papa, and the old wood-yard,' stretching out his foot, 'gets a bit tiresome if I try to do too much. You look tired.'

'I believe that I am, Simeon. I'm not getting any younger, and I haven't the vitality of either Viva or Guido. Look at them, they might be twenty.'

'Look at Aunt Beatrice, I bet she's making Hawkins puff and blow a bit! And Rose Watson, they've neither of them forgotten how to do the light fantastic, have they? She's nice—Mrs. Watson—isn't she, Papa?'

'I like them both, Emmanuel said, sipping his whisky-and-soda. 'You get on well with Charles?'

'Wonderfully, he's such a first-rate chap. Dead keen on his work, and yet never stuffy. He's going over to see Guido, he tells me. I think it's a good idea. Honestly, the less he and Max see of each other, the better. I can see a prize row blowing up there one day—Max can be so damned insulting, and one day Charles will lose his temper. Then—whew!'

'I shall be thankful when he goes back to America.' Emmanuel smiled a little ruefully. 'The fellow isn't our sort, Simeon. If it comes to that, neither was his father—*never*. Yet my mother, and my father, too, both adored him. He was aways the top boy in the Gollantz class in their eyes, bless them both.'

Viva joined them. 'I'm gasping for a drink. Get me something—long and cold, Simeon. Emmanuel, don't you think that we might make an unobtrusive getaway? It's long after eleven, and you look dead to the world my precious. No good trying to persuade Mother and Rose to leave—they think this is one of those fabulous pantomime balls they tell me about, which never end before five in the morning, and everyone dances through a pair of slippers. You and I aren't old enough to have their energy!'

'I think that we might. I'll just have a word with Hawkins, and he can let us out by the side door.'

He returned with Hawkins, who immediately became conspiratorial.

'I trust that you have had a pleasant evening, m'lady. Yes, this way, behind the bar, that's right. May I see you safely into the hall?'

'No thanks, Hawkins, Sir Emmanuel will guide my tottering steps. Let the others know that we've gone, will you. Otherwise my mother and Mrs. Watson will dance all night. Good night.'

He bowed. 'Good morning, m'lady. It struck twelve some minutes ago.' Simeon went upstairs immediately, but Viva and Emmanuel sat by the still bright wood fire, the little dogs snuggling close to their feet, expressing their pleasure at the return of their master and mistress.

Emmanuel said suddenly, 'Do you remember a play called *Milestones*?'

'Dimly—why?'

'The last act—Rose says, "When I think of all this room has seen——" Old John Rhead breathes, "Ah!" and she goes on, "I'm sure it's very pleasant to remember," and the old fellow says, "That's because *you're* pleasant. I've said it before, and I say it again. The women of today aren't what women used to be. . . ." I often think of *Milestones* when it grows late and we sit here together. Ah, Viva, what a lucky chap I've been.'

'Am I part of the—luck?' she asked, smiling.

Emmanuel picked up the little Pug, and Viva got lazily to her feet.

'The major part of it,' Emmanuel said, as they moved towards the staircase.

9

Charles, after a long talk with Emmanuel, left for Milano. Emmanuel had spoken gravely, Charles remembered as the aeroplane carried him on his way south, over the Channel to the coast of France. He had never been abroad in his life, and he knew that the excitement of it all had tired him. He lay back and closed his eyes, thinking of his talk in Emmanuel's office.

'I don't want to r-rush you, Charles,' he had said, 'but I want you to think over what I have to say very carefully. Then the r-rest in your hands—accept or decline, whichever you feel will be for your gr-reater happiness. I am not growing younger, and although I don't propose to stop work *yet* I should like to feel that I could—now and then—take a r-real holiday with a clear conscience.

'No man could have a better son than Simeon, and if this child which they are expecting is a boy, then automatically he will, I hope, come into this business. But that is looking very far into the future. I want you to consider coming into Gollantz and Son. I have talked to Mastock, put my point of view to him, and he tells me that they are distinctly pleased with you, but he—mind, you must form your own opinion—feels that Gollantz can offer you more opportunities than auctioneering.

'Don't attempt to make a quick decision—regard this visit to Milano as part of your education. Guido is perfectly able to advise you, to give you much useful information. He has studied his subject and has made great strides—both Louis Lara and I have the greatest affection and admiration for him. When you come back, which'—and Charles saw that his eyes twinkled—'I am told by Viva must be in plenty of time for the opening of the flat racing on March the twenty-fifth, then give me your answer. Until then, go and fill your eyes and mind with beauty —you will find much of Milano very ugly, and much that is age-old and quite beautiful.'

Charles tried to stammer out his thanks for the trust and belief that Emmanuel placed in him. 'I'll think—hard! I do love beautiful things, and I believe that I can appreciate them. I'll work hard, with Signor Moroni to help and advise me.' He added, half shyly, 'I thought that I might study Italian, sir.'

Emmanuel nodded, 'By all means. I believe that the more languages a man can speak the more valuable he is. Don't worry about money, Guido has my instructions. He knows exactly what I wish.' He held out his hand. 'There, good luck to you, and have a wonderful time.' His eyes looked suddenly a little wistful. 'I almost envy you. To be your age again—though I was even younger—and to be going to Italy for the first time. Guido will show you the little shop where I first started. He begged me not to let it go—so we use it now only for storing our very precious wallpapers.' His eyes were bright again, for Charles had learnt that Emmanuel Gollantz was never so happy as when talking about his beloved Galleries. 'Do you know that we buy really good, hand-printed wallpapers from all over the world—or practically. There, again good luck, and *bon voyage.*' Again his bright eyes clouded. 'Perhaps you will find—a chicken-skin fan, who knows?'

Charles, leaning back in his seat, wondered what he had meant—'a chicken-skin fan'. He had never known that Gollantz's were particularly interested in them, and at the airport where Simeon had come to see him off, he asked him, 'Is the Gov'nor interested in chicken-skin fans?'

Simeon smiled very softly and tenderly. 'It was through a chicken-skin fan that he met my mother—again. Maybe to him it still means finding happiness.'

'Fasten your safety-belts please.'

The voice of the air hostess brought him back to reality. Far below them Charles could see lights—lights which meant they were descending upon the airfield. His new adventure was beginning. Malpensa—dreary as all airfields are dreary; a scramble to find his baggage, laid out on a long counter; a card —which he could not read—handed to him.

He shook his head and said, 'Nothing—no!'

The young official made a mark with chalk on his bags and said, '*Va bene.*'

He followed his fellow passengers, to where a shabby-looking motor bus was waiting. His North Country caution made him hesitate until he saw his bags safely stowed at the back, then he climbed in. The bus seemed very dusty and there was endless chattering and many discussions between the driver and various officials. One elderly woman had apparently brought over with her from England a Pekinese puppy, and had neglected to pay duty on it.

She protested in what, Charles felt, was fluent and incorrect Italian, and finally stalked off to pay the necessary money, using—he heard as she passed him—most violent and highly improper language—in English.

The driver raised his hands in despair. '*Aspettare per un piccolo cane—ma, Dio! Questi Inglesi*!' The only person who remained completely undisturbed was the little fluffy dog.

The woman returned, still fuming, her language unprintable. As she passed him she said, 'English, eh? My God, they drive you up the wall with their silliness. The bother was about the Peke's basket! Not the Peke at all! Can't damn' well beat it, can you? Silly B.F.s.'

But she grinned as she said it, and Charles felt that the beautiful little fluffy dog was going to have a wonderful life.

The long, rather dull drive began, and to Charles it was all new and strange. He watched the villages through which they passed with absorbed interest. He saw women washing clothes at the communal fountain, saw—for the first time in his life—dun-coloured oxen slowly pulling carts, their heads swaying slightly from side to side as they plodded forward. He saw churches—most of them rather ugly—and wondered if there were beautiful pictures inside them.

Then the houses became more numerous and he realized that they were on the outskirts of Milan. His heart beat faster, and he pulled out his diary to make sure that he had the address of the flat where Guido lived. They were actually in Milan! There were wide streets, with huge blocks of modern flats, buses and a great deal of traffic. He saw nothing of any great beauty, and by way of various rather narrow and inconspicuous streets they reached the air station.

The Englishwoman with the Peke tucked under her arm shot out of the bus. She nodded to Charles. 'Just walking him round to Biffi's. Have a good time. I'll come back for my baggage—got to think of the little feller first.'

The Peke trotted off at her heels as if Milan held no sense of strangeness for him. Charles, watching him go, thought, 'One day I'd like a Peke. How self-possessed he is! Not in the least disturbed because everyone is looking at him.'

He stopped a taxi, showed the driver the address in his diary, and leaned back watching everything. There was a big theatre—could that be the famous Scala Opera House? That statue—who was it? How much there was that he must learn! Names to remember, many of which he had never heard. Then the taxi stopped before an imposingly large stone-built house. He could see that there was a charming courtyard, where a little fountain played. The driver climbed down, and going forward with Charles's bags spoke to someone who was inside the little lodge.

A man came out, and took the bags, saying, 'Signor Moroni, *ne*?'

Charles nodded, and taking out some loose money offered it to the driver, saying, 'Please?'

'Inglese, *ne*?' he asked, grinning, while he selected the necessary coins. Charles watched him attentively, and then added another coin to the sum he had taken. The grin widened. '*Grazie, grazie*. Me like Inglesi.'

Charles replied with slightly overdone heartiness, 'Good!'

The porter was waiting for him, and they were taken up in a lift which reminded Charles of an immense gilt birdcage. At the first floor they stopped, and the porter said, 'Pleeze—kom.'

The door of the flat was opened by a man in a white coat, who cried, 'Ah, Signor Carlo Gollantz!' and motioned to him to come in. Charles felt in his pocket for his loose money and found two pieces marked '100'. He gave them to the porter, who smiled, bowed, entered the lift and disappeared from sight.

The manservant said, 'I spik Inglesi ver, mooch goot. Signor

Moroni kom in leetle times. Your chambre—'ere—sees ways. 'E say, very dirty air-voyage. If veesh 'ave bat'. Yes? No, not air-voyage dirty, but auto at Malpensa—— Pah! Chambre aw-rite, no?'

Charles looked round. It was a very large room, with fine furniture, and one or two pictures which he felt sure were valuable.

The man said, 'Me—Luigi. Ver' 'onest chap. I empty baggage? Tak' clo'es to make wiz iron. You take bat'. All is pronto, *subito*. Me—know everysing. Signor Moroni always elegante —w'affror? Luigi attend all clo'es. Yes.'

He was as good as his word, and when Charles emerged from his bath, he found another suit laid out for him, a clean shirt and even a fresh tie. Luigi beamed at him. 'Aw-rite, yes, signor?'

'Splendid. *Grazie*.' He had at least learnt one Italian word.

'*Mia mogile*, Bettina. Goot voman. Cook'—he bunched his fingers and kissed their tips —'*superba!* No ozzer like in Milano. Makea Inglesi thé for signor?'

Again Charles nodded, using his hard-worked word, '*Grazie*.'

Luigi took him along to the big *salotto*. It was a magnificent room, with a very large window, and a large open fireplace where logs were burning. The furniture was dignified and splendid, the grand pianoforte gleamed darkly, looking like a silent monster.

Luigi noticed his glances of admiration. 'Signor Moroni bring flowers, No like apartment *senza* flower. I go bring thé—*subito*.'

Guido arrived before the tea, his arms filled with flowers. Charles tried to imagine a Britisher walking about London carrying a great sheaf of flowers, and being utterly unself-conscious about it.

'Ah,' he rushed forward to greet Charles, 'good trip? Smooth flight?'

Charles reassured him that the flight had been completely uneventful.

'That's fine! Here you will notice I grow the complete Englishman. Sometimes in England I forget and speak ver' poorish damn' bad English, but here many peoples refuse to believe that I am Italian. But it is so, I am Milanese.' At that moment Luigi entered with an elaborately laid tea trolley and Guido gave him the flowers for Bettina to arrange.

Charles noticed that he spoke to the servant in Italian, and wondered if he would ever be able to speak the language even moderately well.

Guido sat down and pulled the trolley a little nearer. 'Now I shall be mother!' He laughed. 'Another English phrase, it means that I will pour the tea into the cups. You prefer sugar and milk or lemon, please? Sugar and milk, that is truly English. I have great love for that country, England. I was P.O.W. —you know what I mean, yes?—in the bloody old war.

'I learn there a great deal English. Many words my master, Gollantz, tell me never, never to use. Others yes, he permit. It was strange,' Guido went on, 'we were taken to this *campo*, and I was unhappy, for to me it is disgrace for soldier to be taken prisoner. We are taken before the commandment—no, commander—of the *campo*. My eyes are filled with tears, I am broken with grief. The officer is writing names, we are what is called a draft. This word—draft—also means a cold wind, but the spelling is differently. The officer don't raise his eyes, only says, "*Come si chiama*." I reply, "Guido Moroni, signor *tenente*." The officer dropped his pen.' Guido's voice shook a little. 'You have guessed who was this *tenente*, yes?'

Charles nodded, 'I think so—Emmanuel Gollantz.'

'You have correctness, it was he. My grief was changed to joy, my tears fell but they were tears shed with happiness. Imagine too my damn' pride when he held out his hand, and said, "My dear Guido!" That *campo* was a happy one. Emmanuel was discipline-fellow, but filled with justice, and always with heart for the below-lying dog. Then when the camp closed and we were sent back to Italy—poor battered Italy—ah, Milano was tragedy!—he sent me to manage his magnificent Galleries. Imagine it! He made me keep on this apartment, so there will be room for Louis Lara when he visits here, for Gilly, and also because in this flat—flat is English for apartment—he has been happy, he has come near to die of wretchedness, like Jewish dish called "sweet and sour"—*dolce e amaro*. Now perhaps he remembers more times of joy than the sad days.'

'I wonder the Germans didn't take your pictures and things.'

Guido smiled, looking like a sly cherub. 'Ah, you don't comprehend this *furbo* Guido. There are at the Galleries cellars —very large, very old. In them was all what Emmanuel calls junk. I move all junk into the Galleries—all fine things down to the cellar. I find honest *muratore*—man who lays bricks—build a wall to shut off the good things—packed close. He plastered the wall with dirty-coloured cement. Looks very ancient. The "Nasties" come. Walk into the Galleries. "This I take!" "That pleases me—I will buy." They fix the price, and pay in paper money not worth a bloody damn! I wait until they go, and laugh until I cry. When Emmanuel came after the war, he looked round, shaking his head. "Nothing much left, eh?" Again I give up the laughter.

'I say, "Now Mister Joshua, bring big trumpet, and make the wall fall down! Come also to the cave of Aladdin, yes?" He tell me not to talk very foolishly. When he see the wall, some of which is already pulled down, he nearly goes crazy—with joy, you understand. "What then did the Huns take?" "Old junk—old masters and when you clean them you find bad painted picture of Mussolini maybe." He also laughed. "Praise God!" he says, "we've for years been trying to get rid of that damned stuff! It took a world war to make it possible." '

There began for Charles a time of complete enjoyment. He went each morning with Guido to the Galleries, and marvelled at what he saw there. Guido explained that from time to time they sent pieces to Louis Lara in Paris and he sent them in exchange such pieces as he thought suitable for Italy.

Sometimes Guido would go with him to show him fine churches, great pictures, and fine antiques. At other times Charles went on voyages of discovery by himself. Slowly he felt that he was gathering knowledge, coming to be able to recognize the style and designs favoured by certain painters. He worked hard at his Italian, and Guido often encouraged him when they sat together in the evenings to make an attempt at conversation. He went to listen to opera which filled him with delight, he heard orchestral music, he even saw the newest films, and rejoiced when he understood a few words here and there.

He saw the 'Last Supper' and thought that he had never felt so deeply moved in his life; he saw the wonderful gold altar at Saint Ambrogio unlocked by many different locks, and no one man held all the keys. He loved the Brera, and it was there that he had his first small adventure. He found that the Crevillis amused him, they were so sophisticated. He stood before the 'Marriage of the Virgin' and marvelled. He lost himself among the beauty created down the ages—almost breathless. Finally he came to a halt before the Mantegna of the Virgin and the cherubs. He stood transfixed, the sheer beauty, the loveliness, and the tenderness holding him.

Charles drew a deep breath, and thought, 'All my life, Mantegna will be the painter I shall love best!' Scarcely thinking what he did, he turned to a girl who was also staring at the picture, and said, 'Oh—isn't it wonderful?'

For a second she stared at him in silence, then answered, 'It is one of my favourite pictures. You're English?'

He nodded, 'Yes—and you, you're not English, are you?'

'I was in school in England—near Epsom—for four years. I am Italian, and I like to study pictures.' He realized then that she was a very beautiful girl, that she was *chic* and had an attraction which was irresistible.

'You like Mantegna?' she asked.

'This is wonderful. I haven't seen much of his work.'

'It is beautiful. In Verona—you must go there—you are tourist, I think?—in San Zeno, on the High Altar, there is one of such beauty that it is unbelievable. He came from Mantua, this painter—there is a memorial—you call it that?—to him in the church there. Oh, such an ugly man! But in the Palace of the Gonzagas there are designs of his which take away your breath. Tapestries so fine, with such colour.'

Charles said, 'Please go on talking, there is so much I wish to learn.'

She smiled. She was very slim, not very tall, with hair which looked as if it would be soft to touch. Her eyes were grey—not usual in Italians, her mouth very soft and yet firm. Charles fumbled in his waistcoat pocket for his little curved card case, pulled one out and offered it to her. He said, 'Might I introduce myself?'

She read, in a voice which was soft yet very clear, 'Charles Gollantz. Are you the son of the man who owns the Gollantz Galleries, please?'

'Not his son—I am his nephew. I am here to learn all that is possible about pictures, furniture and so on. I live in the apartment of Guido Moroni. He is my uncle's partner.'

She raised her hands. 'This is astonishing, signor. Signor Moroni is a friend of my father's. I believe that we dine at the apartment one day of this week—*Giovedi,* surely. You see I have no mother—she died when I was very small, so I go everywhere with my father. The name is Franconi.'

He looked at her, and knew that she was terribly attractive. Who was she? Her short fur coat, her fine gloves, everything about her, was what he had learnt to call *prima classe*. He knew he didn't want her to go, and yet hardly dared ask her to take coffee with him. He flushed, and stammered a little as he said, 'Since, signorina, my friend Guido Moroni is a friend of your father's, would you perhaps come and take coffee with me? I should be so—so grateful. And honoured.'

She looked at him, her eyelids a little lowered, entrancing yet provocative. 'I thought you had come to study paintings, signor.'

'I come so often——'

'So do I.' Did she infer that the Brera might be a meeting-place, he wondered?

'Then—the coffee in the places in Milano is so good. Please come, signorina.'

Her smile was charming, warm and friendly, her tone impulsive. 'Yes, I will. You know of a place perhaps?'

'I don't, signorina. I shall be guided by you entirely. Do you wish me to go down and get a taxi?'

She shrugged her shoulders. 'No, we'll walk, it is not far.'

She walked briskly, and, Charles observed, very gracefully. He had noticed how many girls of her age—and presumably of her class—swaggered, swung their hips and generally adopted a movement which, he felt sure, they thought held tremendous allure. This girl walked swiftly, smoothly and naturally, she had purpose in her movements—she wished to arrive at her destination as quickly as possible.

The café which they entered was small but very attractively appointed. It was evident that the Signorina Franconi was known there, for the waitresses came to her immediately. She greeted them with a smile, a few words, and they left with a backward look of admiration.

She said, 'You like this place? My friends and I come here a great deal. One word, Mistaire Gollantz, do not imagine that I wish this meeting to be—now what is the word?—clandestine, am I right? It is merely that my father is a little rigid, and to know that I had met a young man in the Brera and afterwards taken coffee with him—well, he would be furious! So, when we meet at the apartment of Signor Moroni, can you act well? Can you pretend that you have never seen me before? Yes? That will be splendid.'

Charles said, 'I can pretend that I have never seen you before, but I can't pretend here—now—that I don't hope that I may see you again.'

She laughed, and sipped her coffee. 'The coffee is good, no?' she asked.

'I scarcely know,' he said, 'it seems quite perfect to me—but then at the moment so does everything. Please tell me your name.'

'Maria Angela Françoni,' she answered. 'I am always called by my first name. I am twenty-three years old. Many people say that it is time I was married, but—*che tempo!* I am very happy as I am. I look after the servants in my father's house—we live in Monte Rosa, a villa. I love music, I believe that a great friend of mine comes to dinner with Signor Moroni that same evening that we visit there. She was Iva Alfano—now she is Signora Mancini. She was a great singer—sometimes she sings even now, but voices get tired. She was very great. Her husband, Paulo, was a singer also. Something happened to his voice—and it disappeared. They are both quite charming.' She glanced at her wrist-watch, and Charles noticed that it was very small and set with diamonds. 'Signor Gollantz, it is time that I left you. It has been most enjoyable, and thank you.'

He said eagerly, 'May I see you again? Please say yes.'

She smiled and her eyes crinkled at the corners in a way which he found entrancing. 'Shall I give you instruction concerning painters? Tell me what we shall talk about. Have you seen the Museo at La Scala? No? Ah, you must visit that. I shall show you the only bust—head and shoulders—ever made of the great Russian dancer, Nijinsky. It was made by an English lady—a contessa. I shall remember her name—but it is a difficult one. When? The day after tomorrow—will that be convenient for you? At eleven in the morning. Now, Signor Gollantz, will you get me a taxi, please?'

He found a taxi, she got in and held out her hand. For a moment he longed to ask if he might drive home with her and leave her at her door, but he was suddenly overcome with shyness, and refrained.

Charles walked home, his mind filled with the girl he had met. He had 'walked out' in a mild, inconclusive fashion, with Phoebe Morrison in Dullton; he had fallen wildly and romantically in love with Viva Gollantz. But this meeting was different. The day after tomorrow he would see her again, in the Scala Museum. Somehow the intense interest of that museum seemed to fade into the background. Then—wonder of wonders—she and her father were dining with Guido on the day following. He was not to appear to recognize her—the whole thing was tinged with romance.

How terrible if Guido should say, 'Could you possibly dine out tonight? I have friends—they will all be speaking Italian. To you it might be a bore.' What on earth could he say?

'No, no, unless I should be one too many. I don't mind sitting silent, but I do so want to meet Italians and hear how they speak. The accent, you understand, Guido.'

He couldn't imagine himself saying that!

That evening Guido mentioned his dinner-party.

'I have asked a few friends to have dinner with us on Thursday.' Charles breathed more easily when he heard the word 'us'. 'My beloved Iva Alfano and her gallant husband, Paulo Mancini, also the Baron Franconi and his daughter—oh, so charming, this one! She is Barónessa and also she speak English, having been at some fine school in England. Not maybe good party, four men, only two women. Still—never mind—as you say, 'oo cares? You will like that, Carlo? I must talk with graveness to Bettina of the menu. Iva eats a great deal, and all must be tip-top.'

The next day dragged heavily. Charles wandered about the Galleries, and from time to time Guido joined him, and picking up some piece of china, or a silver ornament, would give him instructions concerning them.

'A gent called R- -uskine, said, Carlo, that you should never have any damn' thing in your house which you do not know to be useful or believe to be beautiful. It was a right opinion. But how can many fine peoples know or even believe what is beautiful if they do not learn? How many peoples have any *belief* in what is beauty? They—silly fools—do not know beauty when they see it. Has a man natural taste for beautiful music? Not often—not when he is baby. Do peoples have immediate taste for caviare? I don't think. Taste!' he waved his hands, 'it is a thing for cultivation. Peoples say with prideful-ness, "I know what I like!" Ah, and who cares a single damn what they like! They have never studied, they are not trained to *see* beauty when it is put before their eyes. Study, dear Carlo, acquaint yourself with what is beautiful. Make the great masters your intimate friends.

'When I first had the great fortune to meet our beloved Emmanuel, I was what you call—scruffy boy. Not very nice boy. Slowly he teached me—no, taught me. For him not only pictures, but silver, metals, enamels, and porcelain—he under-stands all. Yet never is he too *prepotente*—as you say, stuck up—that he will not consult—with humility—others.'

Charles listened, paid close attention—for the little man knew his subjects—and at the same time wished that the hands of the clock could miraculously whirl round in a second so that it might be tomorrow.

The next day was bright and sunny. He asked Guido if it was all right for him to visit the Museo at the Scala.

'I am happy! Music is almost—you might say—sister to painting, no? It is good for you to even *see* the handwriting of the glorious Verdi, the letters of that loved Puccini—all others also—except Wagner. From those I beg you to turn your eyes as you would—I hope—turn your ears away from his terrible Nazi music.'

'But he lived before Nazism was heard of,' Charles said.

Guido's face was white and strained as he answered, '*Forse*—

forse. His music—pah, did I say music?—may Verdi, Bellini, Mozart and the other great ones forgive me—his music held the *seed* of Nazism. It expressed the—then—unborn abomination brought to birth by that fiend, that Hitler! There, I ask pardon, Carlo—I grow hot under the collar when I think of these things. I must fly to my master's Galleries. I have an old trout—how English I grow in my expressions, no?—coming to see me. She wishes to sell a set—mark that, a set—of Dresden of the tomato-coloured decorations. Much as I hate all things Teutonic I still have sufficient love for beauty to understand Dresden—when not too full of sloppy sentiment—and Meissen.'

So Charles set off for the Scala, and on entering found Maria Franconi in the first room, walking about, peering into glass-topped cases, looking more charming, he thought, than ever.

He bowed over her outstretched hand, and when—remembering that he was in Italy—he bent to kiss it, she pulled it away, laughing.

'No, no, the hand kissings are only for married ladies, and then not a real kiss, you understand, just a bow and the mouth as if you made a kiss.'

He said, 'How kind of you to be here, Baronessa. I am so delighted.'

'Signor Moroni has told you we dine with him tomorrow evening?'

He nodded. 'And I expressed no sign of great interest, believe me.'

She laughed. 'That is clever. You must not fall in love with Iva Alfano, please, Paulo is jealous for her.'

Charles met her eyes squarely. 'She may be very beautiful, but I doubt if I shall really see her. My eyes will have other things to do.'

They wandered round, and she pointed out to him all the most interesting exhibits, including the bust of Nijinsky. Then, instinctively, they both realized that they were far more interested in each other than in the show-cases, the prints, the valuable letters.

Charles said, 'And now, is it time to have coffee, Baronessa?'

'I think so, but you must come again here—without me.'

'Ah, I wonder why you say that?'

'Because I believe that I take your mind away from what is—your work.'

He stared at her, and she said, with a touch of shyness which delighted him, 'Perhaps I was very—what do you say—bold, forward—to say that. Come, we will have coffee. Just next door—we are early so that place will be nearly empty. At luncheon and dinner and supper it is filled with the opera singers.'

'Perhaps you will come and have supper with me one day, and point out all the famous people to me. We might even go to the opera first, eh?'

Maria looked doubtful. 'That is difficult. Here girls do not go to the Scala unescorted by another woman, it is regarded as being not suitable. Perhaps one day we mght come in a party—Signor Guido, Iva and Paulo?'

Charles added, 'And you and I?'

She smiled. 'Assuredly.'

As they sipped their coffee and talked, he learned many things about her. How she ran her father's big villa, how she took lessons in playing the pianoforte, how each year her father took her to the sea and the mountains. 'For Milano in summer is an *inferno*,' she said, 'and in winter—oh, the fogs we have here! I love Milano for many things but its climate is——Ugh! Either so hot you can scarcely breathe, or so cold that you turn to ice or are suffocated by fog.'

She asked him to tell her something of his life, and listened with her chin propped on her hand while he spoke. When he said that he was an auctioneer he saw her frown, puzzled.

'You mean one who sells—by *vendita pubblica*. But I thought that you were the nephew of Emmanuel Gollantz?'

'I am, but I began to study for an auctioneer some time ago. Now, if I learn and study, he offers me a place in his firm,' he added with some conscious pride, 'Gollantz, of London, Paris and Milan.'

'Then you don't—how do you say it?—make auctions any more?'

'I haven't decided yet. Even if he accepted me, the knowledge I have of auctioneering would be useful.'

'But why did your mother not make you a lawyer or a doctor—something like that? Am I impertinent?'

'Because, my dear'—that slipped out inadvertently—'because—well, it's a long story, and one day—if you allow me to see you and talk to you, I shall tell it to you.'

Again she glanced at her little watch. 'I must go—quickly. I shall see you tomorrow night—as a complete stranger. Oh, please be very clever!'

10

On Thursday morning Guido talked long and earnestly to Bettina. With imploring actions of his hands, he begged her to scour Milano for the most perfect ingredients for the dishes which she was to make.

Bettina, still attractive, answered very calmly, 'Signor Guido, I was out buying these things while you were still asleep! They are already here!' Charles had made sufficient progress with his Italian to be able to gather the meaning of what she was saying. Had he not understood, Guido's face would have conveyed the meaning to him.

He beamed at her, seized the hand of Luigi and congratulated him on having the perfect wife. Luigi was deeply moved; only Bettina stood watching them both, kindly, tolerantly, saying, 'Oh, la la!'

All day Charles wandered restlessly about Milano. He allowed his imagination to run riot, gazed in the magnificent jewellers' shops, and wondered which of the splendid rings he would give Maria Franconi when they were engaged. When Guido came in that evening, bearing more flowers, so that he looked like a walking bouquet, he gave his last-minute instructions to Luigi. This done, he turned to Charles, and said as if offering a halfhearted apology, 'It may be that to give dinner-party is nossing. I don't know, but to me when friends arrive —it is an occasion! You will wear dinner-jacket, no? Americans say—Tuxedo! I wear with a white *gilet*—waistcoat. I copy your Duc de Vindsor, for whom I have admiration. A very first-class fellow this "David"—Italians all admire with greatness his sacrifice for love.' He sighed deeply. 'Right, wrong—how can you know when it is the 'eart? The bravest 'eart is taken captive by love! I have seen him in Venice—Excelsior

Albergo at the Lido. He come running down the steps, I remove my hat and bow gracefully, and with all respectfulness. He saw, nodded his head in pleasant, friendly style, and said, "Hello!" A memory of great preciousness to Guido.'

He fussed over the dining-table, and he and Luigi almost came to blows. To Charles it seemed that a fight to the death was imminent, then, as suddenly as it had risen, it died and they were beaming at each other.

Charles—a trifle nervous himself—dressed and went into the big *salotto*. Guido, immaculate, looking as if he had been shampooed, manicured, and laundered, was waiting.

'Nearly eight o'clock. On the moment of eight Franconi and his lovely daughter will arrive. He is all right, but *prepotente*. He thinks, poor fathead—another English expression which does not mean that his head is really fat—he thinks that to dine with me because I am partner in the Galleries is to make me a great favour! I don't care a damn, he is gentleman, and good client—never do I say customer, it is not dignified. He collects —imagine this—old coins! So dull, so ugly, but he pays a lot of money for them—so I should have any worry!'

Luigi announced the Franconis, and Charles's heart missed a beat. The Baron was a tall thin man, with a short black spade beard. Maria looked entrancing. Her dress was simple as only a really expensive dress can be, her jewellery a string of pearls which looked soft and almost translucent against her smooth, white skin.

Guido, bowing, presented Charles: 'Charles Gollantz, the nephew of the well-known Emmanuel Gollantz, Bart.'

Charles imitated his bow, and murmured, 'I am delighted.'

The Baron, speaking careful and stilted English, said, 'The nephew, no? I have friendship for Emmanuel Gollantz. A man of character and possessing knowledge.'

'I agree, sir.'

Luigi announced, 'Signor Mancini *e* La Signora.'

The greeting was quite different to the former one. 'Iva, *carissima*!' Guido cried, embracing the lovely, if slightly overblown woman with fervour. Maria also rushed forward crying, 'Iva, Iva, *sono contentissima*!' Paul Mancini, tall, and Charles thought, possibly younger than his wife, smiled and then held Maria's hand while he bowed over it.

They were all introduced, then Iva Mancini—who had been one of the world's most famous *prima donnas*—demanded, 'Cocktail Inglese—*subito*, Guido.'

Paulo Mancini spoke to Charles in English, his voice was very gentle, and a little husky. 'You like Milano? We all curse the climate, say that it is exactly like London—whether the speaker has been to London or not, but we get homesick for it when we have to go away. All Italians believe firmly that England is a country wrapped in perpetual fog. "*Sempre nebbia*" they say, and protest that Milano has at least a few fine, clear days!'

Maria, standing near to them, said, 'But England can be beautiful! The spring in Italy is beautiful, but the spring in England is—what is the word?—something in which you can scarcely believe. Yes, we have primroses and violets—many of the flowers which the spring brings to England, but the spring there is filled with something deeper, more profound. It is like a promise——'

Paulo nodded. 'I know what you mean, Maria. I spent my boyhood in England, and some of the years when I was older, and in those years I lived in the country. I watched the spring come in. Oh, it rained—very often, but when it was fine, there was a beauty about the countryside which was—yes, breathtaking.'

His wife joined them, holding out her empty glass. 'Anudder cocktail, pleaze,' and as Charles took it, she added, 'Sank you. Nice boy, I like 'eem. You talk of England! I was t'ere, *cara* Maria, in the 'orrible war. I lived in a—what you say?—*impermeabile*—rains coat.'

Paulo laughed. 'You did nothing of the kind, you went about in taxi-cabs.'

'Een side of the taxi-keb, I wear—rain *mantella*!' she retorted.

The dinner was magnificent. Charles, seated next to Maria, thought that he had never seen anyone—man or woman—eat with such appetite as did Iva Mancini. Each time Luigi came to stand slightly behind her chair, she nodded at her empty plate and said, '*Si—bene—encora!*'

Maria talked to him in her low, clear voice, behaving exactly as if they were meeting for the first time. Every minute Charles felt that he was falling more deeply in love with her. She seemed the epitome of all that was charming and entrancing; her laughter was melodious, and infectious, he thought it the most beautiful music he had ever heard. Only once or twice during the long and elaborate meal did he catch a sudden sparkle in her eyes which told him that both he and she were playing a part—and playing it very well.

Dinner came to an end at last. Charles could barely remember what he had eaten. It had been very good, delicious, but his mind had been completely filled with the girl who sat next to him. They returned to the *salotto*, and drank exquisite black coffee. Guido said to Luigi, 'Tell Bettina that she excelled herself, and thank her.'

Luigi smiled, shrugged his shoulders and protested, 'It was nothing!'

Charles had made progress with his Italian, and although he missed many of the finer points in a conversation, he could follow it reasonably, and even venture on short sentences himself.

Franconi spoke to him in English, stiltedly and correctly. 'How much do you like Milano, signor?'

'It enchants me, Barone.'

'Ah! Emmanuel Gollantz is your uncle, you say? I know him well. A fine person. I should say—with the exception of Moroni—that he is unique. Antique dealers I do not usually trust with my whole heart, but these two are—above others.'

'It pleases me to hear you say so.'

'One day you must come and inspect my collection of coins—they are wonderful. The result of a lifetime's study. Ah, it appears that my daughter is about to play to us. Here it is a rule—when anyone plays or sings—that no one must speak a word! I have heard Moroni really insult guests who did not strictly observe this rule. Indeed, this is so.'

Maria had walked to the piano. Paulo opened it with some ceremony, and Iva called, 'Goths! Paulo, take that vase of flowers from the pianoforte! 'Ow many times, 'ave I told you, Guido, *nossing* must stand on the pianoforte?'

Paulo answered, 'All right, darling, I should have taken them away!'

Franconi whispered, 'Always the tem-pera-mental *prima donna*!'

Charles watched Maria. She sat with her head a little inclined so that he thought her beautiful slender neck looked like the stem of some graceful flower. He listened enchanted to the exquisite First Prelude of Chopin, and when it ended, as it did all too soon, he knew that he sighed.

She looked up and smiled. 'Oh, more, more,' Guido begged. 'The First is too little and at the same time too much!'

'Liszt?' Maria queried.

Guido replied, 'Anything! Anything!'

Iva Mancini grunted, 'Er—orlright. But not too much of 'eem.'

Again she played, and filled the room with notes which fell like jewels. She played without self-consciousness, remaining very still, almost as if the music had cast a spell over her, as if she played in a dream. Then as the music died, she looked up and met Charles's eyes, she smiled.

'For the guest Englishman,' she said, and played, gently and very touchingly, 'I Attempt From Love's Sickness to Fly.'

Iva struggled to her feet. 'Ah—t'at dinner is settled itself! I seeng!' She stood beside Maria, looking immense but still retaining some of her beauty—her skin, her hair, her features were all, it seemed, enhanced as she waited to exercise her art.

Charles listened, amazed at the purity and flexibility of her voice. The notes came apparently without effort; they sounded, he thought, like golden notes flung into the air, to fall softly into a silver pool. More, her whole face seemed transfigured, to become endowed with a new beauty and spirituality. He had seen her as a woman past her first youth, obviously greedy, loving the good things of the world; now she seemed to have become a creature who, possessing this wonderful gift, allowed it to transform her, to make you regardless of her size, as she became the interpreter of a great musician, a means of transmitting his perfect music to her listeners.

The song ended, Maria said, 'Now, Iva, "When I am Laid in Earth"—yes, to ravish us all.'

Again Charles listened and marvelled. He saw Guido take out his handkerchief and dry his eyes—in fact his own were not completely dry. His mind went back to the resting-place of this musician, with its simple and beautiful epitaph: 'Henry Purcell, who has gone to that blessed place where only his music can be excelled.'

Maria cried, 'Iva, you are wonderful!'

'Eet is a sad song! Beautiful but sad, no? Now, I play leetle song—it is Eenglish song. I don't understand the words, but'—she beamed at them—'I have idea eet is immodest!'

Her husband cried, 'Iva, you must not sing "Coming Down the Mountain!"'

'I doan't seeng 'eem. I seeng for Eenglish boy—Carlo.' She sat down, removing her bracelets, for she was loaded with jewellery, and after a spectacular series of scales played at a tremendous rate, she began to sing.

> 'W'en see lights go oop a-gain in dear ole London,
> Aye'll be leet up as aye neffer vas be-fore——'

Charles said, 'Hetty King. That's her song!'

Maria said, 'What are the "lights" that will go up?'

Iva laughed heartily. 'Lights—zees I know—*intestini*! The rest I don't know—but I t'ink r-rude, no, Carlo?'

He shook his head. 'Sorry to disappoint you, signora, but Hetty King never sang a rude song in her life. You can sing that anywhere with impunity.'

''Oo is 'e—this—Impun—what you called 'eem. It is *duetto*?'

'I mean—it's not at all a rude song.'

'Oh—and for a long time I seeng eet as rude song.' Her disappointment was obvious.

From that evening life seemed to have changed for Charles Gollantz. He had found happiness in Milano, as years ago Emmanuel had found it. Possibly Emmanuel had been more romantic, but Charles was incurably sentimental. His whole mind was set on when and how to meet Maria Franconi. Fortune favoured him, an invitation to dine came from the Barone, and he and Guido went to the immense villa in Monte Rosa, and met a crowd of beautifully dressed women, and perfectly correctly dressed men.

The evening in itself was dull, but Charles managed to have a few words with Maria. She looked—he thought—more lovely than ever.

'Tell me, when can I see you again?' He knew his voice sounded a little breathless.

She met his eyes ; hers were faintly amused but very kind.

'I shall be in the Duomo tomorrow about—about eleven. I do not think, Signor Carlo, that you have yet studied all the interesting things which it holds. I commend it to you.'

After that meeting they met again and again. She even took him to the big cemetery where he saw some of the most hideous memorials he had ever believed to be possible. With every meeting his love grew, and there were times when he felt that it might be possible that she had something more than a moderate liking for him.

He had bought a small second-hand car, a little Fiat, and once she consented to drive with him to Como to visit—ostensibly—the Villa Carlotta. They admired the gardens and Charles admitted that he detested the statue by Canova. When they left the villa, to stand on the long flight of steps looking over the lake, where a wintry sun made the water dance as if it were filled with floating jewels, he knew that now he must speak what was in his heart.

'Darling, I am so much in love.'

She turned towards him, smiling. 'With Italy?'

'Perhaps, but most certainly with the most wonderful treasure that Italy holds. Maria—you know how much I love you, don't you?'

'I don't really know——' He heard her soft laugh. 'It might be that I flatter myself.'

'Will you marry me?'

'We should have to ask my father's permission, Carlo.'

'Have I your permission to ask *his* permission?'

She laid her hand on his arm. 'My dear, he will be difficult. He wants for me—a title greater than his own, a great deal of money, a great family——' She shrugged. 'You know what kind of things my father would want for me.'

'And if he refuses—what then? Will you marry me?'

She hesitated. 'Carlo, I—I don't know. I do love you, yes, I do really and truly. But—I have always been afraid of my father. He is a man of such determination, and perhaps Italy is different from your country. You are not Catholic, are you?'

He shook his head. 'No, I'm not very religious.' Then more

hopefully, 'I'd study it and become one, if you wished, my dearest.'

'That would be a very bad thing, if you had not faith and belief.'

'I might acquire both! Oh, darling, darling Maria, you say that you do love me—I adore you! I've scarcely touched your hand. I want to take you in my arms, to kiss your hair, your eyelids, hear you whisper that you love me—again and again. Maria, when can I see your father?'

She sighed. 'It is going to be very difficult, dear Carlo. I have to warn you that my father can be hard, even insulting. It may not be a pleasant interview. But it shall be arranged. Telephone to him at our villa when you get back to Milano. He will think that you have found some ancient coin for him!

'But,' and the pressure of her hand on his arm increased, 'I have said that I love you, and I mean it. Be patient. However my father protests, we shall attain what we wish—our marriage. He can be firm, so can I. Let me tell this to Iva Mancini—she is a wise person. She can keep secrets. She will offer good advice. Dear Carlo—I am quite determined. Now we must go back to the dear little car—it is like a tiny house just for the two of us.'

They returned to the car, and Charles took her in his arms and kissed her cheek—so soft, so smooth, and at last, greatly daring, his lips found hers and they clung together in an ecstasy of love and happiness

She whispered, 'Now, you believe that I love you?'

'I am the happiest man in all Italy—in all the world.'

'Then see my father; be brave, be patient. Remember that we have the strongest weapon in the world—our love.'

They drove back to Milano in almost complete silence, but a sense of happiness seemed, Charles felt, to envelop them. From time to time he would glance at Maria, and she would smile back at him, a smile which was so warm and so filled with real affection that it warmed his heart. Once or twice she put out her hand and laid it very gently on his arm. He thought that he could actually feel the tenderness of her love for him, and the strength of her trust and belief that their ultimate happiness was secure.

As they drew nearer to Milano, she said softly, 'Stop here, darling.'

He stopped the car, and turned to her. 'In Milano it would be quite impossible, here—is different. I cannot say "Good-bye" to you—as we have always done—ever again. Kiss me, my Carlo, and that will keep me feeling happy until I can see you again.'

With his arms round her, he whispered, 'It's really—true?'

'The most true thing in the world!' she answered. 'I must see you immediately after you have seen my father, yes?'

'Can I telephone to you?'

'I have a telephone in my own sitting-room. Please—what do you say—give me a ring'—she laughed—'I mean on the telephone, not for my finger—though that will come in time.'

'I'll rifle Guido's precious cases for the finest ring they have.'

'Dear, dearest Carlo! There—kiss me once more, and we must drive on. Whatever happens, I am conscious that here—at this moment—I am happy. There, my darling——'

He stopped the car some distance from her villa, and then swung off towards the city. It seemed fantastic, and yet at the same time the most natural thing in the world. How was it possible to come to know her, to listen to the tones of her voice, to watch her changes of expression, to realize that she had not only intelligence but great gentleness and kindliness—without loving her?

The thought of an interview with her father made him nervous, but he was sufficiently filled with North Country determination to remain firm in his decision to see the Barone. When he arrived back at the apartment he went to his room, found the number of Barone Franconi, and asked for the number.

A voice—not particularly encouraging—answered: 'Yes—the Barone Franconi speaks.'

'I am Charles Gollantz—might I ask if you will grant to me a few moments of your time? I have something of importance to tell you.'

The tone of the voice changed perceptibly. 'Ah, I think that you find for me some very old coin, eh? My daughter is dining out this evening, pray come in at—shall we say—nine o'clock? I shall be anxiously waiting.'

Charles heard the telephone click as the Barone relinquished it. He stared at the telephone which he, himself, had been using.

This was a nice complication! There would be the slightly distant Barone waiting excitedly, only to be told that Charles wanted permission to marry his daughter!

When Guido came in, Charles told him of his love for Maria Franconi. Guido beamed at him, and snatching his hand shook it warmly.

'She is a beautiful young lady and as good as she is beautiful. I wish you all happy things, a future which will truly be gold plated.' Then his smile died. 'Her father, the Barone, does he know?'

'We only really knew ourselves this afternoon,' Charles said. 'I am to see him this evening after dinner.'

Guido shook his head gravely. 'Dear Charles, I fear you have 'eavy task before you. This old man with his damned silly coins—I think he has Greek and Roman coins instead of good beating heart. You will have to be very calm, very holding back—he is capable of bloody rudeness. Keep tightly holding on to your temper. You have all my good wishes for everything to completely turn out well.'

Charles sighed. Everything had seemed so splendid, so gloriously simple. Maria loved him, he adored her—but he doubted if Guido felt any more sanguine than he did himself.

He dressed with the utmost care, and after dinner, which was a rather silent and slightly oppressive meal, he drove to the Villa Franconi. The Barone received him in his library, a dark rather gloomy room, with shelves filled with expensively bound books which did not look as if they were much used. The elder man was sipping black coffee, and he looked up when Charles was announced by a servant in a very dark, impressive livery.

'Ah, I thank you for coming to see me. May I see the coin?'

Charles said, 'I'm afraid you are under a misapprehension, Barone, I came about a private matter.'

Franconi put down his coffee-cup and said with what Charles felt was studied insolence, 'What private matters can you possibly wish to discuss with me?'

'May I sit down?'

'Please state your business with me.'

There was no friendliness in his tone, and Charles wondered if he imagined that he had come to attempt to borrow money. The Italian's lips were tightly compressed, his small spade beard seemed to quiver slightly with ill-concealed annoyance. He drummed with his finger-tips on the arm of his chair.

'I wish you to be brief!' the Barone warned him.

Charles bowed. 'I shall do my best. I love your daughter, I believe that she loves me, and I have come to ask your permission to marry her. That is my earnest wish and my request.'

The fingers stopped drumming as the Barone sat stiffly upright.

'I have heard many times of how *prepotente* the English can be, but this is the first time I have ever met—face to face—with such a demonstration of their ability to be so *imprudente*. You know who I am, you know perhaps that my family *albero* is older than most, my daughter has, like myself, a title of distinction, and you—you—have the——' He seemed about to choke, the words appeared to stick in his throat. 'Pah, this is what comes as a result of—democracy. Of treating tradesmen as if they were *signori*!'

Struggling to keep his voice even, Charles said, 'May I remind you that my uncle, Emmanuel Gollantz, also has a title, one which will pass to his son in time.'

'Your uncle keeps a shop!'

'And is respected, trusted and admired by everyone who knows him.'

'Your family are—many of them at least—Jews. I detest Jews! And you, what profession have you?'

'An auctioneer.' He added, 'If I wish and show aptitude, my uncle wishes to take me into his firm—which, as you know, has a branch here and another in Paris.'

Franconi stared at him. 'An—auctioneer!' he said the word as if the very sound of it revolted him. '*Un venditore all' incanto!* Selling to people, shouting "*offerta*" to a crowd of dirty people! Banging with a little hammer! Then yelling, "To go—going—it is gone!" '

'How fully you understand the business of auctioneering,' Charles said. His face was flushed, his eyes hard and very bright. He felt that his heart was suffering definite physical pain. That afternoon they had been so happy; now, facing this infuriated, outraged Italian, he saw their wonderful dreams shattered, his hopes vanishing.

'And you—you—have the stupid conceit to come and tell me

that you wish to marry my daughter! You tradesman Jew! You can go, I do not wish to breathe the same air with you. I have been taught a hard lesson, that I should never have accepted Moroni's invitation to dine, I should have been better advised. Now, go! Go, or my servants shall throw you out, which is what you deserve.'

Charles bowed, then turned on his heel and walked out of the room. As he passed the tall servant, he contrived to hold his head high, and to allow his expression to disclose nothing of the misery which he was feeling. As he reached the hall door, he heard Franconi's door open, and heard him shout to the servant, in Italian, 'That man is never to be admitted here again!'

He ran down the steps, and flung himself into his waiting car. He felt confused, as if he was scarcely awakened from a hideous nightmare. He felt bruised, his mind as well as his body. What would happen now? Dare he telephone to Maria, or might her incensed father forbid her to use her telephone? He drove home slowly, miserable and apprehensive. Guido was waiting for him, resplendent in a velvet smoking-jacket, which Charles fancied he wore in imitation of Emmanuel Gollantz. He sprang to his feet as Charles entered.

'Now—what news! Tell me, I am filled with excitement!'

'He virtually kicked me out! Told his servant that I was never to be admitted again. I kept my temper, but it was horribly difficult. He regards the whole family as—Jew tradesmen! And as for an auctioneer—he appears to think that they are the dregs of humanity. You might imagine that the Galleries are nothing but second-hand junk shops in the lowest quarters of London, Milan or Paris.'

'Ignorant old man! How dare he speak in this manner? Does he not understand that the Gollantz family is one which very fine high-ups are proud to have as friends. I telled you, Carlo, he does not have a beating heart, he has only a lot of dirty old bits of money.'

He paced up and down the big room, muttering imprecations against Franconi. Suddenly he stopped, and hit himself on the forehead, exclaiming, 'I am idiot—cretin—fool! We shall enlist the help of Iva and Paulo Mancini. Paulo is partly Italian, Iva completely so. All Italians—except old *porco* Franconi, have big hearts for people in love. I shall telephone to Iva—now, at once—I shall ask her to telephone to Maria Franconi, asking her—in her turn—to telephone to you from a public box tomorrow! So—as they say at the boxing, there is the first round—it is ours!'

He rushed to the telephone, and on getting the number began to talk to Iva Mancini in rapid and excited Italian. Charles, of course, was not sufficiently fluent to follow all he poured out in a torrent of words. Then apparently Iva began to speak, for Guido merely said, '*Si . . . ma si . . . si*' at intervals. Suddenly he exclaimed. '*Dio mio!* Carlo, come quickly—*subito*——' He pushed the receiver into Charles's hand, beaming. 'It is no less than—her!'

Charles knew that his hand was shaking as he heard her voice saying, 'Carlo, Carlo *mio*. I have confided in Paulo and Iva. They are going to help us. Do not try to telephone to my home. I shall telephone to you either from Iva's or a public box.'

He said, 'Maria—I can't give you up. I love you too much.'

She laughed, very softly, 'I shall not permit you to—give me up! I, too, happen to love you very much. We must be brave, and faithful to each other. Good night, my Carlo. I shall speak to you tomorrow.'

With that he had to be content. Guido wiped his eyes as Charles returned to him. 'Love is beautiful,' Guido said, 'also it is—how do you say?—touches—no, touching. To someone like Guido the thought of what joy love can contain, and also what miserableness when it is not running nicely, makes tears fill up my eyes.'

The days which followed seemed to Charles to be empty except for the daily telephone call from Maria, or the rare occasions when they dared to meet. When Maria first suggested that they might meet in an out-of-the-way church, Charles knew that for a moment the idea shocked him.

Maria realized it, and laughed. 'Carlo, don't you know that half the lovers in the world meet in churches? If they are doing no wrong, if they have no wicked thoughts, but only love and affection for each other, why should the good God mind His house being used for their meetings? We can always thank Him politely and with gratefulness when we leave.'

So they would sit in the rather dim, and slightly dusty churches, and talk in whispers, his hand holding hers. She told him that her father had not even mentioned Charles's visit, neither had he referred to him in any way.

She added, 'But if I am lunching or dining with friends, he always telephones to ask that some message—of no importance whatsoever—may be given to me. Or if I have left, at what time did I go? How silly it all is!'

Once or twice he was able to take the car, while she took one of the numerous autobuses, to meet in some village, and there eat a simple—and often excellent—meal together before she caught another bus which took her back to Milan.

The days passed into weeks, and one day when, greatly daring, they met in Stresa, Charles told her that he must leave Milan in a week's time. 'I promised faithfully that I would be back to see Viva Gollantz's horse run in a very important race. I can't let her down, she's been awfully good to me—and helped me a lot. You do understand, darling?'

She smiled, and nodded. 'I understand, of course. I hope that the horse wins its race. It will be, perhaps, a good omen for us if it does. You'll write to me—send your letters to Iva, yes?'

He hated going, even although the thought of seeing Ordingly, his mother, and Viva filled him with happy expectancy.

'I have written to my uncle—Emmanuel—to tell him that I shall, if my agreement with the firm of auctioneers can be cancelled, be glad and happy to enter his firm instead. That might give me the chance to sometimes come to Milan, to Paris, and to me Milan seems the nearest place to Paradise in the world. Do you ever go to Paris?'

She told him that she had an aunt—a dearly loved aunt—who lived in Paris. She was a contessa married to a very rich and, Maria added quickly, quite charming man. She smiled and her face flushed.

'I have a plan in my mind, but I am too shy to speak it. I shall write it all to you when you go to England. My father will go to New York in June, he tells me, and will be away for two months. He has a great deal of business in America.'

Charles said, a little bitterly, 'I thought he despised all business!'

Maria pursed her lips, and said in a tone of exaggerated dignity, 'Not when it can be referred to as—financial transactions! He suggested that while he is away I should go to my aunt in Paris.'

Charles's little flare of annoyance died. He grinned, looking even younger than his years. 'I shall suggest to my uncle that I visit Paris in June. Won't you tell me your plan, sweetheart?'

But she was adamant, and they sat in the sunshine looking over at the islands, talking softly, telling each other how happy they were to be together, and imagining what the future might hold for them.

A week later Charles left for England.

11

The last thing Charles remembered when leaving Milan was watching Maria who, braving everything, had come to Malpensa to see him begin his journey. As the plane took off and he saw her white handkerchief bravely waving, he felt a lump rise in his throat, and knew that his eyes smarted.

She was so lovely, so young—only twenty-three—so loving and tender. How he hated to leave her with her father, to whom Guido always referred as 'the old pig wallowing in dirtiness'.

Last night, Iva and Paulo had dined at Guido's apartment, and for a few moments Maria—greatly daring—had come in so that they might take their real farewell of each other.

She had looked—as always—beautiful, and Guido with immense and slightly overdone tact had begged Charles to take Maria into the small *salotto* to show her a box magnificently chased and enamelled, of the fifteenth century. They had clung together in something which was almost despair.

'How I shall miss you, my Carlo!'

'Dearest, I shall come back, and soon, but we shall meet in Paris.'

He saw the faint hint of a smile hovering round her lips.

'Ah, Paris. Long before that time arrives, I shall have told you my plan. There, my Carlo. you take my love with you always, and God will protect you. Go, then, with God.'

Now he was being carried away from her, back to England, and his heart felt bruised and hurt. He had liked 'walking out' with Phoebe at Dullton, he had imagined himself to be wildly in love with Viva. Now, assessing everything in the clear flame of real love, he knew that it had been pleasant to walk with Phoebe, because she spoke very little and he was able to propound his ideas and beliefs, and that Viva had attracted him because she was the first really sophisticated woman he had met. Her voice, her clothes, her certainty, had all been something new. Then, that day in the Brera, when, in a burst of admiration for a picture, he had impulsively spoken to Maria Franconi, when he had listened to her soft voice, watched her lovely eyes, he had begun to understand what it might mean to fall in love with such a girl.

Should he tell Viva Gollantz about her? He could imagine Viva listening intently to his story, at times a little smile touching her lips, making perhaps little sounds of sympathy and understanding, and when his recitation ended asking very concise and pertinent questions. Viva would be a good friend to anyone she liked and trusted and Charles felt that she did like him, and also that she had faith and trust in him.

Yes, he would tell Viva the whole story.

Mum might be waiting at the airfield, she had written long and excited letters to him; the house in Dullton had—as she expected—been bought a few days after she put it on the market, sold immediately and at a price higher than she dared hope.

Everyone has been most kind, she had written. *There's a lot to be said for having friends at court, these important people can get things done. Emmanuel found a beautiful flat, just right for the two of us, off Sloane Street. Do you good to walk to work across the Park and stretch your legs, Charlie.*

'Fasten your safety-belts please, put out your cigarettes. Thank you.'

Charles knew that his mother had moved a week before his arrival, and he felt certain that Emmanuel had arranged everything for her, probably sending some of his men to Dullton to do the actual moving with one of Gollantz's big vans. He felt warmed and comforted. It was splendid to be surrounded by good friends.

The plane was descending. He could see the airfield, imagined that he saw his mother waving wildly. Then they landed. He could see her quite plainly now, still waving her greeting to him. When he finally reached her, she was almost crying in her excitement, and could only clutch his arm, while he whispered,

'There, darling, take it easy—that's right. Dearest Mum.'

'No need to go back in their bus,' she told him, still gulping a little, like a child who tries to regain control of its voice after a fit of crying. 'Lady Heriot—that's a grand pal, Charlie!—sent her own car. Oh, yes, she insisted. You're going to love the flat, I know. It's like a flower shop today. Viva sent up enough flowers to fill every vase I've got, and fruit from their hot-houses. Nice little dining-room, largish lounge—oh, I forgot you don't like it called that—well, drawing-room then. Labour-saving kitchen, little study for you, for your books and so forth and, Charlie, two bathrooms, one for each of us! Yours is darkish blue tiled, and mine's rose pink, I feel like a film star when I have a bath! The rent? Trust you to get to the practical part, luv. Well, it appears that Emmanuel has some interest in this block of flats—don't ask me to explain, you know I've no head for business. He took over all the fittings for the electric lights—lovely they are too—and he arranged for the telephone to be left, same number and all.'

'And the rent, Mum?'

'Oh, aye, the rent—well, it seemed a goodish bit to me. But as Emmanuel said, he couldn't have one of the firm living in a dog kennel, he said it would look bad. Anyway, he wants to talk business with you tomorrow. He's as pleased as anything that you're going to join Gollantz's. Did he write and tell you that he'd fixed it all up with those auctioneers you were with? I believe that man could do anything if he set his mind on it.'

Charles said gently, 'And what is the rent, Mum?'

She laughed. 'All right, Mr. Impatience, I'm coming to that. It's four hundred a year—mind we've no rates to pay, only the electric light. Everything's electric, luv. Hoover—that's one of the fittings, floor polisher, the grandest fridge you ever saw! When I said that £400 seemed a big rent, Emmanuel just laughed—nice laugh he has!—and said, "Charles can afford that! I'll see that he can, Rose!" Charlie, we're there! Now, isn't it a grand-looking block of flats? We're among the nobs here, luv. There's a Q.C.—y'know, they used to be called K.C., there's a Lady something or other, Sir George Masters—oh, ever so many swell people. See, uniformed porter—there's two of them.'

His baggage unloaded, Charles and his mother spoke to Lady Heriot's chauffeur. 'Please thank her ladyship for so kindly lending the car,' Rose said, and Charles added, 'Please give her my love, and I hope to see her very soon.'

'Very good, madam. Certainly, sir.'

The porter handed the bags to a man wearing a green baize apron.

'Number seventeen, Jim.' Then to Charles he said, 'Good morning, sir. I hope you had a pleasant flight. I have flown, but I can't say I've ever cared a lot for it. Prefer to be on terra firma myself.'

He closed the lift door in a fashion which was almost reverential. Rose told Charles that he had been most helpful, and had found her a 'daily'. 'It's his wife's sister. She's married and her husband's got a steady job. She felt lonesome in the house—they've got a little tiddley house, but nice as nice, in Chelsea—when he's away all day. So she comes to me every morning, never a minute late. Eh, Charlie, I've been lucky.'

It was a nice flat, Charles thought. The rooms were light, and the decorations in beautiful taste. Mum had made it look charming. She told him that she had sold most of the 'big stuff' and only kept 'Auntie's and Mr. Watson's and my best pieces'.

'You'd have been surprised, Charlie, the prices that stuff fetched! Mind, it had been well kept, and though it wasn't what you could call *old* it wasn't that gimcrack stuff. Oh, and I forgot to tell you, they want us at Ordingly this week-end—seemingly it's the last week-end before this big race. However, Emmanuel 'ul tell you all about it when you see him. Oh, Charlie, it's lovely to have you back.'

She insisted upon their dining at home. Their first night! And she hadn't forgotten how to make a steak-and-kidney pudding just as he liked it. She expected that he'd had to eat some pretty funny food in Italy, and she fully intended to see that he got proper food now that he was home.

That evening they sat in the pleasant room, where flowers filled every possible corner. The dinner had been perfect, for when a North Countrywoman 'gives her mind to it', no one can produce a more delicious dinner.

Leaning back in a big comfortable chair, Charles watched her carefully and with affection in his eyes. How would Maria get on with her? Would some of his mother's queer twists and turns of phrase puzzle her? He dismissed the thought. If Maria—his Maria—could not see the real gold of his mother's character, then she wasn't the girl with whom he had fallen in love. Then, suddenly, he was telling Rose all about Maria, how he had met her, how he had fallen in love with her. He talked just as he used to when he was much younger and 'had something on his mind'.

She listened, her fingers busy with her knitting. It was one of the things upon which she prided herself, that she had always knitted Charlie's socks.

Though I say it myself, I'm a champion knitter. Never mind if it's thick for winter, long for golf, thin for summer, or silk for evenings—my boy has a drawer full of hand-knitted socks!'

She listened in silence, and when he ended she sighed, 'Why luv, it seems strange to me that her father should have turned nasty! Cheek, that's what I call it. But if you love her and she loves you, Charlie, as dear José Collins used to sing, "Love will find a way". Just keep up your heart, m'dear, and everything will come right. I'm glad she and you have a good friend in this lady—I forget her name—who you can trust.'

He slept soundly, and on waking was, momentarily, unable to remember where he was. His mother was standing beside his bed.

'Cupper, Charlie,' she said. 'It will be a change to taste good English tea again. None of those foreigners—never mind how nice—know how to make a decent cup of tea, I know.'

He felt excited. Today he was to see Emmanuel Gollantz, to hear what his plans were for his future. He dressed carefully—as he always did—and set off to walk briskly across the park. Ten o'clock was the time Emmanuel arrived at the Galleries, half past ten was the time he had arranged for his interview with Charles. He looked at the beautifully arranged windows of the Galleries, remembering what Emmanuel had once told him.

'The arrangement of windows is terribly important. They must *say* something. The furniture must be in harmony. Periods—unless you wish to draw compar-risons, with a definite purpose you understand—must be unmixed. If you wish to dr-raw comparisons, then you must make that plain to the people who stand and look. Here a chair in the Jacobean style, here one in the style of Charles the Second, and so on. That must be made plain to the man who looks. Either your windows must be something to catch the eyes and the admiration, or they must be little and charming lesson books!'

Miss Morrison told him that Sir Emmanuel expected him. 'He'll ring in a minute, I expect, Mr. Charles. Had a nice time abroad? Mr. Max came back from Switzerland as brown as a berry. Ah,' as the telephone rang, 'that will be Sir Emmanuel. Yes, that's right—go into his office, Mr. Charles.'

Emmanuel sat at his great carved desk, and held out his hand. 'Nice to see you again, Charles. Sit down. How did you find your mother? She's delighted with the flat—like a child being given a tr-reat. We've grown very fond of your mother, y'know. She gave me a magnificent present the other day—six pairs of hand-knitted silk socks. Needless to say I began to wear them immediately. Look!'

He put up a foot encased in a beautifully polished shoe, and displayed a silk-covered ankle. Emmanuel was proud of his feet and ankles, and justifiably so. He said, 'Nice, aren't they?'

Charles smiled. 'Yes, she's what we call in the north a reit champion knitter. The flat is wonderful, and I suspect would not have been quite so wonderful but for the help which I am sure, sir, you gave so generously.'

'Pooh! I did nothing. The place was there, I have an interest in those flats—well, the rest was easy. Now, Charles, to business. I have had my brother, William, draw up a simple—but water-tight—document. You might call on him and get him to read it over with you, and explain anything which you don't entirely grasp. Simeon is already my junior partner, and you come in as junior to Simeon. That's only fair; he's been in the business for quite a time, you're new to it.'

'Of course, sir, I agree entirely. I shall do my best, but I'm afraid that I shall be something of a passenger for a time.'

'Lots of books to read, study all the time. Study our windows, walk down and learn from the windows of the really fine china shops in King Street, look in silversmiths' shops. All the time be packing knowledge away. Then,' he smiled, 'as my grand-father used to say, at the end of fifty years' hard study, you begin to realize how little you r-really know. There, off you go and talk to Simeon. Oh, and Viva expects you and Rose on

Saturday, to pay a last visit to Hereward. He goes up to Calmering on Monday—the big race is on Tuesday. Viva is desperately excited, says that she has "put her shirt" on him! I told her I daren't lose any of my shirts, but that I'd put my new silk socks on him.' He rose, and held out his hand, and as he spoke his tone was one of friendly formality. Emmanuel, like his father and grandfather, liked to indulge in small formalities, to treat important occasions with dignity.

'I am delighted that we have added another Gollantz to the firm. We're very proud of our business, begun in England by old Emmanuel in a house on Campden Hill. I'm sure that you will br-ring new lustre to the firm. R-remember, Charles, nothing bad is ever cheap! Bad things are the kind of advertisement which we cannot afford.'

Charles took the long-fingered hand and held it firmly.

'You can be sure that I shall do my best, sir.'

'I *am* sure of it. Now, go and talk to Simeon.'

Simeon was delighted to see him, and again Charles felt his heart warmed with the kindness and friendliness of these relations of his. Simeon said that Daphne was well. 'I wish that it was all over, y'know. Pity she was a nurse before she married me, Charles—they *know* too damn' much. Tell me of my dear Guido, of Iva and Paulo—all about Milano. I love the place, and the people.'

'If I *am* to tell you all about these things, don't you think that we might have luncheon together? There are all kinds of things I want to hear too. Miss Morrison told me that Max is back with us! That he is very brown and apparently has had a whale of a time.'

'Yes—he's back. I find that I dislike him more than ever! He hates me, but I think the person he dislikes most is—Viva. Now what on earth has Viva—darling that she is!—done to annoy Max? Have you any idea?'

'Plenty of ideas—but I fancy the right one is the most simple. He's intolerably conceited. Probably imagines every woman will fall for him and—well, I believe that's the answer.'

Simeon whistled softly. 'That's the milk in the coconut, is it? Let's go out to luncheon—somewhere quiet.'

They talked about the new partnership, and Simeon stated that he didn't really know a great deal. 'Compared with my father—literally nothing!' But he promised that he would always be ready to give Charles his advice—'for what it's worth'. He advised Charles to 'hang about the Galleries' in order to orientate himself, and to discover which branch of the business interested him most.

'You might specialize in silver,' Simeon suggested. 'Though it's a devil of a job—means lots of study, and good eyesight. Our last specialist—God help us—was the swine Julian, and a nice mess he nearly got us into—faking silver marks. Nearly broke my father's heart that anyone should be able to hint that Gollantz's weren't playing the game.' He stopped, his face a little flushed. 'I say, I ought not to say things like that to you about your—about Julian. Sorry.'

'I couldn't care less what you said about him. I never want to see him, hear from him or of him. There! Simeon, I've remembered I have to go to Clerkenwell. You remember that picture I gave Viva for Christmas? Well, I only paid the chap—I forget—ten or fifteen shillings for it, and as Emmanuel says it is good, it's only fair to go back and give him a little more. He's a chap called Joe Hindes—or Indes, I don't know which. I suspect that he's not quite on the level somehow, but he did show me how to clean that picture!'

'How? I thought Clapham cleaned it.'

'I started the cleaning,' Charles said gravely, 'with spit!'

He made his way to Clerkenwell, and found the rather mean street without difficulty. There was the chemist's—and the sight of that shop brought back a memory of his detested half-brother—and the German chemist. He glanced into the shop, having to admit that it was considerably cleaner than most shops in the street. The chemist was fiddling about; otherwise the shop was empty. Charles went on to Mr. Joseph Hindes.

Hindes was—apparently—still cleaning his nails, but this time with an old pen nib. He was giving grave attention to the work in hand, but the result on his nails seemed scarcely worth the energy he was expending.

He said, 'Hello, Mr. Hindes, remember me?'

Hindes looked up. 'Carn't sai as I do. Watcher want?'

'Remember that I bought a set of ivory chess-men from you?'

Hindes nodded. 'Nah I do. Lemme tell you, them chess-men

was sold to me by a certain Colonel Moore, they was lef' 'im by 'is Auntie Gertrude. I got the pipers upstairs—all Sir Garnet. So, what are yew botherin' yerself for? Tell me thet, will yer?' His tone was truculent, his eyes narrowed. He added, 'Jest tell me, will yer?'

Charles leaning against the counter, made his explanation. He had come to offer Mr. Hindes a little extra for the picture which he had bought. Hindes stared at him.

'Yew on the damned level?' he asked, and when Charles nodded, he drew a long, deep sigh. 'Gor luv us? Whatcher come ter offer me?'

'I can't honestly afford more than a fiver, Hindes. But any time you've anything that interests me, drop me a card, and I'll come round, have it properly valued, and——'

Hindes said, 'An' Bob's yer uncle! I once yeard of a chap—mind yer it's a longish time ago—'oo went abart wiv a candle. Waffor?—I'll tell yer. Luking fer a 'onest man. Blimey, i' this tahn, 'e'd 'ad wanted a 'underd faasand bloomin' candles ter find one. Joe 'Indes finds one vivout even lukin' fer 'im. 'And it over, mister—I dunno when I see a fiver larst!'

He looked at the note with respect and affection, smoothing it gently, and finally lifting it to his lips and kissing it.

'Superstishon,' he explained. 'Kiss 'em an' some'ow they comes back ter yer. Lot o' damned rubbish, but better ter be on the safe side. 'Ere, mister, w'ats 'appened?'

Charles had caught sight of a tall, elegant figure passing the dirty window. Max, going to visit his chemist—investigating the matter of new cosmetics for export to America.

'Look here, Hindes,' he said, 'I want to know something about that fellow. He's gone to that chemist's——'

'Bloody 'un that chap!'

Charles dived into his pocket and brought out a half-crown. 'Go on, follow him, hang about—ask for some medicine for this or that—I don't care. Listen to what he's saying, to what the chemist says. When he's gone come back and tell me if you've heard anything. I'll give you another half-quid if you've caught anything—I'll watch the shop. Will you?'

'Will I? Once a pal allus a pal. Anyfink ter 'elp a pal. I'm orf. Keep a eye on the till—nuffink in it, but jest keep a eye on it.'

He had gone, and Charles watched him strolling along past the window, hands in his pockets, and a cigarette hanging from his lip. Charles leaned against the dusty counter, and wondered what on earth he hoped to find out? He didn't know, he only knew that he felt suspicious of Max and his little obscure chemist. He had no facts, he actually knew nothing, but there was a queer uneasiness lurking at the back of his mind. He moved restlessly about the grimy shop; there was the same amount of junk and rubbish as he had seen on his previous visit. He wondered if Hindes had sold a single thing since then. The same cracked cups with saucers that didn't match, a few cracked plates, a teapot lacking a spout and a lid. On one shelf he saw an upper part of a set of false teeth, and an ancient and very dirty truss. Did anyone buy these things? It seemed incredible.

The minutes seemed to drag terribly, he hated the stuffy, stale smell, the feeling that the place had not been cleaned for years—and even then cleaned insufficiently. He dared not go too near the window for fear Max might pass and see him, thought it was not particularly likely that even if Max looked he would be able to see through the filthy window.

He looked at his watch. Hindes had been gone nearly a quarter of an hour. Charles moved restlessly. Then the door opened, and Hindes entered, his face wreathed in smiles.

' 'E's gorne, mister. 'ad a taxi waiting dahn the street, walked off an' drove orf. Nah, listen, mister. W'en I got in there, 'im —this swell cove—was talkin' with square 'ead. Confidential like. I 'ung abart, read adverts fer patent pills and so on. Onct the kemist lukes at me, raisin' 'is eyebrows. I shakes me Uncle Ned as if what I gotter say was suthink private, like. You know, like as if I'd got meself in a spot of bother, see?

'I still goes on moochin' abart, but 'ave I got me ears proper skinned?—I'll say I 'ave. The toff says, "It won't kill 'im?" The other 'un shakes 'is 'ead. Now listen, guv'nor—— "Not it," he says, "for twenty-four hours il 'ul make 'im very full o' the joy of spring." I can't give you 'is exact lingo, but this is the meanin'. "After twenty-four hours, 'e won't feel so good. Keep 'im warm, put 'im ter bed, light nourishing grub, an' he'll be on topper the flaming world. See, mister?" Then 'e 'ands over a bottle, not all thet big, an' the swell thanks 'im and money parses but 'ow much I couldn't see. The toff asks a lot o' other questions, which I never 'eard, an' keeps noddin' his Uncle Ned. Then he slings 'is 'ook. Ñar, whatcher mike o' thet, mister? Want me ter tell yer? That toff is backin' one o' these fighting lads. Wants sumthin' ter put exter ginger inter 'im for the fight. Never mind if the bloke's proper laid out after a day, like as not 'e'll 'ave won a nice purse, an' this toff 'ul 'ave 'is rake off of it. W'en 'e'd gorne, I told the ole 'un as I'd 'ad colic for three days. So 'e gives me some muck in a bottle, which 'ul go dahn the sink! Nah, 'ave I done orlright?'

'You've done splendidly, Hindes, and I'm grateful.' Charles handed him a ten-shilling note. 'Have a drink with me.'

'Coo! Best day's work I've done fer donkey's years. Mister, you're not a copper's nark, or from the Yard nor anythink like thet?'

Charles looked at the shabby undersized man, and wondered —as he had done before—what kept the grist rolling into Mr. Joseph Hindes's small and distinctly scruffy mill.

He shook his head. 'No,' he said, 'I used to be an auctioneer in Lancashire, now—only this morning—I've been taken into a business—well, in the same line as your own.'

'Gerron! W'eers it sitiated? Good business?'

'Bond Street.'

'Coo! Some clarse thet. Well, I 'ope you do orlright. Anytime I've anythink spechul, I'll send yer a line. What's the ad-ress?'

'Send it to my home address—there it is on this card.'

'Blimey! Gor' luv uz! You one o' thet fam'ly? I onct saw the old gennelman. I was doin' a bit o' porterin' at the time—it was afore I went inter business on me own. 'E was like suthink outer a play—'andsome, mind yer. It weer a proper lesson ter 'ear 'im biddin'. Calm, biddin' 'underds an' 'underds of pahnds, easy as you or me'd bid for a mixed lot on a ole tin tray. Well, it bin an afternoon. Good luck, an' allus glad ter oblige. Bettcher I'm rite abart thet bloke an' the big fight! S'long.'

Charles walked away, thinking, 'And I'll bet you you're wrong, my friend. Master Max is going to be watched very carefully over this week-end—and I'm the bloke who'll do the watching!'

Later he called on Bill Gollantz, who gave him a hand as large as a small ham, and then went through the proposed agreement line by line, glancing up from time to time to ask, 'That quite clear? Good!'

The reading over, he leaned back in his chair, and said, 'That's the lot then. Both Emmanuel and I dislike long, involved documents of any kind. If anyone shows me an agreement as long as a three-volume novel, I always think, "Hello, hello! I'll lay any money there's a twist in it!" Now all you've got to do is sign on the dotted line, I'll get my secretary in to witness it.'

That done, he leaned back in his chair again and said, 'Care for a drink—not too early, eh?'

He rolled over to a very fine corner cupboard—Charles wondered if all these people had corner cupboards in their offices which held numerous bottles and a stock of admirable glasses of all sizes—and returned with two splendid old tumblers.

'Here's to crime,' Bill toasted.

Charles asked, 'Do you know anything about boxing, sir?'

'Boxing? Good Gad, I barely know a fly-weight from a heavy-weight. I've been to a few fights—y'know, those big affairs when we're mugs enough to pay some fantastic price for a seat and the fight ends in the second round—that's about all. Why?'

'I just wondered. Actually I wondered if you'd ever heard Max mention boxing,' Charles said.

'I've rarely heard Max mention anything,' Bill answered. 'That young man and I are not exactly what you might call buddies. I shall be damned glad when he clears off to the United States. He's going quite soon I believe. He told me that he didn't bet, but he's going down to see Viva's horse run. I don't know that I shall, though I've got something on him of course. Well, I'm glad that bit of business is settled. Emmanuel's as pleased as punch about it. Doesn't say much, but I can tell by his way of speaking. Good luck, Charles. Glad to have you in the family. Wish we had a few of the other members out of it. Good-bye, m'boy.'

On Saturday afternoon he drove Rose to Ordingly. The day was fine, and to Charles, driving along the familiar road, it seemed like going home. Once or twice Rose cried that there were primroses blooming on this or that bank, that she could see the buds in the hedges ready to burst into leaf. The sky was high and clear, the blue was still cold, and the few great white clouds sailed across it slowly, in a kind of splendid majesty. Curiously enough, in their whiteness they looked less cold than the rather pallid blue of the sky.

Charles sniffed with appreciation. There was something in the clear air which made him feel excited, filled with hope, even certainty. That morning he had received a letter from Maria, that letter which now rested in his inside pocket and which had already been read twenty times. It had brought her nearer to him ; he had felt as he read it that he could hear her voice, so gentle and so musical. She told him that she was writing immediately after she had seen his aeroplane leave Malpensa. She had at once driven home and sat down to write to him.

You are in my heart, Carlo, she wrote. *Now I shall tell you my plan—it is wonderful, but may appear to be bold. For this I do not care. I understand you too well to imagine that you will think unfavourably of me when what I write is only to attempt to secure our happiness. My father goes to New York, I go to Paris to my darling aunt. This is when you must come to Paris to see me. We shall talk and make arrangements—for what, you ask?—for our marriage! I am of age, I have my own money left to me by my sweet mother. My uncle is very important, a diplomat, and he must have our confidence. He is not—as I admit that my father is—materialistic, but he is idealistic and romantic. I shall write to you constantly, and you must write to me as frequently as your work allows. If we have real love in our hearts, if we have faith in each other and unlimited trust, all will be well. I am lonely, but Iva and Paulo will do all they can to prevent my being so. Thoughts also of my Carlo will help me—never to forget, but always to remember. I send my love to you, and may God have you in His keeping always.—Maria.*

His heart sang when he remembered that letter, and now he was going to Ordingly, which he loved. How much he hoped that one day Maria would see it, and immediately love it as he did! He could imagine Lady Heriot saying, 'That's a pretty little gal you've got, Charlie,' Emmanuel watching Maria with quiet approval. Viva giving her a greeting which was warm and sincere, and Mum—dear Mum—would beam at Maria and say kind, trite, warm things, talking more and more broadly every moment, as she always did when she felt emotional.

He glanced at his mother, smiling. 'We're just about there!'

She smiled back at him. 'Charlie, luv, I never thought that you and me would be driving, in what you might call a familiar way, to places like this. But then, everything seems to have changed all of a sudden. It's as if Aladdin had rubbed his magic lamp, isn't it?'

'You keep tight hold of that lamp, darling,' he warned her, 'for after all this is every bit due to you and your dear North Country common sense!'

12

It was pleasant to be back at Ordingly. The spring was early, and the flower-beds were filled with flowers—hyacinths, tulips stiff and upright like well-drilled soldiers, and bright-hued crocuses, and the varied brilliant colours of anemones. The trees were bursting into leaf, and the grass had lost its sad grey-green of winter, and was regaining its brilliant hue. Charles knew that in the woods the primroses would be out, and sheltering under their broad leaves the sweet-scented violets which Viva loved. The catkins, too, would be hanging like lambs' tails, giving promise that spring was really asserting herself. He promised himself that tomorrow he would walk in the woods ,to revel in the sweet damp smell of decaying leaves, and watch the birds wildly busy with their nest-building, some of them perhaps already in residence and even sitting on their first clutch of eggs.

There was excitement in the air. Viva—her eyes shining—said that Hereward was in splendid fettle, that Andy Miller expressed himself as satisfied, and that Calft—the jockey who was to ride him—had stated that the Calmering was virtually 'in the bag'.

Charles asked, 'And White Knight, how is he? Do you suppose that he feels a little jealous of all the fuss over Hereward?'

'White Knight jealous! No, rather not. He's too fond of Hereward. You'll see, he'll almost burst with pride when he wins. He's a grand character my White Knight.'

Max came in, looking very handsome and wonderfully tanned by the Swiss sunshine. He greeted Rose politely, nodded in a slightly patronizing fashion to Charles, then sat down and stared at Viva intently. As Charles watched him, he felt once again that feeling of apprehension and discomfort. He wished the fellow would take his eyes away from Viva, she surely must sense that he watched her every movement.

Rose asked when they were going to see the horses. Viva replied that it was too late, Andy liked them to keep early hours.

'We can't go after luncheon tomorrow either,' she added, 'we're all bidden to "Buster" Carteret's place. He's taken a house not far from here, and this is a kind of house-warming. I think it's a hideous place, but "Buster" insists that the central heating, lighting, and all other amenities, are the most modern possible and quite perfect. Old "Buster" loves his comfort, bless him!'

'When shall we be admitted to the stables?' Max asked. It was the first time he had spoken since he came in, except for his brief and formal greeting to Rose, and Charles fancied that he caught a note of sharpness in his tone; then told himself not to let his imagination run away with him, he was growing fanciful.

'We all go on Monday and see them start. By dint of what I am convinced is a tremendous wangle, "Buster" and Miller have contrived to get sufficient petrol for the horse-box. I asked "Buster" how they'd managed it, and he said, a trifle rudely I felt, that people who asked no questions were told no lies. When I asked Miller he screwed up his eyes, scraped his chin and asked if I'd put the question to "Buster"—only, of course, he said "The Major". I told him what "Buster" had answered. He nodded and informed me that he had a great opinion of "the Major's 'eadpiece," adding, "If 'e thinks it's wise ter keep a still tongue —'oo am I ter go agean 'im?" and there the matter dropped.'

'They say there are tricks in all trades,' Rose said. Max turned his eyes from Viva for a second to stare at Rose, as if her cliché had not only hurt but astonished him.

Viva laughed. 'Rose dear, what a very unoriginal remark!'

'But I never pretend to be original,' Rose replied. 'I leave that for cleverer people than me! Anyway, there's a lot of truth in some of those old sayings let me tell you.'

Emmanuel had caught the tail-end of the conversation, and he came forward, smiling. 'I hope that Charles here will pick up the various tricks of the trade at the Galleries,' he said.

'There aren't any tricks to pick up!' Viva said defensively.

Emmanuel put his arm round her shoulder. 'Only one really, my sweet. To learn how hard can you work, and then learn to work even harder! Charles, would you give me a drink? I've been doing a little overtime, pottering about a ver-ry dusty old manor house, wondering why on earth I was wasting my time so. Oh, virtue had its own r-reward,' he winked at Rose, 'and I did find a couple of things—the sale is on Monday. Shall I send Charles to buy them for us?'

'Could he get to Calmering in time for the race on Tuesday?' Viva asked.

With mock severity Emmanuel answered, 'My dear Viva, as one of the junior partners of Gollantz's Charles must learn to put them first, even before the opportunity of seeing Hereward win this gr-reat r-race.'

Charles saw Max watching Emmanuel as he spoke, his face wearing an expression which was almost one of smug satisfaction. He was not actually smiling, but he was watching and listening with intense attention.

Rose Watson said, 'Well, of course, Emmanuel, Charlie knows that. He'd always put business first, you don't need to tell him.'

Viva laughed, saying, 'Oh, you old fraud, you! Adopting that—Mr. Murdstone attitude. I don't expect these "couple of things" are of any great importance!'

Emmanuel nodded. 'Nothing of any importance—a pair of Adam china cabinets—black and gilt——'

'Hideous!' Viva breathed.

Emmanuel raised his hand, enjoining silence. 'And a walnut and gesso table. There were also a couple of Famille Rose vases with covers—nothing really!'

'Then if they're important send someone more—educated—in these things than Charles. He's been used to selling, not buying! Emmanuel, you're an old spoil sport! Anyway, I don't believe you!'

He turned and faced her, his charming smile lighting up his face. 'How easy it is to deceive you, Viva dear! I begin to r-realize that if I planned to live a life which was ir-regular, you would always believe me if I said that I had been kept late at the Galleries.'

Viva shrugged her shoulders, and said to Rose, 'There you

see! He actually boasts that he could deceive me—callous monster!' Then to Emmanuel, 'Who will go to buy these fabulous things?'

'Simeon, my dearest. It's not too far from London, and he can get there and back easily. He says that—at the moment—Calmering is just a little too far for him, though Daphne—thank God—is very well.'

She smiled and laid her hands on his. 'Old fraud that you are! But I saw through you!'

'So you, Max, Charles and I—Rose, Lady Heriot is calling for you—will go and greet the conquering hero. You know that you'll have to lead him in, Viva.'

'I shall be terrified!'

They all lunched the next day with 'Buster' Carteret. It was, as Viva had said, a hideous house, built in the most dreadful late Victorian tradition. It had turrets and balconies which looked as if they were insecurely pinned on to the main building. The rooms were large, and well proportioned, though as 'Buster' Carteret pointed out, 'I've torn down acres of varnished pitch pine, and blotted out quite a few hideously painted ceilings. Still, the gardens are nice—or they will be once we get fairly started.'

As usual the conversation was of Hereward. His price, it appeared, had shortened. 'Aren't you glad we all put our money on early?' 'Buster' Carteret asked. 'I don't know what price you got, Viva, but I got in when he was standing at forties. Last night they were offering three to one! We'll show 'em!'

He was a big, rather boisterous man, with a face the colour of beetroot, and a very bright pair of blue eyes. There was something about him which made Charles feel that he could be trusted anywhere or with anything. He had learnt, through Simeon, that when Viva's second husband—'Toby' Tatten—had been killed in a riding accident, that he had been taken to 'Buster' Carteret's house, and later—months later—Carteret had wanted Viva to marry him. He wondered if he was still in love with her ; if so he didn't show it. He treated her in a rather 'hail fellow well met' fashion—warm, friendly, but utterly unsentimental.

Viva said, 'Some of your furniture's awful, "Buster".'

'I know. I'm waiting for Hereward to bring me in a packet,

then I'll go to Emmanuel on my knees and ask him to refurnish the whole place for me.'

She made a gesture of horror. '"Buster!" He'd fill your house with old oak, and Florentine beds, with Adam cabinets in black and gold, and masses of Chippendale. Not your style, "Buster". You'd be miserable in it.'

Emmanuel said to Charles, 'There you see, do you wonder that I hover on the edge of the bread line, when my wife is so disloyal that in cold blood she deprives me of an excellent client? "Buster" knows nothing about furniture, and I could have unloaded a great many things which have offended me for years.'

'I might even have persuaded my friend in Clerkenwell to part with what he calls his "Almer Taddermer" for a pound or two, and you could have made a heavy profit,' Charles said.

Max asked sharply, 'Who is your friend in—what did you say?—Clerkenwell?'

'Friend of mine who keeps a—well, not to put too fine a point on it—a junk shop.' He turned back to Emmanuel. 'He asked me what I did for a living. I told him that I'd just signed on to work in a business similar to his own.'

'So it will be ver-ry soon, if my wife keeps on—what is the expression?—queering my pitch with possible clients,' Emmanuel answered.

Charles glanced at Max. He had startled him. It had not been premeditated, but the name of Clerkenwell had obviously made him nervous. He wondered if Max had ever seen Joe Hindes's shop, and if so did he realize how close it was to his foreign chemist's?

Charles remembered his step-father—Thomas Watson—had once said to him, 'Don't pull your punches, lad, when you've got to punch; but never 'ustle yer 'orses.' He wouldn't hustle his horses now, but he'd watch and wait. Up to now he had nothing to go on, nothing on which he could base his conviction that Max was waiting to 'get back' at someone—someone in the family, of that Charles felt certain.

The next morning, a bright sunny morning, with just a faint hint of frost in the air, they went round in a body to the stables. The big motor-driven horse-box was already waiting, and little Andy Miller was fussing about, full of importance, energy and efficiency.

''Mornin' m'lady. 'Mornin', Mrs. Watson. 'Ow are you all? This is a grand mornin'. Just suits 'im an' White Knight. Never seen either of 'em in better fettle. Picktures they luke, both on 'em. Tom Willis is ridin' White Knight, as you know, m'lady. It's 'is first big race. 'E's like a kid goin' ter a party is Tom. Yes, carrots is ready, washed 'em meself. Just little 'uns they are.'

They followed him into the stables. There stood the white enamelled bowl with the freshly scrubbed carrots. Max looked at them, and then said, 'By jove, they surely are little ones!'

'They suit my purpose, sir,' Miller said.

The sweet, rather heavy atmosphere of the big loose box seemed to envelop them. Viva's cheeks were shining, her eyes bright with excitement. She slipped her arm over Hereward's neck, and he turned his great affectionate eyes towards her. She offered him a carrot, and he took it, nuzzling his soft nose against her hand.

'Oh, you beauty,' she whispered, 'you're going to do wonders!'

'I must go and see White Knight,' she told Miller. 'After all he's going to immolate himself on the altar of friendship.'

Miller answered that he didn't doubt it, and added that White Knight was a fine old 'oss if ever he'd seen one. Together they walked into the next loose box. Max called to know if he might give Hereward a carrot, and Miller replied in the surly voice which he always used when speaking to Max, 'Aye—gie' 'im two if they're reit little 'uns.'

Max walked over to Hereward, and Charles knew in some indefinable way that this was the culmination of everything, the crystallization of his fear, doubts and speculations. How was he to stop Max giving anything to Hereward? As his mind sought wildly for a plan, there was Max already offering the carrot to Hereward. Charles saw that he had taken it not from the bowl which Miller had placed ready, but from his coat-pocket.

He was not very courageous about feeding it to the horse, and Hereward took it without any great eagerness, rolling up his soft pink lip and baring his big teeth, then taking it delicately and nibbling it.

Charles felt panic-stricken. 'Do something you silly brainless fool,' he urged himself; then walked swiftly over to where Max stood, already putting his hand in his pocket for a second carrot.

Very smoothly Charles slipped his hand into the pocket, and extracting the carrot, began to eat it with every sign of enjoyment. Max spun round, 'What the hell do you think you're doing?' he demanded.

Charles, chewing valiantly—he loathed carrots in any form—grinned, 'It's no good, I can't resist them! The very sight of them so pink and well scrubbed makes my mouth water. Get him another from the bowl there—Miller said that you could!'

Max scowled, but behind his scowl Charles fancied that he detected uneasiness, even fear. He looked white round the nostrils.

'Just tell me what the devil you think you're playing at?' Max demanded. 'What right have you to go diving into my pocket? I guess you've been brought up in a queer way!'

Charles finished his carrot. It had tasted all right, perhaps he had been alarming himself unduly. He grinned again. 'I'll get you another, if you're disappointed,' he said, and walking over to the bowl brought back a carrot and offered it to Max.

'Disappointed be damned,' Max said, pushing away his outstretched hand. 'I'm annoyed at your blasted impertinence! Sticking your hand into my pocket. The first time I saw you I knew that your ideas about decent manners were pretty strange. Coming here, worming your way into the family, claiming to be—a Gollantz! I'll tell you frankly, I've never been taken in by you! That fat old horror, Bill, may have been, but I'm a bit smarter than he is. Yes, sir, I'll say that I am!'

Charles nodded. 'Now we know all about it, eh?'

'You know nothing yet! Gosh, you will before I've finished though, that I will swear.'

'Good! I shall be interested. But leave it for the moment, you've done quite a lot of swearing in a small way. I shall hope to hear some new and original words when you—unmask me. That's the expression, isn't it?'

'You bloody little upstart!' Max almost spat at him, and walked out. They watched the two horses safely boxed, rugged to their eyes, which looked out through the holes in their cloths, mild, unafraid, even interested.

Emmanuel said, 'They look like members of the Ku-Klux-Klan, don't they?'

Miller touched the enormous cap which he wore, saying, 'Get in, Tom lad. 'Ope ter see you ter-morrer m'lady, an' you too, Sir Emmanuel. Like that poem we was learnt at school, it 'ul be a "famous victory".'

'I'll come straight to you when we get to the course, Miller. Good luck to you—all four!' Viva said. The door was closed, and the great horse-box began to move slowly away. She said, 'Don't watch it out of sight—it's desperately unlucky! Where's Max?'

'I think he went back to the house.'

'I don't believe he is really interested in racing,' Viva said. 'He likes horses quite well—to ride for his own pleasure, but he isn't a bit interested in the training and those hundred and one things which absorb people like Andy and Tom Willis—and me, for that matter.'

That evening Charles thought he had rarely felt in such good spirits. There was a great element of relief to account for it. After all, Hereward had only eaten one carrot, and he appeared to be quite all right when he walked so delicately and calmly into the horse-box. If Hereward was all right, if Charles himself felt in splendid form, it might be possible that the whole plan had miscarried—that the chemist had funked giving Max the stuff. Max himself had never mentioned a horse, and had been very 'cagey' with his talk of prize-rings and the like, so it was possible that something had gone wrong somewhere with his plans.

They left early the next morning for Calmering. Max was driving down in his own car, and Emmanuel, "The industrious apprentice"—as Viva called him—left for London and promised to join them on the course. Rose was going with Lady Heriot, who called for her in her massive and exceedingly comfortable car. Charles was going with Viva.

The day was fine and the sky clear; there was a hint of hoar frost on the grass, but the ground was dry. Viva, muffled in a great fur coat and wearing a very smart small hat, looked excited. Lady Heriot was full of good spirits. 'Lovely day, Charlie, for the gee-gees—Hereward likes this kind of going. Got plenty on him, Charlie? He won't go down, but if he does—well, bang goes Auntie Flo's shirt! Now, Viva, keep smiling! Calft's a good jock, and he doesn't fan too much.'

In the car Viva turned to Charles, smiling a little ruefully.

'I'm not too good at quotations, but one comes to my mind now—"O that a man might know the end of this day's doings".'

He smiled back at her. '"But it sufficeth that the end will come, and then the end is known."'

It occurred to him that suddenly he was not feeling as well as he had done; his head felt a little giddy, his legs seemed to have become weak. He tried to put the idea firmly away from him, to assure himself that he was growing nervous and imagining things. He was all right—of course he was all right. He pulled out his handkerchief and wiped his forehead.

Viva said, 'Poor Charles, I believe you're as nervous as I am. I've had butterflies in my tummy for the last three days. Whew!' She lit a cigarette, and almost immediately stubbed it out in the ash-tray, saying, 'The damned thing tastes like straw!'

'I wonder,' she said reflectively, 'if we all take things too seriously. Do you think we do?'

'I don't think it's much use going in for anything—whether it's business or horse-racing, if you don't take it seriously. And when it comes to other things—like love and loyalties, well, they must be taken seriously otherwise—well, it shows that they just don't matter to you.'

'Have you ever been in love, Charles?' she asked.

He managed to grin, though he realized that he was feeling worse every minute. 'When I first came to Ordingly I had the cheek to think that I was in love with you.' He felt he was talking very rapidly, and speaking in an unusual voice. He wondered if, feeling so ill, he was a little feverish and light-headed.

He heard Viva say, her voice coming from a great distance, 'Charles, really? I'm flattered. I'm old enough to be your mother! And then——?'

'When I went to Milan, I met someone—and knew that I should never love anyone else as much as I love her. She's beautiful, and she's as good and intelligent as she is beautiful. Soon she's going to stay in Paris while her father is in America. She'll be staying with her aunt, who's a countess—de Brissac. I'm going over if Emmanuel will give me a few days' leave, and we're going to be married.'

He stopped suddenly like a clock-work toy which has run down, and Viva exclaimed, 'But how romantic! Is she of age?'

He nodded, then said, 'Could the car stop for a minute? I'm afraid that I'm going to be sick. Please forgive me.'

He managed to get out and to stagger to the grass verge, where he was more violently sick than he had ever been in his life. He felt that a violent quarrel was in progress between his stomach and the rest of the universe. At last it was over, leaving the cold sweat running down his face and his whole body trembling. He stumbled back to the car, and dropped into his seat. His eyes closed and he was too spent to open them again.

He felt something cold against his lips, heard Viva saying, 'Try to drink some of this—it will help to pull you round.' He opened his eyes by a great effort and saw her hand holding a silver flask cup to his mouth. He sipped and felt the liquid run down his throat, hot, strong and reviving.

'Once more,' she said, 'yes, make an effort, Charles.'

Again he sipped, and then very gently pushed her hand away. 'No more, please. I'm so sorry. How disgusting! I'm ashamed.'

'Rubbish—that's the kind of thing no one can help. Now, lean back, close your eyes, and rest until we get to Calmering.'

He fancied that he did sleep, for the next thing he heard was Viva's voice, saying, 'You'll have to wake up, my dear. We're just driving in. Or will you stay here and get some more rest?'

'No, no,' he protested urgently. 'I want to see Hereward. That's important. I'll manage. I may look as if I'm tight, but I'll manage.'

The car had barely stopped when Emmanuel stepped forward to greet them. His face was grave with anxiety. He was always pale, but now his face seemed drained of all colour, his lips were set into a thin line.

He said, 'Viva, my dear, I've bad news for you. Hereward can't run.'

'Can't run!' she exclaimed sharply. 'Is he lame? He was all

right yesterday. What is it, Emmanuel, tell me?'

'They don't know. Miller says that he was in great fettle yesterday, really didn't mind the journey a little bit. Then this morning he seemed—Miller says—"hangy"—now—well, come and see him.'

She called back over her shoulder, 'Sure that you can manage, Charles? Right, follow us,' and walked off at Emmanuel's side, moving very rapidly. Charles got out, feeling that his legs were giving at the knees. Emmanuel's chauffeur, standing by the door, asked if he could manage.

'Yes, I'll manage, thanks.'

'Bad news, sir, eh? Her ladyship's powerfully fond of that Hereward. She'd set her heart on him winning this race. Terrible luck for her.'

As Charles made his way to the loose boxes he knew people stared at him, for his course was far from steady and the sweat was pouring from him with the effort he was making. The smell of trampled turf rose to his nostrils; he could hear the raucous voices of the bookmakers as they chanted their prices. There was a subdued chorus of 'Race card, Race card', and another of, 'Mark yer card, sir, mark yer card. Four dead certs ter-day—mark yer card. 'Arf a doller, 'arf a doller, mark yer card.'

Once Charles cannoned into a tall man, who turned on him furiously.

'Damme, can't you see where you're going? You're drunk, man. No right to be here, go and sleep it off.'

Charles said miserably, 'I'm sorry, I beg your pardon. I'm not tight, I swear—I'm ill.'

'Then you should go home and go to bed, damme!'

Tom Willis, the stable-lad who was to ride White Knight, saw Charles and hurried to meet him. Charles scarcely recognized him wearing a big loose tweed coat over his silk jacket and neat breeches.

Tom said, 'Oh, Mr. Charles, isn't it 'orrid? Mr. Miller swears as Hereward's been nobbled. 'Oo could have done it? You're not looking too good, Mr. Charles, kinder green in the face. I'll show you where they're with Hereward.'

Hereward stood with his head hanging, his forelegs splayed out a little, his beautiful satin coat stained with sweat. Viva had her arm round his neck, and her face buried against him. Charles knew she was crying.

Calft, Hereward's jockey, stood watching, his wizened little face twisted with anxiety. He said to Miller in a hoarse whisper, 'If you ask me that horse has been —got at!'

'That's what the vet thinks, and it's what I think. It's plain as the nose on yer face, but 'oo done it! I slept in the stable with him last night, straight I did. There's only me and Tom bin near 'im.'

Viva raised her head, and frankly and openly wiped her eyes. She turned to a tall, horsey-looking man who stood watching Hereward very keenly.

'He can't run, can he?' she asked.

'No, Lady Gollantz, it's all the poor devil can do to stand.'

'He won't die, will he?' Charles heard the catch in her voice.

'I don't think he'll die, in fact I'm pretty certain he won't. The trouble is we don't know exactly what has been given to him. That there has been some dirty work I'm convinced. You're running another horse, aren't you?'

'White Knight. Hereward always runs better if White Knight's with him.'

'I've known several cases like that,' the veterinary surgeon said. 'Buddies, eh? What does White Knight stand at, Miller?'

'Any chance, think you?'

'Twenties—along with Son of the Sea and Druid.'

'He'll put up a good show, plenty o' guts 'as White Knight, but a win'—Miller scraped his chin and looked dubious—'doubt it, sir.'

'Umph.' He was looking at Hereward's eyes, his lips pursed. 'I believe he's on the mend. Eyes clearer. Keep him well rugged up. Let him sweat this damned thing out. Later on try him with gruel—as warm as he'll take it. I'll come back later.' He nodded sympathetically to Viva, muttered that it was a 'damned shame' and left them.

Charles spoke to Miller. 'Has he been sick?'

'Thank God 'e 'asn't, Mr. Charles. It's bart t' finish if you 'ave 'osses spewing 'oop. You're not looking so good yourself, Mr. Charles. Anythink wrong?'

Charles, whose head was aching intolerably, who felt that the ground under his feet was gently rising and falling, as if his eyes were burning and filled with sand, nodded.

'I'm feeling rotten,' he said.

'What is it—nasty bilious attack?'

Charles managed a miserable grin. 'If Hereward could talk he might be able to tell you.'

Miller shot a quick glance at him, and when he spoke his voice had taken on a new edge. 'That's wot I b'lieve they calls a cryptic remark. Oh, well, we'll get round to it later. Hope you've got place money on White Knight—he'll do us all proud!'

He went off to fuss gently round Hereward, cursing softly as he did so. Viva and Emmanuel returned to Charles, who was leaning up against the wall, his face a chalky green.

'Still feeling awful, Charles?' she asked.

'It comes in waves,' he said. 'Almost like seasickness.'

Emmanuel, looking grim, and speaking very quietly said, 'As soon as the race is over we'll get off, I think. Viva, tell him about Calft.'

'He won't ride White Knight, says that little Willis is entitled to his chance. He won't take his fee either. Isn't that rather wonderful of him? Oh, he may have made plenty of money, but not many people willingly forgo their fees. When he was talking to us little Willis was standing there, his lip trembling, his eyes like those of an anxious dog. There's Miller going over to give him instructions now. I'm going to see how my poor Hereward is. Oh, what a damnabe shame it all is!'

Miller was standing talking confidentially and impressively to the young jockey. Tom was listening with concentrated attention.

'You can trust 'im,' Miller was saying, ' 'e's got a 'eart as big as a bullock's. Now, pay attention. Don't fan 'im. Keep yer whale bone quiet—maybe just at the finish, one crack with it—not before. Don't try ter get away wi' a big burst, nurse 'im a bit, then let 'im 'ave 'is 'ead. Don't try to ride for a win—it won't come off. Ride for a place, sitha? A place 'ul do uz all very well. Think on, you've got 'ands, an' knees—use 'em. An' mind Roman Pride—or mind his jockey. I know 'im same as wot a good few more does. Keep away from 'im, or 'e'll 'ave you crowded on to the rails. 'E's crafty. Now, 'ave you got it all, Tom lad?'

'I think so, thank you, Mr. Miller. Will you be there at the finish?'

'O' course I shall, lad. Good luck. No fanning, and mind Roman Pride.'

Viva came out from Hereward's loose box, and laid her hand on Charles's arm. 'He is a little bit better. The veterinary surgeon's pleased with him. Can you face walking down with us to see them start?'

'I think so, only don't be surprised if people eye me coldly, they'll probably think that I'm a drunk.'

Emmanuel growled, 'Let them keep their thoughts to themselves. Gad, there's Max!'

Max saw them and strolled over to meet them. 'This is pleasant! I was delayed And how's the great Hereward?'

'Scratched,' Emmanuel said. 'He was as fit as a fiddle yesterday, but couldn't have run today to save his life. It's Miller's opinion that he's been tampered with. Tom Willis is riding Viva's second string, sporting her alternative colours. They're going down now—can you manage it, Charles?'

Max said sharply, 'What's wrong with Charles? Gosh, he doesn't look too good.'

'For the best r-reason imaginable,' Emmanuel said; 'he isn't feeling too good. All r-right, Max, see you later.'

As they walked down, watching the lovely string of horses, with their little jockeys sitting so easily, their silk jackets billowing in the faint breeze, Charles thought that never again would he be able to enjoy the scent of bruised and trampled turf. The voices of the bookmakers, which he had always found, on his rare visits to a race-course, thrilling and exciting, now fell on his ear as raucous and ugly, the cries of 'Mark yer card, mark yer card!' seemed to go through his aching head like a pneumatic drill. His feet felt as if they were obliged to move incredibly heavy weights with every step he took. He was cold and yet his shirt felt sticky with sweat.

The horses were mincing their way towards the starting-gate, most of them looking slightly supercilious, though Roman Pride was inclined to resent being there at all, and it was obvious that he was going to give trouble at the starting-post. Tom Willis, on White Knight, saw Viva's eager face and raised his whip to the peak of his maroon and fawn cap. She said, as he passed, 'Good luck, Tom ; good luck, White Knight.'

Tom nodded. 'Both on uz 'ull do our best, m'lady.'

There was some trouble at the starting-post. Roman Pride seemed determined to swing round and rush back to his stable ; a big raking chestnut—Forest Glade—flung up his head, showing his huge strong teeth. At last, it seemed to Charles after an eternity, they were off. Roman Pride got off in a fine burst, Forest Glade settled down to a steady controlled turn of speed, and White Knight was lying back, with a huddle of other horses, but always moving steadily up.

Viva said, 'Now the grandstand—can you manage it, Charles?'

He nodded. 'I *will* manage it.' The walk across the few yards of grass seemed to be miles long, but at last they were there. He heard Lady Heriot's voice, then his mother's, and sank down on to a seat, trying to look as if all his interest was centred on the race.

Lady Heriot was saying, 'Damn' shame about Hereward—think some cad got at him? Shocking! But look, look—that gee-gee of yours is creeping up. If you ask me the favourite's beat! I've always noticed Harrap gets off with too much of a burst at the gate, and his mount tuckered out before the finish. Look—here they come. Good old White Knight!—Forest Glade's just a little too fast for him—he'll make a place though, all right. That jockey—we'll hear of him again—he's riding, that's what he's doing—head and hands. By God! White Knight's lying second—it's neck and neck with Forest Glade Forest's gaining—a little—nothing much to it—another half-dozen lengths. It 'ul be a photo finish. If White Knight's second, it's only by a nose—practically nothing!'

Charles heard the shouts of the crowd, closed his eyes, and after a long, blank darkness, heard Emmanuel saying, 'Photo finish—Forest Glade first by half a head—capital lad that Willis. Now Charles, come along to the car. Bed's the best place for you—you coming, Rose? I can send you both back to Ordingly for the night.'

'Kind of you, Emmanuel, but if Charlie's poorly I'd rather he came back to the flat. Whatever is it, Charlie?'

Charles muttered that he didn't know, while Emmanuel—his face looking most unusually grim—answered for him.

'That, R-rose, is what we are going to find out when Charles can bear to answer a few questions. Now can you manage?—Sure? Then Watkins will drive you home, and I'll go with Viva. We'll telephone as soon as we get to Ordingly. Thank you, Charles—I know Viva will be grateful.'

Charles managed to smile. 'For what? For making myself a damned nuisance, and doing no good whatever?'

Emmanuel replied, very drily, 'Well, at least both you and Hereward are alive. Good-bye, R-rose.'

13

Charles lay in bed, and with all his mother's kindness and attention he felt lonely and abandoned. He longed for June, when he might get a few days' leave and join Maria, when they could make plans and be married. It seemed to him that his love for her absorbed him, despite the nightmare of the race-meeting, the disaster which had befallen Hereward, and his own desperate sickness, incidents which seemed to recur to him with horrid vividness, waking him from uneasy sleep and causing his dreadful headaches to come back with renewed fury.

Then there was the problem of Max. He had seen the grim expression on Emmanuel's face, and knew that he was determined to sift this thing to its depths. Emmanuel was a gentle person, full of kindliness, but Charles had realized that he could be adamant when it came to a question of principles. He could imagine Emmanuel, seated at his desk, his pale, handsome face a mask, probing, asking questions, sending back quick replies, and slowly stripping the whole thing down to bare facts.

Charles could imagine himself listening—provided that Charles told all that he knew—and finally saying, 'And now, tell me what motive Max could possibly have? Many years ago I learnt that question from Dickens in *David Copperfield*. You have r-read it? Naturally. I r-remember Mr. Wickfield asking the ador-rable Betsey Trotwood, "And what is the motive, Miss Tr-rotwood? There is always a motive." Now, what is the motive here?'

It was almost impossible to say that Max was—or imagined himself to be—in love with Viva, to recount the incident in the conservatory, which inadvertently Charles had seen and heard. Anyway, he didn't want to get any revenge on Max, he didn't care sufficiently. He did not like Max Gollantz, but he scarcely found it possible to hate him for the sneers and the imputations which he had uttered. In fact, if you came to think of it, there was something almost amusing about it all. Max, the illegitimate son, sneering at, patronizing the legal son of Julian and Rose. What did it all matter? He was accepted by the Gollantz family, he had a position which was sufficiently good and which with time would become even better. More, he had the future—with Maria. Then why disturb himself about Max and his sneers, insinuations and vague threats. He—Charles—was established, he liked Emmanuel—more, he had a profound admiration for him. They had accepted him—after proper investigations—and he had assured them that he had no wish to upset Max Gollantz's world. He had not done this from any sense of nobility, but from the conviction that these things—whether you were legitimate or illegitimate—were neither things for which you could take credit, nor for which you could be blamed.

He had been fortunate, his mother had seen that what she gave to Julian was made secure by 'marriage lines', and whatever might be the outcome of her association she had everything safeguarded.

He could imagine Rose, young and tremendously attractive, even her sound common sense serving to attract the sophisticated Julian. By the time she had realized that she was going to have a child, Julian was off to fresh fields. Charles could not imagine Rose adopting the attitude of the 'abandoned innocent'. She had gone on with her work, growing older, and being forced to take what offered, for the 'show girl', however attractive, could not hope to hold her own for ever. So from the chorus of 'No. 1' musical-comedy companies, she had taken less salary, less adulation, and had taken all those changes 'on the chin'.

He remembered how she had always insisted on his 'speaking nice'. He had gained a scholarship to the Grammar School, and she had engaged a tutor for additional lessons. Fortunately Charles had enjoyed learning, and had understood that if he were to become an auctioneer the fact that he spoke without a pronounced North Country accent would be an asset.

When she married Thomas Watson, he had entered wholeheartedly into the matter of Charles's education ; he had been a modest, efficient little man, and a great reader.

'Beats me,' he used to say, a book open on his knee, 'why

folks want ter be rooshin' about for new bukes. Ninety per cent on 'em have never even started on the classics.' He always spoke the word with a kind of reverence. ''Ow many have read Dickens, or Thackeray, or Trollope? As for George Eliot, or Jane Austen—if you mentioned them they'd just gawp! Shakespeare—there's a gold mine for you! Study 'im and you study 'uman nature, the whole world. Flowers—aye, I love flowers, but you cultivate 'em better if you 'ave cultivated your mind a bit. Oft times when I'm i' t' green-'ouse, I'll talk to t' flowers. Tell them a bit of Shakespeare, a line or two of Wordsworth, or Shelley, or Keats. Does 'em good, Charles, they *respond*.'

He hadn't an enemy in the world, Charles remembered. He had gone on in his quiet hard-working fashion, adoring his wife, being proud of his home, literally 'doing good'.

Now he lay wondering what course he should pursue. He could confide in Emmanuel, answer all his questions with complete frankness and truth, but what good would it all serve? Max was returning to America quite soon; apparently he had gathered together his stock of cosmetics which were to take the United States by storm. Charles sometimes wondered if they really existed, these cosmetics, or if they were figments of Max's imagination. Anyway, what did it matter? He was feeling better. Viva had telephoned that morning that Hereward was home together with the valorous White Knight, and they were both well.

'Perhaps Hereward is still just a little shaky, but nothing that a few days' rest won't put right, so Miller assures me. I saw them both this morning. Hereward—poor sweet—I felt was apologetic, but White Knight was modest and unassuming as ever.'

He himself would be up and about tomorrow. He thought, 'After all the beef tea and the amount of cosseting I've had I ought to be! I'll see Emmanuel, but what the devil is the use of stirring up more dissension, more dislike, more resentment? It's not as if they lived this side of the Atlantic, they don't! "All's well that ends well." The person who has suffered most is Viva, but the rest of us—well, we got place money, and it wasn't so bad. Not that the actual money matters so much, it was Viva's pride in her horse that was hurt, and Emmanuel who was made miserable by seeing her so wretched. No—let's forget all about it!

'I don't know that I can pull wool over Emmanuel's eyes though; I may give myself away more than I wish to, but I'll do my best.'

Then, with his last thoughts of his beautiful Maria, he slipped back into quiet, restful sleep.

The next morning he went to the Galleries. Although he did not feel quite himself again, and from time to time slight attacks of vertigo swept over him, the ghastly headache had gone, and he no longer felt the world rising and falling under his feet.

He walked slowly up Bond Street, realizing that he was enjoying everything as if he were seeing it all for the first time, that all the colours in the shop windows were brighter, fresher, than he had ever seen them. The masses of flowers in the shop in the arcade had never looked so lovely, so entrancing. In his pocket he carried Maria's letter which had come that morning. It gave him the assurance for which he always longed, that she loved him and waited impatiently for the time when they should meet in Paris. The thought of beginning a new life with her filled Charles's heart with joyous expectancy. He wanted to tell her about the events of the last few days, and knew instinctively that she would approve of his determination not to bring any definite charges—however well founded—against Max Gollantz.

It wasn't going to be easy to parry Emmanuel's questions; under his quiet exterior, Charles had always felt that his uncle could be adamant, and that the thought of anyone having indulged in anything which involved unhappiness for Viva, and danger to an animal for the sake of a personal wish for revenge, would meet with his firm and whole-hearted condemnation.

'He must have noticed that Max was sentimental about Viva,' Charles mused. 'I wonder that everyone didn't see it, the way the fellow never took his eyes off her. Perhaps he did. Emmanuel's neither unsentimental nor unimaginative, but I couldn't bring myself to tell him about that scene in the conservatory into which I stumbled. Viva knew that I'd heard Max's voice, and her's answering him, she knew why I cannoned into the flower-pot. If she'd felt it necessary she'd have told Emmanuel herself, and that would have shut the doors of Ordingly on Master Max for good and all. If Viva thought it better not to tell Emmanuel, then I think I have a right to keep my mouth shut, but I shall have to box very clever, and it's going to be very, very difficult.'

Hannah Rosenfeldt greeted him. 'Hope that you're better, Mr. Charles. What a lot of trouble. That race—the disappointment for Viva—for everyone. Sir Emmanuel said very little, in fact he almost declined to talk of it. We know that "a still tongue makes a glad heart", but I could see that there was not much gladness in his. He was upset about you. You're sure that you're fit to come to work, no?'

'I'm practically all right, thank you. Does Sir Emmanuel want to see me?'

She nodded. 'Immediately on your arrival, those were his words. And'—a smile slowly illuminated her plain face—'he added, "Also, a small favour, Hannah. Bring to my office some of your own coffee, made as you have taught me to like it best." So go to him, and I shall go and prepare the coffee already.'

Emmanuel rose when Charles entered. He held out his hand, and said, 'My dear Charles, I hope that you are completely recovered. I can never express the sorrow which Viva and I felt at your—indisposition. Not only sorrow, but a deep sense of humiliation. Sit down, Hannah is to bring us some of her own special coffee—which is very good indeed.'

Charles said, 'And Hereward?'

'Hereward is, I am glad to say, in admir-rable health. Miller says that in another week or ten days he should be back to his old form.'

'That's good!' Charles said, and waited for Emmanuel to open fire.

Emmanuel leaned back in his big chair, first drawing a writing-pad towards him, and laying a gold pencil beside it. He placed the tips of his fingers together as he often did when beginning an interview.

'First, I wish to make the position clear to you, Charles. I wish to get to the r-root of this business not because I am feeling angry that I lost money. I don't like to lose money, not solely owing to my Jewish blood—which one part of the family appears to r-regard as a disgr-raceful thing—but because only fools like to lose money.

'The expenses of the stables, the wages and so forth are not my concern, my wife is the sole owner.' He repeated, 'The sole owner. It gives her happiness, and it gives me happiness to see her happy.'

His keen eyes softened and he smiled gently.

Hannah Rosenfeldt entered with the expected coffee, and his smile widened. 'The ministering angel!' he said. 'Add to your kindness, please, by pouring it out for us. Mine—as if you didn't know—with no milk or sugar.'

'Indeed, and I ought to know when I remember that I've been telling you for years that it is bad for you, already! You lay up for yourself trouble with the liver each time you drink black coffee, and so black too!' she grumbled. 'But no doubt it is too late to reform you now. Charles——?'

'Milk and sugar please, Miss Rosenfeldt.'

'Ah!' she breathed approvingly. 'Please look at him, he has been ill—it might be dangerously——'

'No, not dangerously!' Charles protested.

She waved a fat hand enjoining silence. 'Here he is back, and is his face pale as parchment? Has all the colour left his cheeks? No, his skin is like the skin of young children—and he takes coffee with milk and sugar!' She stooped to pick up the tray on which the coffee-pot stood.

Emmanuel cried, 'Oh, Hannah, after that tirade, after covering me with shame because I am not young and handsome like Charles, leave the coffee-pot!'

'And allow you to continue to poison yourself! Such a year on me if I should do so! Charles—open the door for me—thank you.'

He went back to his chair to find Emmanuel laughing softly.

'What a character she is! And with a heart which is pure gold. Now, as I was saying, my r-reason for wishing to get to the bottom of this matter is not that I am angr-ry at losing money. I lost very little indeed. It was the loss of prestige to my wife, and her deep distress at the suffering of her beloved Hereward—and her natural anxiety r-regarding you. Now—Charles, tell me, have you any suspicions? Tell me fr-rankly.'

Charles frowned, then answered, 'Well, I may have—what

might be suspicions, but I'm not certain that they're not the outcome of a personal dislike, and possibly of wishful thinking.'

Emmanuel glanced at him keenly. 'Ah, personal dislike, eh? You're r-referring to Max, I presume?'

'I suppose so.'

'Yet you've behaved very well towards him. Both my brother Bill and I admire you for it.'

'Yes,' eagerly, 'but Max knows nothing of that! He disliked me on sight, and he has continued to dislike me.'

'I see. Now, tell me, apart from who *did* this dastardly thing, do you believe that Hereward was doped? Miller does, the veterinary surgeon did, Carteret is certain of it, so is Calft. Well?'

Charles thought, 'He's changed his tactics! Taken a different approach'. He said, 'Candidly, and I don't know much about horses, I think it looks like it.'

'And how then do you account for your own—indisposition?' His voice was not unduly curious; rather it was suave, interested but not particularly concerned.

Charles was on his guard. 'Coincidence, possibly.'

For the first time Emmanuel's voice sharpened a little. 'Come, come, Charles. The night before you were in gr-reat shape—so was Hereward. The next morning you appeared to be all right—so did he. Then both of you were taken ill—appar-rently about the same time. You don't live on corn, or bran mash and all the r-rest of it—had you and the horse been given anything to eat—by the same person?'

Charles repeated, 'Given anything to eat . . . certainly no one gave me anything to eat.'

Emmanuel's frown deepened. 'Then possibly—since on your own admission you know Clerkenwell—this may suggest something to you.' He brought out from his breast pocket an eight-ounce bottle, and handed it to Charles. 'That was found in one of the dressing-table drawers in the bedroom of—of a guest who had stayed at Ordingly. R-read the label, if you please.'

Charles obediently read, 'H. Bauer. Analytical chemist' and the address. On the label also were the words 'For the cough'. He handed it back to Emmanuel and said, 'Never heard of the fellow.'

'Please notice the name—Bauer,' Emmanuel said. 'Sufficiently common in Germany, not so common in England. An English chemist writes "cough mixture", not "for the cough". The writing, too, is that of a foreigner. Now you know a second-hand dealer in Clerkenwell. Do you suppose that he could help me to discover this—this blackguard?'

'I shouldn't think so. He isn't the kind of chap who spends much on chemist's bills, I imagine.'

Emmanuel made a sudden gesture of impatience. 'Charles, you're holding out on me! Now, tell me, in God's name—why?'

'Because,' Charles said slowly, almost painfully, 'there is nothing I could tell you that I can *prove* to have any real bearing on the matter. It's over, sir. It was a terrible disappointment for Viva, and it meant loss of money for her, as you said. The fact that I was ill, that Hereward couldn't run, may be quite accidental. The horse is better, so am I. Is it worth trying to drag the whole beastly business up again? If I were involved, I'd fight like mad to defend myself. I'm not, the very fact that I was taken ill puts me out of court on any possible charge in this matter.'

There was a long silence, Emmanuel leaning forward drawing lines on his writing-pad. Charles felt that the tension between them had eased, and he sat perfectly still, waiting for Emmanuel to speak.

The older man raised his head and looked at him. 'Tell me,' he said, 'what is this? Excess of nobility?'

Charles laughed. 'Nobility! I haven't a scrap of nobility in my make-up. It's just sheer common sense. If you could have the race run over again, with Hereward fit as a fiddle, I'd say—by all means pursue your investigations. You can't—the thing's over and done with. You can't put the clock back, so let it go forward and watch it tick out lots of victories for Viva's horses.'

Emmanuel watched him gravely, all irritation gone from his face. His eyes were very kind, even tender. He nodded, then said, 'There is a great deal in you, Charles, of which my father and grandfather would have approved. Looking back on this conversation, I can be sure that you haven't *lied* to me, but that you have not told me the complete tr-ruth I have no doubt whatever.'

'Sir——!' Charles felt that the situation demanded that exclamation.

Emmanuel smiled. 'Excellent, my boy. The typical retort of the hero in melodrama who has been wr-rongfully accused. Well, shall we bring this unsatisfactory interview to a satisfactor-ry conclusion? I think we might have a dry biscuit apiece, and some of my grandfather's dry sher-rry? Hannah would raise her hands in horror, and begin to talk about my liver, but we'll r-ring for Simeon and ask him to join us, eh?'

'It would be very pleasant, sir.'

Simeon came in response to his ring, and Emmanuel became his own charming self once more. Over the sherry—which was admirable—he talked of anything and everything except Hereward and the recent disaster.

He spoke of his grandfather—the founder of the Galleries—for whom it was obvious that he felt something which approached hero worship.

'I wish that Sargent—who could paint, who could delineate character—had called the portrait of old Emmanuel "The Ancestor", but that title had been used for the one he did of Lord Ribblesdale, and a very fine picture—yes, even the drawing—it is. Only never would Emmanuel have worn his neckcloth so untidily! I do not appr-rove of copies, but if Guido can find me a man who can paint—the subject demands a Latin painter I feel—he shall make two. One for you, Simeon, the other for Charles. I myself should like—one day—to be an ancestor. Charles, you will have to mar-ry, as well as Simeon here. I don't say that I want the Gollantz to people the earth, but I don't want there to be the slightest chance of them petering out.'

'I shall bear that in mind, sir. I have every intention of getting married—and quite soon I hope,' Charles assured him.

Emmanuel poured out a second glass of sherry, and glanced at him quizzically. 'Ah!' he murmured, 'I begin to understand—a little. You denied possessing any nobility a short time ago. But all young men who are violently in love assume—and r-rightly—a certain nobility. Didn't you feel noble, Simeon, when Daphne pr-romised to marry you?'

'Relieved, Papa. Distinctly relieved,' Simeon told him.

'You underr-rate your sentiments, I don't doubt.'

'I don't,' his son said. 'Right until I had the engagement ring on her finger I was afraid that she might ditch me'—he laughed—'and in favour of my own father! A pretty state of things!'

'I remember clearly,' Emmanuel mused, twisting the stem of his glass in his long fingers, 'feeling distinctly disgruntled when you walked off with Daphne—the nurse I liked the best—under my very nose. Of course I was in no state to really exert my full and well-known charm'—he turned to Charles—'I had been rather ill for a considerable time, but I still felt that my quiet courage under suffering might have impressed her.'

Simeon laughed. 'Indeed it did! I remember Daphne saying to me one morning, "He's going on splendidly, Simeon—the old devil's too bad tempered for words this morning, grumbling at everything!"'

'The complete and utterly unskilled liar, my son Simeon,' his father said calmly, 'and now after that very abortive and inconclusive interview with you, Charles, and a few ingenuous and very immature lies from my son, I might remind you that the head of the firm *works*, even if the rest of you are content to be merely rather useless ornaments. Charles, I advise you to go home, you still look white about the gills, and if you go home with a headache, Rose will cast me—automatically—as the villain of the piece. May I just remind you—yes, this piece of wisdom is given fr-reely to you both—most rogues, provided that they are given sufficient r-rope, eventually hang themselves. There! Get out both of you.'

As they walked away through the large, heavily carpeted show-rooms, Charles said, 'What did he mean exactly by that last remark?'

Simeon leaned towards him and whispered, 'I think he meant—Max.' A moment later, in his own office, he asked, 'Did you come to any conclusion during your interview?'

'I think I had already come to mine, and I imagine he had done the same. Only we didn't confide them to each other. I hedged, and at one point he became almost irritable with me, but I stuck to my guns. What's the good of stirring up a lot of mud? I doubt if we could *prove* anything, and surely the wretched fellow will be going back to the bosom of his family before long. I should think he's wasted enough time—and money—hanging about London.'

Simeon growled, 'Must have cost his father a pretty penny—or more likely his mother or grandfather! Let's talk about something more pleasant. How do you like that clock? My father doesn't know about it yet. It's a Tampion. I picked it up at a sale yesterday at Northampton, together with a nice pair of George the Second candelabra—beautiful—and a set of miniature, craftsman made furniture.' He smiled and looked suddenly a little shy. 'I'm keeping the furniture—it'll be handy for a doll's house if Emmanuel turns out to be Angela.'

'You'll call her—if it is a her—Angela, not after your own mother?'

Simeon shook his head. 'I don't believe my father could face hearing any child called "Juliet", no matter how much he loved it. He adores Viva, but my mother remains—well, something quite apart. I'm certain that Viva realizes it, and understands.'

That evening Emmanuel and Viva sat alone at the long dining-table. She said that she objected to being marooned at the farther end, and when they were alone always sat on his right. He looked tired, and seemed to her to eat listlessly.

'I shall be thankful when Charles really gets into harness,' she said suddenly. 'I don't believe you either know or care what you've been eating. You listen when I talk, because to do that is part of your exceedingly good manners, but I doubt if much of it penetrated. You not only want to take a holiday, you need one.'

'Hannah Rosenfeldt would tell you that it's an attack of liver, through drinking too much black coffee,' Emmanuel said.

'Is that what you do at Bond Street all day—drink Hannah's black coffee?' she demanded.

'Not entirely,' Emmanuel smiled. 'I also interview a few people, dictate several letters, make a trip of inspection round the Galleries—all new purchases are brought to me for my opinion. Incidentally, Simeon's bought a ver-ry fine Tampion clock, and a r-really beautiful pair of candelabra. He's growing very knowledgeable, that fellow.'

'Interviews! That reminds me, what was the outcome of

your talk with Charles this morning—you didn't tell me.'

Emmanuel spread his hands wide. 'Precisely nothing. Oh, he knew quite a gr-reat deal, and he knew that I knew that he had his own ideas. But he actually divulged nothing. And finally—imagine the self-assurance of these young people—he said that it might be better to allow the whole matter to dr-rop!'

'And you——?' her eyes smiled.

'I agr-reed. But I fancy that our r-reasons were differ-rent.'

'I want you to let the matter drop too! No amount of investigation can give me back the Cup—which Hereward would have won without a doubt. They won't take away from my memory the sight of that lovely animal with his unsteady legs and his drooping head, or the agony that I went through. All that the whole thing *has* given us is a true appreciation of the base and vile character of—well, of the slug who arranged the whole thing.'

'That bottle which Mrs. Cowley found in a drawer——'

'Pooh!'—contemptuously—'confront him with that—what happens? It was stomach mixture, cough mixture! Go to the chemist himself, you'll get the same kind of answer. No, I want you to drop it, because it is a waste of time and energy, quite profitless.'

Emmanuel listened, nodding his head. He loved to watch this attractive wife of his when she allowed herself to be carried away, when she became a little excited. Her eyes became so clear, and seemed to him to send out sparks of cold fire. The colour mounted a little in her cheeks, and her voice took on a slightly deeper note.

He said, 'So all of us wish the same thing, dearest. And how curious, all for different r-reasons. Yours is because it is *inutile*—worthless—a very sane and logical view. With Charles, it is a little different. There is still the same logical approach, but there is added the belief that it will contribute nothing to the dignity of the family, that it is better—since neither he nor your beautiful horse have suffered any permanent damage—that we leave it all alone. Not perhaps to forgive, but to put at the back of our minds.'

'He's a dear, hard-headed little North Countryman,' Viva said. 'And you? Why did you agree?'

Emmanuel leaned back in his beautiful Chippendale arm-chair. 'Give me, if you please, a cigarette, and perhaps we might both have another brandy—it is very fine this '99. Then I will tell you, if it will not make you bor-red.'

'There's your cigarette, and here's your "fine". Now—I am waiting.'

'In my family—and I am very pr-roud of my family—there have always been two kinds of men. The one type who might not be very str-rictly moral, but who in their business dealings r-regard as abhorrent anything which is mean or underhand. The other type is—well, corrupt.

'My grandfather married the beautiful Countess de Lara—Juliana. He loved her to distr-raction, and she loved him passionately. It was necessary for him to make a tour of Europe. In those days travelling was difficult, inns—even the best—might pr-rove to be poor and dirty. She asked him to take her with him, he r-refused. It was impossible, how could he expose her—his wonderful Juliana—to hardships, dirt, possibly even disease. "You expose me to something worse than any of these things if you leave me here," she told him.

'"To what?" he asked.

'"To boredom? When I am bored I forget everything. I might do anything. Hardship, danger, anything I can face—but boredom—never!"

'However, he r-refused to take her, although it nearly broke his heart to leave her. He r-returned and she confessed to him that she had been in Brussels with her cousin—I forget his name, if I ever knew it. Later—within the time which made it possible that this child might be Emmanuel's—a boy was born. Then she died—leaving Emmanuel with two sons—one my father—on him be peace—the other Algernon.

'Always, because he was afr-raid of not being completely just, my grandfather gave Algernon everything. Later he was able to prove that Algernon r-really was his son. But Algernon was bad thr-rough and thr-rough. He lied, he stole, he—ah, he was a *ganef*! Now, in my own gener-ration I have always tried—tried, Viva dar-rling—to be honest and upright as my father and grandfather were. My brother Julian—such a year befall him—no, no,' he added hastily, 'I must not say that, I'd rather say—no ill luck befall him and try'—he smiled drily—'tr-ry to mean it.'

Viva said, 'You don't have to tell me about Julian—I shan't forget what he did if I live to be a thousand!'

'I have not been a very good man, but in my business dealings I have tr-ried to be upright and honest.'

She shrugged her shoulders. 'You satisfy me!'

He lifted her hand and kissed it. 'Dar-rling. But there you see here in this Max, who is Julian repeated. My father and Algernon, myself and Julian, Simeon—he is as good as gold—and Max. It may be that there is some strain which crops up in ever-ry generation. So I agree with Charles—we will let this hor-rible thing die a natural death.'

She looked at him, her face affectionate, if a little contemptuous.

'And haven't men got free-will? Can't they fight down these damned impulses? Do they have to descend to these beastly, foul things just to satisfy some unworthy desire? Emmanuel, of course they can! If they sink to these things—blast it!—it's because they allow, yes, *allow* their baser selves to get the upper hand. This—this *creature*—oh, I'll be quite frank—imagined that he was in love with me! My God, the impertinence of it—when I had you for my husband! I told him exactly what an ass I thought he was making of himself. He used to sit and stare me out of countenance. I wonder that you never noticed it!'

'I did,' Emmanuel said gently, 'but I am used to people staring at you, you are devastatingly attr-ractive.'

'The last time—precious idiot that you are—he was here, he followed me into the conservatory off the drawing-room. He began to plead, to protest and finally he—well, he got ugly. That was when Charles—our nice phlegmatic Charles—came in and heard my voice. Bless him, he knocked down an empty flower-pot, and the other man fled. That was when he determined to get back at me, through my horse. How Charles came to be involved I still don't know and I doubt if Charles will ever tell us. So, the matter is at an end. You and Charles agreed on that? You, because you take this philosophic, very humane outlook, Charles and I because we take the very practical one. I've entered Hereward for the Rowlsey Stakes at—do you know where?'

'I'm afraid I don't——'

'Ignoramus! At Yorchester. It's a big race and he's going to win it.'

'When is this event?'

'May—and let's hope that Max is back with his adoring family, giving New York a thrill, and putting his damned cosmetics on the market!' She laid her hand on Emmanuel's. 'Tell me that you are really, really happy,' she demanded softly.

He rose and took her in his arms. 'My dar-rling—I am married to you—that's my answer.'

14

Spring had really come to London. Every day as Charles walked through the park to Bond Street, he looked about him at the flowers coming into bloom, marvelling at their colours, watched the trees throwing out their new leaves, the horse-chestnuts showing great sticky buds ready to burst, as they shed their winter casing. More than that, there was a feeling of spring in his blood, a sense of increased hope and expectancy. He felt that his step was lighter, that his whole body was invigorated, that his blood seemed to course more freely.

Then, too, every day brought the time nearer when he might ask for a short holiday and go to Paris to join Maria, and marry her. He used to imagine so many scenes—their first meeting after this separation which appeared to stretch to infinity, the first time he took her in his arms, their wedding before the Consul—or whoever officiated at these ceremonies. Then bringing her back with him, watching his mother's delighted welcoming of her new daughter, her admiration for Maria's beauty, her ability to speak English, and the modulations of her charming voice.

So many dreams, so much happiness—sometimes he felt a little giddy with it all. At first he had assumed that Rose would stay with them, but Rose disabused him.

'No, luv, young people want the place to themselves. I shall get me a nice little flat, not too expensive. Emmanuel 'ul help me, and I shall have my old Sarah who aways did for me in Dullton, and swears she'll never leave me. Now, Sarah has a niece—Alice, her sister Mary Ellen's daughter—longing to come to London. Seems to me since Sarah started writing back home, that half the girls in the town want to come to London! This girl, Alice, she'll come to you and—your young lady. Wonderful how everything arranges itself, Charlie, isn't it?'

His work, too, was going well. True he studied very hard, spending any free hours he had in going round the Galleries looking at silver, china, and furniture. Already Emmanuel had sent him to several sales, and acting under instructions, he had bought several things which were noticeable, and which had necessitated very careful bidding.

Emmanuel had praised him, in that moderate but eminently satisfactory way which was his. To have Emmanuel inspect this piece or that and then say, 'It is all that I hoped. You have done very well, Charles,' was sufficient to send Charles away with his heart literally singing. Once or twice he had ventured to buy without instructions. Nothing very valuable—possibly a tray on which reposed a number of discarded, unwanted things. A silver buttonhook, two saucers without cups, a cup with no saucer, a few silver teaspoons and some small piece of rather insignificant china which might be of no value whatever but which might—as Charles always hoped—prove to be Chelsea or Bow.

When the stuff was cleaned he would carry the collection to Emmanuel, who—Charles felt—enjoyed these moments as much as he did.

'Now, Jim Hawkins,' he would say, 'have you found any gold for me?' Gravely he would examine each piece, shaking his head over the dreadful lack of body in the silver buttonhook. 'Terr-ible work!'

'Then,' Charles told Rose, 'he pounces! Picks up the little figure—it has come up since it was cleaned, the colours are bright, and it is charm packed into two and a half inches. Then he holds it out to me.

' "Tell me what is this, please?"

' "I thought that it might be a bit of Bow, sir."

' "Bow! Too small surely for Bow. What is the mark, tell me?"

' "A gold anchor, sir."

'Then he explains that it is Chelsea, that it is a great pity there is only one, but that one is better than nothing. He gives you a little lecture on china marks, on what to avoid—"fingers, Charles, toes—watch for these. The spouts of tea-pots, the handles of cups. These are the danger points." Oh, he is an education in himself.'

Once Charles had brought one of these 'mixed lots' and had taken it to Emmanuel, who examined every article with minute care, shaking his head over them, while he admitted that the two silver dessert spoons might be useful and match up with some already in stock.

Then he said, 'No, Jim Hawkins, I'm afraid there is no gold this morning!' But as Charles was about to carry the lot away, he had become galvanized into attention.

'That tray—where did you get that?'

'It was sold with the rest, sir.'

'Have you had it cleaned?' His questions came like the rattle of a machine-gun.

'Only dusted.'

'Take those things off—put the tray on that side table—the one with the oilcloth cover.' He dashed into his little toilet room, returning with a bowl of warm water and a small fine sponge. He began to clean the tray, and Charles remarked that he used as much tenderness as a woman might have done in washing a small child. Slowly the colours began to show as the layers of dirt were removed and the tray was exposed in all its beauty of delicately painted flowers and fruit, here and there inlaid with mother o' pearl.

Emmanuel stood back and surveyed his work.

'Beautiful, eh? Very good, and early, I think, though I must verify that—papier maché. Viva has been wanting one for a long, long time. So—you found your gold, Jim Hawkins, even if it is hidden under a load of dirt.'

Yes, Charles found life at the Gollantz Galleries an exciting business. On great days when some splendid painting was being offered for sale, some magnificent piece of silver, even a special jewel—though Emmanuel bought very little jewellery—he would go in person to buy. It gave Charles a thrill of pleasure to see his tall, slim figure walk into a sale room, to watch him bowing to his friends, to be greeted by everyone. Then, seating himself, he remained very still allowing one of his staff—Simeon or even Charles—to bid until the great picture or whatever might be the 'high light' of the sale was reached. Then he stiffened slightly, but did not begin to bid until practically the ultimate figure had been reached. Then, speaking very quietly but distinctly, he began to take part ; very often he did not even speak, but signalled his wishes to the auctioneer.

There were times when the auctioneer, watching him closely, would repeat, 'Any advance?' and Emmanuel, smiling slightly, would shake his head and retire from the contest.

Charles, watching him, listening to him, knew that he was gaining knowledge every day. Rarely a day passed without some small addition to his understanding of antiques, and these he would note down in one of the notebooks which he kept with such care, and studied with such application.

And now March had slipped into April, April had given place to May, and June was coming nearer every day. Maria wrote that her uncle by marriage, the Conte de Brissac, had everything in train.

He is occupying himself with our affairs in a most careful and charming way, she wrote. *I am sure that the way will be made very smooth for me and my English sweetheart. Oh, what joy to see you again, Carlo* mio! *It seems an eternity since I saw your aeroplane disappear into the skies, taking you away from me. I shall be a jealous and very possessive wife, who will scarcely be able to allow her husband from her side!*

He had bought her an engagement ring, which he often took out and looked at with pride and affection. He had wished to buy one from the Galleries, but when Emmanuel heard of the idea he had given his decision.

'Yes, there are some fine rings, and later, Charles, later, you can select which you please for birthday pr-resents, Chr-ristmas pr-resents and so forth. But for the engagement r-ring—ah, that must not be one which others have worn, perhaps when they were unhappy, lonely, depr-ressed. It must be new,' he smiled, 'like the life which you will begin together.

'I shall take you to Hatton Garden, to visit my friend and kinsman, Habbemma. There we shall get a stone—or several stones, just as you feel. Then we shall take them to another friend of mine—no, not a kinsman this time—and talk about settings and designs. So—you will have a r-ring which is unique, one which will please the fine taste of this wonderful young woman. Does the idea please you?'

Charles remembered how they had gone to Hatton Garden,

where the little elderly Jew, Habbemma, had treated Emmanuel as if he were a visiting monarch. Stones were brought, and laid on a cushion of pale-covered velvet, Emmanuel and Habbemma, each with a pair of fine pliers, had treated the stones with obvious respect; both were armed with strong magnifying-glasses, both remained grave, absorbed, and almost silent.

Finally Emmanuel turned to Charles. 'My choice would be a square stone, with a much smaller one on either side——'

Habbemma, suddenly almost passionate, cried, 'Im-possible! To hev a r-ring which is perfect, yes—have the square stone, but surr-round it with smaller stones, like what a fr-rame is.'

Emmanuel shook his head. 'And detr-ract from the beauty of the large stone?'

Habbemma gesticulated. 'I say thet eet will enhance its beauty!'

Charles said mildly, 'Which is the square stone, sir?'

It was carefully pushed towards him on its velvet bed. It did seem to Charles a most beautiful stone, and he examined it through the big glass which Emmanuel pushed into his hand, saying, 'Examine it!'

Habbemma almost chanted, 'Pure vhite, cut in the most beautiful vay, by the best peoples in Emsterdamn. A stone like vot you find—maybe—once in a livestimes, not only for the size—I seen plenty of stones, bigger but none effer better.'

Charles said, 'It is beautiful. And the smaller ones?'

Emmanuel answered, 'These were the two I had in my mind.'

'Also—pure vhite—small but of a perfectness,' Habbemma intoned. 'See how both of t'em sparkle, like what rainbows do.'

'I think, Mr. Habbemma, that the idea of the square stone with the small one on either side appeals to me. I am quite sure that your idea would make a most beautiful ring, but for a—well, a young girl—might it not be a little overpowering?'

To his surprise the little elderly man beamed at him. 'Alvays I say eet is Emmanuel Gollantz has the taste vich is perfectness. My poy, always be advised by heem. T'en neffer, neffer vill you go avay from excellence.'

He bustled away to pack the stones, and Charles—somewhat apprehensively—asked Emmanuel about the cost.

'A matter between Habbemma and myself. The stones are Viva's present and mine to your bride. The setting I shall leave to you. Pr-ray say no more about it, for it is a pleasure we have pr-romised ourselves.'

Together that same afternoon they visited a famous jeweller, and once again Charles watched Emmanuel and this admirably dressed man immersed in argument as to the correct setting. Both were grave, their faces serious, they might neither of them have had another thought in the world beyond Maria Franconi's engagement ring.

And now Charles had the finished ring, which Rose declared was the most wonderful she had ever seen, safely locked in the drawer of his dressing-table, but often he could not resist unlocking the drawer and taking it out to hold it up to catch the light, sending out bright flashes of wonderful colours. He felt his heart beat more rapidly when he imagined how he would slip it on to Maria's finger. She had carefully—at his request—drawn the size of her finger from one of her own rings. That charming hand, which he had kissed and fondled so often, so white and deliciously soft!

The long-expected child was born to Daphne and Simeon towards the end of May. Simeon had rushed into the Galleries, his face white as chalk, and had called to Charles to follow him into Emmanuel's office. 'Papa!' he cried, 'at eight o'clock this morning, the future member of the firm made his appearance. Emmanuel the Third. Fit as a fiddle, with a voice like a roaring lion.'

Emmanuel rose and came to his son, threw his arms round him, embraced him tenderly. When he returned to his chair, Charles saw that there were tears on his cheeks, tears which he did not trouble to brush away.

Charles thought, 'That's the oriental in them, I suppose. They're not afraid of allowing emotion to master them, or to care who sees the effects.'

'And the dear clever Daphne—she is well, please God?'

'Tired—in fact she was sleeping when I left, so was Emmanuel. But she's frightfully pleased, and quite well. Meyer Bernstein—he came with his son, who saw the whole thing through—Meyer sat downstairs and insisted upon progress being reported to him at intervals.'

Emmanuel nodded 'Ah, he grows old, this Meyer, the son is

very clever. So! All is well, thanks be to God. And now we celebrate! All in the Galleries must drink *maseltov* to the new little Gollantz. Simeon, have champagne sent up, sufficient for all. If they can't all come in together, then they must come in r-relays. Where is Hannah?'

Simeon laughed. 'Where do you imagine she'd be, Papa? Doing homage to the new infant of course. She swears that he is like you! She wouldn't hear of leaving him. I think she suspects the nurse of some dark plan to kidnap him.'

'If there is any kidnapping to be done,' Emmanuel said, 'Viva and I shall do it. Now this wine, Simeon! Ever-ry moment the little boy grows older, at this r-rate we shall be dr-rinking his health when he is r-ready to go to his first school! Charles, go and bring glasses—good ones. I have not sufficient here.'

He was as excited as a child going to a party, his eyes shone, even his invariably pale cheeks were flushed, his voice had taken on a new note and seemed filled with youth and expectancy. Charles walked through to the big storeroom where the glass, which was one man's duty to clean and polish it every day, was kept.

Charles said, 'Glasses—for champagne, please, Mason. There's a celebration in Sir Emmanuel's room.'

The little man, small, thin and undersized, with sandy hair and a moustache which straggled, of whom no one ever heard, but who Emmanuel and Simeon avowed knew more about glass than any man in England, blinked his pale blue eyes.

He said, 'It 'ul no be the bairn that's arrived, eh?'

Charles nodded. 'It's the bairn. A boy.'

'A wee laddie! Noo, this ca's for glasses that arre a bit oot o' the ordinary. And,' he was busy assembling glasses as he spoke, 'may Gawd help the feller who damages yin o' them. Mister Charles, every one o' these is worth awe o' five pun'. Na, na, I'll carry them there mysen. I'll no trust them to even you, Mister Chairles'

They returned to find Emmanuel fussing happily. He spun round and greeted Mason, who said, 'Na, na, wait a wee minute whiles I pit doon the tray. There's valuse there, sir.'

'My dear Mason, you've heard the news?'

'Aye, and I'll wager that you're a prood mon the day, sir.'

The others employed in the galleries began to come in, smart young men in black coats and striped trousers, all wearing ties which were rich but eminently discreet. Charles remembered when they first entered his employ, Emmanuel presented them with two ties each, bought from his own haberdasher. After that they were expected to—as Simeon said—'live up to them'. There was the bustling housekeeper, the very old, very astute accountant, Reuben Davis who had grown old in the service of the firm.

Emmanuel greeted him with outstretched hands.

'Reuben, you've heard?'

The old man nodded. 'No evil befall him! It is splendid! I am happy like it was my own daughter gave me a grandchild! *Mazeltov*.'

'Time passes so quickly,' Emmanuel said, 'before long he will be here, working with us, eh?'

Davis sighed. 'I wish to bring no sadness to this day, Emmanuel, but how happy I should be to live to see him *bar-mitzvah*.'

Emmanuel patted his shoulder. 'Dear Reuben, these young people must make their own decisions. I don't believe that I was ever given a *bar-mitzvah*. There, drink your wine!'

Charles, watching, thought, 'Fundamentally how Jewish they all are, these Gollantzes and their intimate friends. At a time like this Emmanuel is a complete patriarch, the head of the tribe. They have no self-consciousness. He can embrace his son, tears on his cheeks, as he embraced old Reuben Davis. These very correct young men in their black coats don't affect him in the least. Then he switches to talk to the housekeeper, to Wilson and Bentley, and slips back into being completely British. They are an astonishing race, and nothing—hundred of years, tribulation, persecution—will ever eradicate their essential Jewishness. Given moments of emotion they immediately revert to type.

'Emmanuel has probably never attended a Jewish service in his life. He may know what this—*bar-mitzvah* is, I certainly don't. Some kind of ceremony I imagine. But although he was married first in an English church—I've heard my mother say so—there remains in his heart that love for the religion of his own race. He may not practise it, but he loves, admires and respects it. In fact, although he may be completely British, he remains, and always will remain, a Jew.'

They drank the infant's health, Emmanuel obviously deeply moved, and then dispersed. Emmanuel sat down as if the effort had exhausted him; the colour had drained from his cheeks, his whole figure seemed to droop.

Simeon stood near him. 'Papa, Hannah has just come—shall she make you some coffee?'

His father smiled. 'I should enjoy that, thank you.'

A moment later she bustled in. 'The moment I heard of this health drinking, I said, "He will want coffee!" and began to make it. Always this coffee drinking! Do we wish that your grandson enters the world—no evil eye befall him!—to find you leaving it? There, drink your cup of poison! This child—you have not seen him, drinking champagne here and allowing yourself to become overset by your emotions—he is beautiful. He lies there, sleeping, his mouth like a small rose-bud, his tiny hands like little models of hands—he has the long fingers of the first Emmanuel—on him be peace.'

Emmanuel, sipping his coffee with relish, asked, 'His eyes?'

Hannah eyed him tolerantly. 'Do you not know that the eyes of all young things are blue—kittens, puppies, even babies?'

Simeon said, 'Calves? I never saw a calf with blue eyes.'

'When did you ever see a very young calf, tell me?' Hannah retorted.

Emmanuel finished his coffee, and rose. 'The *festa* is over, I am going to drive down to see my gr-randson.'

Charles watched Simeon's glowing face as they worked together in his office. He found himself wondering what it must feel like to have a son. In another year—or rather longer—he night be sitting here half-smiling with a happiness which he did not attempt to conceal, thinking and dreaming of his beautiful Maria and of a small round head, a mouth 'like a small rose-bud', of tiny hand with miniature nails like the little sea shells which he used to hunt for when Rose took him to Blackpool or Morecambe.

During the days and weeks that followed it appeared that there had never been a child who advanced with such miraculous rapidity. Every day either Simeon or Hannah Rosenfeldt had some new and astonishing piece of news regarding the youngest Emmanuel. He had smiled, a most delightful smile, when Hannah went near him.

'The nurse—it is my belief that she is *meshoogah* this one, a crazy woman—said, "They smile when they have—wind!" I told her, that it is well known that small babies smile because the angels whisper to them beautiful words and that makes them happy. Wind!'

Emmanuel produced a Charles the Second silver porringer, a rattle with silvery bells which some child had swung when James the First was king, a fine leather case which held an elaborate knife, fork and spoon. The child's perambulator was the finest procurable. 'The man who sold it,' Hannah boasted, 'told me—on his word of honour—that it was exactly like the one the Queen had for Princess Anne.' His wardrobe was so extensive that he could have clothed a large orphanage with comparative ease. Rose Watson knitted—it seemed to Charles —small and exquisite garments perpetually. Lady Heriot tried to follow her example, but only succeeded in getting the wool into a terrible tangle which someone had to unravel for her. Little Gilbert sent all the way from Australia a magnificent cricket bat and a crate of the finest honey that Australia could produce.

Viva declared that she intended having him measured for his first suit as soon as he could stand to allow the tailor to measure him! She told Charles that they were 'all set' to make a fool of the boy, but he noticed that again and again she brought the conversation back to him, her chief delight in the child being that he gave such an added interest to Emmanuel.

It was when she talked of him that Charles realized how deep her love for Emmanuel was. To an outsider she might have been taken for a rather worldly middle-aged woman, capable of a considerable amount of rather mildly bad language, but when she spoke of Emmanuel her whole face softened, and her voice became tender, her eyes almost sentimental.

He had come to regard Viva Gollantz as one of his best friends. He could talk to her frankly of Maria, of his high hopes, and she always listened with grave interest.

Max was still in London, and when he came to Ordingly—at longer and longer intervals—he told them of the wonderful toilet preparations which were to stagger America.

'And who is the chemist who prepares them?' Emmanuel asked.

Charles fancied that there was an edge to his voice, and that his eyes suddenly turned cold.

Max laughed, 'Say, that's something I've got to keep to myself. Once people get wise to him, he'll never come over to the States, which is something I've got in mind.'

Emmanuel answered coldly, 'You have nothing to fear fr-rom me. I am not inter-rested in cosmetics, Max.'

'Well, things do get around after all.'

'Possibly you're wise.'

June came in, a warm beautiful month. There were more flowers in the Bond Street shop as Charles passed on his way to the Galleries, women were wearing light dresses, and even Simeon—who was restrained in his dress—wore what he called 'summer ties'. Emmanuel changed into a thin silk jacket when he got to the office. Hannah Rosenfeldt mopped her face, and declared that 'this heat will slaughter me already'.

Maria wrote that her father had left for New York, and she was on the point of leaving for Paris. When could her 'Carlo' join her?

Charles went to Emmanuel, asking if he might have ten days' leave.

'Ah, to go to Paris, my dear boy, whenever you wish. I should have liked the wedding to have been a gr-reat family reunion, but I can see that—under the circumstances—it is impossible. Give our gr-reetings to your beautiful Mar-ria, and assure her what a warm welcome awaits her. *Mazeltov,* and all good attend you both.'

Rose cried a little when he left, saying, 'I'm longing to see her but, remember, Charlie dear, "Your son's your son 'til he gets him a wife". Nay, I mustn't talk that road, all I want is your happiness. Go on, and bring me back a luvely daughter. My word, she'll have such a welcome! God bless you both.'

He felt slightly giddy during the journey to Paris. It all seemed so incredible, almost impossible. The girl he had met in the Brera, to whom he had exclaimed at the beauty of the Mantegna at which they were both gazing, was waiting in Paris to become his wife. In his waistcoat pocket was the engagement ring, and in the other pocket the thin gold ring—he disliked platinum and so did Maria—which meant the culmination of all his hopes.

Paris, the drive through the city, a great house in the Champs-Elysées, with window-boxes aflame with flowers, a courtyard, a man in dark livery who opened the wonderful door with its hand-wrought ironwork. A hall with dark green-and-white tiles, and he was ushered into a drawing-room which was a vision of wonderful furniture, magnificent curtains. A woman rose to greet him.

She held out her hands. 'You are Maria's Carlo, yes? I am Hortense de Brissac. Maria will be here in a moment. How happy she will be to see you again. Oh, what a dear girl this is! Everything is arranged, my husband has occupied himself over the ceremony. I should have wished to be able to ask you to stay, but it would not be—convenable. So—the Crillon is across the road, there you will sleep, but as you say in England—I love this England, excepting always your climate—you must run in and out as you wish. Ah, here is Maria!'

He turned; there she stood, her lovely face alight with happiness. He forgot the Contessa, and went to her, taking her in his arms, whispering to her his joy at being with her again. He felt that time had ceased to exist. There she was with his arms round her, the scent of her hair reaching him; he could feel the soft roundness of her young body, her lips on his, and when he held her from him, he saw the gladness in her eyes, saw the wonderful flush which had risen to her cheeks, and heard her say, 'Oh, Carlo *mio*—what joy to see you again!' He let her go, and hand in hand they went back to the stout, elegant little Contessa who was frankly wiping her eyes with a wisp of cambric.

'It is so touching,' she explained, 'that it forces the tears. Now, I have many letters to write, and so I must leave you here. That is something which will not cause you any grief, eh? I shall see you later, for you, Carlo, will dine with us this evening.'

They sat together on the Empire sofa, their hands clasped. She told him how long the separation had been, and how wonderful it was to see him again. He said exactly the same—in different words—and the one listened to the other with rapt attention. He brought out the engagement ring, told her its history, and she exclaimed at its beauty. He told her how

Emmanuel had chosen the stones, that they were a gift from him and his wife—'an engagement present'.

'Ah, these wonderful people,' Maria exclaimed, 'how much I long to meet them all. And your loving mother, Carlo—I shall feel for her as if I were her own daughter.'

'That is exactly what you will be, my darling. She said that to me this morning, just as I was leaving. And your father?'

'He has never mentioned you, never! As you know all your letters—ah, your precious letters!—have come to me through that beloved woman, Iva Mancini. He sailed six days ago, and will be away for a month at least. Once we are married—Carlo, how wonderful it sounds—we shall send him a cablegram. He will be furious, but he will—how do you say?—relent if we are a little patient, eh?'

That night he dined with them. The dinner was elaborate, the glass and china magnificent. The Conte, a small rather stout man, with heavily rimmed tortoiseshell glasses, a carefully trimmed moustache, and a small very neat 'imperial'. He was suave, kindly, and very courteous. He had arranged everything. There must be two ceremonies, as Maria was a Catholic. One at the Embassy, the other at a church not far away. Very quiet, for, as he said, 'It must all be most discreet.'

'Not tomorrow,' he explained. 'Tomorrow you and our dear Maria may play happily in Paris—eat at superb restaurants, and perhaps go to a performance, though you must leave in time for her to be in here before midnight. Otherwise it means bad fortune.'

He chuckled at the superstition, but the Contessa said gravely, 'This is very true.'

'The next day you will meet us at the Embassy. I have provided for you a—groom' man. A nice young man, my godson, Anatole de Rigney He will call for you. Is this all clear?'

'Perfectly, sir, and I am deeply grateful to both you and the Contessa.'

De Brissac dismissed his thanks with a gesture. 'It is nothing—it is less than nothing. Let us not mention these thanks again, if you please.'

That evening Maria played the pianoforte, and Charles knew that his mind went rushing back to the evening in Milan, when she had come to Guido Moroni's apartment, and he had stood listening to her, entranced. Now, he was with her again, she was on the eve of becoming his wife. Life together stretched before them, and he felt his hands clench with the intensity of his emotion. It was almost beyond his powers not to say, audibly, 'Oh, my darling, I'll be so good to you!'

The next morning he called for her quite early, and together they went out into the lovely city, so filled with life, glamour and gaiety. Charles was a stranger to its beauties, but Maria knew it intimately.

'The Louvre, Carlo? You have visited it?'

'Well, no, darling, I can't say that I have. You forget—this is my first visit.'

'Then it is essential. Not to see everything—this requires many weeks, but the "Mona Lisa", you must see, the "Winged Victory". In all I will show you not more than five pictures—the "Winged Victory" is not a picture—she is a glorious statue.'

So they stood hand in hand like wondering children before the splendid statue, and Maria confessed to him that she had never been able to stand directly in front of it. 'For,' she said, 'at any moment I feel that she may come flying down and she must have a clear passage.'

They agreed that they didn't really like the 'Mona Lisa'. Charles said, 'She looks what we call in the north suttil.'

'What exactly is this—suttil?' Maria asked.

Charles frowned, puzzled. 'I don't know how to explain—it's just that her expression is—well, suttil!'

They lunched—luxuriously, elegantly, and exquisitely at Larue's, where they ate *caille a la Souvaroff, becasse flambee,* and *crêpes Suzette*. They drank wonderful wine, and delicious coffee. They talked without ceasing, they laughed, and were quite consciously happy.

It was June, they were in Paris, the streets seemed full of flowers, and—tomorrow would be their wedding day.

'And this evening——?' Charles asked.

She held up a warning finger. 'We must say "Good night" before the clock strikes twelve, remember! I should love—yes, really love—to go to the Casino de Paris. Yes, it may be sometimes just a little naughty, but it is pleasantly naughty. I have been once or twice with my aunt and uncle, and since within twenty-four hours you will be my husband, surely it is correct, no?'

'What do I care for what is correct, if you wish it!'

They drove back to the de Brissac villa, for Charles insisted that she must rest for a little. As they entered the dignified butler handed Maria a cablegram, meticulously placed on a silver salver.

She tore it open, saying with that quick, courteous turn of her head, 'Please excuse me.'

He watched her reading it. It seemed terribly long, and as she read all the colour seemed to drain from her face. She breathed a long deep sigh, and then turned to him, the cablegram crumpled in her hand.

'Oh—Charles—this is terrible!' She handed him the form.

The Barone Franconi suffered grave stroke last night stop his condition is very serious stop advice you fly from Paris at the earliest possible moment stop cable me I shall await you at the airfield. Mario Casagrandi.

Charles felt giddy; he blinked his eyes as if to clear his vision and reassure himself that he had read correctly. It wasn't possible that she was to be snatched from him at this late hour. Their wedding—his return with her to London—he felt that his whole world was crashing into fragments.

'But—but—our wedding——' he stammered in his dismay.

Maria answered firmly, 'If there is a plane I must go at once. Let me find my uncle, he will arrange everything for me. If there is no plane then—Carlo *mio*—we will be married in the morning, even if I must leave immediately after the wedding Oh, my dear, dear love, that this should happen now—of all times! Yet, what can I do? He is my papa, he has been kind and good to me, now this friend of his, Casagrandi, says that his condition is—critical. Imagine how I should for ever reproach myself if—if anything dreadful happened, and he was left alone, without me to stand beside him, to perhaps speak gently to him—my life would be one long regret. Oh, Carlo, say that you understand.'

He nodded, and when he spoke his voice sounded dull and heavy.

'Yes, dearest, I understand. Go and talk to your uncle.'

He sat there in the elaborate drawing-room of the Contessa, his head in his hands. Maria was right, of course; she must go to her father. If only they could be married before she left he knew he would feel that he had that fact to cling to—that she was his wife. The day had been so filled with joy, with laughter, that it seemed almost cruel that this news should have come at such a moment, when life seemed to be stretching before them, a life filled with brightness and happiness.

Maria came back to him. She sat beside him and slipped her hand into his. 'My poor Carlo! Now I begin to wonder if this is a kind of punishment—my punishment—for having been ready to deceive him. That is one additional reason why I must go. Yes, there is a plane leaving at twelve midday. My uncle has telephoned, and he is going now to collect my ticket. We can be married before I leave, my dear one. Then although I shall have to rush away to the airfield, I shall at least be your wife.'

'That means so much to you?' Charles asked, conscious that his voice shook with emotion.

'It means almost everything. Have no fear, my Carlo, I shall come back to you. I could not live without you, I should die.'

He put his arms round her and held her to him. 'If I know that, realize that you will come back to me, I can bear this separation. I'm not good enough for you, but I swear on everything that I hold sacred that no woman—not in all the world—shall have a husband who loves her as I love you.'

She tilted back his head and looked into his eyes, her own very grave and steadfast. 'Be assured that happiness will be ours. We're young, my dear one, and we can afford to make this sacrifice to bring comfort to this poor man. We shall never regret it. Patience, darling, just a little longer.'

He nodded. 'I'll do my best to be patient.'

15

This time he had watched Maria's plane slowly mount into the air, had watched her last wave to him, and knew that his eyes had been blotted with tears. She looked so young, so lonely, so forlorn. And this was to have been the happiest day that either of them had ever known. He walked slowly back to where the aeroplane for England was waiting. His mind was still confused—so much had happened that day. An exquisite young man had called for him at the Crillon, incredibly suave, almost meticulously shaved and his hair shone with much brushing. He bowed as he shook hands with Charles, and murmured that he wished him all felicitations.

'A disaster—the illness of the father of the enchanting Maria!'

'Yes, bad luck.'

'But if he lives, she will return to you, and if'—he shrugged his shoulders—'he does not live, she will also return. It is a delayed joy only, not something which is extinguished, no?'

Charles nodded. 'That's right.'

'My uncle—who is also my godfather, instructed me that we were to share a bottle of champagne—it is customary for the bridegroom and his—what do you call it?—best man, to drink a glass of champagne. I have ordered it, in one moment it will be here.'

A pleasant young man, Charles decided, but how he wished that he had not arrived, just when Charles was fighting to keep calm, to stifle his unhappiness, to get ready to face the immaculate Conte, his elegant wife and most of all—Maria, with a certain amount of equanimity.

He said, conscious that he was growing more and more

'North Country' with every moment. 'It's very thoughtful of you. You'll understand that I am rather—well, knocked off my perch by what has happened. Forgive me if I'm not exactly gay, won't you?'

Again the young man bowed. 'Monsieur Gollantz, I am young, but I, too, have known grief—grief of the heart. My heart has been completely broken—three times—and I am only twenty-four. Ah, here is the wine. Now, as we lift our glasses and see the bubbles rising, our hearts will rise too, I think. For a few moments at least. Then, it may be that sadness will descend, but for those moments we must be thankful.' He raised his glass. 'To your complete happiness, to a life of beauty and love with the charming Maria Franconi, and all prosperity. I read once a poem which said that the night is always darkest before the arrival of the dawn. A beautiful thought, no?'

Charles remembered how he had drunk his wine, and had felt his spirits rise a little. He and Maria were young, life was before them, they had only—as she had said—to be a little patient.

His bags were packed, for his aeroplane left soon after the one on which Maria would travel. There was no sense in remaining in Paris, seeing again places which would remind him of yesterday. He would get back as quickly to Mum—dear Mum—to Emmanuel, to the Galleries, there to immerse himself in work.

The young man—Charles had completely forgotten his name—treated him as if he were a patient recovering from a long and dangerous illness. He was almost ready to offer Charles his arm to assist him into the immense and splendid car which was waiting.

'A small church,' he was explaining, 'for the religious ceremony. There will be—alas!—no music or flowers, as it is a mixed marriage. The priest will wish for your assurance—it only takes a moment—that any children of this marriage shall be brought up as Catholics. That is understood, no?'

'I understand.'

'Then to the representative of the British Government, and there the ceremony will be even shorter, less than ten minutes, I think. My godfather wishes that you and Maria—that sweet person—take his car and drive immediately to the airfield. No one will go with you. He is a very fine, sensitive man. No one will be present except himself and his charming wife, and his family lawyer. Perhaps,' with sudden expectancy, 'when Maria returns, you may be able to be married again! A beautfiul wedding, with bridesmaids, and guests of the most distinguished. This may be, indeed I hope that I may have the honour of being your best man once again under circumstances which will be more happier. With all my heart.'

The church was small and very dark, the priest was waiting, and the young man and he between them managed to explain to Charles the matter of these children. Charles, depression almost submerging him, felt that he would have promised that they should be brought up as Mormons or Plymouth Brethren.

They went back to stand by the altar rails, and the young man said in a loud and piercing whisper, 'The ring—you have it? Give it to me please. I hand it to you at the proper moment. Maria will kneel beside you. I shall show you exactly. Ah, she arrives with my godfather.'

She was coming up the aisle towards him, on the arm of her uncle. Charles felt his heart miss a beat. She looked very pale, but self-controlled. As their eyes met, she sent him the flicker of a smile.

They knelt together, the priest's voice, speaking slowly and with great distinctness, uttered words which meant nothing to Charles. He was only conscious that he was renewing his vows to always be good to her, to cherish and protect her, and because he was a practical North Countryman he added, 'and to work hard for you'.

They exchanged rings, they received a blessing, they signed a register, and the young man handed over certain monies to the little priest. It was over. In the eyes of the Church, they were man and wife.

The atmosphere at the Embassy—was it an Embassy or a Consulate?—Charles neither knew nor cared. The room was very large, and if in the church there had been no flowers, here it seemed that half the florists in Paris must have been ransacked. A short man wearing formal morning dress greeted them. He smiled, shook hands with them both, with the Conte and his wife and with the exquisite young man.

Then, rubbing his hands briskly, he said, 'Now! Stand there—yes, you here, signorina—ah, I forgot you're signora now! Forgive me.'

It was over in under ten minutes. Again there was handshaking, and then there was the Conte's great Mercédes waiting. The Contessa wiped her eyes, Maria's filled and overflowed. More handshaking, as they entered the car which slid away smoothly towards the airport.

Maria dried her eyes, and Charles took her hand. 'Whatever happens we belong to each other now, my dearest,' he said.

'That makes me so happy, Carlo *mio*.'

There at the airfield the great trans-Atlantic plane was waiting. Charles said, 'I feel that it is some immensely strong and fierce dragon waiting to carry you off to his den.'

She tried to smile. It was a brave effort but not completely successful. 'Then somewhere there is another dragon, but a good dragon, who will rescue me and bring me back to you,' she said.

He wondered later how often he had said, 'You'll send me a cable the moment you get there, won't you? Promise!'

'This is a day of promises,' Maria said. 'I have made promises in that dark little church, before the British representative, now I make promises to you, Carlo. I shall keep every one that I have made, have no fears.'

She insisted that he should not wait until the aeroplane left. 'I shall wave when I get to the top of the gangway,' she said, 'and please wave to me, then turn very quickly and walk away. From my window I shall watch your dear broad shoulders, and the rest will just be waiting.'

He put his arms round her, kissed her passionately, and knew that both of them were almost overcome by the emotion which stirred them so deeply. The dreary airfield seemed to melt away and for a few brief seconds they stood trying, Charles felt, to make time stand still for them. Maria tore herself away, whispering, 'God bless and take care of you, my dearest. *Au revoir*.' Then she turned from him and hurried to the waiting aeroplane. At the entrance she turned and waved to him. He waved back, then kept his promise and walked rapidly away.

The aeroplane for England seemed to be crawling through

the skies. He longed for the journey to be over, wanted to hear Mum's voice, warm, kind and reassuring. There would be explanations to make to Emmanuel, and it would be good to hear his quiet voice, speaking with gentle sympathy, perhaps because of his sincerity he would duplicate his 'r's' rather more than he usually did.

Then from time to time the full realization that this was his wedding day, and that with each moment that passed his wife was being carried farther and farther away from him, swept over him. Again he experienced that sense of desolation, though now it was tinged with a feeling that it was impossible that it could be really true. It was a fantastic and horrible dream ; he would wake in his elaborate bedroom at the Crillon, and bath and dress ; the pleasant godson of the Conte would arrive, they would drink champagne, and then he would go to meet Maria at the altar. Then he glanced down at the finger bearing the wedding ring which Maria had given him, and the realization that this was all no dream, but a heartbreaking reality, would fling him again into the depths of depression.

At last he heard, 'Fasten your safety-belts, please,' and looking up saw the illuminated sign, 'No smoking'. Then again the voice of the air-hostess, 'Put out your cigarettes, please.'

The journey was over.

He drove direct to the flat, gave his beautiful new bags to the porter—they had been part of Simeon's wedding present—and let himself in with his latch key. Sarah rushed out from the kitchen calling, 'Noo, noo, 'oo's that for any favour? Why it's you, Mister Charles, we weren't expecting you while a few more days. The mistress is out, but she'll be back for tea. And where's Mrs. Charles?'

'Mrs. Charles,' he said heavily, 'is on her way to America. Her father is gravely, critically ill, and she was cabled to go to him.'

'Nay,' Sarah gave the word several 'a's' in her surprise, 'nay, that's a reit do, yon is Eh, but I'm proper grieved.'

Charles nodded. 'Thank you, Sarah. Don't talk about it just now. I'll wait tea for my mother. I'll go and unpack.'

'I'll do that for you, Mister Charles, I know wheer your things go as well as what you do yourself. Leave it to me. Just go and have a nice wash and brush up, and by then the mistress 'ul be back. She's fetching some teacakes wi' her, though why we've got to buy teacakes wi' me in the place, I'd not know.'

He washed and 'brushed up', then went into the pleasant little sitting-room—he refused to call it lounge—to await his mother. She came in, her eyes anxious and troubled, saying, 'Why, Charlie luv, what's this Sarah tells me? That bonny girl gone off to America! On your wedding day! Nay, it's about the hardest thing I ever knew happen to anyone. Oh, my poor dear luv.'

She kissed him tenderly, and he felt glad that he had been able to come home to Mum—his own, understanding mother, who had such limitless stores of love to draw upon. Sarah brought in the tea trolley, and remarked, 'Them teacakes don't luke so bad to me.'

'They're from a French shop I passed on my way home,' Rose said.

'I'd like to know what French folk know about making teacakes!' remarked Sarah, contemptuously.

He found that he was hungry, and longing for a cup of tea which his mother handed to him.

'There, luv, nothing like a cup of tea when you're feeling dowly. Don't talk till you've had some tea ; yes, and a piece or two of teacake. Sarah can say what she likes, that's all jealousy. They're beautiful.'

He drank his tea, found that he ate the teacake with a certain appetite, and then he began to tell his mother all about everything. The magnificent house of the de Brissacs ; how Maria had played after the elaborate dinner ; the next day when they had been to the Louvre and Maria had said that she would show him no more than five pictures. He spoke of their wonderful luncheon, their happiness at being together, and then the cable waiting for her when they got back. Maria's decision, and the realization that she was to be torn from him immediately after the two weddings.

Rose, her hands clasped, murmured, 'Eh, Charlie, how cruel! But she was right, she'd never have forgiven herself for not going, or you for trying to keep her, if anything happened to the old gentleman.'

He said, rather helplessly, 'If everything goes well, how soon will she be able to leave him, or bring him back to Italy?'

'That's hard to say, dear. We don't know how serious it all is.'

Charles shivered. 'I can't bear to think of her finding him all twisted and distorted. Have you ever seen anyone who had had a stroke, Mum?'

'Why, yes, luv. Auntie Bella Dickson—mother's sister. She lived at Colne, and I was sent for. She looked much as usual, poor thing. One side of her mouth was a bit twisted, and one eyelid drooped a little. But there was nothing to—well, distress anyone.'

'Did she get better?' his voice was sharp with anxiety.

'She got a bit better, and she could sit up in her arm-chair. Then she slipped back, poor thing—had another stroke—and she passed over.'

'How long was she ill?'

Rose was not an adept at tempering the wind to the shorn lamb. 'Well, luv, she was about three months getting over the first one, then she was sitting about as I told you for another month or so, and then came this second stroke, and she was gone in a few days. Charlie, whatever happens you mustn't *look forward* to the old gentleman leaving this world. That wouldn't be right, or Christian. You must hope—we all must—for his recovery. Be sure he'll have the best treatment, every luxury. Happen he wasn't very nice to you—in fact it's my opinion that he was downright *rude*, saying things he did—but Maria's his daughter, and if she loves him we must all—yes, all—hope for the best. There, I've said my say!'

'I'll do my best, dear. I must send a cable to her. I can telephone it, can't I? Then tomorrow I must tell Emmanuel.'

He went to Bond Street quite early the next day. He knew that Emmanuel would not be there but he wanted to see Simeon. He had grown very attached to Simeon; he liked his ability, his completely straight outlook on everything, and his essential kindness. He left word that they were to telephone to Simeon's office when Sir Emmanuel arrived.

Simeon was not alone; much to Charles's dismay Max Gollantz was with him Max, cool, arrogant as always, said,

'Hello, how's the happy bridegroom? I'm leaving for the States in a couple of days, on the *Queen Elizabeth*. I've finished my business, and it's time I went back to see the old folks.' His eyes narrowed suddenly. 'I want a talk with Emmanuel—yes, and Uncle William before I go. That's why I came down this morning—to fix it.'

Simeon said, 'I'm sure they'll both be very much pleased.'

Max laughed. 'Why? Because I want to see them or because I'm off to the States? Might be taken both ways.'

'Take the one you prefer. Now, Charles, let's hear all about it.'

Calmly and dispassionately Charles told his story. He felt he had told it so often that it was beginning to sound mechanical. He ended by saying, 'So—there it is. I must just hope for the best, eh?'

'My dear fellow, I'm awfully sorry. It's terribly hard luck,' exclaimed Simeon. The telephone rang, and he answered it. 'That's my father. He'll see you at once, Charles. Again—I'm awfully sorry.'

As the door closed behind Charles, Max lay back in his chair and laughed. Simeon stared at him, frowning.

'What exactly is the joke?' he asked.

Max wiped his eyes. 'That's the lamest story I ever heard! Gee, he's got pretty poor inventive faculties, that blue-eyed boy of the family. It's obvious the old father saw through him from the first, went to the States and sent his daughter to these people in Paris for them to take Charles's measure. They were not impressed, so I imagine they cabled to the father. Probably when the girl saw him in those surroundings—in Paris—she realized it was a hopeless mistake. So she made off. He'll never see her again!'

Simeon said drily, 'Remarkable! Brilliant fellow you are! Only one flaw in your excellent argument. Why did she marry him if she was going to leave him?'

'How do we know that she did? He says so—we've no proof.'

'Well, well! Most interesting. Now, d'you mind getting out of here? To be quite frank, you *stink*! Thank God, you're going back to your own home. They may think everything of you there—we don't think anything of you here.'

'Oh, I know that you've none of you ever really liked me! And of course I know why. I shall have many pertinent questions to put to your father in the morning.'

'Pertinent, eh?' Simeon said. '*Im*pertinent in all probability. Now—get out!'

Emmanuel stood up as Charles entered, holding out his hand, and saying, 'My dear Charles, I am dr-readfully sorry about this.'

'You know?'

'Your mother telephoned to us last night. She thought—and r-rightly—that it would be less painful for you, and spare you having to tell your stor-ry all over again. Viva sends her love, and said, "Tell him that she'll be back very soon."' He smiled. 'She added, "She'll come back, as I did to you. Once women get their talons r-really dug in no man on earth has a chance." Sit down, Charles, I have a proposal to make to you. You look terr-ribly tired.'

'I've had rather a tempestuous few days,' Charles admitted.

Too much emotion, he reflected, the pendulum swinging backwards and forwards too quickly, the consciousness of minutes slipping past with tragic inevitability, so many high hopes crashing down on to a miserably cold hearth-stone. London, Paris, the Contessa's beautiful drawing-room, their equally splendid dining-room. His own luxurious bedroom at the Crillon, the dignified comfort of Larue's, the 'Winged Victory', that 'Mona Lisa', which he remembered with an almost personal dislike. The Contessa's drawing-room again and the cablegram. A church, an Embassy, and the aeroplane again. Now this room of Emmanuel's seemed like a very peaceful back-water after a roaring torrent.

The fine panelling which old Emmanuel had installed, the dark, rich curtains, the massive and beautiful desk at which Emmanuel sat, it stood—this room—for dignity, integrity, as if it challenged the right of anyone to bring what was not genuine there.

'Yes, I have a pr-roposal to put to you,' Emmanuel said, breaking the silence. 'I wish to send you off on a voyage of discovery.' He watched Charles intently, he and Viva had discussed this idea last night at length. 'There are still many places in England where there are fine things to be found. The

Cotswolds, Gloucestershire, Lancashire, Yorkshire, in such small places as Skipton, Battersby, Westmorland—I shall have a list pr-repared for your itinerary. How does the idea appeal to you?'

'It would be interesting, sir but,' Charles hesitated, 'my letters, perhaps a cable to say that Maria was returning, how could I deal with them?'

'In the case of letters, your mother will have a list of your ports of call, she will immediately send them on—"express". As for cables, if you will allow her to open them, she can telephone the contents to my private number here and I shall see that it is r-relayed immediately. You can r-rely on both of us. Well?'

'I should like you to brief me, sir. Give me an idea of the kind of things you wish me to look for.'

'My dear boy, you have eyes, you have considerable knowledge, you know something of pr-rices. Buy what is good, let the dealers have the r-rest. Only, I beg you with all possible sincerity, don't buy Welsh dressers—or exquisite models in ivory—or any other substance—of the Taj Mahal! Watch the posters for sales—they're often amusing in the north. They hold them in the open, and if you get a chair, it's quite likely that they'll turn you out when they're ready to sell it. Oh, there are some ver'ry pleasant things to be found at sales, I assure you.'

Charles nodded. 'It might be quite exciting.'

'I hope that it will be. And now'—briskly—'I want you to go to Hampstead this afternoon.' He consulted a slip of paper. 'Fifty-nine King's Avenue. Household effects. I happen to know that the late owner had some ver-ry pleasant china. See what you can do. Nothing extr-ravagant, there may be nothing at all. Just look r-round.'

Viva had said, last night, 'Poor Charles, take my advice and keep him busy, even if you overwork him a little. Otherwise he'll begin to go "broody".'

Emmanuel gave it as his opinion that Charles should have flown to America with Maria. The idea was received coldly.

'Oh, be yourself, darling,' Viva exclaimed. 'How in heaven's name could he? This old man lying at death's door, the news that they were married might have killed him. This Villafranco—or whatever his name is—would have raised his eyebrows at the idea of them crossing the Atlantic together.'

Emmanuel said mildly, 'His name is Casagrandi.'

'It can be Garibaldi or Mussolini for all I care. Charles did right and so did the girl. But keep him hard at it, his nose to the grindstone, until you hear that she's coming back.'

Now he said, 'Come in and get your briefing tomorrow. Make it late in the morning—I have Max coming for an interview at half past ten or eleven. He's leaving in a few days, and has the insolence to ask if my brother William and I will meet him here! I have agr-reed, because it suits both William and me best to do so. Say twelve o'clock, eh?'

'I shall be here, sir And—thank you.'

'There is nothing to thank me for. There, go to Hampstead and buy for me a perfect tea-service in R-rockingham, for the pr-rice of half what a r-really cheap modern one would cost!'

Emmanuel sat for a long time after Charles had left. He was terribly sorry for the fellow—such a decent fellow too. It was all the hardest of hard luck. Viva had been right—Viva was invariably right—about keeping him busy. It might not *seem* to be the kindest method of treating Charles, but it was the right one.

Now this interview with Max. The impertinence of the man! What did he want to say? Nothing pleasant, Emmanuel was certain of that. He knew his brother William; Bill could hold his tongue until something rattled him, and once he was rattled—out everything came. Not that he, Emmanuel, cared. It mattered very little to him how much either Max or his father were humiliated. He had long been convinced that the illness of Hereward and Charles, coinciding as they had done in so exact a manner, was due to some roguery on Max's part. Charles wouldn't talk, but he was completely convinced that Charles knew. Very well, if Max became too tiresome tomorrow, he would openly accuse him of tampering with the horse. Admittedly the whole thing seemed rather pointless, because after all the fact that Hereward couldn't run scarcely affected Charles—the person really affected was Viva. He must talk it over with Viva tonight; her brain was very clear; her outlook balanced and unswayed by sentiment.

He refused to go on thinking about the wretched Max and his detestable father. To think of Julian invariably seemed to make that awful scar—the end of which just showed where his hair ceased on his forehead—throb and ache afresh. Resolutely he turned to the various catalogues which lay on his desk and immersed himself in them.

At half past ten the next morning Bill Gollantz eased himself out of a taxi and rolled into the Galleries.

'My brother here?' he asked.

'He arrived a few minutes ago, Mr. William. Said that you were to go direct to him.'

'Thanks.' Bill made his way to Emmanuel's office. As he opened the door his brother looked up from his desk, where he sat reading the morning's post.

'Hello, Bill,' he greeted him, 'come for this momentous interview?'

Bill grumbled, 'The damned cheek of the fellow! Seen Charles?'

'Yes, on Viva's advice I'm going to work him to death until his wife r-returns from the States.'

'Very sensible. Now—what about sending for this young cub? I've work waiting for me at my office.'

Max came in, unperturbed and completely at his ease. Emmanuel said, 'Sit down, won't you?' Bill merely grunted, ' 'Morning.'

He asked in his deep voice, which always sounded as if he were ready to grumble, 'Now, what can we do for you? I've not got time to waste.'

Max looked very handsome, and was as usual perfectly groomed. He sat with one leg crossed over the other, showing a good deal of very fine silk sock and an admirable ankle.

'Let's get this straight,' he said. 'I've no intention of allowing anyone to "do" me. I leave that to the astute family of Gollantz. Whether you've allowed yourselves to be tricked, or whether it is part of a plan to oust me from any possible interest—either present or in the future—I don't quite know; but I've been just a little smart for you all. I've seen through it all, your pretty story won't wash.'

Emmanuel sat very still, his face firm, his eyes hard. Bill moved restlessly in his big chair, which creaked a little.

'Now, after having heard that preamble,' Bill said, 'let's

listen to the whole story of your discovery. As I said, we're both pressed for time.'

Max nodded and produced a small notebook with gold corners. 'Certainly. About this Charles Gollantz. You told me that Emmanuel Gollantz had two sons—Max and Algernon. Algernon was the elder. Algernon had a son called Frank, who married someone called Morrie—afterwards Lady Stansfield. I'm right there?'

'Up to this point you are perfectly correct.'

'You told me that this Charles was the son of Frank Gollantz and his wife Morrie—whatever her name was.'

'Allow me to correct you,' Bill said with overdone courtesy. 'I think I said that Charles was Frank's second son by his marriage to a chorus girl, who after his death married a man called Watson.'

'That suits me,' Max agreed, 'because Frank never had a second son, he was killed fighting. So now, kindly elucidate the whole thing for me.'

'On what compulsion must I?' Bill said. '*The Merchant of Venice*—in case you don't know.'

Max frowned. 'You can cut out that superior line of talk! I've a right to know. I come here and see this Charles installed as a member of the family, given a partnership—even though it's a junior one. The man's a liar. He goes to Paris to be married and it's obvious that the girl and her family realized that he just wasn't good enough. Do you really believe that they were married! Say, he's pulled the wool over your eyes, the pair of you! Tell me another! The man's a bastard, and you're gullible enough to believe in him. Anyway, I'm not standing for it, and neither will my father when I tell him the whole story.

'Of course I've heard how you hate my father, he has told me so himself. You lied to my grandfather about him, and when he came to Milan, to your precious Galleries, you incited some wretched little pansy Italian to attack him and left him crippled for life. He wanted to come into this business; he was—and is—an expert in silver; on some pretext you came to his office when he was working late, and tried to kill him. That was when he went to the States, he couldn't stand this persecution any longer. I suppose you got this thing cooking to get another dirty blow at him—through me, eh? Very pretty.'

Emmanuel sat still, his hand clenched on the edge of his desk, his face ghastly. Once his hand went to his forehead, as if with his finger-tips he felt the old scar still painful. Bill sat unmoved.

Finally he said, 'Well, after that burst of eloquence—incidentally, your father has not got his facts perfectly right. But then he never allowed plain facts to limit a good story. You have made one glaring mistake however. This, I may tell you, Charles Gollantz wished—most sincerely—should not be mentioned to you. He is not a bastard. You fool, do you think that at my age, in my profession, I don't sift everything! I have his mother's marriage lines, his birth certificate. No, he's no bastard—you, Max, are that!'

'You're a damned liar! Then who was his bloody father? Tell me that.'

'I intend to. Charles's father married Rose Hughes, known on the stage as "Rosemary Hallet". He met her when she was in pantomime in Manchester, and left her. He married again, unfortunately not mentioning to his new wife or her family that he had neglected to terminate his marriage with Rose Hughes. His father was—as you have possibly guessed—Julian Gollantz. That is why, when I called you a bastard, I was not indulging in mere abuse. I was stating a fact.'

Max was breathing heavily. Emmanuel saw the sweat gather on his forehead. 'My father will institute proceedings for slander!' he gasped.

'If he does he's a greater fool than I take him for! We have all the proofs—"all" being the operative word. Charles never wished you to know this, he asked my brother and myself not to tell you, but you forced my hand. Charles need never know about this interview, if you keep your mouth shut.'

'God, you loathesome lot of Jews!' Max burst out. 'How I hate the lot of you A lot of damned tradesmen, no wonder my father used to call this junk shop of yours—just that—*the shop*.'

For the first time Emmanuel spoke, his voice was very quiet, almost without expression. Bill knew that he was exercising tremendous control, but Max wondered what was wrong with the man.

'And just before you leave us,' Emmanuel said, 'will you r-remember that if there is any tr-rouble, if your father is so misguided as to attempt to indulge in such folly as legal pr-roceedings, I shall warn him that I shall br-ring forward everything I know—and it is a gr-reat deal—concerning your wicked and malicious attempt to dope my wife's horse, Hereward, almost killing both the horse and the man you hate.'

'Charles was never in any danger!' Max almost shouted.

Emmanuel asked, 'Who mentioned Charles? Well, r-remember what I have said. And now—go. I don't wish to see you again.'

Max leaned across the desk, his face almost touching Emmanuel's, and shouted, 'D'you think I'd stay, d'you think that I want to see any of you again, particularly you—you wretched lisping old Jew!'

The door closed behind him, and Bill said, 'Open the window wider, this room is full of evilness! That young brute will come to a bad end.'

16

He went home after the sale in King's Avenue, where he felt that he had done reasonably well. He had bought—not a Rockingham—but a Bloor Derby tea-service, and remembering Emmanuel's advice, he had examined the tea-pot spout, the handles of the cups, and found them all perfect, with the exception of one tea-plate which had a small superficial crack. There had been a beautiful pair of Georgian candlesticks, but he judged the price too high, and left his rival bidder with them on his hands.

He told Mum of Emmanuel's plans for him. She listened and nodded, then said, 'It 'ul be a bit lonely, Charlie, won't it?'

For a moment he longed to say that everywhere, all places, any conditions would be lonely until he could have Maria with him again, but he realized that such a statement would hurt her, and merely shrugged and said, 'Oh, I don't know, dear, I've got to do my job.'

He knew that in his heart he wanted to be off on this tour, wanted to win his spurs. A line came to him, 'Go, say I sent thee out to purchase honour!' That's what he wanted to do, that was what he would do. Take this roving assignment, and do his best to return like the good spies from the Promised Land.

He had cables from Maria, air mail letters, and they were full of affection, full of her longing to see him again. But her father's condition was unchanged and it was impossible to leave him.

There are times, Maria wrote, *when he knows me, even smiles at me. I don't think he realizes where he is, for sometimes he talks of Milan, of the villa, even of the servants. Then again—he slips into unconsciousness. He seems to sleep for many hours, and the doctors say that it is good for him, that in sleep he regains a little strength. Carlo* mio, *how I long for there to be improvement in his state, so that I might admit to him that I have married the only man in the whole world who means anything to me. Be patient,* mio marito, *I shall spend the remainder of my life making you happy to repay you—in a small way—for your understanding at this time.*

He kept all her letters carefully, writing the date of their arrival and of his reply on every envelope, then laying them away carefully in an old cedar-wood box which had belonged to his grandmother.

He saw Emmanuel the following day, received his careful praise concerning the Bloor Derby service, and his usual—apparently casual—brief lecture concerning that type of china. Those small talks with Emmanuel concerning china, furniture, and silver, were things which Charles treasured, and which immediately on reaching home he transcribed as careful notes. Ten minutes with Emmanuel gave him more information, he told Simeon, than ten books.

'He takes it all so easily,' he said, 'it's not like a lecture. It's as if everything of which he talks is a kind of passion with him.'

'It is,' Simeon assured him. 'He's ready to spend as much time over half a dozen silver tea-spoons as he is over some splendid work by Fabergé. He's so full of knowledge that he likes to get rid of some of it by imparting it to half-baked idiots like you and me.'

'How is the youngest Emmanuel?' Charles asked.

Simeon smiled. 'That child is apparently the most marvellous infant prodigy. Every day either my wife or Hannah recount at length some fresh achievement—invariably untrue—of his. He is, they tell me, evidently cut out to be an antique expert, for he stretched out his hand towards *Chaffer's Silvermarks* as they carried him past the bookshelf where it is kept! No, joking apart, he's a grand little baby.'

'I'm off on this roving commission tomorrow. There are some enchanting names in the Cotswolds, in Dorset and—oh, I've forgotten the others. So long, Simeon, and my respects to Daphne and my love to the youngest Emmanuel.'

'Good luck, Charles—all the best.'

As Charles drove in his little car through the lovely English countryside, everywhere there was this entrancing new green, a green still unsullied by the dust of passing cars and heavy buses. Pale dog-roses bloomed in the hedges, placid-eyed dog-daisies, and in the places where there was water, great satisfying kingcups showed their handsome heads. Larks sang overhead, merely tiny specks in the sky, and yet their song reached him clearly. He passed through entrancing villages, where the cottage gardens blazed with colour, the cottages which looked newly scrubbed, and the windows shone like jewels. Past farm-yards where hens scratched and clucked, where dogs, obviously pretending to be fierce, rushed to the gate barking defiance, where pigeons strutted pompously and reminded him of town councillors.

He stopped to eat at small public-houses, where the tables were milk white with much scrubbing, where the floors were of worn and mellow red tiles and sometimes of old brick faded to a colour which was almost rose. He found great open fireplaces, large 'marmalade' cats who stared him out of countenance with their arrogant green or yellow eyes. The inn-keepers were invariably stout, and beamed at him when he asked if he could have a meal. Their speech was slow and rather drawling.

'Whoi Oi beant soa shore. Oi got sum niceish cold beef, if you fancy that. 'Ow d'ye loike it? Well cooked or a bit on the rare soide?'

Charles smiled. 'Shall we say half and half?'

'Sum bread? Wife cuukes it at 'ome. Butter's made at 'ome as well. Oi've a nicish bit o' cheese. Whomely, but wholesum,' he laughed.

'Perhaps a drink? Bitter, eh?'

'An' you'll find noa better i' these parts,' he assured him as he drew it. 'All from the wood 'ere. Oi doan't 'old wi' them 'ere ingines. Oi 'olds as it ruuins good beear.'

Charles, sampling the beer said, 'And this is first-rate.'

'Theer's sum as says, "Wot no 'ead on it!" Not knowing nothing about beer, pure fools think as it's same as Bass or Worthington. Nay, they make yew praper toired.'

He enjoyed his meal, in fact for the first time since he left Maria he felt that the sunshine was breaking through. Tonight he could write to her and really *tell* her something, tell her of the country, the things he had seen, this delightful village 'pub' and the excellent cold beer which he was actually enjoying.

The names of the villages and small market towns delighted him, and at first he could scarcely believe that such names actually existed—Old Sodbury, Chipping Sodbury, Pucklechurch and the rest. It was difficult to find places where good furniture and china might linger, and once, acting on the advice of the local butcher, who Charles met in a charming little public house over bread and cheese and beer, he went five miles out of his way on what proved to be a wild-goose chase.

'Choina, eh? Ah, you're in-ter-ested in choina! Now, I did hear as Mrs. Revelstone was talking o' selling her collection. Moving away tew live wi' her daughter i' Bournemouth. I've heard about this collection for years, seemly it's right out o' the ordinary. It 'ul be just 'bout five mile from y'ere. Can't miss the place, right on the Frampton Cotterell road, red brick 'tis. Name o' Revelstone. The house is called The Limes, though what for, doan't ask me, for so far as I know there bean't a lime tree within twenty moile!'

Charles thanked him, offered him another beer, which was accepted. 'I don't moind if I due. Mention my name—it might help—name o' Liggett, butcher and grazier.'

Charles drove away, his mind filled with visions of old Crown Derby, Royal Worcester, Minton—of the best period—Wedgwood. Or it might be a famous mixed collection—lovely little pieces and figures of Bow or Chelsea, Meissen cherubs, Capo di Monte—a regular treasure trove.

He found The Limes, and felt disappointed. It was a square red-brick house with a neat—perhaps over-neat—garden where geraniums, calceolarias and lobelias grew in a restrained and orderly fashion. An elderly wizened servant wearing a sprigged print dress opened the door to him.

He asked if he might see Mrs. Revelstone.

The elderly maid asked, 'Not about sellin' 'oovers? 'Cos we 'ave one.'

'No, it's about Mrs. Revelstone's china collection.'

'I see. Siddown, please. I'll see.'

He sat down on one of the uncomfortable hall chairs, and

thought it was obvious that the household possessed a Hoover and every other machine making for the elimination of dust and dirt, for the place was so clean and polished that even on this warm June morning it felt positively chilly with cleanliness.

The maid returned. 'This way—she'll see you.'

He entered a room which was filled with brightly coloured chintz-covered furniture, and flowers in small stiff vases standing on little French-polished tables. Mrs. Revelstone came forward to greet him. She was a plump bird-like woman, who reminded him of a well-fed thrush. Her voice was bird-like, high and chirping. He gave his name, and explained his reason for the visit.

'Gollantz,' she repeated. 'Ah, you'll be a foreigner, no doubt?'

'No, madam, the family came originally from Vienna, but that is many years ago. We're completely British.'

'Really, how interesting. And so Liggett sent you here? Ah! that man knows everything that goes on, though I must admit he is an excellent butcher. I always say that no one can beat Liggett for early lamb—though I must say I prefer Caldicott's for sausages. Oh, how we missed his sausages during the war! Can I offer you a glass of sherry, Mr.—er—Gollantz? Yes, pray do have one. I get my sherry from Hodgson's in Chipping Sodbury, they're an excellent firm, most reliable, most.' She rang, and gave the order, 'The sherry, Charlotte, and biscuits and glasses, please.' She turned back to Charles. 'I always believe in being polite to servants. My dear husband—he died many years ago—always said, "My dear Henrietta"—Henrietta is my name, I was callcd after my dear mother's elder sister—"politeness costs nothing and yet it often pays excellent dividends".'

Charles, feeling slightly dizzy with the flood of chatter, managed to ask about the collection.

'Ah, my collection—the fruits of over fifty years. I am assured that it is practically unique, but I am going to live with my daughter—my only daughter—in Bournemouth—such a charming place, I think—so well laid out too. She has a charming house on Canford Cliffs, but the space is limited. Alas, no room for my cabinets! There, drink your sherry—and a dry biscuit—Romary's, I always have theirs, as my husband used to say, "My tastes are simple but I must have the best and only the best." How right, don't you think?'

'Indeed I do——'

'Yes, and the sherry, that is to your taste I hope?'

'Excellent, thank you.'

'When next I go into Hodgson's I shall tell them that a gentleman from London liked their dry sherry. They'll be delighted. I always have a chat when I go into their shop.'

Charles thought bitterly, 'I'll lay any money that you do!'

Mrs. Revelstone finished her sherry. 'Now for the collection! Come with me. I keep it in the dining-room. It's rather a dark room and the china seems to light it up. Of course I have special lighting in the cabinets.'

Charles turned his eyes towards four large, obviously expensive, though modern, china cabinets. It was difficult to see what they held, but he caught the gleam of beautifully kept, and very smooth china, of small objects with scarcely a splash of colour.

He laughed a trifle nervously. 'I am anxiously waiting.'

Mrs. Revelstone laughed, chirruping like a bird. 'Now!' she cried, and switched on the concealed lighting. 'There you are—absolutely unique, I began collecting when I was—imagine it!—seven years old. My first piece was bought in Bournemouth. I remember I was with my dear Uncle Herbert, he was a great collector himself, and he said—oh, I remember it so well! "Start a collection, my dear, it will give you tremendous joy." And indeed it has.'

Charles had moved nearer to the cabinet on his right. He peered at the little objects displayed there—white china with a good high glaze, and a small armorial bearing on each one. Some of the shapes were tortured, some were quite simple and pleasing. But—what the devil were they?

He took a deep breath and said, 'Remarkable.'

'Now,' the old lady cried, 'the others—three more.'

He swallowed hard. 'Mrs. Revelstone, I have not been with my firm very long, I am not as knowledgeable as no doubt I should be, but what exactly is this very charming china?'

She clapped her hands and laughed. 'Mr. Gollantz, it is called Goss.' Dimly it came back to him that once, when his mother had been to Morecambe, she had returned with a small 'amphora' as a present for Aunt Bertha. She had declared that Aunt Bertha's collection was without this particular piece, and that she would be 'over the moon' to have it.

He moved on to the other cabinets, and wondered what Emmanuel would say if he returned with the whole lot. He could scarcely imagine it, except as in some horrid dream.

'Wonderful, isn't it?' she chirruped, 'quite unique. Are you interested?'

Charles hoped that the Recording Angel was sleeping, as he said firmly, 'Tremendously, Mrs. Revelstone, tremendously. But,' he sighed, 'this is too vast a collection for us to purchase. This is something which is—I dare to say—of almost national importance.'

She was in no way depressed. 'I'm not surprised, not at all. In fact I'm rather relieved. It's not that I *need* the money, you understand, and I am attached to my collection, and I wish to find a—well, a home for it, where it will receive attention and stimulate interest. I thought of Bournemouth—the Revelstone Collection—might look very nice there. Then my mind flew to my own birthplace. I'm a Warwickshire woman, Mr. Gollantz, and I thought I might offer it to the museum or art gallery—if they have one—at Sutton Coldfield. Then there is Hanley—the very heart of the Potteries. No, no, it will not have to beg for a home, but I would prefer—actually—to make a gift of it, than to make money out of something which has given me pleasure for years. I am glad that you called. Anytime you are passing—provided that I have not gone to my daughter in Bournemouth—do stop and have a pleasant talk. I've enjoyed our conversation so much.'

Feeling slightly weak and drained of strength, Charles thanked her and bade her 'Good-bye'. He had it in his mind to return, find the butcher, and do him some bodily harm, but wiser counsels prevailed.

The next day, as if in compensation, he found a small but quite charming antique shop in a little market town, and managed to pick up a pair of square Longton bowls, in perfect condition, and beautifully painted with flowers and fruit.

He drove on into Wiltshire, and here again, as he wrote to Maria, the names of the villages and market towns seemed to him to be unbelievable. He wrote:

Over, Middle and Nether Wallop! I have always thought that 'wallop' meant to chastise heavily, now I find these peaceful little places called by that name. Some of their names are beautiful—listen—Compton Chamberlayne, and Steeple Langford. Someday we will visit these places, and investigate how they come by their names, and—think of the joy of it—we'll be together!

He recounted all his day's doing to her, his interview with the lady of the 'collection', though he realized that she would have no idea what 'Goss China' meant. He told her of his simple lunches in old-fashioned inns and public-houses, of the kindly landlords. He tried to draw verbal pictures of the loveliness of the English countryside, and always ended with the same statement: *It is so beautiful, but when we can see it—together—it will seem to me, incomparably more wonderful.*

He had moved on to Dorset, to other places with strange names, and discovered beautiful old cottages—half timbered or washed with a faint golden yellow, their gardens blazing with flowers. He always arranged to spend the night at the places which Emmanuel had indicated on his itinerary, for there he knew there would be a post office, be it never so small—generally only a counter cut like a slice out of a grocer's shop, where from behind a brass barrier like a glorified chicken coop, rather acidulated elderly ladies of very certain age, eyed him with suspicion when he called for letters or telegrams. His pleasant smile went for nothing, and when he ventured to ask if they knew of anyone who might have interesting furniture or china which they wished to dispose of they stared at him like Gorgons.

'No, Aye can't say as Aye due. We're not an information buroo.'

Landladies and landlord, and the 'locals' he met in the evening when he went into the public bar for a beer, were his best means of information.

'W'at kinder things be you after, mister? Farmer Willis 'e has some foine things——'

'Nay, doan't send t'pore chap theer!' another man cried. 'We 'arl know what 'is temper be loike! Nay, mister, leave Farmer Willis alone—onless you want your crown broken.'

''Ow 'bart Miss Darcy? She be a gentle creature. 'Er got some chice things I've 'eard. Roight gentle laady is Miss Darcy, an' Oi did y'ear as brass weren't all that plentiful.'

Another grunted, 'Better she saw this y'ere gennleman then git in some o' they sharks as due come along, eh?'

The landlady said warmly, for Charles had stood pints all round, 'They're right, mister. A luvely laady, Miss Darcy. What I calls a reel laady. It's Briar Cottage, jest down along the road. Tell 'er as Mrs. Prossit sent you—no offence meant, and I trust none taken. Give Miss Darcy that message, sir, and why, yes, I'll take a small port.'

Charles walked down to Briar Cottage, and a tall, very thin woman wearing clothes which had been very good but now were distinctly shabby, opened the door to him. She told him that she was Miss Darcy.

'Mrs. Prossit told me to call here,' Charles said.

The rather thin lips smiled, and he noticed that when her eyes lit up they were very fine. She said, 'Ah, Ellen Prossit—she's a dear good creature. Many years ago she was our cook. Won't you come in?'

The cottage was very old, and although it was spotlessly clean, with furniture and silver beautifully polished, everything was woefully shabby. Charles told her why he had come, and she listened intently, her hands—they were beautiful hands, with long slim fingers—relaxed in her lap. She said earnestly, 'Oh, I am pleased. That's why Ellen sent you. You see I have far more furniture—more of everything—than I need or can keep clean.' Suddenly she laughed. 'What rubbish we talk,' she said, 'I have too much of everything—except money! That is practically non-existent!'

'But,' he glanced round the room, 'haven't you tried to sell anything?'

'I'm so stupid about selling anything! I did have a man here, and he was so offensive that—to get rid of him—I let him have a dear little Queen Anne oak bureau. He offered me ten pounds for it. I tried to assert myself, and said very firmly "Twelve". He took it.'

Charles almost groaned. 'I should think he did—it was his lucky day, wasn't it?'

'You see,' she spoke more confidingly now, 'I've never

thought what these things are *worth*, they've been in my life ever since I can remember. I want only to save enough to furnish a tiny cottage—there is one in the village, it belongs to Ellen's brother, Silas, and he is going to Canada. The rent is only ten shillings a week, and it has a little garden. So now, Mr. Gollantz, if there is anything you think you'd like to buy—except a few pieces which I must keep—please look round and I'll make some coffee.'

There was a splendid pair of Chippendale chairs with fine needlework seats, a beautiful Crown Derby tankard, with gilt decorations and flowers in wonderful colours, a Hepplewhite Pembroke table with cabriole legs and decorations—Chinese influence, Charles thought, which he had never seen before. A sofa table—mahogany, in perfect condition, and only recently he had heard Emmanuel deploring the scarcity of good sofa tables. A Carlton House writing-desk—with drawers, and a back panel which slid along as if it ran on velvet. There was a small picture—it needed cleaning but it was—he felt certain—a David Cox.

Then, in a table with a glass top, he peered, gasped, and took out his torch. An Easter egg, pale blue and ornamented with stones—primary and secondary. There were initials—'N—A', chased in gold, and heavily decorated. Very gently he raised the glass lid, and took out the exquisite egg. It opened, and there was a cockatoo carved in amber, standing on a perch in a tiny cage made of gold wire. He closed the egg almost reverently. It was—he couldn't doubt it—Fabergé, the man who has devised lovely, trivial things for the kings, grand-dukes, and aristocracy—particularly in Russia. This might even be one of the Easter eggs which the unfortunate Czar Nicholas had designed to give the Empress—as he did every year—for the Easter Festival.

'Mr. Gollantz, come and have your coffee!'

He walked back to the tiny drawing-room, feeling slightly giddy. Miss Darcy smiled as he entered, and it struck him that years ago she must have been an exceedingly handsome woman. When she smiled he felt that years slipped away from her.

The coffee-cups were old tomato-coloured Dresden, the tiny spoons of silver which had worn to almost paper thinness through the years, and there was one brandy goblet—very large, very fine.

'I thought,' Miss Darcy said almost shyly, 'that you might like a brandy. It is '75 and my father had a friend in France who distilled in some château. This was never—or very seldom—listed. I still have a few bottles, because—frankly—I don't care for it. I hope your coffee is as you like it.'

He nodded. 'It's perfect. Now, Miss Darcy, I'm going back to spend the night at the Leopard.'

He saw her face lose some of its animation. 'There is nothing that interests you?' she asked anxiously.

'On the contrary, there is too much that interests me. I am sending a telegram or telephoning for my senior partner to come down. I'm only a very junior person in the firm. He'll come round if he may, and perhaps you'll be gracious enough to let him look round.'

'Who is he—this senior partner?' she asked.

'He's known to be straighter than anyone in the antique business. He has a place in Milan, another in Paris and the headquarters are in Bond Street. He is Sir Emmanuel Gollantz.'

'I've heard of him. Didn't he give some tremendous Old Master to the nation?'

'That was his father—Max Gollantz.'

She gave a sigh of relief. 'I believe that I will join you in a brandy,' she said. 'I must drink to tomorrow. Yes, even though I don't like it very much.'

They sat and talked. She told him the history of the Fabergé Easter egg, enumerated the things which she must keep for her little cottage, recounted how her father, who had been born into a very rich family, cared only for old furniture, old china and—in a lesser degree—pictures. He had died, many years ago, leaving her a small but—as they believed then—certain income. Its value had steadily deteriorated, until now—she shrugged her shoulders and laughed, 'Well, life has been barely bread—the scraping of butter hasn't really been noticeable.'

Charles walked back to the Leopard, taking with him the memory of Miss Darcy, her face faintly flushed, her eyes very bright, saying as she bade him 'Good night', 'Oh, I can scarcely wait for the morning!'

Charles put through a long-distance call to Ordingly. Fortunately Emmanuel was at home, and he came to the telephone.

Charles said, 'I believe—no, I'm certain—that Jim Hawkins had found gold. Can you possibly come down tomorrow, sir? It's worth it, I'm convinced. Cerne Abbas—I am at the Leopard. I meant to go on tonight to Yetminster, but I daren't—I mean that—take this chance entirely upon myself.'

'You were perfectly r-right. I shall be there, without fail, by eleven in the morning. I might persuade Viva to dr-rive down with me in her car, it is consider-rably faster than mine. You're well? Good. I am ver-ry much pleased with you, Jim Hawkins. Good night.'

Charles was slightly 'flustered'. He sought out the pleasant Mrs. Prossit, and discovered that she was more than willing to arrange luncheon for four people.

'What 'a'd yew say, sir, to ducklings, my own green peas, and potatoes as are *new*—not them as 'as been buried in a sand heap all winter thro. Apple pie—and theer's few as 'ave a lighter 'and then Ellen Prossit, no matter wheer the next cums from. Cream—natcherly. An' a nice bit of local cheese, varry good it is. We've got a few bottles of goodish wine i' the celler, not much call fer it 'ere. 'Ow many did you say as there'd be, sir?'

'Four—Sir Emmanuel and Lady Gollantz, Miss Darcy and myself.'

'Lardy! Titled folk. Well, my Miss Darcy can hold her own wi' any o' 'em. Praper lady she is, our Miss Rosemund. Eh, the Leopard's luking up, seemly.'

As the church clock struck eleven the next morning, Viva's car drew up and Charles rushed to greet them. He had enjoyed his journeys, but he had felt marooned and very often lonely, almost as if he were in banishment.

Viva, looking ravishing, cried, 'Charles, if the game isn't worth a considerable number of candles, I shall have something to say. There ought—in a properly constituted world—to be no such time as seven in the morning! What have you found—some Victorian sideboards?'

He smiled. 'Indeed yes, and some delicious crewel work and

a copy of "The Monarch of the Glen"—I think you'll like that!'

Emmanuel, looking very tall and elegant, sipped his sherry. 'This is remarkably good sherry—quite astonishing to find such sherry in a small place.' He smiled and gave his little formal bow to Mrs. Prossit, saying, 'My compliments, madam—excellent.'

'I y'ear as you're goin' to see Miss Darcy, sir?'

'Indeed, I look forward to that pleasure.'

'An' pleasure you'll say as it is ar'ter you seen 'er. For years I 'ad the h'onour of servin' 'er and 'er father—grand gentleman, 'e was! Yes, cuke, I was.' She laughed. 'Not lost my 'and yet, as I hope yew an' your good laady 'ul say ar'ter lunch.'

They found Miss Darcy waiting for them eagerly. She looked younger Charles thought, she laughed more easily, and her eyes were very bright and expectant. Emmanuel brought out his notebook and gold pencil. 'Now, Miss Darcy, if you'll tell me exactly what pieces you wish to r-retain, it will be kind. Ah, mostly small pieces?' He nodded rather ruefully. 'Those madam, are exactly what ever-ryone wants! Still, let me see. Charles, please check everything I select, subject to Miss Darcy's appr-roval.'

Emmanuel, except when he was, as he expressed it, 'after big game', never hesitated to show his delight at beautiful things. The pieces which Charles had noted the previous day called forth his complete approval.

'Charming! This Pembr-roke—on principle I dislike them, but this is charming. How vastly differ-rent when a great artist like Hepplewhite turned his attention to a design. Those chairs—delightful, yes indeed. The Carlton House desk—admirable, oh, admirable. Miss Darcy, what taste your father possessed!'

His list grew, and Charles felt inward delight. The little picture, Emmanuel decided, was indeed a David Cox. 'Not possibly his best, but in these days—well there is a vogue for him.' The Crown Derby tankard pleased him, and he murmured, 'The richness they introduced—never overdid it.'

When they came to the Fabergé Easter egg he turned it over reverently in his beautiful fingers, and opened it with almost exaggerated care.

'I always think of Fabergé as being the last of the Benvenuto Cellini line,' he said. 'This may not be very old, but oh, the care, the thought, the workmanship that went into such things! You can bear to part with it?' he asked Miss Darcy, half quizzically. 'I don't know that I shall be able to!' He selected other pieces, entering them all in his notebook, his face grave and intent as he worked.

'And that,' he said at last, 'is all I think. I have to thank you most sincerely for your courtesy, Miss Darcy. Now, if I may talk of business without offending you?—thank you. I must go into what I pr-ropose to offer for these charming things, but I feel that I must ask you to allow me to leave—what do you say? —"something on deposit"! I shall take nothing away of course, and shall await your r-reply with anxiety—and a good deal of excitement.'

He took out a cheque book, went over to the Carlton House desk, and wrote out a cheque. Charles watched him run his hands over the smooth wood as if he offered it a brief caress. He folded the cheque carefully and handed it to Miss Darcy. 'I am deeply obliged to you,' he said.

She glanced at the cheque. 'Sir Emmanuel—do you realize what you've written?'

He smiled. 'I gener-rally do.'

'Six hundred pounds!'

His smile broadened. 'That is only deposit money.'

17

Charles moved towards the north. At leaving, Emmanuel, who had been his most charming self during luncheon, laid his hand on his shoulder and said that he had done well.

'The going may be harder in the north—in Lancashire and Yorkshire they pr-ride themselves on being—what we call—tough. They're as honest as the day, and under their str-range rather hard exter-rior, you can find the kindest hearts imaginable.'

As Charles drove north, he watched the country change. The lush green was left behind and in its place there were mill chimneys and coal stacks. Even the green grass assumed a dingy hue, but there was still a beauty to be found if you looked around with imagination. You might drive past men who had just left the pits, who looked as if they were made up for a Christy minstrel show; he saw cotton mills 'losing' with streams of rather pale-faced people crowding through the factory gates; he passed through heavily industrial towns where men sat—their work over—crouched on their haunches leaning against the walls of houses. Then he drove into Rochdale and remembered that this was Gracie Fields's own town, where she was greeted like a visiting queen. The town hall astonished him, he was used to town halls which were monuments of hideousness and bad taste, but this one rose splendid as a great cathedral. Slipping back into his own speech, even in thought, he mused, 'Nay, theer's nout wrang wi' Rochdale!'

Emmanuel had given him the name of a hotel in Southport, and there he found a cable waiting for him from Maria:

My dear father began his journey to God yesterday at half past three. My love to you. Maria.

For a moment his heart leapt, then he remembered what his mother had said, and imagined Maria's distress. His dear Maria, alone in America, with the exception of her father's friends. She must feel as desolate as he had done when he returned to England without her. Perhaps the de Brissacs would fly over to be at her side, to help her in the business which must inevitably ensue after the death of Franconi. He sent a long and affectionately worded cable, resisting the temptation to ask when she might be leaving for England.

His heart felt lighter—in spite of his attempt to feel as Rose had insisted. Now Maria—his wonderful Maria—was free; she would come to England and they would begin their real life together.

Lancashire yielded very little—a good corner cupboard which a woman sold 'Becos' Ah'd rather 'ave a TV. It weer my Auntie Mary's. Happen TV. 'ul keep my old man at 'ome nights, corner cupboard weant'.

An unexpected find of four beautiful silver lustre jugs, all in perfect condition, enchanted him but after all they were 'small beer'. In an old cottage he listened to an old lady—he thought she must be nearly ninety—declaring, 'Somewheer Ah've a pair o' silver candlesticks. Get rid on 'em, Mary Lizzie, they'll pay for my funeral.' She chuckled. 'An' see as it's a good 'un! Go get 'em, Mary Lizzie, an' gie t' young chap a sup o' my rhubarb wine. Nay,' she admonished him, 'dean't luke sideways—it's all o' five years old, an' kep' in them little ole brandy casks. That's t' secret! Sup *that* up, young man.'

Charles 'supped it up' and found it very little inferior to good champagne. The candlesticks were an ordinary but reasonably handsome pair, late Georgian. Well kept, and dignified. He asked what she wanted for them. She replied, rather testily, that she had told him already—sufficient to pay for her funeral.

He laughed, 'I'm not an undertaker, Madam.'

She nodded agreement. 'Aye, well, time was when I could ha' gotten t'whole thing, aye, an' done praperly, for fifteen pounds. Now I doot it 'ul be more.'

He looked at her placid old face, with the blue eyes still bright, wrinkled at the corners as if she had faced the high winds on the moors. He smiled.

'Would twenty be all right, madam?'

She nodded. 'It 'ul be a bit of a tight squeeze, but I've my insurance. Threepence a week for over fifty year. Aye, I can manage on that. Mind, I could ha' done better bi takin' 'em to Colne.'

Charles knew his Lancashire people. 'Then why didn't you?'

She smiled, showing terribly artificial teeth. 'Why? I'll tell you for why—I don't like t'chap as 'ud buy them! That's why!'

He took leave of her, holding her thin hand which felt as if the skin were tissue paper. 'You'll not need to cash in on that insurance for another ten years, madam.'

'Eh, lad,' she told him, 'you get a bit wearied wi' it all. You can be i't' world ovver long. Tak' care on yoursen.'

He was in Huddersfield when Maria's cable was sent on to him, announcing that her father had died. The letter which followed it told him that the de Brissacs had flown over to New York, and that her uncle would help her to settle all the business affairs of her father.

He had so many interests, she wrote, *and I am afraid that I am terribly foolish about anything connected with business, so I am grateful indeed to my uncle for so willingly promising to help me. How long it will take I cannot say, but be sure that my clever uncle will expedite matters as much as is possible. Then* caro mio—*I shall fly to you—in all the meanings of the word, but my thoughts are always flying like white doves to you, I think of you so much and so often. The thought of you during this unhappy time—which has seemed so terribly long—has helped and sustained me—We must be patient for a little time longer,* Carlo caro.

He longed to write back and ask for a time-limit, to beg her to leave everything to her uncle and at all costs come back to him, but in spite of his loneliness, and his burning desire to be with her again, that streak of hard-headed North Country common sense asserted itself. He felt certain that Franconi must have died a very wealthy man, and that in all probability Maria would be an exceedingly rich young woman. He felt no elation at the prospect, he would have liked it better if she had been completely dependent on him, so that he might have had the satisfaction of earning everything for her, so that he could have congratulated himself that with each step forward he took in his business he was able to afford some additional luxury and comfort for her.

He took himself to task for his attitude, told himself that he was conceited and selfish. Why should Maria be forced to live in a style less elegant and luxurious than that to which she had been accustomed so that his self-esteem should be encouraged!

'Damn it,' he addressed his reflection in the looking-glass in the bedroom of the rather grim hotel where he was staying. 'Damn it, I'm lucky—I've got a niceish flat, it shall be nicer afore I've done with it! I can support her, in comfort—and maybe a bit more than just comfort. Her own money will be her own, I'll not have her wanting to pay her share or any rubbish of that kind, but as it's her money she can spend it on whatever she fancies.'

He plodded round Yorkshire, thinking—as he had thought of Dorset and Gloucestershire—that it was the most beautiful county imaginable. He drove over the moors to Whitby, Robin Hood's Bay, Runswick and Staithes, discovering that each has its own separate charm. He grew to love the broad, comfortable vowels, the rather slow speech, and the sense of humour which invariably held something of the macabre. He fell in love with little market towns such as Yarm, and the villages—some of them were sufficiently large to call towns—of Skipton—where he bought some Wedgwood, Northallerton, Stokesley and Great Ayton, which charmed him completely.

It was there that he made his usual tentative inquiries at the little hotel, where incidentally he had been given a remarkably good luncheon.

'Old furniture—or china? Nay, most folks have some o' both, but whether they want to sell or not, why that's a different matter. You can but try, sir,' he was told.

They talked, other people being pressed into the group to give their opinions. There was Mrs. This or Miss That, then head waggings, and doubts expressed. Charles saw a house on the other side of what they called 't'beck', a stream which meandered slowly through the village.

'Nay, that's Manor House. I'd not know as t'laady theer 'ud want ter sell onnything. Lovely laady, 'er people have lived here and hereabouts for years an' years, 'aven't they, Garge?'

'Aye, they're no offcomers them isn't.'

'Gotten some luvely pieces, if all you 'ear is trew. You can but ask, mister.'

So Charles made his way to the charming old stone house, set in a beautiful garden, walked into a yard where the paving-stones looked as if they were newly scrubbed each morning, and rang the door bell.

A thin elderly maid opened the door; he asked—already feeling that he had made a dreadful mistake—if he might see the lady of the house. The maid said, rather grudgingly, 'Why yes, I'll ask her.'

She returned and said, 'That's right, come in.'

He followed her, and found a woman in the charming room. Immediately he thought, 'Their own word—bonnie—describes her!' He rather stumblingly told her the reason for his call, and she smiled—kindly, warmly. Then she shook her head. 'No, Mr.'—the slightest hesitation while she glanced at his card—'Gollantz, I'm far too attached to my china and furniture to want to sell any of it. If it interests you, look at it. I've some rather nice pieces in the dining-room and in the drawing-room, only not for sale.' She laughed, a warm, kindly laugh which soothed his feelings, for he realized that he had made—though inadvertently—a dreadful gaffe. 'What I can do is to offer you a cup of tea. Oh, yes do, it will be here in a minute.' She rose and called, 'Florence, two cups, and at once, please.'

He drank his tea, he ate thin bread-and-butter, teacake, and all the time, for some unknown reason, he felt impelled to talk to this woman of his own affairs. She listened gravely, from time to time asking some brief question, or uttering some sound which conveyed sympathy. He told her of his marriage, of Maria's departure for New York, of his hopes and his ambitions.

His story ended, she said, 'And now you can expect her any time? How wonderful that will be. I'm sure that you are going to be happy. Next time I come to London, I shall call at your Galleries—oh, not that I can afford Gollantz prices!—but just to say "How do you do".'

He said sincerely, 'Yes, please do, and meet my rather wonderful uncle, Emmanuel.'

'I've heard of him. That would be nice!'

She showed him some of her fine china, her magnificent chairs, all with evident pride and yet without a trace of undue ostentation. Charles thought that one day he and Maria would have a house like this one, solidly built, facing the wild winds of winter, and yet cool in the heat of summer. They, too, would collect with discrimination, and be kind and tolerant to unknown young men who came trying to buy old furniture. He even showed his new acquaintance the picture of Maria which he carried in his pocket-book. She examined it carefully, and then exclaimed, 'Why she's perfectly beautiful! Oh, you must be very, very happy.'

She shook hands when he left, wished him good luck, and he drove away feeling that he had been accepted as a friend. He might never meet her again, but he would never forget her warm, friendly kindness.

He drove on towards Bradford, where there was a house where, he had been told, they sometimes sold old furniture. It stood on rather a lonely, grim road on what he had been told was 'Blubberhouse Moor'. He imagined what it must be like in winter, and shivered. The scenery was wild and magnificent, but it struck something of a chill into his heart. The whole prospect was unfriendly, however much you might admire its grandeur. The house itself was as forbidding as the country round. A notice hanging on the railings announced 'Tea served. Eggs. Cut flowers. Antiques'. He walked up the paved path and knocked. A middle-aged woman opened the door and Charles told her his business. She nodded—she was old and grim like the house and the surrounding country, but she proved to be garrulous.

'Nay, they're all oot, gone ter Bradford. Why, we due sell antiques. Ah'd not know what you want exackerly. Ah've a reight nice Welsh dresser. Cum this way an' see for yerself. My daughter says it's a proper beauty. Luke!'

He examined it, recalling Emmanuel's warning. It was an excellent fake, but fake it undoubtedly was. He asked if it came from Wales.

'Nay, my daughter gets 'em fra a chap i' as lives somew'eer i't'Dales. Carpenter 'e is. We sell a lot on 'em. This un's partickerly nice, Ah reckon. Thirty-five pound—cheap an' all, eh?'

Charles shook his head. 'No, I think not—not for me. Anything else, madam?'

'Some luvely old Sunnerland ware, proper pretty it is.'

'Where do you get that?' he asked.

'Ah deant rightly know. Some plaace i' Staffordshire, Ah fancy.'

Again Charles marvelled that people could be such fools as to buy these palpable fakes. 'I expect you do pretty well here,' he said.

'Aye, i' summer-time, when theer's plenty o' touwerists, an' Americans an' sic like. I' winter t'place is dead as a door-nail. We shut opp, and Ah goa ter my married daughter i' Manningham, my other daughter goes ter 'er 'usband's muther i' Wakefield. She's a widder, is our Clarice. Makes a change. Then we oppen oop i't' spring. Folks stops ter watch lambs skippin' abart, then cum in fer tea. Ah'm sorry, mister as yew wean't tak' t' Welsh dresser, fer it's worth 'aving, my daughter says soa. Sas it's abart t'best 'e's ever sent uz. Well, 'appen you cum rhand 'ere agean, stop an' see if we've summat as takes yer fancy. Good arternoon.'

So, slowly he drove back to London, and in spite of all the beauty of the country-side, he knew that his heart felt lighter as he saw the distance from London decreasing with every milestone. One day, he and Maria would make such a tour as he was ending. He'd show her the lovely villages, she should go with him to look at fine old churches, she should smell the scent of meadow-sweet in the hedges, see the pale dog-roses. He would find 'Lords and Ladies' growing for her, and teach her what a glass of good English beer, taken with home-baked bread, fresh butter and cheese, tasted like.

His whole future was bound up in Maria Franconi.

Mum was happy to have him home. She said that he looked thinner, but Charles remembered that whenever he had been away, if only for a week's holiday to Eastbourne and Torquay, she had always said the same.

They sat that evening and 'tired the sun with talking'. He recounted his experiences and Rose found the story of the Welsh dressers particularly to her taste.

'They're cautions some of them, I don't doubt. But—well, it's all experience, Charlie, isn't it?'

He saw Emmanuel the next morning, and it was pleasant to know that everyone seemed glad to see him back again. Pleasant, too, not to be obliged to rush off to some out-of-the-way village or market town, but to feel that—for a time at least—he could 'stay put' as his mother said.

Emmanuel told him of the last interview with Max, speaking gravely and with marked distaste. 'I was sorry to have to go against your wishes, Charles, but it was necessary to give that wr-retched young man a lesson. I doubt ver-ry much if we shall hear anything from him again.

'It is curious how this hatred of Jews runs through our family. My father's brother, Algernon, had it, so has Julian, and here it is repeated in Julian's son. All of them r-regard it as a shameful thing to have any Jewish blood, they despise the whole r-race. I r-remember when I first read *Trilby*—that wonderful human book du Maurier wrote—I was so impressed that I learnt the passage by heart—"that strong, sturdy, irrepressible, indomitable, indelible blood". You've no sense of—why, it amounts to actual r-revulsion—at having Jewish blood, have you, Charles?'

'None at all, sir. I'm proud of it.'

'I'm glad of it. I have always felt that the only Jew who merits all the scorn one can possibly feel, is the Jew who is ashamed of his race. I r-regard him as nothing short of a traitor. I have often wondered if Hitler and his abominable Jew-baiters were not—in part at least—Jews who were ashamed of being Jews. It's not merely a matter of religion, I am not a particularly religious man, it's pride of race that every decent Jew should feel.

'As a very small boy I was taken to see *The Merchant of Venice*. I forget who played Shylock, but he was played as a cringing, whining old creature. I told my grandfather how I disliked it, and he said, "Ah, yes indeed. You should have been born much earlier. Then you could have seen Shylock played as a gentleman by Henry Irving." I love and admire Dickens's novels, but I have never quite forgiven him for Fagin. A vile caricature! There, Charles, I must not r-ramble on like this. Keep your pr-ride of race, live up to your Jewish blood. It may be diluted, but no one can eradicate it'

Charles smiled, and Emmanuel thought what a nice, frank

smile it was. 'I'll try to do so, sir, and I'll try to live up—so far as I can—to the present head of the house.'

'Ah, you should have known my father and my grandfather! There, get along and see what Simeon has to tell you about the youngest Emmanuel. He wasn't talking two days ago, but no doubt by this time he is talking with perfect fluency.'

A few days later Maria wrote that the end of the business was in sight. Her uncle had worked with tremendous energy; he said that the Americans might boast of their ability to 'hustle', but in this case it was he—a Frenchman—who had 'hustled' them.

So, dearest Carlo, before long we shall be together again. I only hope that I shall recognize you after this long separation. I hope also that you will not find your ever-loving Maria too unattractive and hideous. I feel that I go about with a silly smile on my lips, whispering 'Soon, soon, soon'.

Her cable announcing that she was leaving New York arrived as Charles was leaving Bond Street. Rose, watching him, wondered if the cable held bad news, for he sat down suddenly, his face drained of all its healthy colour.

'Nothing bad, Charlie?'

He contrived to smile, and handed her the cable.

'The finest news in the world, Mum.'

'Charlie, how wonderful! At last—and you've been so good and brave.'

'Not really, dear.'

'Well, I think you have,' her tone was defiant. 'I'm properly proud of you, so there.'

He told Simeon, who smote him on the back by way of congratulation, and nearly knocked him off his chair. He told Hannah Rosenfeldt, who beamed at him and said, 'Tell Sir Emmanuel, quickly while it is too early for him to say "Now we drink coffee!" How happy she will be, this dear little wife, to see young Emmanuel! So envious I t'ink that she will not rest until she has a baby herself, as like little Emmanuel as possible, no?'

Emmanuel looked up as he entered. 'Good morning, Charles, to what do I owe the honour of this early visit?'

'I came to ask if I might have the day free, sir?'

Emmanuel's eyes twinkled, and Charles thought, 'I bet Mum telephoned him as soon as I left the flat!'

'For what exact r-reason, Charles?'

'To meet someone at the airfield, sir.'

'Am I permitted to ask whom?'

Charles grinned. 'Certainly, sir. A lady called Mrs. Charles Gollantz.'

'Pray give Mrs. Charles Gollantz my compliments, and ask her to take you off on that ter-ribly belated honeymoon for the r-remainder of the week. Oh, and as you go out, ask Hannah to let me have some coffee. I won't ask you to join me—that would pr-rove a lack of consideration, eh? Off you go, Charles. *Mazeltov.*'

Sirmione
Prov. di Brescia
Italia